Camino Royale

Camino Royale

ROSS O'CARROLL-KELLY
(as told to Paul Howard)

Illustrated by Alan Clarke

SANDYCOVE

an imprint of

PENGUIN BOOKS

SANDYCOVE

UK | USA | Canada | Ireland | Australia
India | New Zealand | South Africa

Sandycove is part of the Penguin Random House group of companies
whose addresses can be found at global.penguinrandomhouse.com

First published 2023
001

Copyright © Paul Howard, 2023
Illustrator copyright © Alan Clarke, 2023

Penguin Books thanks O'Brien Press for its agreement to Sandycove using
the same design approach and typography, and the same artist, as O'Brien Press
used in the first four Ross O'Carroll-Kelly titles.

Set in 12/14.75pt Dante MT Std
Typeset by Jouve (UK), Milton Keynes
Printed and bound in Great Britain by Clays Ltd, Elcograf S.p.A.

The authorized representative in the EEA is Penguin Random House Ireland,
Morrison Chambers, 32 Nassau Street, Dublin D02 YH68

A CIP catalogue record for this book is available from the British Library

ISBN: 978–1–844–88627–2

www.greenpenguin.co.uk

For Faith O'Grady

Contents

Prologue

I'm an optimist – yeah, no, *famously* so? When an Ireland squad is announced, I always check to see if I'm in it. Even at thirty-nine years old. That's just how I am. Full of dumb confidence. So when Sorcha sends me a text and asks me to pop over to the house tonight, after the kids have gone to bed, I instantly assume it's because she wants me back.

I spend the early port of the evening doing sits-ups, then I throw on the black Deliveroo hoodie I bought on eBay back in the day after Sorcha drunkenly confessed that one of her fantasies was having sex on the stairs with a random food delivery goy.

I got a lot of wear out of the thing on our role-play nights, which quite possibly Roe McDermott in the *Irish Times* magazine said were a good way of keeping a relationship fresh and interesting. Jesus, I even splashed out on a mountain bike, really committing to the port. I should give myself more credit as a husband.

Sorcha was so seriously into it – even adding little storyline twists, like pretending that she couldn't find her purse and asking me if I could think of any other way she could pay for her Nando's pitta triangles with hummus and PERi-PERi drizzle – that I storted to genuinely worry whenever she phoned for takeout and I wasn't actually home.

Anyway, I throw it on me as I'm on my way out the door. As I said, an optimist. Such an optimist, in fact, that it's only when I'm taking the turn off the roundabout onto Ballinclea Road that I stort to think that maybe she's *not* looking for sex and what if the reason she wants to see me has something to do with her sister (still don't know her name) being pregnant and me being potentially the father?

As I pull up outside the house, I actually consider taking the hoodie off, but the optimist in me ends up winning out, as it usually does, which is one of the things I love about myself. But then, as I press the doorbell, I notice her old man's cor in the driveway and my hort storts to beat faster, wondering do they know.

Sorcha answers the door. She's still dressed for work, even though it's, like, ten o'clock at night. She looks wrecked – so much so that she doesn't even notice the hoodie as she opens the door wider and invites me in.

I'm there, 'Er, how *are* you?' still not knowing if I'm walking into an ambush here. For all I know, the sister might have told her that she pretty much seduced me on the day I moved out.

'Tired,' she goes – which I can see with my own eyes.

'You don't *look* tired,' I go. 'You look amazing, in fairness to you.'

It's possibly the tone of my voice – I'm going to use the word *seductive*? – that suddenly brings her to her senses. She notices the Deliveroo logo on my chest, then also, at my feet, the giant, cube-shaped thermal delivery bag – I forgot to mention that we also bought a giant, cube-shaped thermal delivery bag – and she goes, 'Oh my God!' in a highly outraged voice. 'I can't *believe* you thought you were coming here for *that*!'

I'm there, 'Maybe I misread the text.'

But – again – she's like, 'We are never, *ever* doing that again! Get that through your thick focking skull!'

'Doing *what* again?' a voice goes.

Yeah, no, it ends up being her old man. He steps out of the kitchen and stares at me like I'm a focking fan dancer at a funeral.

Sorcha quickly goes, 'Nothing,' because she obviously doesn't want her precious dad to know the kind of shit his little princess gets up to when she's in the mood, like asking me to whisper, 'Your rider is Julio!' in her ear while we're doing it and I hope that doesn't come across as indiscreet.

Sorcha looks me in the eye and goes, 'I don't know if you heard but my sister is pregnant.'

Shit.

I'm there, 'No way.'

But she's like, 'Yes way,' and she carries on staring at me – we're talking full eye contact.

I'm there, 'I hope you don't think –'

She's like, 'What?' and she seems to genuinely *mean* it?

'Yeah, no, nothing,' I go, sorry I even opened my mouth. 'You can continue saying stuff.'

She's like, 'After everything I said to Oisinn and Magnus about her not being an appropriate person to carry their baby, they went ahead and chose her as a surrogate anyway. I'm furious with *her*, of course. But mostly I'm angry with *them*?'

I'm there, 'That's, em, pretty out of order alright. Which sister is it again?' hoping that she'll finally give me the name.

She's like, 'Which sister? I only have one sister and that's –'

But her old man is obviously terrified by the prospect of me worming my way back in there and, before she manages to say the name, he goes, 'Can we get on with this thing?'

Sorcha's there, 'Yes, let's skip the pleasantries and do that.'

I'm like, 'What's this thing? As in, what am I actually doing here?'

Sorcha looks at her old man, who nods once, then she looks back at me again.

'I want you to sign something,' she goes.

I'm there, 'If it's the divorce papers, I might need to think about it. I'm not sure I even *believe* in divorce?'

'No, you're getting it confused with monogamy,' she goes. 'It's monogamy you don't believe in.'

He sort of, like, chuckles to himself. He's loving every minute of this. He's waited long enough for it, in fairness to the dude.

She goes, 'We *are* getting divorced, Ross. But, in the meantime, I need you to sign a piece of paper – basically, a statement.'

'A statement? Saying?'

'Excuse me?'

'As in, what does the statement supposably say?'

She takes a deep breath and it comes back out as a sigh.

'It says that we've been separated for the last five years,' she goes. 'We continued to cohabitate for the sake of our children, but we've been living very much separate lives under the same roof for all of that time.'

I'm there, 'But that'd be a lie, Sorcha.'

She's like, 'Yes, I know that,' and she can't even look at me when she says it.

Sister Austrebertha would be spinning like a rotisserie chicken in her grave. She knows it and I know it. She looks down at her feet.

I'm there, 'So why do you want me to sign a statement telling a lie?' and for a few seconds I have her on the big-time back foot. 'You know, especially given that you led the Rosary at the last Mount Anville Past Pupils Union Prayers and Prosecco event.'

'Because,' *he* ends up going, trying to spare her blushes, 'you're about to go to prison for exposing yourself in public and pinning the blame on someone else. So my daughter, naturally, wants to put distance between you both.'

I'm there, 'I didn't expose myself. I took my orse out in a pub. And that was back in the pre-woke days when that kind of thing was considered hilarious.'

Of course, he wouldn't know that, having zero interest in rugby. He just gives me a look that's as filthy as my internet search history. We're talking, like, genuine, genuine contempt. I'm sure this is all very triggering for him, reminding him of the night in Pearl Brasserie when I got focked up on tequila, turned my trouser pockets inside-out and did my famous elephant impression that still makes Seán O'Brien honk with laughter to this day.

I'm there, 'Is me doing a mooner in The Thomond Bor really what's upsetting you? Or was it me taking my mickey out in front of your family and friends at your twenty-fifth wedding anniversary dinner?'

In that moment, he looks mad enough to kill me with his bare hands.

'Ross, please,' Sorcha goes, 'you being chorged with indecent exposure and perverting the course of justice is obviously very embarrassing for me and I'm talking politically. But if you end up going to prison –'

I'm there, 'I might not go to prison.'

'– if you end up going to prison, that could be the end of my political career.'

'And, what, working for my old man, who burned down the Dáil himself, Sorcha, that *isn't* embarrassing politically?'

'Ross, I don't want this overshadowing my legislative agenda for the rest of 2019!' she pretty much roars at me – and then, in a softer voice, she goes, 'Ross, you owe me this.'

I look at her and it's weird because I know in that moment that it's, like, definitely, definitely *over* between us? And I feel sad thinking that she'll never again dig her fingernails into my head and shout, 'Oh, Julio! Ride me like I'm your delivery bike and you've a bagful of orders going cold!' and I'll never get to use my brilliant 'Order Successfully Delivered!' line as she lies on the stairs in a post-sexual daze.

'Fine,' I go, realizing that the game is up here. 'I'll do it.'

Sorcha smiles. She's like, 'Thank you, Ross.'

But *he* goes, 'Don't thank him. It's the least you deserve after what he's put you through for the last – *how* many years? Let him go to jail and rot there, I say.'

I'm like, 'Where is it? As in, this famous statement?'

'It's in the kitchen,' she goes, then she leads the way. He makes sure to come too. Yeah, no, he doesn't want any slip-ups at this late stage.

The statement is sitting on top of the island. It's, like, ten lines long but I don't bother my hole even reading it. I just pick up the pen that's sitting beside it and I scribble my name at the bottom with a big flourish – like when I used to practise my autograph back in school.

'Can you put your second name as well?' she goes, so I add the O'Carroll and the Kelly.

She's like, 'Thank you.'

I'm just about to ask if I can pop upstairs to see Brian, Johnny and Leo, but then I remember that I saw them last weekend – they were very focking annoying – and that was probably enough. And that's when, out of nowhere, her old man ends up suddenly *losing* it with me?

He goes, 'Why the *hell* are you wearing that?' and I just assume he's talking about the Deliveroo hoodie. Having had enough of his shit for one night, I end up going, 'What, this thing? If you must know, me and your daughter used to play this kinky game where she ordered food for delivery and paid for it with sex.'

'Oh! My God!' Sorcha goes, putting her hand over her mouth.

I'm there, 'The reason she was limping at your twenty-fifth anniversary dinner, by the way, was corpet burns on her orse.'

Sorcha's like, 'Oh my God! Oh my God! Oh my God!'

And that's when the dude goes, 'I'm *talking* about your wedding ring!'

I'm there, 'Alriiighty – *slight* breakdown in communication there.'

He goes, 'Take it off!' and he grabs me violently by the wrist and – I shit you not – storts literally trying to pull the thing off my finger.

Sorcha screams. She's like, 'Dad! Stop it!'

And I'm there going, 'What the fock? What the *actual* focking fock?' because he's hurting me. Yeah, no, I don't mind admitting, I'm not the whippet-thin number ten I was when Sorcha and I first got hitched.

'Get it off you!' the dude goes – in an absolute *rage*, by the way? 'You're not married to my daughter any more!'

I'm there, 'I am still *technically*?' but he's having none of it.

Still clutching my wrist, he literally drags me over to the fridge, tears open the door and whips out the Low Low Gold.

Sorcha's like, 'What are you doing?' and she's practically hysterical.

He's there, 'If it won't come off naturally, I'm going to have to use this,' and the next thing I know he's sticking his hand into the tub and smearing my finger in butter.

He storts pulling again and, I swear to fock, I'm in absolute agony. I should deck the focker – God knows, he's had it coming for years – but it's like he's suddenly got this, I don't know, superhuman strength. It's like all the shit I've thrown at him over the years has turned him into a monster – one who's in serious danger of dislocating my finger.

Sorcha's still going, 'Dad, stop! Dad, please, stop!' but the dude won't be told.

I end up just howling. I'm like, 'Oooooouuuuuuwwwwww!!!!!!'

The ring still won't budge, even with my left hand covered in butter, which makes him even angrier.

I'm like, 'Dude, chillax. I'll lose a bit of weight – especially now that it looks like I'm going to be back on the dating scene,' but he's not listening to reason.

He drags me over to the counter where the chopping board sits and that's when Sorcha ends up totally losing it. She's, like, screaming at the top of her voice, going, 'Dad, no! No! I don't *want* this!'

And of course I have no idea what *this* is until he throws open the cutlery drawer with his free hand and pulls out the good Sabatier bread knife.

I'm like, 'What the fock?' as he slams my hand down on the chopping board. And now it's *my* turn to scream? Because the mad bastard is going to do it – he's going to saw off my actual finger.

I'm there, 'Dude, no! No! Noooooo!!!!!!'

And that's when I hear a sudden clunk behind me. Sorcha's old man drops the knife and falls to the ground. I turn around and Brian, Johnny and Leo are standing there in their pyjamas, Leo with a wok in his hand, having pretty much knocked Sorcha's old man out cold.

'What . . . the hell –' the dude grumbles, no idea what day of the week it is.

I'm like, 'Boys! It's great to see you!' and I'm not actually lying for once.

Brian snatches the wok out of Leo's hand, steps forward and gives his grandfather a second crack over the head with the thing. And while I'm tempted to step out of the room and leave them to it, Sorcha insists on taking it out of his hand.

'Ross,' she goes, 'just get out of the house – before my dad comes round.'

So I decide to call it a day – down a wife, but at least with all my fingers still attached.

Sorcha gets down on her hunkers to see if he's okay. A second or two later, he raises his head.

He goes, 'Get him out of here, Sorcha! Please! Before I kill him!'

Moonfaker

So – yeah, no – I'm in Erika's gaff on Ailesbury Road, which is, like, *home* to me and Honor now? Or at least for the moment. Erika has taken Amelie and Honor shopping for the morning and I decide to make myself useful by doing the laundry. I tip into Erika's room and I stort pulling things out of her, like, laundry basket.

I absolutely love the smell of her clothes and I don't mean that in, like, a pervy way. She's my actual half-sister – as I'm constantly reminding myself. What I mean is that I've always loved the smell of *Symphony* by Louis Vuitton, which is, like, her signature scent. I hold her light blue Adriano Goldschmied shirt up to my nose and mouth and I breathe in. It smells unbelievable – gorgeous, even.

After about five minutes of doing this, I end up feeling a little bit faint and that's when I hear a voice go, 'What the fock are you doing?'

Yeah, no, Erika is standing at the door of her bedroom, shopping bags swinging from her fingers and a look of horror on her face.

I'm like, 'Hey, Erika, how was Dundrum?' trying to style it out.

She's there, 'I asked you a focking question,' snatching her shirt out of my hand and also a pair of black lace knickers that I also just so happen to be holding. 'What are you doing?'

I'm there, 'In a word, laundry.'

'You were sniffing my dirty clothes.'

'Hey, I happen to love the smell of *Symphony* by Louis Vuitton. I'm not going to apologize for that.'

'Just stay out of my focking room. You're sick in the focking head.'

I'm like, 'Fair enough. Does Helen have anything for the wash, do you know?'

'Stay away from my mother's clothes as well. Jesus Christ, Ross, what the fock is wrong with you? You've already been cancelled for being a focking pervert.'

'Can I just remind you – and the rest of the public – that I haven't been found guilty of *anything* yet?'

'The coach of the Ireland women's team exposing himself in public. You know you're never going to get a job in rugby again?'

'Yeah, no, they weren't exactly queueing up to employ me *before* I took my orse out in The Thomond Bor.'

As I'm heading for the door, she goes, 'You heard that Sorcha's sister is pregnant, did you?'

I'm there, 'Er, yeah, no, I did. Sorcha's not happy about it.'

'What focking business is it of hers?' Erika goes – this is the girl who used to be her bezzy mate, by the way. 'Oisinn and Magnus are happy. They're going to be parents.'

I'm like, 'Hmmm,' not wanting to commit myself one way or the other. 'Hmmm-hmmm.'

'Anyway,' she goes, 'can you fock off now because I need to get changed?'

'Are you going out again?'

'I'm going to Dóchas.'

'Is that the new coffee shop on Monkstown Crescent? I've heard good things.'

'It's the focking women's prison, Ross.'

'Oh . . . *that* Dóchas. That's why you're changing out of your good clothes. You're presumably going to visit See-mon?'

'It's pronounced Sea-mon.'

'Yeah, I'm pretty sure that's what I'm saying. How the hell is she?'

'How do you think she is?'

Yeah, no, Simone is Sorcha's former Special Adviser, who's been chorged with burning down the Dáil, even though we all know she was fitted up by Hennessy.

I'm there, 'Have they set a date for, like, her *trial* yet?'

She goes, 'They're saying it could be November or December. I've got her a new solicitor and he's pretty confident that he can get her out on bail until then.'

'Fair focks, Erika. Here, tell her I said hello, will you?'

'Why?'

'I don't know. It's a figure of speech, isn't it?'

'It's not exactly going to make her day, is it?'

'Probably not.'

I step out onto the landing, then I turn back – just as she's taking her good sweater off over her head. Yeah, no, she's standing there in just her bra.

She's like, 'For fock's sake, Ross.'

'Sorry,' I go, 'I just wanted to ask you something.'

She still has a great bod in fairness to her – and I mean that in a *non*-sexual way? Her boozies are like two scoops of butter pecan sorbet and I'm saying that as a technically blood relative.

'What?' she goes, trying to cover up with her orms.

I'm like, 'Errr,' totally thrown for a minute.

My face feels suddenly hot.

She's there, 'You said you wanted to ask me something.'

'Oh, yeah, sorry,' I go. 'Tell me this, will you? What's Sorcha's sister's name?'

'Her name?' she goes.

'Yeah, no, what is it – as in what actually?'

She looks at me like I'm as dippy as a dump truck.

She goes, 'How could you not know your wife's sister's name? Jesus Christ, you've slept with her, haven't you?'

I'm like, 'Hmmm.'

'Did you come back to ask me that just so you could see me in my bra?'

'No.'

But she goes, 'Fock's sake, Ross! You sick focker!' and she slams the bedroom door in my face.

So – yeah, no – I tip downstairs and I find Honor in the kitchen, giving little Amelie a – believe it or not – *makeover*?

'Hi, Uncle Ross!' the kid goes. 'Honor is plucking my eyebrows!'

And I'm like, 'That's good! How was Dundrum?'

'Oh my God,' she goes, 'Honor bought me my first ever pair of, like, high-heel shoes and she's going to teach me how to, like, *walk* in them?'

I sort of, like, smile to myself. It's nice to see them bonding like this, my daughter and Erika's daughter, whatever they are to each other – half-cousins, I suppose.

'Amelie,' Honor goes, 'will you go upstairs and get my Charlotte Tilbury eyebrow pencil? It's on my dressing table.'

Off the kid runs.

I laugh. I'm there, 'Looks like she's turning into your Mini-Me!'

Except Honor isn't listening. She's reading a text and sort of, like, smiling to herself.

They say you should always take an interest in what your kids are up to, so I go, 'Who's that, Honor?'

She's like, 'Mind your own focking business.'

And I'm there, 'Hey, I was just asking, Honor. Ticking a box.'

She sends a text back, then she goes, 'It's just a boy.'

I'm like, 'A boy?'

'Before you ask,' she goes, 'the answer is Blackrock College.'

I nod and try not to let my feelings show in my face.

'Excuse me?' she goes.

I'm there, 'I didn't say anything.'

'You said "focking wanker",' she goes.

Yeah, no, it's quite possible I did – it's, like, an *automatic* thing?

I'm there, 'Does he have a name, this focking –'

She goes, 'His name is Joel.'

I'm like, 'Joel? Yeah, no, I can already picture him. And what, are you, like, going out with each other?'

'Oh my God,' she goes, 'your generation are, like, so obsessed with labels.'

I'm there, 'Yeah, no, maybe you're right. Back in my day, relationships were a lot simpler. There was going out with someone and then there was seeing someone. There was also being with someone. And obviously being *with* with someone. It's a lot more complicated now.'

'Whatever.'

'I saw your old dear last night. She was asking for you.'

'Was that a lie?'

'Yeah, no, pretty much.'

'She hates my focking guts.'

'I wouldn't say she hates your guts, Honor.'

'Then why did she throw me out of the house?'

'She's just upset. I mean, you kidnapped that boy.'

'It wasn't focking kidnapping.'

'Well, you smashed him over the head, put him in the boot of your old dear's cor and drove up him to the Sally Gap. He missed the Leinster Schools Senior Cup final.'

'He deserved everything he got.'

'He did deserve everything he got.'

Except missing the Leinster Schools Senior Cup final. No one deserves that.

'She's just terrified that it's going to get out,' she goes, 'like you exposing yourself in public –'

I'm there, 'It was a mooner, Honor. I thought you were on my side.'

'– and it'll damage her so-called political career.'

'Well, that one won't get out. Hennessy paid everyone off.'

Yeah, no, including Reese's old pair – and the Feds, who agreed to forget the entire incident.

'How are the boys?' Honor goes.

She misses them.

I'm there, 'Yeah, no, I only saw them briefly. Leo smashed Sorcha's old man over the head with a wok.'

She's like, 'Hill! Air!'

'Yeah, no, the dude was trying to saw my finger off at the time.'

'Oh! My God!'

'That's what your old dear said. Word for word. Her sister's pregnant, by the way.'

'I know. I saw it on her Instagram. So the baby will be, like, my cousin, right?'

If I end up being the father, God focking knows what it'll be.

I'm there, 'So she's, em, on Instagram, is she?'

'Yeah, hilarious,' she goes, 'she's just storted working in this, like, hair removal salon in, like, Bray of all places. It's called, like, The Waxy Dorgle!'

I'm like, 'Jesus. No wonder the family have practically disowned her. I must give her a follow on – like you said – Instagram.'

She's there, 'Whatever.'

'What's her name again?'

She looks at me like I'm out of my bin.

She's there, 'Her what?'

I'm like, 'Her name.'

'You don't know your sister-in-law's name?'

'Yeah, no, I've just forgotten it. I think I've got a touch of that old-timer's disease!'

She sighs and goes, 'Her name is –'

And at that exact moment, her phone rings. She looks at the screen.

'Oh my God,' she goes, 'it's Joel! Dad, can you please fock off so that I can talk to him in private?'

'So what do you think?' the old man goes.

I'm there, 'What do you mean, what do I think? It's just, like, a banknote with, I don't know, some random old dude on it.'

I fock it back across the table at him – which is something I wouldn't *usually* do? It's just that it looks like the kind of funny money they try to slip into your change in Ronan's old local in Finglas.

The old man laughs.

He's there, 'Did you hear that, Fionnuala? That *random old dude* – as you call him, Kicker – just so happens to be the late, great CJH!'

I'm like, 'Who?' and I genuinely mean it.

'Aha!' he goes. 'I can see where you're going with this, Ross! Trying to entice your *old dad*, as you call me, into one of our famous political dissensions on the subject of the great man's legacy! He's incorrigible, Fionnuala! Absolutely incorrigible!'

I have literally no idea what he's talking about. But I decide to ask him – making the effort, as you do with your parents.

'What the fock does it have to do with me,' I go, 'focking, I don't know, Dick Features?'

He's like, 'Excellent question, Kicker! The answer is that you're going to be seeing these everywhere in a few short weeks! Because on the first day of July, in the year two thousand and nineteen – Anno Domini! – we shall be leaving the Euro and returning to the punt!'

I'm there, 'On second thoughts, give me that back, will you?'

I snatch it back from him and throw my eyes over it again. Yeah, no, it's, like, a *fifty*?

He's like, 'I knew you'd want one of the first ones to roll off the presses, Ross! Notwithstanding your reservations about Haughey as a statesman on the world stage!'

I'm there, 'Can you get me more of these?'

He's like, 'Of course I can! I'm the bloody well Taoiseach!'

I'm there, 'About two or three hundred of them would be great. Like you said, they're collector's items.'

'And you'll never guess whose face I've chosen to adorn the twenty-pound note!' he goes. 'Your friend and mine – Seánie Fitz! Oh, the chap was cock-a-hoop when I phoned him personally with the news, Ross! Cock-a-hoop!'

'I'll take five hundred of those. No, make it a thousand.'

'You see, I knew you were a fan!'

The old dear goes, 'Did you tell him the other news, Chorles?'

Jesus Christ, I thought her without make-up was the most disgusting sight I'd ever seen until I saw her eating a breakfast frittata without her dental plate in.

'We're returning to the southside,' she goes.

I'm there, 'Can you maybe *not* talk with your mouth full? You're focking spraying me with egg here. Hang on, what do you mean you're returning to the southside? You mean you're moving out of the Áras?'

'Oh, no, we have no intention of leaving the Áras,' she goes. 'Your father is going to move the river.'

I actually laugh.

I'm like, 'You're shitting me,' and I look at him when I say it, because he's the one who supposably *doesn't* have dementia? 'Please tell me you're shitting me.'

He goes, 'I have requested the Office of Public Works to undertake – as a matter of the utmost urgency – the job of rerouting the famous River Liffey! Exclamation mork! Exclamation mork! Exclamation mork!'

Again, I laugh.

I'm like, 'Rerouting it? Rerouting it where?'

'Well, initially,' he goes, 'through Cabra and Ashtown.'

'Are those the names of places on the northside?'

'Correct! Then through Castleknock! That's the route they feel will involve the least disruption and require the fewest number of houses to be demolished!'

'So, what, you're knocking down people's actual homes to do this?'

'Only about two hundred or so! They'll be compensated, Hennessy has assured me! Provided they have the stomach for the legal fight! You know what he's like, Kicker! An absolute bastard, of course! I'm just glad he's *our* bastard!'

'And all just so you can say that you live on the southside?'

The old dear goes, 'What's wrong with that?'

I end up just shaking my head. I'm like, 'Nothing – for you two anyway. I suppose it's, like, por for the course.'

The old man reaches into his jacket pocket and whips out a Montecristo the size of a child of school-going age.

He goes, 'By the way, Ross, your mother and I were very saddened to hear the news that you and Sorcha have decided to port ways! She's a much-loved member of this family as well as a valued Cabinet colleague.'

I'm there, 'We didn't decide to port ways. She focked me out. Because I did a mooner in a pub in Cork and tried to pin the entire thing on Fionn.'

The old man just shakes his head.

'Since when did taking your orse out in public become a matter for the Gordaí?' he goes. 'It's political what's-it gone mad! Quote-unquote!'

I'm like, 'Yeah, whatever.'

'Ross, you really must let Hennessy do something about those chorges! I mean, what's the point of *having* the Attorney General as your godfather if you can't ask him to help you out of the occasional – inverted commas – pickle?'

'Because I've decided to own it. For once in my life, I'm taking responsibility for my own shit.'

'But why on earth would you want to do that? Hennessy could make the case just disappear! Or make sure it's heard by a sympathetic judge! Dare I say it, a rugby judge! This is still bloody well Ireland after all.'

'And what would the cost of that be?'

'What do you mean? No money would change hands! It's rugby, Ross!'

'Bullshit. The dude told me himself that he'd only help me if I persuaded Ronan to come back from the States to work for him.'

'Well, you know how I feel about that particular issue! Young Ronan belongs here! With Shadden and Rihanna-what's-it! And, yes – as you say – it *was* Hennessy's dream that Ronan would one day take over the business from him!'

'And what business *is* that exactly?'

He tries to go, 'The legal business, of course!'

I'm there, 'Yeah, right,' at the same time getting to my feet. I'm suddenly not hungry any more.

'Oh, one last thing,' the old man goes, 'before you leave, Kicker – tell me, what are you doing a week on Friday?'

I'm like, 'The usual. Getting pissed in The Bridge – that's if I'm not still borred. I'll have to check with Heaslip.'

'Well, forget all of that! The future Prime Minister of Great Britain and Northern Ireland – the famous Boris Johnson! – is visiting and I'm hosting an informal dinner for the chap! Want to put on a bit of a show for him! He's going to be the greatest leader the United Kingdom has had since Winston Churchill – once the Tories see sense and get rid of that frightful Theresa May woman! I want our countries to be friends, Ross, especially once we've both freed ourselves from the shackles of EU membership!'

'And this affects me *how* exactly?'

'I'd just like you to be there, Kicker! I think you two would get along famously! The famous Vladimir Putin still asks for you, by the way!'

'I've got better things to be doing.'

He goes, 'How many of those Chorles J. Haugheys did you say you wanted again?' because he's no focking fool, even though he comes across as one. 'I could have them here for you on the night!'

I'm there, 'Fine. I'll see you then. I'm going to pop into the nursery to see the kids – if that's okay with you two, I'm just going to come out and say it, *knobs*.'

'Be careful of Cassiopeia,' the old dear goes. 'She's become a bit of a biter since she storted teething. She almost took my nose off yesterday – although I think she may have had a sip from my Margarita when I wasn't looking. Must be a family thing. Tequila made my mother aggressive too.'

I walk out and leave them to their breakfast. Honestly, with those two as parents, it's a genuine wonder that I turned out as well as I did.

Into the nursery I go. Astrid, their German nanny, is looking after my – still so random – brother and sisters, we're talking Hugo, we're talking Cassiopeia, we're talking Diana, we're talking Mellicent, we're talking Louisa May, we're talking Emily.

They're all walkers at this stage and they're tipping around the room happily.

I'm like, 'Astrid, how are you?' but not in a flirty way, because – with the greatest will in the world – she's not great in terms of looks.

'I am good,' she goes, 'if a little tired. They are much, much work.'

I'm there, 'Yeah, no,' picking up Cassiopeia, 'I believe this little one nearly took the old dear's nose off yesterday.'

Astrid suddenly goes quiet. There's something on her mind.

I'm like, 'What's wrong? You can tell me.'

She goes, 'She give her tequila to drink.'

'Excuse me?'

'Your mother. I see her. She thinks she is in The Shelbourne Bar with her friend – is it Blothnid?'

'Yeah, no, that'd be Bláthnaid Ní Chofaigh. They go way, way back.'

'She say, "Here you are, Blothnid – down the hatch!" and she gives tequila to the baby.'

'Jesus Christ.'

'I say to your father. I say, Fionnuala is sick, sick woman. She cannot be around children. But it is me that he blames. He says that if I am watching the children properly, then no one could give them alcohol.'

He actually has a point, in fairness, although I don't say that.

She's there, 'I would tell him what to do with his job except then I would worry what would happen to these children if I was not here.'

I'm like, 'Fock.'

'You must persuade your father,' she goes, 'that your mother needs full-time care – even more than these children.'

All of a sudden, my phone rings. I can see from the screen that it's Oisinn.

Shit.

I'm thinking, Does he know? As in, does he know that Sorcha's sister's baby might possibly be mine? I'm going to have to stort simplifying my life at some point. Whatever he does or doesn't know, I decide to just, like, brazen it out with him.

I answer the phone, going, 'Oisinn, how the hell *are* you?'

He's like, 'Hey, Ross, how are you?' and he sounds in alright form.

I'm guessing he knows fock-all.

I'm there, 'All good this end – except the old man is about to reroute the Liffey and the old dear is pouring tequila into her children.'

'Jesus,' he goes, in fairness to him. 'Hey, I've got a bit of news. Me and Magnus are taking a lease on Gerald Kean's old gaff in Brittas Bay.'

I'm there, 'Whoa! Fair focking focks!'

'We're going to turn it into an in-patient care facility for former ad-tech and fin-tech employees struggling to readjust to the real world.'

'You're getting a second fair focking focks for that, Dude – like it or like it not.'

'By the way, Sorcha's sister had her first scan yesterday.'

'And the good news keeps on coming.'

'Oh my God, Ross, I can't even begin to tell you how it felt. Well, you've been through it before, so there's no need to tell you.'

I'm trying to remember was I there for any of Sorcha's scans.

I'm there, 'It stays with you for life, Dude.'

And that's when he goes, 'So which one of us do you think is the father?'

I end up nearly having a prolapse on the spot.

I'm there, 'What? What do you mean?'

He goes, 'Exactly that, Ross. Which one of us is the father?'

I'm like, 'What the fock has she said? She's a focking liar, Oisinn. If we know one thing about her, it's that she's not to be trusted.'

He's there, 'What are you talking about?'

I'm like, 'Er, what are *you* talking about?'

'I'm saying I wonder which one of us is the father – me or Magnus? Because we both provided sperm for the transfer. We've both said we don't want to know, but I suppose it'll become obvious as the baby gets older.'

Jesus focking Christ, my nerves are in ribbons here.

I'm there, 'Yeah, no, it's all ahead of you, Dude.'

He becomes a bit, I don't know, *emotional* then?

He goes, 'You know, I don't care which one of us provided the actual DNA. I'm going to be a father, Ross. I'm going to be a –'

His voices cracks and I decide that I can't listen to any more.

I go, 'Dude, you're just breaking up there,' and I blow into the phone two or three times, then I hang up, knowing that I have to find out the truth, even though it could destroy our friendship forever.

The Waxy Dorgle is on Florence Road, between Vape Nation and The Vape Academy and directly opposite The Vape of Things to Come. Three e-cigarette shops on one street. Seriously, I've never said a word about Bray that wasn't one hundred per cent true – although you would have to admire the confidence of whoever came along when there were only two and thought to themselves, 'You know what this street really needs?'

I push the door and walk up the stairs. There's a bird standing behind the counter wearing glasses and a long, white coat, looking like a doctor, although I'm guessing she's about as medically qualified as the women you see in Holland & Barrett, flogging cod liver oil capsules and muesli bors that soften your shit.

I'm like, 'Hey,' in my sexiest voice, because I just have a thing for women in glasses – well, good-looking women anyway.

She's there, 'Can I help you?'

I'm like, 'Yeah, no, I was looking for, em –'

She thinks I've come in to be waxed but lost my nerve.

She's there, 'Do you want to make an appointment for another day?'

I'm like, 'Yeah, no, I'm looking for a girl. She's just storted working here.'

'Oh,' she goes, 'you must mean –'

But she doesn't get to finish her sentence because Sorcha's sister suddenly appears from one of the treatment rooms and goes, 'He's here to see me, Vanessa.'

Fock sake.

She's like, 'Hello, Ross?' drinking me in with her eyes – the way she *always* does? 'Do you want to come through?' and I follow her into the – like I said – treatment room.

She closes the door behind us.

'How *are* you?' she goes.

I'm like, 'Jesus Christ, how the fock do you *think* I am?'

'I heard my dad tried to cut off your finger.'

'Yeah, no, he seriously lost it with me.'

'He'll cut off more than your finger if he finds out that you're the father of this baby I'm carrying.'

'Well, am I? That's what I'm here to find out.'

She goes, 'Who knows?' and she smiles at me like *she* knows – like she *knows* but isn't telling.

I'm there, 'Is this fun for you, er –' and I look to see if she's wearing a name badge. Unfortunately, she's not.

She goes, 'Of course it's fun. It's *so* much fun.'

I'm there, 'Look, this isn't you trying to pull me off in the doorway of Select Stores the night Sorcha was named the Dalkey Lobster Festival Queen with her and your old pair walking ten metres ahead of us. This is focking serious.'

Suddenly, totally out of left field, she storts unbuttoning my shirt.

I'm like, 'What the fock are you doing?' although – typical me – I'm not exactly pushing her away.

'You are *so* hairy,' she goes. 'Oh my God, look at you!'

I'm like, 'Yeah, no, thanks,' because I can take a compliment as well as the next man, even if the next man is Dylan Hortley.

'That wasn't a compliment,' she goes. 'You're like a walking corpet.'

I'm there, 'Am I?'

'Okay, maybe that look *used* to be in – but it's not any more.'

'Isn't it?'

'Do you ever watch *Love Island*?'

She's obviously talking about those hairless dudes with the spray tans and the Turkey teeth.

I'm there, 'I think they look weird – random, even.'

She goes, 'Ross, if you're back on the dating scene, you're going to have to get with the times. No girl wants *this*,' and she runs the tips of her fingers through my chest hair. 'Oh my God, some of these hairs are actually grey.'

Jesus Christ, I can feel myself getting a chubby here. What the fock is wrong with me?

I'm there, 'I came here to ask you if I'm the father of this baby,' and at the same time I'm wondering if she can see the old fat intruder.

She goes, 'I told you. I don't know.'

I'm like, 'You do know. You have to know.'

She smiles at me. She's loving every second of it.

'I can't believe you've got a boner,' she goes.

I'm there, 'Will you stop focking around? Look, Oisinn is a friend of mine. So is Magnus. I don't want you stringing them along. If I'm the father, you need to tell me.'

She goes, 'Do you mind me saying, I never understood what you saw in my sister,' and she carries on fingering my chest hair.

I'm there, 'In terms of?' and I am extremely turned on now.

She's there, 'I've been listening to it since I was a child – you know, just how focking perfect she is. Mom *and* Dad, letting me know that, no matter what I did in life, I was never going to measure up. I've had a focking lifetime of it. From the moment I took my first steps, I was told, "Sorcha learned to walk when she was a year younger than you!" When I learned to read, it was, "Sorcha was reading at three!" Do you know what it's like to be constantly reminded of someone else's achievements?'

I'm like, 'Yeah, no, it'd be a similar situation with me and Brian O'Dris–'

'And when I got older, it got worse. Commendation in the Young Scientist of the Year competition. All Ireland Debating Champion. Head Girl. Maximum points in the focking Leaving Cert. And now look at her. She's got the career that her daddy always wanted her to have – whereas I'm a total fock-up. Except when it came to you. It was always a comfort for me to know that I could have her husband any time I focking wanted.'

'And you did, in fairness to you. You could probably have me right now. Would that treatment table hold our weight?'

She goes, 'I hate her! I focking HATE her!'

I'm like, 'Yeah, no, I'm picking up on that. So, like, are you going to tell me?'

She's there, 'Tell you what?' and she stops playing with my chest hair.

I'm like, 'Tell me whether or not I'm the father of your baby.'

I swear to fock, she goes, 'How would I know?'

I'm there, 'Er, simple maths?' even though I was the goy in school who thought Henry the Eighth was the inventor of fractions.

I'm not even joking.

She goes, 'Ross, I had sex with you the day after the sperm transfer. There's no actual *way* of knowing.'

I'm there, 'But you can get, like, a DNA test done before you even *have* the baby?' at the same time buttoning up my shirt.

'Unfortunately,' she goes, 'I'm afraid of needles.'

I'm like, 'Afraid of needles? You're covered in, like, tattoos.'

But all she does is smile at me. She's there, 'I'm going to enjoy the intrigue over the next nine months. And I'll tell you something else,

Ross. I really, really hope that it ends up being *your* baby? Just to see the look on that focking bitch's face.'

I'm there, 'I'd like to speak to Fionn de Barra, please?'

Yeah, no, I'm talking to Ciara Casaubon, who isn't even his secretary, by the way. She's a focking maths teacher, who went to – believe it or not – King's Hos and who snowballed Gussie Grennan, the Gonzaga number eight, in the jacks in Hollywood Nights back in the day.

She goes, 'I'm afraid Mr de Barra is busy.'

I'm thinking, A school principal? Busy? Yeah, give me a focking break.

I'm like, 'Yeah, you're not even his focking secretary, can I just remind you?'

'His secretary is at lunch,' she tries to go, 'and I told him I'd make sure he isn't disturbed.'

I'm there, 'How's Gussie Grennan? Do you ever hear from him?'

'Who?' she tries to go.

You wouldn't focking blame her wanting to forget him. Gussie had a face like a roofer's knee.

I'm there, 'Doesn't matter. Can you maybe just go in there and tell Fionn that Ross O'Carroll-Kelly is here to see him?'

'He doesn't want to see anyone,' she goes, 'and he especially doesn't want to see you.'

I'm there, 'I've come here to apologize to him.'

'He doesn't want your apologies.'

'Who the fock are you to say what he wants and doesn't want? Correct me if I'm wrong but you didn't play rugby with him.'

'Please leave – or I'll call the Gords.'

I'm like, 'Call the focking Gords,' and I just push my way past her and into his office.

I'm the last person in the world he expects to see – that's judging by his reaction.

He's like, 'What are you doing here?'

I'm there, 'Believe it or not, I've come to apologize.'

'I don't want your apologies,' he goes.

I'm like, 'Look, Dude, I'm sorry I told the Feds that it was you who flashed his orse in The Thomond Bor!'

He ends up totally flying off the handle then.

He's like, 'That's *not* what you focking did!' seriously, seriously losing it with me. 'You appeared in court, pretending to be me. You pleaded guilty to indecent exposure using my identity and you allowed my name to be put on the register of sex offenders. And when I was suspended from this job because of it, you said absolutely nothing.'

I'm there, 'I was Head Coach of the Ireland women's team. I swear to fock, I was going to come clean *after* the Six Nations?'

He's like, 'You stood idly by while I was labelled as a sexual deviant and ostracized by colleagues who once respected me.'

'Well,' I go, 'I'm sorry for *all* of that.'

He's there, 'No, Ross! You don't *get* to say sorry! Why are you apologizing anyway? Oh, let me guess – they've set your trial date and you want me to go to court to speak on your behalf.'

'Sorry to disappoint you,' I go, 'but no.'

'What, your old man's crooked solicitor is fixing it for you?'

'No, he's not. I've told Hennessy to stay the fock out of it. When the time comes, I'm going to plead guilty. I've already been – Erika used the word – *cancelled*? I mean, the shit that people are saying about me on Twitter. But I'm happy to take whatever punishment is coming my way.'

He goes, 'Sorry, are you expecting a round of applause or something?'

I sort of *am*? And that's me being brutally honest.

I'm there, 'Dude, like I said, I don't care what people out there are saying – a brilliant coaching career has come to an end, I'm a sexual deviant, blah, blah, blah. I just don't want to lose your friendship.'

He goes, 'My friendship? We're not friends! We were *never* friends!'

'I disagree.'

'A friend would never do something like that.'

'Again, I beg to differ. I've done way worse than this on you.'

'Yes, you have. You've spent half your life focking me over. Not just me, but Christian, JP and Oisinn as well.'

At the mention of Oisinn, I go suddenly quiet.

He's there, 'You're toxic, Ross. You're poison.'

'Well, if one good thing has come out of all of this,' Ciara goes, walking around to his side of the desk and standing next to his chair, 'it's that we've finally faced up to the problem with the culture in this – and *all* – same-sex schools.'

'The fock are *you* banging on about?' I go. 'The fock is she banging on about, Dude?'

Fionn sits back in his chair and gives me a big, smug smile. 'As the Principal of Castlerock College,' he goes, 'I've made the decision that, from September of next year, the school will be going . . . co-ed.'

I'm like, 'Co-ed? Does that mean you'll be letting –'

'Letting girls in,' *she* goes. 'Yes, that's exactly what it means.'

I'm like, 'I can't believe what I'm actually hearing here.'

'Well, whether you believe it or not,' *he* goes, 'it's happening.'

I'm there, 'I'm trying to imagine what Father Fehily would say if he was alive today. Jesus Christ, he didn't believe that women should be educated at all.'

Fionn just goes, 'The world has moved on since Father Fehily's time. We have to accept that a lot of the things he held dear have no place in modern society.'

'The only thing that all-male schools succeed in doing,' this – again – Ciara one goes, 'is turning out people like you,' meaning me, and she doesn't mean that in a good way.

And then I suddenly notice something. It's in, like, their body language. Fionn never could hide it when he was into a bird and then I notice her put a supposedly comforting hand on *his* shoulder.

'Oh my God,' I go, 'you're, like, riding each other.'

Fionn's like, 'Get out of my office,' which is as good as an admission of guilt.

I'm there, 'I don't focking believe it. *She's* put you up to this, hasn't she?'

Now it's her turn to go, 'Get out. I *will* call the Gords.'

I'm there, 'Don't worry, I'm going,' all the time staring at Fionn. 'You do know she snowballed Gussie Grennan in the jacks in Hollywood Nights, don't you? It was the night that Ulster won the – mad when you think about it now – Heineken Cup.'

Again, *she* goes, 'Who the fock is Gussie Grennan?' and I suddenly remember that it actually *wasn't* her? It was another girl called Eilish Tunney. I don't know how I forgot because the same girl tried to snowball *me* at a house porty in Foxrock, even though it was probably more Cornelscourt.

I'm there, 'Actually, it doesn't matter.'

I turn around and I storm out of there. On my way out the door, Fionn shouts after me, 'You and I are finished, Ross. I want nothing to do with you – ever again!' which obviously hurts.

I walk back to my cor in an absolute fouler. I feel like I need to take it out on someone, which explains why I end up doing what I do next. I whip out my phone, Google the number of The Waxy Dorgle in Bray and dial it. The phone is answered on the third ring.

'The Waxy Dargle, Bray,' the receptionist goes. 'Can I help you?'

I'm like, 'Yeah, no, can I speak to the manager, please?'

Thirty seconds later, some random dude comes on the line.

He's like, 'This is Deco Gahan. I'm the manager. How can I help you?'

I'm there, 'Yeah, no, just to let you know, Deco, that I was in your place for a wax the other day and I ended up itching all over.'

'I'm so sorry to hear that,' Deco goes. 'Who was your therapist?'

I'm there, 'I, er, don't know what she's called. She's, like, *new* there?'

'It's probably folliculitis.'

'That could be her name alright. Although I thought there was a Z in it.'

'No, I'm saying that's likely what you have,' Deco goes. 'Did you indicate on your client intake form that you had sensitive skin?'

I'm there, 'Er, I wasn't *given* a form?'

He's there, 'You should have been given a form.'

'Woulda, shoulda, coulda,' I go. 'Seriously, whatever her name is, the girl should be focking sacked.'

Honor's got her nose stuck in her phone as per usual and she's smiling, which is something she literally *never* does, except when something has gone disastrously wrong for someone else.

I'm there, 'Is that Joel? Not that it's any of my business.'

'No, it's not Joel,' she goes, not even looking up. 'It's MacDara.'

I'm like, 'MacDara? Jesus! And do you mind me asking –'

'Clongowes,' she goes.

I'm there, 'I was actually going to ask is MacDara his first name or his second name?'

She's like, 'It's his first name.'

I actually make a fist and punch the air.

I'm like, 'Fair focks, Honor! Fair focking focks! And do you like this dude? This MacDara?' because I love saying his name. He clearly comes from money.

She just shrugs. She's there, 'He's okay.'

All I can do is just shake my head.

I'm there, 'Your old dear probably wouldn't thank me for saying this, Honor, but I think you cracking Reese over the head and then driving him up the mountains in the boot of a cor is one of the best things you ever did?'

She looks at me. She's like, 'Really?' because – yeah, no – she's always loved positive feedback. Takes after me in that regord.

I'm there, 'It's created a whiff of danger about you, Honor. Dudes love that. I mean, first Joel, now MacDara. They're all over you like flies on –'

The doorbell all of a sudden rings.

She goes, 'That might *be* Joel. He said he might call in.'

I stand up and I'm there, 'What'll I tell him?'

'Tell him I'm busy,' she goes.

I'm there, 'You know how to play them, Honor. What am I saying? You learned from the master!'

I tip out to the front door, ready to give Joel the big F.O. But when I open it, it ends up not being him at all. It ends up being Ross Junior – as in, like, Christian and Lauren's *eldest*?

I'm there, 'The fock do *you* want?' which is no way to greet your supposed godson, I accept.

Out of nowhere, he suddenly bursts into tears. And I'm like, 'Sorry, kid, I'm not having the best of weeks.'

'Roth,' he goes, 'I neeth your help. Thomeone ith trying to black-mail me.'

I'm like, 'Blackmail you?' and that's when I see the laptop in his hand.

'Yeth,' he goes. 'I thidn't know whath elth thoo thoo.'

I'm there, 'Fock's sake – I suppose you'd better come in.'

I bring him down to the kitchen. He sits down at Erika's old dear's table and I'm like, 'Show me.'

He slides the laptop across to me and I open it.

The first thing I see is this, like, pop-up screen, which is all black with, like, white writing on it. It's like:

WARNING! We have gained access to your device, including your contacts, webcam and internet browsing history! We are aware of all the websites you have visited in the past two weeks and we have in our possession intimate recordings of you perusing those sites!

I'm like, 'Perusing? Is that an actual word?'

'I think tho,' Ross Junior goes.

I'm there, 'Perusing? It's definitely a random one.'

I carry on reading. It's like:

These videos, as well as your browsing history, will be sent to all of your contacts unless you give us $10,000.

And then that's followed by some small print, saying that they accept Bitcoin, which seems to be the way a lot of businesses are going.

I'm there, 'Yeah, no, you're not being blackmailed, kid, you're being sextorted.'

'Thexthorthed?' he goes.

And I'm like, 'Er, yeah, no, that's it.'

He turns on the waterworks again. He goes, 'Whath am I going thoo thoo, Roth? Thith ith my mom and thad'th computher. Theeth people are going thoo thend e-mailth to everyone in their contacth litht.'

I'm there, 'Well, what kind of shit have you been looking at anyway?' and I check out his browser history.

It's mostly, like, lingerie websites. Exotica. Sultry Sleepware. Bra Bra Black Sleep.

Yeah, no, I'm no stranger to one or two of them myself.

The Lace Lounge. Pleasure Chest. Knickers to You.

He's there, 'My mom thaith ith only natural for me to be curi-outh about my thexualithy.'

I'm like, 'Your old dear has got a lot to answer for, kid. I've been saying it for years. On the focking record.'

Jesus Christ, he's only twelve.

I'm there, 'But if she's so open-minded, I don't understand why you can't just tell her you were looking at knickers and bras.'

But then I scroll further down through his history and that's when I see the – yeah, no – porn sites.

I'm like, 'Foooccckkk!!!'

He tries to go, 'I thidn't look at them, Roth! They mutht have jutht popped up when I opened other pageth!'

I'm like, 'Yeah, no, that's what I used to tell Sorcha whenever I forgot to clear my search history. Focking hell, kid.'

'Roth,' he goes, getting upset again – he can really turn it on and off, this kid, 'you have thoo help me!'

I'm like, 'Me? Why me?'

'Becauth you're my godfather!' he goes.

I'm there, 'Look, I've never said this to you before but the whole godfather idea is a bit of a bullshit thing.'

Yeah, no, I showed my face at the christening, Sorcha set up a monthly direct debit for his college fund and that was pretty much that.

'As a matter of fact,' I go, 'Lauren actually sacked me as your godfather – didn't she?'

He goes, 'Roth, pleeeaaath! I'm begging you! My mom can'th finth outh!' and this time the tears *really* stort flowing?

I'm like, 'Fine! Jesus Christ, stop crying! I'll focking handle it, okay?'

He goes, 'How?'

I'm like, 'How do you think? We're going to have to pay these fockers off.'

I call Honor. I'm like, 'Honor? Honor, will you come in here?'

Twenty seconds later, Honor walks into the room. She sees Ross Junior sitting there in tears.

He goes, 'Hi, Honor,' because he's terrified of her.

She's like, 'What's going on?'

I'm there, 'Don't ask. You know how to use Bitcoin, don't you?'

She goes, 'Er, *yeah?*' like it's the most ridiculous question she's ever heard.

I'm there, 'I need you to send ten K's to someone. It's urgent.'

Ross Junior wipes the tears from his face and goes, 'Thank you, Roth! Thank you *tho* much!'

I'm like, 'Don't thank me. It's coming out of your focking college fund.'

'As regular readers of the Letters to the Editor page in the *Irish Times* will no doubt know,' the old man goes – two bottles of wine inside him, 'I have long been of the view that independence from Britain was the greatest mistake that Ireland ever made! I would further suggest that, since severing its link with wonderful Albion, Ireland has not had one . . . good . . . day!'

The famous Boris Johnson is like 'Hear! Hear!' and he storts clapping his hands so violently that he ends up nearly knocking over my pint of Heineken.

'Now that our two countries have committed to freeing ourselves from the real oppressor that is the European Union,' the old man goes, 'I hope that we can forge bonds so strong that we can forget the divisions of history and pretend that 1921 never even happened!'

Out of the corner of her mouth, Sorcha goes, 'I can't focking believe that the Taoiseach put us sitting next to each other,' and she practically spits the words at me.

I'm there, 'Hey, I'm still your technically *husband*, bear in mind?'

She goes, 'Well, you needn't think *I'm* playing happy focking families. Like I said, I have my reputation to think of.'

The old man goes, 'To mork this new era of friendship between Ireland and Britain, I want to suggest a brand-new, non-contentious term to describe our two islands collectively! That term is the Sovereign Islands!'

'The Sovereign Islands,' Boris Johnson repeats. 'I think that's rather wonderful,' and everyone in the packed ballroom of the Áras applauds.

He goes, 'I know that you, Boris, are a keen scholar of the language of Ancient Rome, so I'm going to leave you with the following thought! *Nemo nisi per amicitiam cognoscitur!*'

Boris Johnson jumps to his feet and storts clapping again and shouting, '*Ex amicitial pax! Ex amicitial pax!*'

The old man returns to the table and sits down next to the old dear, who goes, 'Is Theresa May going to speak now?'

But the old man is like, 'No, Theresa May isn't here, Dorling! No point! She's a lame bloody well duck! You mork my words, Boris here will be Prime Minister before the end of the summer!'

'Ah, *very* flattered!' Boris goes.

The old dear is like, 'Oh,' sounding definitely disappointed, and then – I shit you not – she goes, 'People say you're a bit of a wanker, don't they?'

I end up nearly choking on a mouthful of Ken.

But Boris must cop that my old dear is losing her morbles and in fairness to him goes, 'Yes – and that's just the Cabinet!'

The old man cracks his hole laughing.

'Wonderful!' he goes. '*Castigat ridendo mores* – eh, Boris!'

'*Quid rides?*' Boris Johnson goes. '*Mutato nominee de te fabula narratur!*'

The old dear looks at me then and goes, 'Am I having a stroke, Ross?'

And I'm there, 'No, they're just talking in Latin, Mom.'

'Mom!' she goes, sort of, like, chuckling to herself. 'I can't remember the last time you called me Mom! You know, I'm not sure I like it.'

It's Carrie – as in, Boris Johnson's, I suppose, girlfriend – who ends up breaking the awkward silence that follows.

She goes, 'So, Sorcha – you're the minister who's in the process of banning sheep and cows from Ireland, are you?'

Of course, Sorcha is straight on the defensive. She's there, 'Well, Carrie, ruminant animals are responsible for the vast majority of our hormful greenhouse gas emissions –'

But Carrie goes, 'I think it's wonderfully brave of you, Sorcha – and I'm saying that as a committed vegan.'

34

Sorcha's there, 'A vegan?' because it's something that she's always dreamt of being herself, except she's naturally low on iron and willpower.

'Yes, I honestly think,' Carrie goes, 'that our exploitation of animals is something that future generations will look back on with horror. It's a stain on all of us.'

It's definitely a stain on Sorcha. She's having the beef tortore. But the second she hears that Carrie is a vegan, she pushes the plate away and goes, 'I feel like I should be doing even more – as a legislator, I mean. I've actually asked my deportment to draw up a white paper on a possible law that will restrict everyone in the country to three servings of meat per week from the year 2025.'

'Three still sounds like a lot,' Carrie goes.

Sorcha's like, 'Two, then. Or even one. I'm also hoping to persuade the Taoiseach to introduce legislation capping the number of flights that all Irish citizens are permitted to take each year – and also the number of miles that motorists are allowed to drive.'

Boris Johnson is just, like, staring at her like she's a focking rabbit reading the *Nuacht*.

He's like, 'So, em, Ross, how long have you two been married?'

'How long?' I go. 'Now you're putting me on the spot, Boris.'

Sorcha's there, 'We're not married,' letting me down in a big-time way. 'We're separated.'

'Oh,' the dude goes, 'I'm sorry to hear that!'

Sorcha's there, 'Please don't be. It's a blessed relief.'

'*Amor et melle et felle est fecundissimus!*' Boris Johnson goes, raising his glass.

The old man's there, '*Cras amet qui nunquam amavit; quique amavit, cras amet!*' returning the toast.

Except Sorcha's not happy to just leave it at that. There's a lot of bitterness in the girl.

She's there, 'He took his orse out in a pub – in case you're wondering.'

Boris Johnson has a good chuckle at that one. I presume he went to the same kind of school as me.

'Not only that,' she goes, 'but he gave the police someone else's name when he was arrested.'

He's there, 'What, they arrested you?' and he says it in a definite non-*judgy* way? 'For *that*? Oh, what rotten luck!'

'He gave the police the name of one of his best friends,' Sorcha goes, 'who ended up on the register of sex offenders and almost lost his job as a school principal.'

The old man tries to interrupt her flow. He's there, 'Carrie, how are you feeling about the prospect of being Britain's – inverted commas – First Lady, once the Remainer, Theresa May, has been removed from the stage, of course?' except Sorcha is on a roll now.

She's there. 'The last straw was when he had sex with his mom's friend, Delma, in the side passage of her house.'

'He did *what*?' the old dear goes – because, yeah, no, it's a new one on her.

Sorcha's there, 'But, then, he was never faithful to me, were you, Ross? He's had sex with all my friends, all my bridesmaids and every nanny we ever had. He did the actual dirt on me at my 18th, my 21st, my 25th and my 30th. He brought a prostitute to my graduation –'

She was actually a stripper, but I decide not to pull her up on it. No point.

She goes, 'He cheated on me at my debs and at his debs and he hit on the singer at my granny's funeral. He gave me gonorrhoea for our 5th wedding anniversary and genital herpes for our 10th. Am I missing anything, Ross?'

She's missing hundreds but I try to stick to the ones she actually *knows* about?

I'm there, 'One of the ones you were most upset about, I remember, was me getting off with your Deputy Head Girl.'

She's like, 'I didn't know you were with Birch.'

Oh, fock, I think, sorry that I even opened my mouth.

I'm there, 'Yeah, no, I was – the night of your graduation. I wouldn't have said anything if I thought you didn't know.'

She's like, 'Oh my God, I can't believe you were with Birch Kennedy. I also did grinds with her in the Institute.'

Hey, I did grinds with her *after* the Institute.

In that very moment, I notice that Boris Johnson is just, like, staring at me in that exact same way that, I'm told, I stare at Johnny Sexton – with pure love in my eyes and saliva dribbling from the side of my open mouth.

I'm there, 'I'm, er, just going to go for a slash,' because my tonsils are floating here.

I head for the jacks and I bleed the boiler. I'm standing at the sink, washing my hands – random, I know – when the door opens and in he walks, Boris Johnson himself.

He tips over to the trough and while he's wetting the porcelain he goes, 'I have to confess, Ross, to being rather an admirer of yours!'

I'm there, 'In terms of?'

'I just mean, you know, what I heard about you out there! You've successfully managed to lower the bar for me and men everywhere!'

'Yeah, no, I've been hearing that all my life.'

'I mean, just listening to your wife's stories there,' he goes, 'I'm sure even the biggest shit in the world would feel like Husband of the Year material compared to you!'

I'm there, 'Again, thanks.'

At that exact moment, the door of the Gents' swings open again and this time – oh, fock-a-doodle-doo – in walks Sorcha's sister.

She walks straight up to me and she grabs me by the throat, squeezing my windpipe to the point where I can't actually breathe.

She's there, 'I want a focking word with you,' and I can see that Boris – who's giving the old lizard a shake – is already smiling.

She goes, 'You nearly got me sacked from my focking job.'

'Sorry,' I manage to gasp, 'I was in . . . a fouler . . . shouldn't have taken . . . it out on you.'

She's like, 'How would you like me to walk out there and tell Sorcha that there's a fifty–fifty chance that the baby I'm carrying is yours?'

I'm there, 'I wouldn't . . . like that . . . at all.'

Boris Johnson makes his way over to the sink with a big, delighted head on him. Yeah, no, he definitely loves a bit of drama, this dude.

Sorcha's sister goes, 'You ever pull a focking stunt like that again and I'll tell your wife everything. And my dad will cut your focking balls off, Ross – and you *know* that's not an idle threat.'

She lets go of my throat, then walks out of the jacks.

Boris finishes washing his hands and he's looking at me all gooey-eyed again. He's like, 'Who in the name of Hades was that, Ross?'

'Believe it or not,' I go, 'that was Sorcha's sister.'

All the dude can do is just laugh.

He's there, 'Good God! Your sister-in-law! Pregnant with your child!'

'Well, it's either mine,' I go, 'or one of my friends. They're paying her to be their surrogate and – yeah, no – I just happened to ride her the day after the sperm transfer.'

He's, like, shocked by that. He's, like, genuinely, genuinely shocked.

He goes, 'What's her name?'

And I'm there, 'I have literally no idea.'

Ronan is in cracking form, it has to be said.

He's there, 'Ine arthur being in Bostodden, so I am,' and you can hear the excitement in his voice.

I'm like, 'Boston?' because I'm pretty sure that's what he's trying to say. 'What were you doing down there – up there, whatever?'

He's like, 'I was at an open week in Heervoord.'

'Horvord?' Honor goes – yeah, no, he's going to be studying Law there from September. I'm so proud of the dude. It seems like only yesterday we were walking up and down Talbot Street and Abbey Street on our unsupervised access days together, with him pointing out which shops were legitimate businesses and which shops were – as he called them – 'fruddents'.

He's like, 'Yeah, Heervoord. Ah, Hodor, it's some place, so it is. You'll hab to cub oaber and visit me, so you widdle.'

'Oh my God,' she goes, 'I would love that!'

We're all huddled around the computer, chatting to the dude on, like, FaceTime.

Erika can read Ronan like a book. Always could.

She goes, 'You met someone there, didn't you?'

And Ronan – I swear to fock – turns red.

He shrugs and he's there, 'I myra dudden,' and he goes all, I don't know, bashful. We've all been there.

I'm like, 'Answer me this – is she hot?' because Ronan, unlike yours truly, has never being especially interested in looks – Shadden being a prime example, the focking woofer.

He goes, 'I think she's lubbly,' which could mean literally anything. She could have two focking noses and a hump on her back. 'She's cubben down to New York for the weekend.'

Erika's like, 'So what's her name, Ro?'

And he goes, 'Avoddy.'

Erika's there, 'Avoddy?'

'No,' he goes, 'Avoddy!'

I'm like, 'How are you spelling that, Ro?'

He's there, 'A.'

I'm like, 'Okay.'

'V'

'Right.'

'E.'

'Keep going.'

'R.'

'R – right.'

'Y.'

'Y?'

'Avoddy.'

'Oh, Avery!' Erika goes. 'Oh my God, that's a beautiful name.'

I'm there, 'It's still proof of nothing, Erika. It's still proof of nothing.'

Erika's like, 'Ronan, I'm going to have to be really rude now and go. Ross and I have to drive down to Brittas Bay this afternoon.'

I'm there, 'Yeah, no, Oisinn and Magnus are renting Gerald Kean's old gaff. They're turning it into, like, a treatment centre for people struggling to readjust to the world post-Facebook and Google.'

'Ah, feer boddicks to them,' he goes. 'Can I joost hab a woord in private with Rosser before yous head off?'

Erika is like, 'Of course!' and Honor goes, 'I'll FaceTime you at the weekend, Ro! Bye!' and then off the two of them fock.

When he gets me alone, he goes, 'How's things, Rosser?'

I'm like, 'Yeah, no, all is good in the 'hood.'

'What's happening with yisser case?'

'What case?'

'Conspidacy to perveert the cowurse of justice, perveerting the cowurse of justice –'

'Oh, *that* case.'

'– taking your mickey out in public.'

'Yeah, it was my orse, Mr focking Law Student.'

'Hab thee set a date for yisser thrial yet?'

'No, they're saying the middle of August.'

'Who's your solicitodder?'

'His name's Hugo Mangan. He was, like, the duty solicitor in the station the day I was chorged.'

'Do you want me to hab a woord with Buckets of Blood? He can inthroduce you to the fedda what got he's brutter off for eermed robbedy.'

'No, you're good, Ro.'

'He was acquithed, Rosser – even though thee found the muddy and a bleaten rod in he's posseshidden.'

'No, I'm going to stick with this Hugo Mangan dude. He went to Blackrock College, so there's an eighty–twenty chance he'll know the judge.'

'Rosser,' he goes – and he looks and sounds definitely worried about me – 'you don't really think the fact that you played rubby is going to save you from jayult, do you?'

And I'm there, 'I have every faith in this country's justice system, Ro.'

Erika goes, 'So?'

And I'm there, 'Did you even hear what I said?'

Yeah, no, we're all sitting in her Porsche Cayenne – on the way to

Brittas Bay to check out Oisinn and Magnus's new gaff – and I'm presuming the only reason she doesn't kick off is because little Amelie is sitting in the child seat in the back.

I'm there, 'Castlerock College . . . is going co-ed, Erika. This is Fionn's revenge on me.'

But she goes, 'But why would I give a fock one way or another?'

'Mommy!' Amelie goes.

And Erika's like, 'I'm sorry for swearing, Dorling.'

I'm there, 'I suppose you were never that much into rugby anyway – or rugby goys, for that matter, and I'm including myself in that.'

She has no response to that. She just shakes her head and rolls her eyes.

A few minutes later, we're flying up the gravel driveway to Drayton Manor and I'm having flashbacks to the night that me and Christian crashed one of Gerald Kean's costume porties. We pass the swing chair where I spent twenty minutes – totally shit-faced – trying to chat up a girl with long, curly hair before realizing it was Gavin Lambe-Murphy in a powdered wig, trying to roll a cigarette.

'Wait until the goys hear about what Fionn is doing,' I go. 'They're going to go literally ballistic. Literally, Erika.'

Erika pulls up in front of the gaff. A few seconds later, Christian porks beside us – yeah, no, I forgot to mention that him and Lychee were following us in *his* Ferrori Dino. He's wearing a hoodie and Converse, by the way, obviously trying to look younger and less like her old man.

'Here, Christian,' I go, getting out of Erika's cor, 'I was just remembering the night me and you turned up uninvited to one of Gerald Kean's porties here.'

Lychee – I shit you not – goes, 'Who's Gerald Kean?' which will give you an idea of how young and utterly clueless the girl is. Christian – I'm not making this up – pulls a face like he's trying to place the dude, which is un-focking-forgivable in my book, even if he is trying to spare her embarrassment, the focking dizzy little ride.

'The man was a focking legend back in the day,' I make sure to go. 'And one of Ireland's best ever people. He didn't throw us out of his gaff – even when your boyfriend there slashed one of his Graham Knuttels with a duelling sword that once belonged to Daniel O'Donnell.'

'Daniel O'Connell,' Christian goes. 'It belonged to Daniel O'Connell,' and, even though I've never heard of Daniel O'Connell, I dare say he's right. I always wondered what Daniel O'Donnell was doing with a duelling sword.

I'm there, 'I stand corrected. He slashed one of Gerald Kean's Graham Knuttels with a duelling sword that once belonged to Daniel O'Connell.'

God, the Celtic Tiger was great when you think about it.

'Who's Graham Knuttel?' Lychee goes.

She's more to be pitied than anything.

Then she goes, 'Chrissy,' because that's what she calls him, 'will you take a picture of me in front of the house? And don't make me look cross-eyed in this one.'

JP pulls up then in his vintage 8 Serious, with Delma in the front passenger seat and little Isa and Hillary in the back – along with Fionn. It's, like, high-fives and hugs and how-the-fock-are-you's between me and JP, but Delma is a bit stand-offish – she's not a fan, even though I rode her in my old dear's gorden – and Fionn ends up blanking me altogether. He just lifts Hillary out of the cor and goes over to talk to Erika.

JP's there, 'What's the story, Ross?' and I think about mentioning the whole Castlerock going co-ed thing but I decide to maybe bide my time, not wanting to spoil the moment for Oisinn and Magnus.

I'm there, 'All good, my friend. So, are we going in or what?'

Christian, by the way, is still trying to take a photo that Lychee finds acceptable. She's going, 'Okay, *why* do you keep making my orms look fat?' and I'm honestly wondering how he puts up with it.

The door is wide open, so we make our way inside. We find Magnus in the main hallway, down on his hands and knees, sanding the floor.

It's so random that Oisinn has ended up married to a man who actually *enjoys* manual labour.

'Hey, guysh!' Magnus goes.

He stands up and it's, like, hugs for all of us, then he calls Oisinn, who tips down the stairs thirty seconds later with his orms out-stretched, going, 'What do you think?'

I'm there, 'It's bringing back one or two memories for me, Dude. I got sick on Georgia Salpa's coat – over there, where Gerald used to have the hormonium that once belonged to Enya – and she was surprisingly fine about it. Mind you, I think it turned out it was Leigh Arnold's coat all along.'

JP goes, 'It's the perfect location, Oisinn,' the estate agent genes still strong in him. 'Away from everything.'

'Plush,' Magnus goes, 'one of the added benefitsh for people try-ing to eshcape Fashebook and Google and all of theesh kindsh of companiesh ish that the broadband in thish area ish sho poor.'

Oisinn smiles at Erika. Yeah, no, they've always had a connection.

'You're looking great,' he goes. And he's not wrong. She's wear-ing leather trousers and a tight black poloneck that really shows off her lunchables.

'Thanks,' she goes, giving him a big hug. Then she's like, 'Con-gratulations! I heard about Sorcha's sister!'

Sorry, what is the problem with using her name?

He goes, 'Yeah, no, Sorcha's not happy,' snatching a sly look at me. I don't know where to focking look. 'But Magnus and I are very excited.'

Magnus goes, 'Hey, let ush show you the nurshery! Come thish way,' and he leads us all upstairs and along the corridor to Gerald Kean's old smoking room, which they've turned into a – like he said – nursery, painted in neutral colours.

'So you've no idea whose baby it actually is?' Fionn goes.

I end up letting out an involuntary squeak, which I then try to turn into a cough.

'Well, we hope it ish one of us!' Magnus goes.

Fionn laughs. He's there, 'What I mean is, you don't know if it's your DNA or Oisinn's?'

'I'm sure it'll be pretty obvious when the baby is born,' Oisinn goes, 'especially if he or she has blond hair and blue eyes – like this

43

gorgeous man here,' then he and Magnus share a kiss and – yeah, no – I'm totally, totally cool with that.

'I shtill can't believe that we are going to be parentsh,' Magnus goes – and I decide that it's time to move the conversation along.

'So,' I go, 'I notice we're all avoiding the, em, elephant in the room. I don't know if you heard, but Fionn here is talking about opening the doors of the school to – I'm just going to come out and say it – *girls*?'

'Yeah, no,' JP goes, 'I read about it in the Castlerock College Past Pupils Union newsletter. I think it's a great idea.'

I can't believe he actually reads that thing.

I'm like, 'Excuse me?'

He's there, 'I just think, you know, real life is co-ed – so doesn't it make sense for students to spend their formative years in a learning environment that better prepares them for the future beyond school in a more diverse society?'

'I agree,' Delma goes.

No surprise there. She went to, like, The High School, Rathgor, who, by the way, haven't won a Leinster Schools Senior Cup since they opened the doors to girls.

Christian walks in then with Lychee and catches the orse-end of the conversation.

He's there, 'Yeah, we're actually sending Ross Junior to St Andrew's in September.'

I'm like, 'Andrew's?' unable to hide my out-and-out contempt for the place. 'And why was I not consulted about this?'

He's there, 'Why would we consult you?'

I'm like, 'Er, as his supposed godfather?'

He goes, 'It was Lauren's idea. But my cousin's kids went there – they're both goys – and it's had a definite civilizing effect on them. They're not only thriving academically but they're developing social skills that *we* never had. They're a lot more respectful of women than I was at their age. And they're more mature and confident in themselves. That all comes from the new experiences and fresh perspectives they've gained from being educated alongside – I'm going to say it, Ross – but *girls*?'

A focking definite *civilizing* effect? I am *this* close to mentioning the visit I had from his son last week, the little focking pervert.

But I don't. Instead, I'm like, 'Do you know who I'm thinking about? St Claude of Bethany, the founder of the order, who, in 1572 – can I just remind you all? – swam to Ireland from France with a rugby ball under his orm.'

Everyone – I shit you not – bursts out laughing.

I'm there, 'What? Are you saying that's, like, bullshit?'

Oisinn goes, 'We're saying that, like a lot of Father Fehily's stories, Ross, it wasn't meant to be taken literally.'

'Well, *I* took it literally.'

'How could he swim to Ireland using only one orm?' Christian – I'm surprised at *him* – goes. 'Wouldn't he just keep going around in circles?'

I'm there, 'Yeah, that's focking blasphemy. And he'd be furious about what's happening to the school today – if he hadn't been burned at the stake by the GAA.'

Oisinn goes, 'I'm sorry, Ross, but I have to agree with Christian and JP. I want *our* baby – when it arrives – to go to a co-educational and – I'm going to say it, Fionn – non-denominational Castlerock College. Because, frankly, if it ends up being a boy, I don't want him to be the kind of boorish, misogynistic idiot that I was in my teens and twenties. I want him to have female as well as male role models and a wider, more diverse network of friends.'

I end up not knowing *what* to say? I'm basically speechless. But also I'm picking up on a sudden vibe between the goys – as in, they're all on the same page and I'm suddenly no longer port of the crew. I've never felt more on the outside.

It actually saddens me, especially when Fionn turns around with a big, smug look on his face and goes, 'By the way, I have a bit of an announcement to make.'

I'm there, 'Let me guess, you're going to abolish fees and let poor kids into the school as well as girls?'

He doesn't even respond. I might as well be dead to him.

He's there, 'Well, as you know, my fortieth birthday is coming up. All of our fortieths are coming up.'

Oisinn's like, 'How did we get so old?'

'It turns out,' Fionn goes, 'that Father Fehily left us some money.'

JP is like, 'Money? What are you talking about?'

'I got a letter,' he goes, 'from the solicitor who handled his will. It turns out that he left each of us €10,000 – to be paid when the first of us turned forty.'

'Which is you,' Christian goes, 'next week – right?'

JP's there, 'I don't understand. Why is he giving us ten K's each?'

'Because he wants us to walk the Camino de Santiago this summer,' Fionn goes.

Oisinn's like, 'What? Why?'

'I don't know the answer to that question,' Fionn goes. 'All I know is that he did the pilgrimage himself when he turned forty – and presumably he wants us to follow in his footsteps.'

I'm there, 'Well, *I'm* definitely up for it.'

And there ends up being this, like, silence in the room.

'Er, *you* won't be able to come with us,' Christian goes.

I'm like, 'Why not? You're all taking Fionn's side, are you?'

'It has nothing to do with taking sides,' JP goes. 'It's just that, well, your court case is in August. Presumably, you're not allowed to leave the country before then?'

I'm there, 'Hey, why don't we just put it off until afterwards?'

And that's when Fionn says it – the same thing that's on all their minds and that I've been trying my best not to think about.

He goes, 'What makes you think you'll still be around? You're probably going to be in prison by then,' and it's the first time that it feels suddenly real to me. 'That's if there's any justice in the world.'

And I'm just like, fock!

2.

A View to a Grill

So – yeah, no – I'm back in the gym in Riverview, trying to get myself – and I can't even believe I'm *using* this phrase? – but prison-body-ready. I'm thinking, If I do get sent down, I want to be in the kind of shape I was in when I won the Leinster Schools Senior Cup. I don't want to end up being my cellmate's, I don't know, *plaything*?

Today is orms day and I'm sitting on a Swiss ball in front of a long mirror, with an eight-kilo dumbbell in either hand, thinking how fantastic I look for a man of, like, thirty-nine.

All of a sudden, I spot Mallorie Kennedy – the mother of Honor's classmate Courage Kennedy – staring at me across the floor of the gym with a look of, I want to say, *revulsion* on her face?

I'm there, 'Is there something wrong, Mallorie?' because I've been getting dirty looks in here all focking week.

'You're absolutely disgusting,' she goes.

I'm there, 'Am I? Didn't know that.'

'Exposing yourself like that – you're absolutely vile.'

'Nothing's been proven yet, can I just remind you?'

Yeah, no, I'm storting to know what being cancelled *feels* like?

'You make me sick to my stomach,' she goes.

I'm like, 'Whatever.'

I keep working the shoulders for five more minutes, then I lie down on the floor and stort putting The Six through their paces with five sets of twenty sit-ups. I'm about six or seven into my second set when I all of a sudden notice Grainne Power – as in, like, Conwenna Power's old dear – staring at me from her yoga mat opposite me.

She goes, 'I suppose you think it's hilarious, do you?'

47

I'm there, 'I do as matter of fact. So did everyone else – until the whole world lost its sense of humour.'

'Well, *I* don't think it's funny. I think it's repulsive. I think *you're* repulsive!'

'It's called rugby banter. I don't know why I have to keep explaining myself.'

She goes, 'Well, I can't stand to be in the same room as you. You're a disgusting person.'

I'm there, 'Wait until you hear the full facts. It'll all come out in court,' which I realize sounds possibly dodgy.

I keep doing the sit-ups, at the same time wondering what life is going to be like behind bors. Then I stort thinking about the goys – we're talking Christian, we're talking Oisinn, we're talking JP, we're talking even Fionn, walking the famous Camino without me and I end up having major, major FOMO. Weirdly, I think I'm more upset about missing out on that than I am about going to possibly prison.

Just as I'm finishing the last of the sit-ups, I notice that Roz Matthews, the mother of Sincerity Matthews – although she's back to being Roz Carew since her divorce – is standing over me.

'Ross –' she storts to go.

And I'm there, 'I don't want to hear it, Roz. Not from you of all people,' because this is a woman I went on, like, four dates with when me and Sorcha were on one of our famous breaks. I was actually a little bit in love with her.

She goes, 'Are you okay? Ross, you're crying,' and I realize that she's right. I've got literally tears rolling down my face.

I'm there, 'I'm sorry, Roz,' as I climb to my feet. 'I don't know what the fock is wrong with me.'

She goes, 'Come on over here – take a break,' and she leads me over to a nearby weights bench. I sit down and she plonks herself down beside me. She looks like a slightly less annoying version of Allison Williams but with a smaller mouth and I'm saying that as a compliment to the girl.

'Here,' she goes, offering me her Lululemon water bottle. 'Drink something.'

I'm there, 'You sure you don't mind?' and then I remember that

I've had my lips in far more intimate places than the spout of her water bottle and if germs weren't an issue then, they shouldn't be an issue now.

I knock back a mouthful of water.

'Oh my God,' Roz goes, 'you're shaking.'

I'm there, 'Yeah, no, I'm not surprised. I'm in seriously deep S, H, one, T at the moment, Roz.'

'Well,' she goes, 'I can't pretend I haven't heard.'

I'm like, 'Everyone's talking about it, I presume.'

'Some people are talking about it,' she goes – just being nice.

I'm there, 'I don't know if you heard, but me and Sorcha are finished.'

I look at her to see how she feels about this, but she doesn't give anything away one way or the other.

'Yes,' she just goes, 'I saw her statement in the *Irish Times*.'

I'm there, 'To be honest, I think I was only ever a trophy husband to her.'

She goes, 'Sincerity tells me that Honor is living with you.'

'Yeah, no,' I go, 'we're staying in Erika's for the moment.'

She's there, 'Will you get your own place?'

I'm like, 'No point. I'm quite possibly going to prison.'

She goes, 'You don't really think that, do you?'

I'm there, 'I don't know what to think any more. I mean, mooning a room full of people used to be funny, right?'

'Well,' she goes, 'I'm not sure if I was ever the right audience for that kind of thing.'

I'm there, 'It was so long ago as well. Everybody had their holes out in those days – at the slightest provocation. I never thought that years later it would come back to bite me on the – pordon the pun – but *orse*?'

'It does sound like you're paying a very high price for what you did,' she goes.

She's so easy to talk to, even though she's a totally different character in the bedroom. To chat to her at the school gates, you'd swear that butter wouldn't melt in her mouth, but you wouldn't believe the filthy talk that comes out of her when she's on the job.

I'm there, 'I've lost everything, Roz. I've lost my wife. I've lost my boys. I've lost my home. I've lost my job. I'm *losing* my friends. And before the summer is over, I'm going to lose my freedom. I mean, my kids are going to be visiting me in, like, prison.'

She puts a comforting hand on my thigh and instantly – Jesus Christ – I'm horder than Drimnagh.

'You don't know that,' she goes. 'Isn't your father's solicitor the Attorney General now?'

I'm like, 'Hennessy? Yeah, no, I can't ask him to help me.'

'Why not?' she goes.

I'm there, 'Long story. Can't afford the price.'

She rubs her hand up and down my thigh. I swear to God, I could shuck oysters with the focking swellington I've suddenly got on me.

I'm there, 'You're being very nice to me.'

'Hey,' she goes, 'we're old friends.'

We both know it was more than that, but I'm too much of a gentleman to mention it. I remember riding her once on top of her Hotpoint top-loader washing machine when she had a high-agitation, non-eco wash on.

I'm there, 'I finally know what it feels like to be cancelled. It's been coming, a lot of my critics would probably say.'

'What do you mean by cancelled?' Roz goes – again, being nice.

I'm there, 'Mallorie Kennedy and Grainne Power told me I was disgusting and they couldn't bring themselves to look at me. Jesus, Grainne's husband *played* rugby. He was on the seconds in Lansdowne and I could tell her some stories about what happened on a certain Leinster away trip.'

Roz just laughs.

I'm there, 'Yeah, no, I'm glad you find it so funny.'

She's like, 'Ross, where did you get those shorts?'

'What, *these* shorts?' I go. 'Yeah, no, these are ones that the great Rob Henderson wore for the Lions against Australia in the First Test in 2001. My old man bought them at a charity auction in the Shelbourne Hotel to raise awareness of, em . . . well, who even *knows* what now. All I remember is that Seán Dunne outbid him for the jersey and the old man ended up paying eight grand for these bad boys as a sort of, like, consolation prize. I can't believe they still fit me.'

She's there, 'Do you, em, really think so?'

'Thirty-nine years old with a thirty-two-inch waist,' I go, grabbing the waistband to show her how much room there is in them. 'They're practically falling off me – look!'

She's like, 'I'm not talking about *there*. I'm talking about – oh God, how can I put this delicately?'

I'm there, 'What are you talking about?'

She goes, 'Clothes change shape with repeated washings, Ross. The legs of those shorts have become a little, well, *slacker* over the years?'

I'm like, 'Look, I'm famously slow on the uptake, as you know. You're going to have to be a bit more pacific.'

She's there, 'We can all see one of your testicles, Ross.'

'What?'

'We see can right up the leg and your left testicle is visible.'

The penny suddenly drops.

I'm there, 'Holy fock, is that what Mallorie and Grainne meant when they said –'

She's like, 'Yes.'

'– that I was vile for exposing myself?' I go. 'Okay, I get it now. I did wonder. Grainne's husband rode a lap-dancer in Exeter and she was eight and a half months pregnant.'

She doesn't say anything in response to this. I suppose there's not much *to* say?

I take a long, hord look at myself in the mirror – at possibly my favourite item of clothing in the world, which has been a port of my life for, like, practically twenty years now.

'That's what I came over here to tell you,' Roz goes. 'You need to bin those shorts.'

I'm like, 'Do you think Rob Henderson would understand?'

She goes, 'After all the things you've lost, Ross – you don't want to lose your Riverview membership as well.'

I nod sadly.

I'm there, 'I couldn't do one last set of sit-ups in them, could I?'

She squeezes my thigh really tightly.

'No more sit-ups!' she goes. 'For the sake of decency, Ross, no more sit-ups!'

We both laugh and suddenly I have this flash of memory of the first time I ever kissed her, standing outside Kielys on Donnybrook Road, and how she tasted of jojoba lipgloss and elderflower gin, and I realize that I'm actually falling for her again, the complete and utter ride of a woman.

I'm having one of my famous – I want to say – *philosophical* moments, just thinking about how quickly the years go by. As in, it seems like only yesterday I was enjoying unsupervised access days with Ronan in Stephen's Green and now I'm enjoying un-supervised access days with Brian, Johnny and Leo in the exact same spot.

There's quite possibly a lesson in there – as I used to say at school when I passed the biology lab on my way to rugby training.

Anyway, it's, like, the first day of June and it's absolutely swelter-ing out, but the boys are being weirdly *quiet* today? They'd usually be running amok right now, spitting at the ducks and making wanker signs at people on rollerblades. But they're not. They're just sitting on a bench, saying and doing fock-all.

I turn around to Honor and I'm there, 'Do you think there's something, I don't know, wrong with them?'

Honor's like, 'They've been very quiet all day.'

And I'm there, 'Boring would be my word. Usually, they'd be making shit of the place and I'd have at least five people telling me that my children are a disgrace.'

Yeah, no, it's worrying.

Honor's like, 'Boys, are you okay?'

They look up – three sad little faces on them – and they all nod.

'Brian, look,' I go, 'there's a little girl over there with a helium balloon. A big number five. Must be her birthday. Why don't you go over, grab it out of her hand and then let it go?'

Brian looks in the direction I'm pointing – but there isn't even a flicker of interest on his face.

I'm there, 'Go on, Brian. I'll deal with her old man if he decides to make an issue out of it. I'll tell him to fock off.'

I swear to fock, Johnny turns around and he's like, 'But that would be mean.'

'It'd also be funny,' Honor goes. '*Very* funny.'

I'm there, 'Listen to your sister. She has no conscience when it comes to this kind of thing.'

Brian just shakes his little head.

I look at Honor. I'm there, 'Holy focking shit. I wonder does this have anything to do with –'

She's like, 'What?'

'Well, you know, me and Sorcha getting separated.'

'Why would you think that?'

'It's just you see it all the time in movies and on TV. Parents break up and the kids end up being messed up over it. Although it does seem to be mostly an American thing.'

'You're being paranoid, Dad.'

'That's good to hear.'

'I mean, you and *her* got, like, separated when I was around their age – and I've turned out okay, haven't I?'

'You've put my mind at ease, Honor. You've put my mind at definite ease.'

'Hey, Johnny,' she goes, 'look at that family over there, having a focking picnic.'

All of the boys have a look and – yeah, no – I do as well. It's, like, mom, dad, son and daughter, eating all sorts out of, like, Tupperware containers. There's no excuse for it.

Honor's like, 'Hey, Johnny, do you remember that time in Powerscourt when that family were having a picnic and you pulled down your trousers and pissed in their taramasalata?'

'I think it was vegan tzatziki,' I go.

She's like, 'Yeah, whatever – it was focking hilarious, wasn't it, Dad?'

'It was one of the best days ever,' I go. 'Remember the face on the dude when I told him that I didn't need parenting advice from a man who drives a Hyundai focking anything.'

Honor's there, 'Johnny, go and piss on their picnic.'

55

'Yeah, no, do it,' I go. 'The focking nerve of them with their focking Tupperware containers.'

But Johnny just gives us a tight little shake of his head.

I'm there, 'Johnny, piss on their picnic – that's a focking order.'

But Brian goes, 'Don't do it, Johnny, because that will make those people sad.'

I look at Honor. I don't think either of us can believe what we're actually hearing here.

I'm like, 'Leo, what about you?'

And that's when I suddenly notice that Leo is – I'm not making this up – reading a book.

'The fock did you get that?' I go, then I snatch it out of his hand. I look at the cover. It's called – randomly – *Charlotte's Web*. I walk six or seven steps, drop it in a bin and go, 'That's where books belong.'

He doesn't call me a focking prick or try to punch me in the balls like he usually would. He just sits there and takes it.

I'm like, 'Leo, look at that kid chasing the pigeons. He actually kicked one a minute ago. Why don't you push him in the pond? See how focking hord he is then.'

He goes, 'I don't want to.'

I'm there, 'What do you mean you don't want to?'

'That would be bullying,' he goes. 'And bullying is wrong.'

I'm like, 'That something you learned from a book, is it? From focking reading?'

That's when, totally out of the blue, Johnny goes, 'Daddy, are you going to prison?' and – I swear to fock – my hort *literally* breaks in two?

I'm there, 'Of course I'm not going to prison. Who told you I was going to prison?'

'Granddad Lalor,' Brian goes.

I'm there, 'He said what?'

'He said that you did a very bad thing,' Johnny goes, 'and you were going to be sent to prison for years and years.'

Jesus Christ, I think, who tells a six-year-old something like that? I'm suddenly in an absolute rage.

I turn around to Honor and I'm like, 'No wonder they're zero craic. He's put the focking fear of God into them, the focking wanker.'

'Daddy, that's a bad word,' Brian goes.

I'm there, 'Well, you'd better cover your ears when we meet that prize fockwit because you're going to be hearing a hell of a lot –'

I suddenly stop because I notice that Leo has gone to the bin and fished out his book. He's, like, reading it again.

I'm there, 'There's one way to fix that.' I snatch his glasses off his face. 'See how you get on with your so-called book when you can't see six inches in front of your nose.'

That's how much of a *rage* I'm in? Again, he doesn't call me a thundering clownfock, or a bastarding fockpig, or a bolloxing wank-dog, like he used to back in the day. He just sits there and stares sadly into space.

I'm there, 'Honor, that focking orseprick has traumatized them.'

She looks at the time on her phone.

'Oh my God,' she goes, 'we were supposed to meet him, like, half an hour ago.'

I'm there, 'Normally I would say let the focker wait another half an hour, but there's shit I have to say to him and I need to say it to him while I'm still angry. Come on, goys.'

So off we tramp in the direction of the Leeson Street gate, which is the supposed drop-off point. *He's* waiting there with the usual face on him – like a focking half-sucked mango.

He's like, 'You're thirty-five minutes late.'

He's got balls like focking dinosaur eggs.

I'm there, 'Why are you telling my children that I'm going to prison?'

He doesn't even try to deny it.

He goes, 'Well, *someone* has to tell them.'

I'm there, 'I might very well get off. What makes you such a focking expert?'

'Oh, my forty years working as a barrister,' he tries to go.

Honor's there, 'Yeah, in focking *family* law,' backing me to the hilt.

I change the angle of attack.

I'm there, 'Who gave Leo that book?'

'My wife,' he goes. 'It was a favourite of Sorcha's when she was a child. *And* her sister.'

I am *this* close to telling him that I rode that sister. But I don't. Instead, I go, 'You're some prick.'

And that's when Johnny decides to pipe up. He's like, 'Daddy, you said a bad word!' and this coming from the kid who said nothing *but* bad words for the first three years after he learned to talk.

'The fock have you done to my kids?' I go.

The dude's like, 'What do you mean?'

'I think you *know* what I mean. A few weeks ago they tried to cave your head in with a wok and I should have focking let them. Now they're pulling me up on my *language*?'

He actually laughs in my face and how I don't deck him on the spot is a genuine, genuine mystery.

He goes, 'This is how children behave when you introduce rules and boundaries and stability to their lives.'

'They're focking boring,' Honor goes.

The dude points at Honor. He's like, 'And *this* is what happens when you don't.'

I'm there, 'I still say you're a wanker – focking telling them that they're going to be visiting their father in prison. What kind of thing is that to put in their heads?'

'Oh, they *won't* be,' he goes.

I'm like, 'Excuse *me*?'

He goes, 'What, bring children of *their* age into a prison environment? Surrounded by bars and barbed-wire? To talk to their sexual deviant father through an inch of bulletproof glass? Oh, no, that would be too, too traumatizing for them – especially when we've come so far in getting their behaviour under control.'

That ends up being the final straw. I close my fist and I take a swing at him. But Honor grabs my orm and stops the punch mid-flight.

She's like, 'Dad, don't. He'll only use it to stop you seeing the boys altogether.'

I'm there, 'We'll see what Sorcha has to say about this.'

But he goes, 'Sorcha is fully onboard with the idea. When you go to prison, you'll be saying goodbye to your children.'

I'm there, 'You're a focking wankbag.'

And Brian goes, 'Daddy, you said two bad words.'

A dude on the radio says that residents on Dublin's northside have responded angrily to the Government's plans to reroute the Liffey.

Yeah, no, this is while I'm actually crossing the thing, on the way to the Áras to see my brother and sisters and – if she happens to be sober – my old dear.

The dude goes, 'According to a report in this morning's *Irish Independent*, the Taoiseach, Charles O'Carroll-Kelly, is planning to alter the course of the River Liffey to place his current home, Áras an Uachtaráin, on the southside of the city. A leaked document *seen* by the newspaper says the plan will mean that hundreds of homes in the north city areas of Cabra, Ashtown, Smithfield, Stoneybatter and Castleknock will have to be demolished. Opposition leaders are calling for the Dáil to be recalled to discuss the matter. It hasn't sat since Leinster House was destroyed by fire last year. Fine Gael leader Leo Varadkar has said that the ongoing uncertainty over when the Dáil would return, to discuss this and other matters, was leading people to ask whether Ireland is still a parliamentary democracy.'

I switch off the radio as I'm swinging the cor through the gates of the Áras, then into the actual gaff I go. I head straight for the nursery, where I find the old dear stretched out on, like, a day-bed while Astrid – I want to say – *recites* nursery rhymes for the kids.

'Ross!' the old dear goes. 'How lovely to see you!'

I'm there, 'Jesus Christ, will you fasten at least three more buttons on that focking nightdress if that's what it's supposed to be. No one wants to see your nungas.'

She goes, 'He's obsessed with my breasts, Astrid. Couldn't keep his greedy hands off them as a child and can't keep his greedy eyes off them as an adult.'

I'm like, 'For fock sake – seriously?'

The old dear's there, 'I suppose you've *heard* the news. There's absolute war going on over our plans to move the house to the southside.'

I'm like, 'I'm not surprised. You're putting the river through people's actual homes.'

'Think of the number of people who are going to benefit, Ross, from their homes being suddenly transported to a better postcode. The value of their properties is going to soar. But no one wants to hear from them. All anyone wants to know about is what's going to happen to the people who are going to be thrown out onto the street.'

'Weird that, isn't it?'

'I said it to your father. I said, "Why don't you just explain to people that you promised this to me as a belated sixtieth-birthday present?"'

'Very belated,' I go, 'given that you're at least two years north of seventy.'

She's there, 'I think our problem is one of communication.'

'Yeah, no, it's *one* of your problems,' I go. 'Will you *please* put your focking rattlers away?'

She does up *one* button.

She's there, 'I've asked your father to put a balcony on the building. Can you believe that a house such as this doesn't have a balcony, Ross?'

'The fock do you want a balcony for?' I go.

'I need a place from which to speak – to my people.'

I actually laugh at that one.

I'm like, 'What people?'

She's there, 'The people of Ireland, of course! I'm the First Lady, Ross. The public want to hear what I have to say – about all manner of things.'

'You've always thought that anyway. The focking volume of your voice in The Gables back in the day – they could hear you in Stillorgan.'

'I want to be like Evita.'

'Evita? As in, like, Madonna?'

'I'm talking about Eva Perón, Ross. And, yes, Madonna portrayed her in the movie.'

'I didn't realize that story was actual – as in, like, based on real events?'

'Well, your father and I watched it the other night and I shouted, "Chorles, that's me!"'

'You must have been gee-eyed, were you?'

'I said, "You being the leader of this country has given me a plat-form and I'm not using it! I should be conducting an ongoing conversation with the public – one-way, of course."'

'Obviously.'

'I have views on all sorts of things, Ross, from childhood obesity to UNESCO World Heritage recognition for Dublin 4 . . . Do they have it in burgundy, Celia, or does it just come in taupe?'

I'm suddenly confused. I'm like, 'What the fock are you on about?'

She goes, 'I'll tell you what, why don't I ask her to hold it for me, and we'll go to the Westbury for some bubbles?'

Jesus Christ, she thinks she's out shopping with Celia Holman Lee. I turn around to Astrid and she just, like, shrugs, as if to say, 'This is how she *always* is?'

I'm there, 'Hey, you should get yourself up to bed.'

She goes, 'Bed? Ross, it's four o'clock in the afternoon.'

I'm like, 'It's, er, eleven o'clock in the morning. Come on, just have a little lie-down,' and I help her up off the day-bed and I walk her up the stairs to her – yeah, no – bedroom.

'I *am* rather tired,' she goes, getting under the covers.

And I'm like, 'Then bed is the best place for you.'

As I pull the curtains, she goes, 'And don't you worry, Ross, about me standing out on that balcony and telling everyone about the time I caught you masturbating when you were fifteen.'

I'm like, 'Jesus Christ.'

She's there, 'I was wondering where my Freemans Ireland cata-logues had disappeared to – and then I walked in on you. Do you remember that, Ross?'

'Unfortunately, yes,' I go. 'Now get some rest.'

I pull the door closed behind me, then I tip downstairs – and I end up running straight into, believe it or not, Sorcha. I've been ringing her ever since my conversation with her old man last week, except she won't answer my calls or return any of my messages.

I'm there, 'Sorcha, can I've a word?'

She goes, 'No, Ross, I'm on my way to see An Taoiseach.'

'This is important.'

'What, and my commitment to Ireland achieving corbon neutrality by 2024 *isn't*?'

She actually goes to walk past me.

'Sorcha,' I go, grabbing her by the actual orm, 'your old man said I'm not going to get to see the kids if I'm sent down.'

She's like, 'Let *focking* go of me,' shaking her orm free, then fixing me with a look of anger I haven't seen since I told her that a leather jacket made her look a bit Sandra Dee at the end of *Grease*. Hey, she asked for my opinion.

I'm there, 'I want to know is it true?'

She's like, 'Yes, it's focking true.'

'Sorcha, you can't do that to me.'

'Er, yes, I can.'

'As their father, I have rights.'

'No, you don't, Ross.'

I wasn't actually sure if I did. I was just taking a punt.

She goes, 'I am not allowing the boys to be brought into a prison once a week to see their father incorcerated. I don't want to undo all the progress they've made. They're different children since you and Honor moved out.'

'Zero craic is what they are, Sorcha.'

'They're not zero craic. They're beautiful, calm, well-adjusted children – and that's all down to them not being around you and *her*.'

'That's a very hord thing for me to hear.'

She's there, 'Ross, I can't be seen around you. The press are already dubious about my statement that our marriage ended five years ago.'

'It's horseshit,' I go. 'I'm not surprised.'

'Ross,' she goes, walking away from me, 'just get on with your life and let me get on with living mine.'

And off she – like I said – focks.

I stand there for, like, thirty seconds and I think about what she said. Then I think, you know what? She's focking right. I *do* need to move on? And that's when I decide to give the famous Roz a bell.

I step outside and I call up her number. She answers on the fifth ring.

She's like, 'Hello? Ross?' because she's obviously got my number in her phone.

I'm there, 'Roz, how the hell are you?'

She goes, 'I'm fine . . . thank you,' and she sounds – yeah, no – out of breath. 'Sorry, I've just finished my spin class.'

I'm like, 'Coola bualadh. Look, I just wanted to say – whatever – thank you for last week, talking to me when I was upset in the gym, reminding me about all the amazing things I still had going for me, even telling me that you could see my – yeah, no – left nut up the leg of my shorts.'

She laughs. I think she gets a genuine kick out of me.

She's there, 'You're welcome. Like I said, we're old friends. And our daughters are in school together.'

'Yeah, no,' I go, 'I was wondering would you be interested in going for, like, a drink – just so I can say a proper thank-you?'

She goes quiet for a while.

I'm like, 'Are you still there, Roz?'

'Yes,' she goes, 'I'm still here. Are you talking about, like, an actual date?'

I'm there, 'Hey, if you want it to be.'

She's like, 'I don't.'

'Oh,' I go, failing to hide my disappointment. I honestly thought she'd bite my hand off.

She goes, 'Look, Ross, we tried it, didn't we? A few years back?'

I'm like, 'Yeah, no, I thought we got on well.'

If you'd heard the animal noises she made when we had sex, you'd think so too.

She goes, 'We did, Ross. And then you went back to your wife.'

I'm there, 'Like her statement said, we were only together because of the kids.'

'I'll never forget that night, Ross, just before Christmas, when you were supposed to call over. I had a goose and everything.'

'I remember the goose.'

'And you rang to say that you and Sorcha were giving it another go.'

'You seemed cool with it.'

'Well, I wasn't cool with it. You hurt me, Ross – very, very badly.'

'I wasn't expecting this. No offence, but I honestly thought you'd have my hand off.'

She goes, 'You're a really, really nice goy,' and I'm thinking, Oh fock, I'm about to be friend-zoned here. 'But I see you mainly as a fellow Mount Anville parent who I quite enjoy talking to when I meet him.'

Shit. So this is what it feels like to be Fionn.

'Fair enough,' I go.

She's like, 'I'll see you around, okay?'

I'm like, 'Yeah, no, cool.'

As she hangs up, I suddenly hear the old dear's voice behind me. I turn around and – yeah, no – she's got her head sticking out of her bedroom window. At the top of her voice, she's going, 'Ross! Ross! It wasn't a Freemans Ireland catalogue that you were masturbating to!' and I notice that the two Gordaí posted at the front door are cracking their holes laughing. 'No, you were masturbating to one of my *Image* magazines!'

Hugo Mangan has a Kermit the Frog pen. Yeah, no, I can't stop looking at the thing. Every time he writes a word, Kermit storts waving his orms around like a mad thing and all I can think is that whether I go to prison or not is in the hands of a solicitor who writes with a Kermit the Frog pen. He looks up from whatever he's doing and he catches me staring at the thing.

'Birthday present from my daughter,' he goes – then he chuckles like I should find it funny as *well*?

This is in his office on, like, Baggot Street, by the way.

I'm like, 'Yeah, no, as long as you don't bring it into court – and use it to try to, I don't know, emphasize a point.'

'Oh, I won't be going to court,' he goes.

I'm there, 'Excuse me? I thought you were going to represent me?'

'What I mean is, *I* won't be presenting your case to the jury. It'll be a barrister – that's if you choose to let this thing proceed to trial.'

'What do you mean? I can just, like, walk away if I want to?'

He laughs like he can't believe how stupid I am. Focking typical Blackrock College, I'm *sorely* tempted to say.

'No, you shan't be walking away from anything,' he goes.

Shan't. What an absolute prick.

He's there, 'What I mean is, if you change your plea to guilty, there will *be* no trial – just a sentencing hearing.'

'Okay,' I go, 'and in that case how long do you reckon I'd get?'

'Best-case scenario?'

'Yeah, best-case. Sorry, can you put that focking pen down for a minute? We're talking about me doing possible jail time and Kermit the Frog there is introducing the next act.'

'My apologies,' he goes, laying it down on the desk. 'Best-case would be a suspended sentence, but I'm going to have to warn you, Jeff –'

'Ross.'

'Sorry – Ross. It doesn't look good for you.'

'Fock's sake, you're my solicitor – you're supposed to make me feel *better*.'

'Well, that's *not* part of my brief, as it happens. Look, the fact is, Ross, you're in a lot of trouble. The public indecency –'

'It was a mooner.'

'It was just a moment of juvenile stupidity.'

'Well, you weren't there, so you're not in a position to say how funny or unfunny it was.'

'A young man, drunk and acting like an idiot.'

'Jesus Christ,' I go. 'I thought you'd appreciate the comedy given that you went to Blackrock.'

He's there, 'Well, I wasn't part of the rugby crowd, you see.'

I'm thinking, What the fock am I paying you for, then?

'No,' he goes, 'I think any decent barrister would be able to get you off with a suspended sentence for exposing yourself, but it's this other business of giving the Gardaí someone else's name and

65

address and pinning the whole thing on them. That's very, very serious.'

I'm like, 'Dude, level with me. Worst-case scenario – how long are we talking?'

'If you plead not guilty? Something in the order of ten years.'

What the fock?

I'm there, 'Ten years?'

'Yes,' he goes.

'What about the rugby thing that I mentioned before?'

'Rugby isn't going to help you. Not with a case as serious as this. There's also the fact that your father is the leader of the country.'

'I know that.'

'Which means everyone is going to be taking an interest in this trial. Plus, you have a bit of a public profile yourself, as the former coach of the, em –'

He reaches for his file.

'The Ireland women's rugby team,' I go, to save him the trouble. 'Grand Slam-winning, I *could* add?'

'Unfortunately,' he goes, 'none of that is going to save you from prison.'

I'm there, 'Even if I get fifteen or twenty players to go to court and say what a good goy I am and what a laugh? I'm talking about actual internationals here – men as *well* as women?'

'I think it'd make things worse. It would shine an even bigger spotlight on the case, if that's even possible. Like I said, it's already bad enough that your father is the Taoiseach. With the whole country watching, the judge is going to feel under enormous pressure to give you a custodial sentence. I can't stress enough that the courts tend to take a very dim view of the more serious charges you're facing.'

I'm there, 'Ten years, though! Ten *focking* years!'

'Again, that's worst-case,' he goes. 'And you'd only *serve* eight – tops.'

I'm like, 'I've another question to ask you. Would I be entitled to see my children while I'm, like, inside?'

'Of course,' he goes, 'you'll be allowed visitors.'

'Yeah, no, what I mean is, if my wife – slash, ex-wife – didn't want to bring them in to see me – could I, like, *force* her?'

He laughs. Focking Blackrock.

He's there, 'No, if she decides that she doesn't want to bring the children into a prison environment, there's nothing you can do to compel her.'

'But the boys are, like, six years old,' I go. 'They'll be pretty much teenagers when I get out.'

He's there, 'As I told you before, it doesn't look good for you, Jeff,' and he picks up his Kermit the Frog pen and storts writing with it again.

'It's Ross,' I go.

He's there, 'Excuse me?'

'My *name* is Ross!' I go. 'My *name* is *focking* Ross!' and I snatch the pen out of his hand and fock it across the room. 'How are you going to save me from prison if you can't even get my focking name right?'

He goes, 'There's no cause to be losing our tempers,' and he stands up and walks across the room to pick up the pen.

In that moment, I just happen to notice his phone on the desk. He's on the focking line to someone. And even reading it upside-down – oh, holy focking shit! – I recognize the name on the screen. I reach across the desk, pick it up and hold it to my ear.

Hugo goes, 'What the hell do you think you're doing? Give me that phone this instant.'

But I'm like, 'Hey, Hennessy. Having a good focking listen, are you?'

Hennessy all of a sudden hangs up. Busted and disgusted.

I look my so-called solicitor up and down. I'm there, 'So he got to you, huh?'

The dude can't even look at me. If anything, I've gone far too easy on that school over the years.

He goes, 'He just wanted me to frighten you a little bit. He thought if I told you the worst-case scenario, you might change your mind and let him represent you in court.'

I'm there, 'What did he promise you?' I stand up. 'Actually, don't answer that question. He's the Attorney General, he can give you pretty much anything you want.'

'Well, yes,' he goes.

I'm there, 'I'm not sure if this needs saying, dude, but I'm going to say it anyway. You're focking fired.'

Ronan can't believe it when I tell him.

He goes, 'He was *what*?'

This is over, like, FaceTime.

I'm there, 'He was listening to the entire conversation. Hugo focking Mangan, my so-called solicitor, rang his number and let Hennessy hear every single word that was said.'

He goes, 'Rosser, that's a breach of prividege.'

'I've no idea what you just said.'

'What goes on in the roowum between you and your solicitodder is apposed to be private, Rosser. You should repowurt him to the Lor Societoddy.'

'Dude, my priority for now is staying out of prison. Who was that dude you mentioned who got Buckets of Blood's brother off for ormed robbery?'

'*Ormed* robbery,' he goes, mocking my accent. 'It's eermed robbedy, Rosser. Addyhow, the fedda's nayum is Frankie de Felice. Thee call him The Chiseller.'

I'm there, 'Any reason? Do I even *want* to know?'

'He was up befower for passing a chisel to a fedda on the witness stand.'

'You know some *seriously* shady people.'

'He represented himself in cowurt and was fowunt not giddlety.'

'Okay, he sounds ideal.'

'Knows evoddy thrick in the buke, Rosser – he *writ* the bleaten buke.'

'But how do I know I can trust him? As in, how do I know Hennessy won't get to him?'

'In moy peert of the wordled, Rosser, every wooden stays loyal – do you get me?'

'Er, yeah, no, I *think* I do?'

'Frankie hates authoditty. He dudn't do what he does for the muddy. He's motivashidden is to beat the systoddem.'

'Is he on, like, LinkedIn?'

'LinkedIn?'

'Yeah, no, I'm just wondering how do I reach out to him?'

'Fooken *LinkedIn*? This fedda dudn't move in that wurdled, Rosser.'

'So how do I get in touch with the dude? I'm guessing he doesn't have a website either.'

'No, he dudn't hab a website. I'll ast Buckets to serrup an appointment wirrem for you.'

'Yeah, no, that'd be great. Thanks, Ro.'

He's there, 'Afore you go, Rosser, I want you to meet some wooden.'

I'm like, 'Yeah, no, who?'

'Avoddy.'

'Avery? As in, like, Avery from Boston?'

'Yeah, she's arthur cubben to New York for the weekend,' he goes, then he calls her over to the computer. 'Avoddy, I want you to meet Rosser.'

And then a girl of pretty much Ronan's age sits down at the table beside him and goes, 'Ah, Ronan's famous *auld fedda*. It's lovely to meet you, Ross!'

And I end up just freezing.

'Rosser?' Ronan goes. 'Is evoddy thing alreet?'

But I don't respond.

'The screen has frozen,' Avery goes. 'I think we've lost the connection.'

'N . . . n . . . n . . . n . . . no,' I go, sounding like the famous Kennet. 'I'm, like, still here.'

Ronan's there, 'What's the stordee, Rosser? You look like you're arthur seeing a ghost.'

I'm like, 'Yeah, no, I'm fine. It's, em, lovely to meet you, Avery. I've heard so much about you.'

'Likewise,' she goes. 'Are you okay? You look a little pale.'

I'm there, 'Yeah, no, I was just thinking, I should go and get

Honor and Amelie. And Erika obviously. And Erika's old dear. Wait there.'

I race down the stairs and into the kitchen, where Erika and Helen are making dinner and Honor is teaching Amelie how to flip someone the bird like you actually mean it.

I'm there, 'Goys, I've got Ronan on FaceTime upstairs. He wants you all to meet his girlfriend.'

'Yay!' Honor goes and races for the door.

I'm there, 'Not so fast, Honor. There's something you need to know about her before you go putting your foot in it like *I* possibly did?'

She's like, 'What?'

And I go, 'She's black.'

Erika's like, 'Black? You mean African-American?'

I'm there, 'I don't know, Erika. I mean, I've no idea what you can and can't say any more.'

Honor goes, 'But so *what* if she's black. What's the big deal?'

I'm there, 'I'm not saying it's a big deal. I'm just telling you so that you don't make the same mistake that I made – which was to sit there for, like, twenty seconds, just staring and saying fock-all. They thought the screen had frozen.'

Erika's like, 'I don't understand why the colour of her skin is an issue for you.'

'Jesus Christ,' I go, 'it's *not* an issue for me. I'm just saying that Ro could have at least given us a heads-up.'

Honor's like, 'What, he should have said, "I've met someone. And she's black"?'

Helen – in fairness to her – steps in then.

'I think what Ross is saying,' she goes, 'is that he was just surprised – am I right, Ross?'

I'm like, 'Yes, thank you, Helen – that's exactly what I'm saying.'

'That's just down to social conditioning,' she goes. 'Because he grew up in a monocultural bubble, he had an expectation that his son's girlfriend would be of the same ethnicity as him.'

I'm like, 'Er – yeah, no – again, thanks, Helen,' even though it doesn't sound like she's *defending* me any more?

Honor goes, 'Sorry, are we going to stand around here talking about my dad being a racist or are we going to meet her?'

Up the stairs we trot. I let them go first. Ten seconds later, we're all gathered around the computer and it's all, 'Hi, Avery – lovely to meet you!' and there's literally no weirdness – *I think* – because they were *pre-warned*?

Honor's going, 'Oh my God, Avery, you *have* to come to Ireland!'

And Avery looks at Ro and goes, 'Well, Ronan and I were talking about going over there this summer.'

Erika's like, 'You're staying here with us, Ro – no arguments!'

I'm there, 'Yeah, no, Avery, you definitely do *not* want see where Ronan grew up. Talk about the 'hood!'

'Why are you are mentioning the 'hood?' Erika goes.

I'm like, 'Jesus Christ, Erika, you've *been* to Finglas.'

Honor's there, 'But why did you use that phrase?'

I'm suddenly sweating.

I'm like, 'I always use that phrase. The 'hood. It's short for the neighbourhood, isn't it? Jesus, I can't believe you're throwing shade at me for slagging off the northside, Honor – a girl who used to hyperventilate if she heard the *Fair City* theme tune.'

Ronan gets in on the act then. He goes, 'Hee-or, Rosser, Ine joost arthur figurding out why you weddent all quiet a midute ago.'

I'm there, 'Did I? When?'

'When you met Avoddy for the foorst toyum,' he goes. 'Is it because she's black?'

I'm like, 'Black?' like it hadn't actually occurred to me before.

Ronan's there, 'Yeah, black, Rosser.'

'I didn't even notice,' I go, then I push my face a little closer to the screen. 'Oh, yeah, now that you say it.'

There's, like, silence from everyone, on both sides of the – I want to say – *Aclantic*?

After ten seconds, which feels like ten minutes, Avery goes, 'Rosser, they're just being mean to you,' and then – I shit you not – everyone laughs, including, thankfully, Avery herself.

I'm like, 'For fock's sake, goys, I've already been cancelled – don't get me cancelled any further.'

And that's when my phone all of a sudden beeps. I whip it out of my pocket and it ends up being a text message from the famous Roz.

And it's like, 'Okay, ONE date.'

'So is the rumour true?' Roz goes, looking at me over a forkful of scallop ceviche. 'I have to know.'

I'm like, 'You wouldn't want to listen to rumours, Roz – although I would be interested in knowing which rumour you're talking about *pacifically*?'

'The one about Honor,' she goes.

And, of course, I'm instantly relieved that it's not about me.

I'm there, 'Honor? Yeah, no, whatever you've heard, it's almost certainly true.'

Her eyes go wide.

'What,' she goes, 'she drove a boy up the Wicklow Mountains in the boot of Sorcha's car so that he'd miss the Leinster Schools Senior Cup final?'

I feel suddenly bad. I don't want to let Honor down, so I make a big point of laughing like it's the most ridiculous thing I've ever heard.

'Talk about giving a dog a bad name,' I go. 'It's something I've suffered from over the years as well, in fairness to me.'

We're sitting in Glovers Alley on Stephen's Green, by the way. We're on bottle of wine number two and we're getting on like Bang and Olufsen.

She goes, 'It didn't *sound* true,' missing the point that most stories involving Honor never do. That's generally how you know they *are*? 'People can be so horrible, can't they?'

I'm like, 'Who are you telling? Where did you hear it, by the way?'

'Some of the mothers in Gleesons were talking.'

'Gleesons – say no more.'

'I know! I think the only reason I go for coffee there is because I'm terrified of what will be said about me behind my back!'

'I'm sure they're having a field day talking about the Rossmeister,' I go.

She's like, 'The Rossmeister?'

'Yeah, no, sorry,' I go. 'I mean me.'

'Oh, em, yeah, they are a little bit.'

'Seriously? What are they saying – as in, like, what *actually*?'

'Oh, you know, just the kind of things you'd expect from those girls.'

'Yeah, the same ones who never missed a match of mine back in the day. And they're suddenly offended by a man taking his orse out in Cork. The world has gone mad.'

I'm having the Dublin Bay prawns with fennel, hollandaise and lordo, by the way, and I've pushed the boat out by paying the €18 supplement for the Oscietra cavior. I just thought, fock it, I could be eating prison food in three months' time.

'Oh my God,' she goes, laying her knife and fork down on the plate, 'Andy McFadden is an absolute genius.'

I'm there, 'Yeah, no orguments from me on that score.'

She looks incredible, I should have mentioned earlier. She's wearing a tight, black shirt that really shows off her bips and she hasn't got a wrinkle on her face. I'd say she's no stranger to a bit of Botox.

'Do you know what I'd really love?' she goes.

I'm there, 'What's that? Bearing in mind that I never put out on a first date.'

She laughs. Roz has always *got* me. And by that I mean she's always had a lorger-than-average capacity for my bullshit.

'What I'd really love,' she goes, 'is for Sincerity and Honor to be friends.'

I end up nearly choking on my last prawn.

'What?' I go, at the same time thumping my chest as I try to cough it up again. 'Jesus Christ, are you absolutely sure about that?'

Roz goes, 'Sincerity talks about her all the time.'

I'm like, 'Yeah, no, Honor talks about Sincerity all the time too.'

Usually about how much she hates her and would love to stick a pen in her eye.

'I would love it if they could become friends,' she goes, as the waiter takes away our storter plates. 'I think it would be very good for Sincerity.'

I'm there, 'As long as you don't mind signing a waiver to say it was your idea.'

She laughs. She thinks I'm joking.

'The thing is,' she goes, 'Sincerity could do with toughening up. She's a great kid but she's a bit of a goody-goody.'

I'm there, 'Yeah, no, Honor may have mentioned something about that. Continue.'

'Honor isn't scared of anything, is she?'

'Nothing. She takes no shit and she gives no focks.'

'I just want Sincerity to toughen up a little bit. I don't want her to be pushed around. Could I ask you for a favour?'

'You can certainly ask.'

'Would you ask Honor if Sincerity can hang around with her for the summer?'

'Er – yeah, no – I'll mention it to her and we'll see what she says.'

'Thank you,' she goes, then she gives me the full-tooth smile across the table, just as the waiter brings her wild turbot with brassicas, chorizo and red dulse and my sika deer with black curry, carrot purée, dates, endive and foie gras – this time for a €15 supplement, because I'm determined to go down in a blaze of glory.

'So can I ask you another question?' she goes. 'And I want an honest answer.'

I'm there, 'Let me hear the question before I commit myself.'

She goes, 'Do you think you're going to go to jail?'

I'm thinking, Shit, she's wondering if there's any future in this or is she just wasting her time?

So I go, 'Honestly? No,' even though it's total horseshit.

She's there, 'Because – again – the girls in Gleesons–'

And I'm like, 'Forget about the girls in Gleesons, Roz!' and I end up actually *shouting* it? Quite a few people at the other tables are suddenly staring at us. 'Look, just between ourselves, a mate of Ronan's is fixing me up with a shit-hot lawyer called Frankie de Felice.'

'I've never heard of him. What school did he go to?'

'He's not that kind of lawyer, Roz.'

'Oh.'

'They call him The Chiseller. Don't even ask. I'm seeing him tomorrow in his office in Cabra. That's a place on the northside.'

'Yeah, no, I've heard of Cabra.'

'Then you'll know the kind of solicitor I'm talking about. There's not a chance of me getting sent down, Roz. That's a promise.'

She smiles and gets stuck into her turbot and the rest of the meal goes really well. Conversationally, it has to be said, I'm at the very top of my game.

An hour later, we're in a taxi, telling the driver to take us to Ailesbury Road and then on to Goatstown, where *she* lives? Although, to be totally honest, I'm kind of waiting for her to say, 'Let's just go back to mine. I am going to go to absolute focking town on you when I get you home.'

Except she *doesn't*? Instead, she goes, 'That was a lovely meal.'

I'm there, 'Like you said, Andy McFadden.'

'Ross,' she goes, suddenly looking deep into my eyes, 'I don't want to get hurt again, okay?'

I'm there, 'I'm not the hurting kind, Roz.'

I hate myself for lying to her. But that's dating in your late thirties – get used to it.

She goes, 'I need to know if it's definitely over between you and Sorcha.'

I'm there, 'Hey, *it's* over.'

'Definitely, definitely?'

'Definitely, definitely, *definitely*.'

We end up staring into each other's eyes as we cross Leeson Street Bridge and then we both lean in for the kiss. Her tongue tastes of Îles Flottante, mango and Madagascan vanilla and I've a bone in my chinos that could jam the jaws of the focking Rancor.

When I finally pull away from her, it just happens that we're passing Energia Pork, scene of some of my happiest days, both as a schools rugby player and as the coach of the Ireland women's team. And – yeah, no – this one is very nearly up there with them.

Roz puts her head on my shoulder. Her hair smells of, I don't know, something and something else.

'I just have one rule,' she goes. 'No secrets.'

I'm there, 'Well, that's good news because I don't have any. I'm an open kimono, baby,' which is a line we used to use back in my estate agent days.

'That's good to hear,' she goes, then I notice that I have a text message from, like, Ross Junior, saying that the sextortion crowd are looking for another ten K's, otherwise everyone in his old pair's contacts list is going to find out about the – yeah, no – *gay* porn.

Frankie de Felice works out of an office above a bookies shop on Annamoe Terrace. You have to walk through the actual bookies – with punters looking you up and down and muttering, 'Fooken southsiders' and 'Where's your bleaten yacht, you fooken yuppie?' – before you climb the stairs to a little waiting room, where there's no receptionist, just a sign that says, 'Sit Down and Wait to be Called – CCTV is in Operation on These Premises. Thieves Will be Dealt With'.

We sit down on a couple of, like, hord plastic chairs. Honor whips out her phone and storts replying to a text message while I stare at the dude's collection of framed tabloid front pages on the wall, with headlines containing words like 'Cleared', 'Freed', 'Acquitted' and 'Walks'.

I'm thinking, Fair focks to him.

I'm there, 'Who are you texting, Honor?'

She goes, 'MacDara.'

'MacDara,' I go. And I smile – can't help it. 'I really like the sound of this dude.'

She's there, 'You don't know anything about him.'

'Hey, sometimes you can just judge someone by their name.'

'I'm also texting Sebastian.'

'See? Now you're focking talking. Who's Sebastian?'

'He goes to, like, Belvedere College.'

'Focking Belvo. You're certainly getting around – and that's not me slut-shaming you. And what about Joel? Is he gone from the scene?'

'No, I'm still seeing him.'

'That's great news. The thing is, Honor, you're hot property at the moment. Enjoy every moment of it. I know I did.'

There's, like, an awkward pause in the conversation then, and that's when I go, 'So, Honor, can I ask you a question?'

She's there, 'No, Sebastian isn't on the Senior Cup team. He's only in, like, Transition Year.'

'Yeah, no, I was going to ask you about Sincerity.'

'Sincerity? What about her?'

'What do you think of her? Honestly?'

'I'd like to stab her in the eye with a pen.'

'Yeah, no, you've made that point in the past.'

'Why are you asking me about that focking sap?'

'Well – okay, don't go mad, Honor – but I went out on a date with her old dear the other night.'

She suddenly looks up from her phone.

She's like, 'Roz?'

I'm there, 'Er, yeah.'

'You went on a date with her?'

'Now that doesn't mean that I never loved your mother, Honor.'

'Fock my mother.'

'Oh, er, right.'

'You went on a date – with Roz Matthews!'

'Yeah, no, I think she's gone back to calling herself Roz *Carew* again?'

'She's, like, *so* hot.'

'You're taking this surprisingly well, it has to be said.'

'She looks like Allison Williams from *Girls* – except not as annoying-looking.'

'That's exactly what *I* think! And with a smaller mouth.'

'She's, like, a really cool person as well. Not like her stupid bitch of a daughter.'

'Yeah, no, about her daughter – see, I was wondering, and I realize this is a big ask, Honor, but would you be prepared to hang out with Sincerity over the summer?'

'What? Er, *why*?'

'Well, Roz thinks it'd be good for her – might, you know, toughen her up a bit.'

'Roz thinks it would be good for her daughter – to hang out with *me*?'

'I know! It's insane!'

She shrugs. She's like, 'Fine, then, I'll do it.'

I'm there, 'Really?'

'Whatever.'

'That's brilliant. And you definitely, definitely don't mind that I'm back dating?'

'I just can't wait to see that focking wagon's face when she finds out you're with someone else.'

'Er, we're back talking about your old *dear*, I presume?'

'Exactly.'

My phone all of a sudden beeps. It's, like, a text message from Christian, reminding me about the borbecue in Booterstown this weekend.

'Shit,' I go, 'I forgot that was this Saturday.'

Honor's like, 'What are you talking about?'

'Yeah, no, Christian's just reminding me about Lauren's fortieth.'

She goes, 'Isn't it, like, weird the way he's still involved in her life?'

I'm there, 'I suppose they're just putting on a show for the sake of the kids,' and then I notice the line at the very end of the text. 'Why the fock does he need to say that?'

'What did he say?'

'He's like, This is a big deal, Ross. It's Lauren's fortieth – so please don't do anything to ruin the day!'

'Patronizing prick. You should bring Roz!'

'No, what if your old dear is there? There might be a scene.'

'Er, she's the one who made you sign a statement saying your marriage was over five years ago. Anyway, I doubt if she'll *be* there. She's too busy making the world a better, corbon-neutral place even to have a relationship with her children these days.'

'Very good point, Honor. *Very* good point.'

All of a sudden, the door opens and out walks this old dude, we're talking possibly late sixties, short, with a weatherbeaten face, grey sideburns and – hilariously – a head of reddish-brown hair that's one hundred per cent definitely a wig. An even worse one than my old man's, if you can believe that.

'You Ross?' he goes.

I'm there, 'Yeah, no, Ross O'Carroll-Kelly. You come highly recommended.'

He refuses my offer of a handshake and we follow him into his office and sit down on the opposite side of the desk to him. On the wall, I can't help but notice, in a glass presentation case, is a chisel.

I'm there, 'Ah, this must be the famous –'

'The famous what?' he goes – he's definitely not a fan of mine.

I'm there, 'The famous chisel that you tried to pass to a dude on the stand.'

He's like, 'I was acquitted of those charges. What's your point?'

'Yeah, no, I was saying it as a *compliment* to you?'

'Buckets of Blood said you were an acquired taste. Who's this with you?'

Honor goes, 'His daughter. My name is Honor. Are you going to keep my dad out of prison?'

'I'm going to try,' he goes, then he looks at me. 'Even though scumbags like him sicken me.'

I'm like, 'Er, *excuse* me?'

'Oh, I've read the Book of Evidence,' he goes. 'Taking your arse out in a pub full of people.'

'Er, they were *Munster* fans?'

He suddenly roars at me. 'THERE COULD HAVE BEEN WOMEN AND CHILDREN THERE! No, you piece of human filth, you *belong* in jail.'

I'm like, 'That's *your* view.'

'Yes, it is my view. There's only one reason I've decided to take your case. And that's because of Buckets.'

'Thank God for that. I thought you were going to say you were a mate of my old man's.'

He ends up just roaring at me then. He's like, 'I DESPISE YOUR FATHER!'

I'm there, 'Er, okay.'

'He's trying to reroute the Liffey – put us all on the southside.'

'In fairness, property values around here will go through the roof.'

'I DON'T WANT TO LIVE ON THE SOUTHSIDE! NO ONE AROUND HERE DOES!'

'Fair enough – takes all sorts.'

'He's talking about knocking down people's homes! *Good* people!'

'He's a dick. I've been saying it for thirty years. The rest of the world is only catching up now.'

He gives me an absolute filthy then. He's there, 'I despise him. I despise you. But I'll do it for Buckets.'

Honor goes, 'Do you think you can, like, get him off?'

'Well,' he goes, 'let me put it to you this way, Princess – if anyone can, Frankie de Felice can,' and then he looks at *me* again? 'This consultation,' he goes, in one continuous sentence, 'has cost you two thousand euros you can Revolut me the money now get the hell out of my sight you sorry piece of human waste.'

On the way down the stairs, Honor goes, 'Oh my God, he's amazing, isn't he?'

And I'm like, 'Yeah, no, I've a good, em, feeling about him alright.'

Christian answers the door. He's got, like, a spatula in his hand and he's wearing his borbecue apron, the one with 'Daddio of the Patio!' on it. He goes, 'Hey, Ross,' then he cops Roz standing next to me and his facial expression changes like he's forted and followed through. 'Oh, em, hello – it's Roz, isn't it?'

And Roz is there, 'Yes – you must be Christian.'

Don't do anything to ruin the day. The focking balls on him – when you think about it.

He goes, 'You'd, em, better come through.'

And I'm like, 'You'd better come through? What kind of welcome is that for your so-called best mate?'

So through the house we walk. The back gorden is, like, already rammers and the smell of burning meat – we're talking steaks, we're talking chicken, we're talking sausages – hits me straight away. I notice Hennessy – as in, like, Lauren's old man – giving me serious daggers from the other side of the picnic bench, but I keep smiling and refuse to make *eye* contact with the dude?

Roz looks fantastic – and I'm only pointing that out to give the story some context. She's wearing, like, tight jeans and a black, lacy camisole that really shows off the old stress balls. She tells me she's just seen a girl she knows from PT and she'll be back in a minute and I laugh like she's said something hilarious because I know it focks with Hennessy's head to see me happy.

I go looking for the goys, but I end up running into Chloe, Sophie and Amie with an ie, who are doing the usual – standing in a little huddle next to Oliver's trampoline, drinking prosecco and speculating about people's weight out of the corners of their mouths.

'Oh my God, Ross!' Sophie goes. 'I'm surprised to see *you* here!'

I'm like, 'Er, why wouldn't *I* be here?'

She goes, 'I'm just saying, I thought you'd be hiding your face away – after your public disgrace.'

She's actually focking serious.

I'm like, 'Public disgrace?'

'I couldn't believe it when my mom showed me the piece in the paper,' Amie with an ie goes. 'Former Ireland Women's Rugby Coach Chorged with Public Indecency. I was like, Oh! My God!'

I'm there, 'It was a focking mooner. I seem to remember you found it hilarious when I stuck my orse in the window of the exam hall in Muckross while you were doing your mocks.'

She's like, 'Those were different times, Ross. What was appropriate back then isn't appropriate now.'

Chloe goes, 'So are you, like, going *out* with Roz Matthews now?'

I'm there, 'Yeah, no, but she's gone back to being Roz Carew.'

'We both did our Jis in Nantucket. What does she weigh, Ross?'

'I've no idea what she weighs, Chloe.'

'At a guess – what would you say?'

'I don't know and I don't care.'

'Oh my God,' Sophie goes, at the same time laughing, 'did you not bring Lauren a present, Ross?' because – yeah, no – I arrived with my orms swinging.

But I'm just there, 'I'll see you later,' and I end up walking away from them because I suddenly need a drink. I tip back into the kitchen, where I notice that the table is full of presents. I make sure no one is looking, then I have a bit of a rummage through them, checking all the tags. I find Sophie's present – it's, like, a flat box the size of a laptop – and I yank off the tag.

'Ross?' a voice behind me goes.

I turn around and it ends up being Lauren. She looks well, although I've always said she could do a lot more with herself.

I'm like, 'Hey – *there's* the birthday girl!' trying to keep it easy-breezy, but at the same time I'm wondering did she see me take the present from the table. It turns out that she didn't.

She goes, 'Did you bring a focking date to my birthday porty?'

I'm there, 'Yeah, no, I thought you'd be cool with it. She said you were in the same spin class a few years ago.'

'I don't *give* a shit,' she goes. 'I told Christian to tell you not to do anything to ruin the day. Sorcha's on her way – and you're here with someone else.'

I spot Lychee outside in the gorden, taking a selfie of her and Christian standing next to the borbecue, presumably for her Insta-gram or her TikTok or her whatever-the-fock. He flips a burger high in the air and catches it on his spatula and she goes, 'Do it again! I wasn't filming!' and I'm wondering is Lauren more pissed off with him bringing a date than me bringing one.

I'm like, 'Hey, me and Sorcha have been separated for five years, Lauren – did you not read her statement?'

Then I go, 'Here,' and I hand her the present. 'Happy birthday,' giving her a big kiss on the cheek.

She sort of, like, stiffens. It's hord to believe it sometimes but she used to be a fan of mine.

I'm there, 'Where's Ross Junior, by the way?'

She goes, 'He's not Ross *Junior*. He exists in his own right – not in relation to you.'

I'm like, 'Fair enough.'

'He's somewhere in the gorden,' she goes, 'with Emer, his girlfriend.'

I actually laugh in her face.

She's there, 'What's so focking funny?'

I'm there, 'Yeah, no, nothing, Lauren.'

I grab a stick of Heinemite from the fridge, then I head back out-side to try to find him. I eventually do. He's lying on a sun-lounger, catching a few rays along with – like Lauren said – a girl. *She* doesn't even register with me, so I'm not in a position to describe her, although plain as fock covers pretty much everything.

I go, 'Get the fock out of here – I need to talk to my godson alone.'

She gets the message and off she jolly well focks.

I'm like, 'That's your girlfriend, is it?'

He goes, 'Yeth, her name ith Emer.'

I'm there, 'Yeah, no, I'm sure it is. Just to let you know, I paid that crowd another ten K's.'

He's like, 'Thank you *tho*, tho much, Roth!'

'But that's the end of it,' I go. 'I'm not handing over another cent. The good news is that they're off your case now. The bad news is you won't be going to college.'

I take a swig out of the bottle, then I head off and mingle some more, something I've always been pretty excellent at. I find Roz. She's smiling. I love her smile.

She goes, 'I'm picking up on a vibe.'

I'm there, 'What kind of vibe?'

'Like I shouldn't *be* here? I just met some girl called Chloe, who said we were in Nantucket together. Then she asked me how much I weighed.'

I just shake my head.

I'm there, 'They're focking vultures, that crew. Come on, I'll introduce you to the goys,' and I grab her by the hand and lead her over to Oisinn, Magnus, JP and – yeah, no, fock *him* – Fionn.

I'm there, 'Goys, this is Roz. You probably remember her. She went to Alex back in the day.'

The goys are all like, 'Hey, Roz, how the hell *are* you?' and it's, like, handshakes and air-kisses all round. They really make her feel like port of the group, except for Fionn, who says to me out of the corner of his mouth, 'You do know Sorcha is coming, don't you?'

I'm there, 'So? We've been living separate lives for years – that's according to her.'

He goes – and this is, like, word for word – 'I just think someone should tell her that you're here with someone else – just so she's not embarrassed.'

He's such a knob.

Everyone is getting on famously and then Delma arrives over with a glass of wine. She storts picking, I don't know, lint or something from the shoulder of JP's shirt, then they smile at each other. And that's when Roz ends up saying *the* most unbelievable thing.

She goes, 'Oh, you must be JP's mum!'

Holy focking shitcakes, it's a moment! It's like everything goes instantly quiet. Delma just, like, stares her out of it, then turns around and storms off in tears.

JP goes, 'Fock's sake!' and runs after her, going, 'Delma! Delma, she didn't mean anything by it!'

Roz looks at each of us and goes, 'What did I say?'

Oisinn's there, 'That's, em, JP's *wife*, Roz?'

She's like, 'His wife?' and she puts her hand over her mouth. I love her mouth. 'Oh my God, I feel awful.'

I'm there, 'Hey, it's an easy mistake to make. I'd probably think the same thing if I didn't already know her as a mate of my old dear's.'

'I feel terrible,' Roz goes.

But there's no time to discuss it any further because Sorcha suddenly shows up. She's obviously been tipped off – I'm presuming Fionn texted her – because she morches straight up to Roz with her orm outstretched and shakes her hand like she's looking for her vote.

She's like, 'Roz – so lovely to see you! How *are* you?'

Roz ends up being a little bit thrown by this, like she's never experienced falseness before – and her from focking Goatstown.

She's there, 'Oh, em, lovely to see you too, Sorcha.'

'How's Sincerity?' Sorcha goes. 'Is she still getting amazing, amazing grades?'

Roz is like, 'Well, yes – but, as I said to Ross the other day, they're not the most important thing.'

'Well,' Sorcha goes, 'you're pushing an open door with *him*!'

Everyone laughs – everyone, that is, *except* Roz, in fairness to her.

Instead, she goes, 'I just wish sometimes she wasn't such a goody-goody.'

'There's nothing wrong with being a goody-goody,' Sorcha goes.

'*I* was a goody-goody!' and the words 'and look at me now' are left unspoken.

Sorcha turns to Oisinn then. She's there, 'Fionn tells me that you and the goys are doing the Camino this summer!' and it's a definite smackdown for me for bringing a date here.

Oisinn goes, 'Yeah, Magnus is letting me have one last blow-out. It's all going to change once the baby –'

Then he stops because he knows that Sorcha is not a happy camper about it.

She goes, 'It's fine, Oisinn. Look, I'm over it now. I said what I had to say about my sister not being a fit person to be a mother to your baby – she's a focking bitch – and that's that.'

Magnus is like, 'Thanksh, Shorcha.'

Christian arrives over then with a plate of chicken and also with Lychee, who moves like she's hearing catwalk music in her head.

She goes, 'Okay, I want to get a photograph of all the boys together!' and we each take a drumstick, then arrange ourselves in a bunch and smile for her.

'Actually,' she goes, 'maybe *you* should take it, Ross?'

I'm like, 'Me?' horsing into the chicken. 'But then I won't be in it,' and, as I say the words, the penny suddenly drops. 'Ah – you don't want me *in* the photograph, do you?'

'Well, I want to post it on my Instagram,' she goes, 'and I don't want haters in my replies going, "Oh my God! I can't believe you're friends with him!"'

I just shake my head and throw the bone from my chicken leg over my shoulder. I'm there, 'I'm going to go and grab another beer.'

As I'm walking away, I hear Roz go, 'What kind of a thing was that to say?'

And Lychee is like, 'Hey, he was the one who got *himself* cancelled?'

It suddenly storts to rain then, out of literally nowhere, and Lauren announces that we should all go back inside to watch her opening her presents. So I'm walking towards the back door when Hennessy suddenly intercepts me. He's got a massive

Romeo y Julieta – unlit – between his fingers and the blood from his steak has dribbled out of the corners of his mouth and dried on his face.

'So you sacked Hugo Mangan?' he goes.

—I'm there, 'Well, *obviously* – given that he was working for you.'

He's like, 'So who've you got representing you now?'

I'm there, 'Yeah – like I'm going to tell *you*.'

'Hey, I'll find out.'

'Fine, then, it's Frankie de Felice.'

He cracks his hole laughing. He's like, 'The Chiseller?'

I'm there, 'Yes, The Chiseller.'

'You're going to get five years inside.'

'He thinks he can get me off.'

'He's a crook.'

'And you're *not*?'

'I am – but juries focking love me.'

'Well, I've every faith in him. His reception area is full of framed newspaper cuttings of all the people he's helped walk free from justice. In fairness to him.'

'Tell Ronan to come home,' he goes, 'and I'll make sure you don't do a day in prison.'

I'm like, 'Not a focking chance, Dude.'

The rain is really storting to come down now. I step past Hennessy and into the gaff. Everyone is crammed into the kitchen. I notice that Lauren is holding the present I gave her and she goes, 'I might as well open this one first.'

Sophie's like, 'Oh my God, Lauren, it's only a novelty present – please open it when everyone's gone.'

But Lauren goes, 'No, this one's from Ross!' and Sophie turns around to me with a look of, like, total confusion on her face.

At the top of my voice, I go, 'I hope you don't already have one, Lauren!' just to really rub it in with Sophie.

There's, like, total silence while Lauren tears off the wrapping paper to reveal a box. I've literally no idea what the fock is in it. She takes the lid off and pulls out this, like, beaded necklace.

There ends up being, like, *gasps*?

I'm like, 'What do you think, Lauren?' and then – like a focking idiot – I take it out of her hands and I put it around her neck. I go to fasten the thing at the back, but there's, like, no clasps or anything.

I'm there, 'Okay, how does this thing tie together?'

I notice that Lauren is staring at me with a look of horror on her face.

I'm like, 'What's wrong?'

'Ross,' Sophie goes, grinning from ear to ear, 'I think those are *anal* beads?'

Everyone is just staring at me, looking appalled.

'Oh my God!' Lychee goes. 'I'd actually put this on TikTok except I don't want people to know that I *know* him?'

I'm there, 'I don't understand.'

Lauren goes, 'I can't believe you would buy me a sex toy for my birthday and let me open it in front of all these people. Including my son and his girlfriend.'

I do my best not to react.

'What?' she goes.

I'm like, 'Nothing.'

'You laughed again when I mentioned his girlfriend.'

I'm there, 'Sorry, can you all just go back to your conversations,' because I'm not enjoying having everyone at the porty staring at me.

Lauren goes, 'What's so focking funny, Ross? I want to know.'

So I end up just saying it. I'm like, 'Your son's gay, Lauren.'

Again, there's gasps – yeah, like this is breaking news to *anyone* in this room. I look at Roz. Her mouth is wide open. If there's an upside for her from all of this, it's that no one is going to remember her asking Delma if she was JP's old dear.

'Gay?' Lauren goes – like the thought has never occurred to her. 'What are you talking about?'

Christian – my so-called best friend – goes, 'Ross, get the fock out of here.'

I'm there, 'Dude, you're walking around with your head in the clouds if you can't see it.'

He goes, 'I'm sorry I ever asked you to be his godfather.'

I'm there, 'I've been a better godfather to him than you'll ever know.'

I look at Ross Junior, who's looking back at me with – I want to say – *pleading* eyes?

I'm there, 'He's cost me twenty focking grand this month.'

'Roth,' the kid goes, 'pleath don't thay anything.'

I'm there, 'I'm sorry, kid, I have to say it,' and then I fix Lauren with a look. 'Your son was being sextorted.'

Again – gasps. They love a bit of drama, this crowd.

'What?' Christian goes.

I'm like, 'Oh, yeah – blackmailed. For looking up websites. And I don't just mean the ones selling knickers and bras – even though there were quite a few of those as well. I'm talking about porn sites. And I'm not going to say what kind because I want to respect his choices.'

Ross Junior goes, 'I thidn't open thothe pageth! They mutht have opened themthelvth.'

I'm there, 'Don't embarrass yourself, kid.'

Lauren goes, 'Why didn't you tell us this?' and she's talking to, like, *me*?

I'm like, 'Hey, I paid the blackmailer off. Put my hand in my own pocket. Well, sort of. He's not going to third-level, by the way – unless he pays for it himself.'

Christian all of a sudden grabs me by the scruff of the shirt. I've never seen him so angry – and I'm including the time I rode his mother. He literally manhandles me out of the room, then out of the house, throwing me out into the front gorden with such a force that I end up hitting the deck.

'Get the fock out of here,' he goes. 'I never want anything to do with you again.'

3.

Blockedapussy

In fairness to Roz, a day or two later she's prepared to laugh the entire thing off.

She goes, 'So do all porties end that way for you?'

And then *I'm* the one who's laughing?

I'm like, 'Pretty much, Roz. Pretty, pretty much.'

Yeah, no, this is us talking on the *phone*, by the way?

'Did you really buy a set of anal beads,' she goes, 'thinking you were buying a necklace?'

I'm there, 'Hey, I arrived with you. If you remember, I brought fock-all. It was actually Sophie's present – supposed to be a hilarious joke between the focking girlies – and of course it's, like, totally inappropriate when she thinks it's from me.'

There's, like, silence between us then.

She goes, 'Have you spoken to Christian?' because she knows he's my best friend in the world.

I'm like, 'Yeah, no, I'm going to wait until he cools off. Jesus Christ, I shelled out twenty K's to stop his son's internet search history from going viral. He should have been thanking me instead of focking me out on my ear.'

'It definitely seemed unfair,' she goes. 'Oh, well – at least no one is talking about what I said to Delma.'

I laugh.

I'm there, 'Yeah, no, I jumped on that grenade for you, Roz, in all fairness to me. Anyway, listen, I have to go here. We're just about to pull up outside the prison.'

I tell her I'll ring her later on, then I hang up. I can tell that Erika is itching to say something as she reverses the cor into a space on the – believe it or not – North Circular Road.

I'm like, 'What? If you've got something to say, Erika –'

She goes, 'I heard what she said to Delma.'

I'm there, 'Easy mistake to make. I thought the woman totally overreacted, by the way.'

'Well, it's just that, from talking to JP, it's not the first time that she's been mistaken for his mother.'

I laugh – no choice in the matter.

'Erika,' I go, 'she's old enough to *be* his mother. What the fock does she expect?'

She's there, 'What you did to Christian and Lauren, by the way – that was unforgivable.'

I'm like, 'Excuse me?'

'How could you not tell them that their son was being blackmailed?'

'Because he focking begged me not to. And I was just trying to be a brilliant godfather to him – as per focking usual.'

We both get out of the cor and Erika puts the coins in the meter.

I'm there, 'I mean, Lauren doesn't even accept that the kid is gay – even though it's been obvious to everyone since he said his first word. Which was *rainbow*, by the way?'

'Yeah,' she goes, 'she used to bring him on all the Pride morches.'

I'm like, 'Yeah, just to be seen. And now she's pushing this horse-shit story that he has a girlfriend?'

She's there, 'I've no idea. Either way, I think you owe both of them an apology.'

I'm like, '*She's* not getting one. Not a focking chance. She's not even married to him any more. *And* she's Hennessy's daughter. I'll have a word with Christian, though. Yeah, no, I'm going to drive up to Donegal on Friday. Him and JP are up there for the week. Apparently the famous Malingrad is really storting to take shape.'

We stort walking towards the – again, I'm saying it – prison. Or Dóchas, as Erika insists on calling it. I was actually *with* a girl called Dóchas on Peter Stringer's stag weekend – in Pallas focking Paintball, of all places, in Galway. She wanked me off in the undergrowth while I was hiding from a psychopathic hen from – I want to say – Borris-in-*Ossory*? Although, now that I think about it, her name might have been Dorchas.

We turn the corner and that's when I see the twenty-foot-high wall with the razor wire on top and a cold shiver runs down my spine.

Erika goes, 'Are you okay?' because I actually stop walking.

I'm like, 'Er, yeah, no, I was just thinking about a girl I used to know. She worked as a something-or-other in Corrib Foods,' but I'm not thinking about Dóchas slash Dorchas at all. I'm thinking about prison. I'm thinking that, by the end of the summer, I could be living in a place like this. I've been, like, *inside* before, of course – visiting my old man and obviously my old dear. But it's different when it's, like, *you* behind bors?

We approach the giant metal doors and my hort is beating so fast it feels like it's going to possibly *explode*? We step through and we're directed to a room where a dude who's built like a Fitzwilliam Square door checks our paperwork, then directs us into another room, where we're told to empty our pockets and remove our belts and shoes before walking through a scanner, the kind you see at the airport.

There's, like, metal bors everywhere. And the sound of alorms ringing and doors squealing on hinges in serious need of oiling and then – worst of all – clanging shut. And screws shouting at us in take-no-shit voices, 'Remove the laces from your shoes and leave your belts! Remove the laces from your shoes and leave your belts!'

I turn to this woman – I don't want to call her a screw because she's not great in terms of looks and it might sound like I'm being a dick – and I go, 'What about Dubes?' holding up my shoes. 'They've only got, like, tiny laces in them.'

She looks at them – I swear to God – like I'm showing her where I wiped my knob on one of her good tea towels.

I'm there, 'The laces in these wouldn't be long enough to, well, you know –'

She's just there, 'If they have laces, remove them!'

'It's just that they're very difficult to put back in,' I go. 'There's, like, a *knack* to it?'

Erika pulls on her Uggs and goes, 'Ross, just take your focking laces out, will you?'

So I do – and I notice that my fingers are literally trembling – then I step into my now suddenly slip-on shoes.

Along with a group of other visitors, we're led along a corridor that smells weirdly of sweat, then left into a second corridor that also smells weirdly of sweat, then into a massive room that looks like the visitors' room in every prison movie you've ever seen.

It brings me back to the time when – like I said – my old dear was in here for killing that dude she married. What's the word – illegibly?

There's, like, a prisoner sitting at each table – and while I generally try to focus on the positive when it comes to women, there are no beauty queens amongst them. I've watched all seven seasons of *Orange is the New Black* but there's no Alex Vause in here and there's most definitely no Piper Chapman.

It's Erika who first spots Simone across the floor. She's – yeah, no – sitting at a table with her orms folded, sort of, like, rocking backwards and forwards, like she's trying to get warm.

We walk over to her and I'm like, 'See-mon, how the hell are you?' trying to keep it light, even though I'm shitting Ready Brek here.

'It's Sea-mon,' she goes, without even looking at me. 'What the fock is *he* doing here?'

Erika's there, 'He wants to see justice done every bit as much as I do, Sea-mon.'

The girl sort of, like, snorts at that one. She looks absolutely horrendous, by the way – not that she was any focking scene-stealer before she came in here. But she looks like she's lost about two stone in weight – her clothes are hanging off her – and even her dreadlocks look somehow *dirtier* than they did before this all happened?

She goes, 'I see your wife wants to put a cap on the number of miles that motorists are allowed to drive each year.'

I'm like, 'She's lost her focking mind.'

'That was *my* idea as well,' she goes. '*And* the cap on air miles.'

I'm there, 'If it's any consolation to you, our marriage is over and I'm seeing someone else now.'

It's no consolation to her. I don't know why I thought it would be.

'Ross,' Erika goes, 'would you mind shutting the fock up while I talk to Sea-mon, please?'

I'm there, 'Er, yeah, no, whatever.'

'Sea-mon,' she goes, 'I was talking to your solicitor.'

Simone's like, 'Yeah? So?' and I feel like nearly pointing out to her that we don't *have* to be here? I, for one, would definitely rather *not* be, except Erika talked me into it.

'He said that he's spoken to you about lodging an application for bail,' Erika goes.

Simone's like, 'I don't want bail.'

'Why not?'

'Because.'

'Because isn't an answer. Sea-mon, you can't arrive in court each day and then leave again in a prison van. These things leave a huge impression on juries.'

Simone's like, 'I feel safer here.'

'How could you feel safer here?' Erika goes – and, just as she says it, I hear raised voices coming from a table a few feet away. It's obviously someone getting bad news because I hear a woman go, 'What do you mee-in, *you're* wirrem now? He's maddied to *me*!'

Jesus, it's like watching the *Fair City* Christmas omnibus. I'm purely guessing, of course.

Simone goes, 'Hennessy can't let me take the stand. If I get out, I'm a dead woman.'

Erika looks at me, then back at Simone.

She's there, 'I think you're being a little bit paranoid.'

'Oh, I'm not,' Simone goes – and she's got a sort of, like, *laugh* in her voice? 'He burned down the focking Dáil. If you think he's above having someone killed, then you don't know the man at all.'

Erika goes, 'But even if that's true, surely you'd be safer outside than you would be in here. I mean, you're a sitting duck in here.'

Simone just shakes her head. She's there, 'At least in here, I'd see it coming.'

All of a sudden, the woman who's getting the bad news stands up and grabs the hair of the woman who – from what I can follow of the conversation – is riding her husband. She goes, 'You doorty fooken bitch!' and she slams the woman's head down on the table like she's bouncing a ball.

There's, like, a sickening sound of skull hitting Formica and the visiting room is suddenly filled with sirens. Screws – men *and* women – come running from every direction and they grab the woman and wrestle her to the floor. While that's happening, fights stort breaking out at other tables and it ends up turning into an actual riot.

A message over the intercom is telling us to evacuate the room. It's like, 'All visitors, leave the room immediately! All visitors, leave the room immediately!'

Me and Erika both stand up. To my immediate left, I watch a woman knock a man out with the best punch I've ever seen thrown by someone whose name wasn't Mirco Bergamasco.

'Think about what I said,' Erika goes. 'Sea-mon, you won't survive in prison.'

And, as we're fleeing the scene of, like, total and utter cornage, all I can think is, neither will I.

I can't believe my eyes. It looks like an – honestly? – asteroid has hit the Earth. There isn't a tree in sight and there's, like, holes in the ground everywhere, each one big enough to swallow the – yeah, no – Aviva Stadium. I'm driving along this long and winding road and once or twice I end up nearly driving off it into one of these pretty much *craters*?

There's, like, JCBs and other digging machines everywhere and construction workers who look like little toy men – and, for all I know, women – from up here. I keep driving until I run out of road and I end up coming to this basically *city* of shipping containers. There's, like, hundreds of the things, as far as the eye can see. On the sides of quite a few of them it says 'Produce of the Philippines', and I think, holy fock, these must be the Vampire Beds and the Homedrobes where the population of Malingrad will sleep. And, if that's the case, the goys have to be around here somewhere.

It doesn't take me long to find JP. He's standing around, wearing a yellow hord hat – Father Fehily would have a focking stroke if he could see him – and staring at this, like, clipboard. I pull up in the old A8 and give him a big friendly beep.

He ends up just staring at me like I'm, I don't know, a turd in a bidet. As a matter of fact, that's exactly it, because I actually *did* a dump in JP's old pair's bidet while they were away on a wellness retreat in Ard Nahoo and I was too wankered drunk to tell the difference between *it* and the toilet. Yeah, no, JP is looking at me now the same way he looked at me when he was picking my big black dookie out of there with a long borbecue tongs.

He's like, 'What the fock are you doing here?' and that's before I'm even out of the cor.

I'm there, 'I just decided to go for a bit of a drive. See how Malingrad is coming on. Are these things all full of beds?' and I flick my thumb at one of the containers.

He goes, 'Fifty thousand of them, yeah.'

I'm there, 'You're getting a fair focks, Dude – irregordless of what happens here.'

I hang my hand up there for a high-five. He gives me one but without any real, I don't know, enthusiasm.

He goes, 'Christian is *not* going to be happy to see you.'

I'm there, 'Christian needs to get over himself. As does *Delma*, by the way?'

He goes, 'She was just upset by what Roz said.'

I'm like, 'Dude, she didn't say it to be a bitch. She genuinely thought that Delma was your old dear. I don't want to rub it in, but the woman *is* a lot older than you. And, from what I'm hearing, Roz isn't the first person to make that mistake.'

JP just sighs. He's there, 'The worst thing was that it had happened in La Bodega in Ranelagh the night before.'

I'm like, 'See?'

He's there, 'One of her customers came in and said, "I haven't seen this young man since the famous 21st in the tennis club."'

'He thought you were, em –'

'Bingley.'

'I'm still laughing at that name, by the way.'

'She's just very sensitive to it – you know, the age difference.'

'Dude, she's another one who could make more of an effort. The best thing you could do for her is to go through her wardrobe, find every turtle-neck and pair of Ecco sandals she owns and fock them in the bin. And I'm saying that as your mate.'

All of a sudden I hear a voice go, 'What the fock is *he* doing here?'

Except it's not Christian who says it. It's – yeah, no – Lychee.

I might easily ask her the same question, the focking gorgeous-looking dunderhead.

I'm there, 'I might easily ask you the same question, you focking gorgeous-looking dunderhead.'

The two of them are standing, like, ten feet away from me, both of them wearing – again – yellow hord hats, as well as fluorescent orange bibs. He's still got the goatee. I actually want to shake him.

'After what you did,' *she* goes, 'you have a nerve coming here.'

I'm like, 'I want to talk to Christian in private.'

But Christian – I swear to fock – goes, 'Anything you have to say to me, you can say it in front of Lychee,' which is totally against the code of bro's before ho's.

He's always been a sucker when it comes to women. He married Lauren, for fock's sake.

I'm there, 'Okay, I drove here all the way from Dublin to apologize.'

She laughs and shakes her head.

I'm like, 'What is she, a focking ventriloquist's dummy or something?'

Christian goes, 'What you did, Ross, was focking unforgivable.'

I'm there, 'Are we talking about the anal beads or are we talking about me paying off Ross Junior's sextortionist?'

'My son was in distress about something,' he goes. 'He should have come to me or Lauren.'

I'm there, 'He didn't feel comfortable going to you or Lauren. He was embarrassed. He knew I wouldn't judge him – as someone who's in no position to judge anyone.'

I can see from Christian's expression that he's beginning to, I don't know, weaken. He's not only a sucker for women, he's a sucker for me too. I rode his mother, I can't stress that enough, and he even agreed to put that behind us.

But that's when *she* pipes up again. She goes, 'Christian, just tell him.'

I'm like, 'Tell me what?'

She goes, 'He doesn't want anything to do with you any more.'

I'm there, 'I'd prefer to hear that from him.'

'Being friends with you could potentially damage his brand,' she goes.

I'm like, 'What focking brand? The fock are you on about?'

She's there, 'I'm talking about his social media identity.'

'Fock's sake, Christian,' I go, 'what are you *doing* with this focking airhead?'

JP tries to stop me from saying anything further that I might regret. He's like, 'Come on, Ross, there's no need for that.'

But that's when Christian goes, 'It's cool, JP. This is the last conversation that Ross and I are ever going to have.'

I'm there, 'Dude, you said that when I rode your mother.'

Lychee smiles and shakes her head – like I'm digging a grave for myself. He's obviously filled her in on one or two of my previous crimes.

'Fionn is right about you,' Christian goes, pointing an angry finger at me. 'And Sorcha as well.'

I'm there, 'What does Sorcha have to do with this?'

He goes, 'You're toxic, Ross. You bring misery into people's lives and you've nothing more to contribute than that. Focking goodbye – and focking good riddance.'

And the hordest thing for me to take is that he seems to mean every single word.

Frankie de Felice looks at me like I'm a dog who's just walked in with a used rubber-johnny in his mouth.

He's like, 'Your kind – you're the scum of the Earth, you know that?'

I'm there, 'Have we not been over this ground before?'

Yeah, no, I'm back in his office, supposably to discuss the State's case against me and the possibility of me pleading guilty to all chorges in return for a lighter – meaning non-custodial – sentence.

'That was before I saw the CCTV footage,' he goes. 'You with your arse in your hands.'

I'm there, 'Sorry, how much am I paying for this abuse again?'

The answer is a grand an hour, by the way. One thing he definitely knows how to do is chorge.

'And women and children looking on,' he goes. 'It's taking every ounce of self-restraint I have to stop myself from taking off my shoe and using it to hammer that chisel into your frontal lobe.'

I'm like, 'Dude, can we maybe move on?' because I'm storting to wonder is he trying to drag this so-called consultation into a second billable hour. 'I've been thinking about possibly admitting everything.'

He's there, 'Have you now?'

'As in, like, holding my hands up,' I go, 'and saying, yeah, no, I did it. As long as I don't end up having to do time.'

'That's very big of you.'

'I'd do Community Service. As long it's not, I don't know, cleaning up after other people. You give people an inch and they take – whatever the phrase is – the piss.'

'That sounds great.'

I'm there, 'Seriously?'

He picks up the phone. 'Yeah,' he goes, 'I'll get straight on to the Director of Public Prosecutions himself.'

I'm there, 'Are you being sorcastic?'

'You really need to ask?' he goes, replacing the receiver. 'Let me tell you something, you middle-class yob, they're not interested in doing any kind of deal with you. You don't have a leg to stand on. You're on video, you filthy animal. You haven't got zip to bargain with. And the jury, by the way, is going to hate you.'

'How can you be so sure?'

He goes, 'Because I've met you,' and then he laughs like it's the funniest thing anyone has ever said. 'Another rugby idiot who thinks he can do whatever he wants and walk away from his responsibilities. Well, let me tell something, you good-time Charlie, you're not going to be walking away from this one that easily.'

I look at the stopwatch on my phone. We've been sitting here for, like, fifty-eight minutes and thirty-two seconds.

'You degenerate,' he goes. 'You lowlife. You morally debased, sick animal.'

I'm there, 'Are you calling me these names to try to stretch the meeting into a second hour?'

'There's only one way you're getting out of this,' he goes. 'Only one way.'

I'm there, 'Go on – what is it?'

'Will I tell you?'

'Yeah, no, tell me.'

'Do you definitely want to know?'

'Yes.'

'Definitely, definitely, definitely?'

'For fock's sake.'

'Because I'll tell you – and I have no qualms about saying it.'

'Look, I know it's going to end up costing me another grand before you manage to get the words out.'

'The only way you're getting out of this,' he goes, 'is if I have one of the best days of my life in court.'

I'm there, 'Right,' and at the same time I stand up.

'Wait a second,' he goes, 'I've got something else to say.'

I'm there, 'What is it?'

He stares at his watch for a good, like, ten seconds, saying fock-all, then he goes, 'You know what? I forget. Well, it looks like our meeting has run over into a second billable hour.'

I'm there, 'Imagine that.'

He goes, 'Hey, *you* were the one who made an appointment to see *me*.'

I'm like, 'Presumably, though, I have you for the next, I don't know, fifty-nine minutes – seeing as I'm paying for it.'

'If I had to look at you for sixty seconds more,' he goes, 'I couldn't be responsible for what I'd do. It's two grand. Revolut me. Now get out of here before I throw you down the stairs on your head.'

I tip down the stairs, then walk through the bookies and out onto the street. I'm just about to send the money to the dude when I notice that I have a WhatsApp message from Ronan.

It's like, 'How'd it go?'

I decide to, like, ring him rather than message him back. He answers pretty much straight away.

He's there, 'Weddle?'

I'm like, 'Yeah, no, the DPP have decided they're not interested in doing a deal.'

He goes, 'Thee wanth to thrun the buke at you?'

I'm there, 'I've no idea what that even means. They want me to face the full, I don't know, rigour of the law.'

He's like, 'That's good, Rosser.'

I'm there, 'Is it?'

'Mee-uns you know what you're facing,' he goes. 'And The Chiseller knows what he has to do – am I reet?'

'Er, I suppose.'

'He's the fooken business, Rosser. Did you see all he's pitchers of the people he's arthur getting off oaber the yee-ors?'

'I did, yeah. I'm just waiting for him to sound like he's, I don't know, on *my* side?'

'He's a ball-buster, Rosser, but he'll get you off. Thrust me – I've evoddy fait in him.'

I'm there, 'And what if he doesn't get me off, Ro?'

He goes, 'You're not skeered, are you, Rosser?'

I want to tell him that, yes, I focking am scared. I want to tell him that I've had actual nightmares of being in prison ever since I went to visit Simone with Erika last week. And that was just the women's prison. I actually don't think that I could physically do the time. But I can't let Ronan know that because I know he'd give up everything and come home to work for Hennessy.

I'm there, 'Scared? It'd take a lot more than going to prison for a few years to frighten me. I played for Seapoint against Bruff, bear in mind.'

He laughs, even though it's a rugby rather than a soccer or GAA joke.

'Look, eeben if the woorst cuddems to the woorst,' he goes, 'you'll be looked arthur.'

I'm like, 'Will I, though?'

He's there, 'You bethor belieb it, Rosser. Gull has two brutters who are screws in the Joy and Buckets is a mate of wooden of the Kidihans.'

I'm like, 'That's great news. Yeah, no, that's made me feel a *whole* lot better.'

Erika walks into the kitchen wearing a pair of jodhpurs that leave nothing to the imagination. I can nearly tell you the year that the coins in her pocket were minted.

I'm there, 'Are you riding? *Going* riding, I mean.'

I can feel my face redden as Erika exchanges a look with Helen.

'It was a slip of the tongue,' I go. 'I didn't mean it in terms of, like, sex.'

Erika's there, 'If he's going to go on living here, we're going to have to get him focking gelded.'

Helen just laughs. She's always been a massive supporter of mine over the years.

'By the way,' Erika goes, 'what's going on with Honor?'

I'm there, 'In terms of?'

'Well, I asked her if she wanted to go to the horses with Amelie and me – but she said Sincerity was calling over.'

'Yeah, they're having, like, a *girls* day together?'

'But she hates Sincerity. She's always saying how she wishes she was dead.'

'Yeah, no, she's grown on her.'

'Grown on her?'

'That's the thing about Sincerity – she's a *grower*?'

Erika's like, 'This wouldn't have anything to do with Ròz, would it?'

Helen's there, 'Who's Roz?'

'Roz Carew is Sincerity's mother,' Erika goes. 'She's also Ross's new girlfriend.'

I'm like, 'Jealous, are you? I bet you wish it was you, don't you?' and then I'm like, 'Again, sorry – I don't know what the fock is wrong with me this morning.'

It's the jodhpurs. It's definitely the jodhpurs. And the knee-high leather boots.

I'm there, 'Anyway, in answer to your question, yes, Roz asked me if Honor wouldn't mind maybe taking Sincerity under her wing for the summer. She's worried that the girl is possibly *too* much of a goody-goody?'

Erika laughs. 'Honor will certainly knock that out of her,' she goes. 'It'll make her summer.'

Helen puts a cup of coffee down in front of me. Like I said, she's a big, big fan.

'So have you seen the new notes?' she goes.

I'm like, 'The ones that are replacing the yoyos? Yeah, no, the old man gave me some samples. Seán FitzPatrick is on, like, the twenty and Chorlie Haughey is on, like, the fifty.'

'Have you see who's on the hundred?' she goes.

I'm like, 'No, who?'

She opens her purse and whips out a note, then smoothes it out on the surface of the island.

It's, like, holy fock.

I'm there, 'He put his own face on the hundred-pound note? What a wanker,' and then I go, 'Sorry, Helen,' because I forget sometimes that she was once married to the dick.

She goes, 'He told the *Irish Times* that it was a complete surprise to him. He said he asked for Michael Collins but Hennessy swapped it out for Charles's face as a surprise.'

Erika goes, 'You know he *actually* texted me last night? To invite me to this focking porty to mork the moment when Ireland officially leaves the EU.'

Yeah, no, I got the same text. I'll probably go if there's free drink at it.

Erika's there, 'I mean, the focking cheek of him.'

Helen goes, 'He's still your dad, Erika.'

'He's *not* my focking dad,' she goes. 'And I'm not giving up until I destroy him once and for all.'

I just nod and agree with her – you'd have to with the mood she's in.

All of a sudden, the doorbell rings.

I'm there, 'I'll get that. It'll probably be Sincerity.'

Out to the front door I trot and – yeah, no – it ends up *being* her alright? She's standing on the doorstep with – I shit you not – her schoolbag on her back. Roz waves at me from the driver's seat of her black BMW X5 and tells me that she'll ring me later.

Sincerity goes, 'Hello, Mr O'Carroll-Kelly.'

I laugh. She's so focking polite.

I'm there, 'Yeah, no, call me Ross. You're making me feel like a teacher here.'

She goes, 'Honor texted me!' like all her Christmases have come at once. 'She invited me over for a playdate!'

I'm there, 'Jesus Christ, Sincerity, have you brought, like, your schoolbooks with you?'

'Yes,' she goes, 'I made a list this morning of all the things we could do today. One of them was make a headstort on our Junior Cert novel. It's *To Kill a Mockingbird* by Horper Lee.'

I'm there, 'Know your audience is the probably best advice I could give anyone when it comes to Honor. I wouldn't mention books at all.'

That's when I hear her coming down the stairs behind me.

I'm there, 'Anyway, come in, Sincerity.'

But Honor goes, 'Don't bother – we're going out. Dad, we need a lift.'

Honor is wearing cut-off shorts, a pink t-shirt and white Havaianas. She also has, like, Chloé sunnies on her head and her Gucci beach bag slung over her shoulder.

I'm like, 'Where are you going? And, before you stort abusing me, Honor, the only reason I'm asking is because I have to know if I'm going to, like, *drive* you there?'

She's there, 'We're going to the Forty Foot.'

So out we step onto Ailesbury Road and we head for the cor.

'So, the thing is,' Sincerity goes, running to try to match the length of Honor's stride, 'I can't actually *swim?*'

Honor's there, 'We're not going to swim, you focking sap.'

'So why are we going?' Sincerity goes.

Honor's there, 'Why the fock do you think? To hang out with boys.'

I pretend to be totally cool with it as I get into the driver's seat. Honor and Sincerity hop into the back, then I stort the cor and point it in the direction of Sandycove.

Sincerity is quiet for a good five minutes and I can tell from her expression in the rear-view mirror that she's not happy with the turn this day has taken.

'So, like, who are these boys?' she eventually goes. 'Do you know their parents?'

Jesus Christ, I'm thinking, Honor has her work cut out here.

'They're just boys I know,' she goes. 'Blackrock boys. Clongowes boys. Gonzaga boys.'

This doesn't seem to put Sincerity's mind at ease.

'It's just that I made myself a promise,' she goes, 'that I wouldn't have anything to do with boys until I have my degree – and maybe even my Master's?'

Even I burst out laughing at that line.

Honor's there, 'Yeah, you don't have to focking marry them. We're just going to hang out with them.'

'Hang out with them?' Sincerity goes. 'Okay.'

Honor's there, 'Look, just try to be cool – not the focking dweeb you are in school.'

There's, like, silence then until we hit Blackrock.

'Will there be a chance for us to read today?' Sincerity goes.

Honestly, it's like she's trying to focking provoke her.

Honor's there, 'Read?' and she's fully within her rights.

I watch Sincerity produce a book from her bag. She's there, 'It's *To Kill a Mockingbird*. We're going to be doing it for the Junior Cert. I'm actually *re*reading it at the moment?'

Honor goes, 'Oh, that's very interesting,' and she takes the book from her. She doesn't even look at the thing, just opens the window and focks it out. It ends up hitting the windscreen of a silver Toyota Avensis behind us and the driver ends up giving me an angry beep of his horn.

'Oh my God!' Sincerity goes. 'Oh! My *actual*! God!'

I've a feeling she's going to be saying that a lot this summer.

Honor's like, 'Whoa, whoa, whoa – is that your focking schoolbag?'

'Yeah,' Sincerity goes, 'Mrs Claffey said not to let our books become strangers to us just because it's the summer holidays.'

I swear to fock, Honor yanks the bag out of Sincerity's hands and she focks that out of the window. The Toyota Avensis ends up having to swerve to avoid it and very nearly drives head-first into a white van driving in the opposite direction.

'That was my schoolbag!' Sincerity goes. 'Mr O'Carroll-Kelly, can we turn back – just to get my schoolbag?'

Honor's there, 'We're not turning back. And you mention that schoolbag again and you'll be the next thing going out the focking window.'

There's, like, silence again – understandably enough – until we hit Dún Laoghaire. Then Honor suddenly goes, 'Oh my God, you are, like, *so* white!'

It's probably focking shock, I nearly feel like saying.

Sincerity goes, 'What factor sun cream are we wearing?'

Honor's there, 'We're not.'

'Honor, the sun can be, like, *so* damaging to your skin.'

'Whatever,' Honor goes, then she storts rooting around in her – like I said – *beach* bag? 'Okay, I've got a bikini for you here somewhere.'

Sincerity goes, 'Er, I don't *want* to wear a bikini?'

Honor's there, 'Why are you making me fight with you? You are *not* sitting on the beach in, like, jeans and a jumper. Everyone will be laughing at you.'

Honor drops the bikini on Sincerity's lap, then Sincerity picks it up and storts, I don't know, *inspecting* it?

'Is this . . . all of it?' she goes.

Honor's like, 'Yes, that's all of it. You can change into it when we get there.'

Five minutes later, I'm pulling up right next to the beach. Honor and Sincerity get out and straight away I hear some random dude call my daughter's name.

He's like, 'Honor! Honor O'Carroll-Kelly!' and I notice this goy – he's got some focking six-pack on him – waving from the sort of, like, *diving* platform? Yeah, no, he's with a load of other dudes as well.

Honor waves back at him and through the window I go, 'Is that Joel or MacDara?'

She's there, 'It's MacDara,' just as he shouts, 'Fock you, St Michael's!' and then he jumps into the sea – we're talking cannonball-stylee.

I'm there, 'He seems great, Honor.'

She's like, 'Whatever – I'll ring you when we're ready to come home.'

I'm there, 'Yeah, just go easy on Sincerity, will you? I'm still figuring out how to make my move on her mother.'

Fock. I suddenly notice that Sincerity is standing, like, two feet away and heard everything. She looks at me in, like, shock.

I'm there, 'I'll, er, take the same route home, Sincerity, and see can I find that schoolbag of yours.'

Roz says she's got Malaysian bulgogi and it'll tell you where my mind is at that my first thought is, will that stop us from having sex tonight? After, like, a month of dating, we still haven't sealed the deal – a record for me by at least three weeks.

She must see the disappointment on my face because she goes, 'You're not vegetarian, are you?'

And I'm there, 'Oh – you're talking about dinner!'

'Supper,' she goes.

Supper. God, I love Protestants.

I'm there, 'Yeah, no, I eat pretty much everything,' as she leads me down the hallway to the kitchen. 'It smells great, in fairness to it.'

So does *she*, by the way? I'm pretty sure it's Tom Ford *Portofino*.

'I did an Asian cooking course,' she goes, 'the year I got divorced.'

I'm there, 'Fair focks would be my reaction.'

She's wearing, like, a black wool dress and knee-high boots and it's doing it for me in a big-time way.

I'm there, 'Is, em, Sincerity home?'

She goes, 'No, she's at her dad's tonight. Okay, why are you smiling?'

And I'm like, 'No reason,' even though she knows very well why I'm smiling. 'Sorry again about her schoolbag.'

She's there, 'I'm glad it's gone,' as she hands me a glass of Pinot Grigio. 'I thought she was going to be carrying it around all summer. She told me she didn't want her schoolbooks to become strangers to her just because she was on her holidays.'

'Yeah, no, she said that to Honor. I think that's what provoked her.'

'She had a great day.'

'Did she?'

'She was all talk about this boy and that boy. And Honor, of course. She absolutely adores her.'

'Yeah, no, that's good to hear.'

'I want Sincerity to be a normal teenager like her.'

'Jesus, there's nothing normal about Honor, Roz.'

'It's just that Sincerity can be so serious. I want her teenage years to be fun.'

'Well, Honor loves fun – especially if it's at someone else's expense.'

I take a sip of my wine while she lights a candle in the middle of the table, then switches off the lights.

I go, '*Very* romantic,' and I can feel that big sleazy smile on my face again.

'So tomorrow's the big day,' she goes.

I'm there, 'In terms of?'

'Ireland's last day in the EU,' she goes.

I'm like, 'Oh, that. It hopefully won't affect me. My old man is having a bit of a porty in the Áras tomorrow night – sort of, like, a countdown to midnight thing, if you're interested?'

'I might pass on that.'

'There's going to be free drink at it.'

'To be honest, Ross, I voted to Remain. I think leaving Europe is going to be an absolute disaster for the country and definitely not something to celebrate.'

'I didn't vote at all. I just found the whole thing a bit boring.'

'Anyway,' she goes, stirring the pot, 'I don't think Sorcha would be pleased to see me there.'

I'm there, 'Hey, I'm a free agent, Roz.'

She's like, 'I know, but it was so awkward seeing her at the borbecue that day.'

She spoons the, whatever, Malaysian bulgogi onto two plates.

I'm there, 'I thought you handled it well, in fairness to you.'

'It was just such a cringe moment,' she goes, carrying the plates over to the table. I sit down. 'I've known Sorcha for years as one of the other school moms. One minute we're drawing up a new constitution for the Parents Association in the Merrion Tree Bistro – and the next I'm sleeping with her husband.'

I'm there, 'Are you?' as she puts my plate down in front of me. 'Sleeping with me, I mean?'

She smiles.

'You know what I mean,' she goes. 'As far as *she* knows, we're at it like –'

I grab her hand and I hold it while staring deep into her eyes – an old seduction trick of mine. Her expression turns suddenly serious. She leans down and she kisses me very focking passionately. I stort kissing her back – be weird not to – and after, like, sixty seconds of this, she hoicks up her wool dress and sort of, like, straddles me in the chair, with her hair hanging down over my face.

I've suddenly got a hammer in my chinos that could tenderize a thirty-ounce New York strip.

She storts sort of, like, rubbing herself up and down my lap while I have a good, old-fashioned feel of her flabbergasters, the dinner slash supper totally forgotten.

She goes, 'That's nice. Oh my God, that's so nice.'

They're absolutely fantastic, since we're giving out compliments, and I can feel her nipples horden under my thumbs even through her bra and the wool of her dress.

She's there, 'You're not going to be able to focking walk tomorrow,' and I remember how much she likes to talk dirty – often in the way of threats – while she's riding the old Bologna pony. 'I don't know what you're focking smiling about. You're going to be leaving here in a focking ambulance.'

I'm suddenly horder than a tank trap. She stands up and she tears open my chinos like it's a bag of Kettle chips. She yanks them down along with my boxer shorts, pulls her Diana Vickers to one side and moves our respective pieces into place.

And there, like a film director, I'm going to shout, 'Cut!' because I don't think it would serve any purpose to go into the ins and outs of what happened except to give everyone a cheap sexual thrill.

All I will say, for the purpose of filling out the story, is that she ends up bouncing up and down on me like Tayto riding Tír na nÓg into the focking West and the whole grubby affair comes to a quick and shuddering end with me squinting my eyes and with my bottom teeth sticking out like I've an underbite and with her shouting, 'Jesus focking Christ, don't come! Don't you focking come already!'

When it's all over, she – yeah, no – *alights*, as they say in the airline business, and she fixes up her clothes while I catch my breath and pull up my chinos, noticing as I do that I've lost a button or two in the exchanges.

'That was, em, quick,' she goes as she sits down opposite me and I'm trying to figure out from her voice if she's pleased or disappointed by that.

I pick up my fork and I try a mouthful of her Malaysian bulgogi.

'This is gorgeous,' I go. '*And* it's still hot.'

And she's like, 'I can't say that I'm surprised.'

The old man is in his total element. And why wouldn't he be? He loves being the centre of attention. He's buzzing around the room, wishing people a – yeah, no – Happy Independence Day and people are saying Happy Independence Day back to him and they're saying Happy Independence Day to each other.

I check the time. It's, like, half eleven. There's a crowd of maybe ten thousand people gathered outside in the grounds of the Áras, waiting for the old man to appear for the first time on the new balcony to lead the countdown to midnight.

Sorcha looks amazing in this, like, sporkly green dress. She catches me staring at her and she tips over to me.

She's there, 'So . . . Roz Matthews.'

I'm like, 'What about her?' and I can hear the sudden, I don't know, *defensiveness* in my voice? The thing is, she hasn't been returning my texts all day and I'm wondering is she pissed off about something.

'I'm just saying, I think you've done well,' she goes. 'She looks like Mornie from *Girls* but with a smaller mouth.'

I'm there, 'And not as annoying-looking. She's gone back to using her maiden name, by the way.'

'She was Roz Carew when I first knew her,' Sorcha goes. 'We debated with Alex – oh my God – loads of times. Does she still have amazing Spanish?'

I'm there, 'I don't know. It, em, hasn't come up.'

'Did she mention that she and I drew up the new constitution for the Mount Anville Parents Association in the Merrion Tree Bistro?'

'Weirdly, yes, she did.'

'I always thought it was a bit random,' she goes, 'that she kept her married name for, like, years after she got divorced.'

I'm wondering is she saying it just to be a bitch?

I'm there, 'It was for their daughter's sake. She thought it would be confusing if she was called one thing and Sincerity was called something else.'

She goes, 'Oh my God, Ross, I'm just making conversation.'

'Fine – whatever.'

'You don't feel threatened by her still being really, really close to Sincerity's dad, do you?'

I'm like, 'No, the divorce was – I want to say – *amicable*? They just realized that they were too young when they got married.'

And that's when she goes, 'I actually saw them together today. I'm not being a bitch, Ross, but they still look like a married couple.'

I'm there, 'What? Where? When?' and I hate myself for sounding so desperate. 'When did you see them? Where?'

'They were having lunch in Cinnamon in Monkstown,' she goes. '*He* was having a club sandwich and *she* was having the falafel and hummus wrap with a side of wilted spinach. Oh my God, she's *so* teeny-tiny. What does she weigh, Ross?'

I'm there, 'I don't focking know what she weighs!' and I end up roaring it at her. 'Jesus Christ, you're as bad as the others.'

'Oh my God, you're not, like, jealous, are you? How funny that you're finally getting a taste of your own medicine! Anyway, I just came over to ask you for a favour.'

'What favour?'

'Are you planning to go out onto the balcony for the countdown?'

'I suppose. My old man is the Taoiseach. He wants me there.'

'Well,' she goes, 'would you mind standing at the opposite end of the balcony to me?'

I'm like, 'Excuse me?'

'Ross, I don't want people to look at us the way they look at Roz and Ray and think – oh my God – they're still secretly together. As my dad said, any association with you coming up to your trial could be construed as, like, a show of support. I'm not only Ireland's first ever Minister for Climate Action, Ross, I'm also a woman – and the optics wouldn't be good. I'd even prefer it if you stood at the back.'

Then off she focking focks.

I'm, like, staring at her old man across the ballroom – him and Sorcha's old dear in a way-too-short dress – chatting away to the famous Boris Johnson and Carrie.

I spot the triplets and I tip over to them. They're all dressed in, like, identical grey suits and their hair is combed to the side. They look like basically choirboys. I hand them each a cocktail stick.

I'm like, 'Here you go?' and they look at me like they've never seen one before.

'What's this for?' Johnny goes.

I'm there, 'Go and stab Sorcha's old man in the orse with it.'

Brian's like, 'Why?'

'Because it'd be focking hilarious.'

'But it would hurt him,' Leo goes. 'He's our granddad.'

I'm there, 'What about Sorcha's old dear, then?'

She should *not* be showing off her knees at her age, by the way. The last time I saw legs like that I was being shoed by Denis Leamy after finding myself on the wrong side of a Rockwell College ruck.

Brian goes, 'But she's our grandma,' like it should be somehow obvious to me.

I'm there, 'You've changed your tune. You used to hate them – all of you.'

Johnny goes, 'We're good boys now, Dad.'

I'm like, 'Okay, get the fock out of my sight. You're making me sick to my stomach.'

I whip out my phone and I send Roz a message. I type the words, 'What the fock?' but then I delete them and instead I write, 'Hey, is everything okay? You're very quiet today,' and then I send that. Five seconds later I see that it's been delivered and I wait for the message to tell me that she's typing, except it doesn't appear.

'Howiya, R . . . R . . . R . . . R . . . R . . . Rosser,' a voice suddenly goes.

It's Ronan's father-in-law, Kennet, the stuttering fock. He's walking around, giving out little plastic Ireland flags.

He's like, 'Here you go, Rosser, there's w . . . w . . . w . . . w . . . w . . . w . . . wooden for you. It's a great day for the c . . . c . . . c . . . c . . . cunthroddy, idn't it?'

I'm there, 'The what?'

'The c . . . c . . . cunthroddy,' he goes.

I'm like, 'I've no idea what you're trying to say. I might as well be listening to a focking crow as you.'

I notice that he's given Johnny, Brian and Leo little flags too.

He goes, 'You m . . . m . . . m . . . m . . . moost be getting neerbous, are you, R . . . R . . . Rosser?'

I'm like, 'Nervous? Why?'

'Anutter few weeks,' he goes, 'you're probley headon to j . . . j . . . j . . . j . . . j . . . jayult.'

I'm there, 'You might be surprised. I've got The Chiseller in my corner.'

'The Ch . . . Ch . . . Ch . . . Chiseller hasn't wood a case for b . . . b . . . b . . . b . . . bleaten yee-ors. You're godda get seddent dowun, Rosser – udless you do the s . . . s . . . s . . . smeert thing.'

'I'm not asking Ronan to come home.'

'Do you know what th . . . th . . . th . . . thee do to good-looking f . . . f . . . f . . . f . . . f . . . feddas like you in prison. Thee'll fooken r . . . r . . . r . . . r . . . r . . . r . . .'

'Yeah, don't finish that sentence.'

'R . . . r . . . r . . . r . . . r . . . r . . . r . . . r . . .'

'For fock's sake.'

'R . . . r . . . r . . . r . . . r . . . r . . . r . . . r . . .'

'Yeah, I can *guess* where this is going, Kennet?'

'R . . . r . . . r . . . r . . . r . . . r . . . r . . . royid the eerse off you.'

'Yeah, thanks for that – very focking helpful.'

'I've d . . . d . . . d . . . *dudden* toyum, Rosser. Ine oately warden you.'

'Whatever.'

'Of cowurse – as Heddessy says to you – it could all be m . . . m . . . m . . . med go away if you joost t . . . t . . . t . . . t . . . t . . . t . . . teddle Ro to cuddem howum to he's woyuf and thaughter – wheer he b . . . b . . . b . . . b . . . beloggens?'

I'm like, 'Yeah, fock off, Kennet – and shove your *Arelunt* flags up your focking *eerse*.'

All of a sudden, I spot Christian and Lychee over at the prosecco bor. I tip over there – again, the optimist winning the day. Christian is filming Lychee going, 'Happy Independence Day!' and performing a toast to the camera, except – as usual – she's not happy with the results.

She goes, 'For fock's sake, Chrissy – are you, like, *deliberately* trying to make me look fat? This is for focking TikTok.'

The poor focker.

I'm there, 'So have you calmed down yet?' trying to break the ice in, like, a light-horted way.

He turns his head and looks at me and I feel this overwhelming urge to pin him to the ground and shave off that focking ridiculous goatee that he has going on.

'Ross, I focking told you,' he goes, his voice rising in volume, 'we're not focking friends any more – so stay the fock away from us, okay?'

Off the two of them go, making me feel about as welcome as puke in a punchbowl.

'*Ira furor brevis est*, eh?' a voice beside me goes.

It turns out it's, like, Boris Johnson again.

I'm there, 'Sorry, what?'

'Anger is but a brief madness,' he goes. 'Your father said you were something of a Latin purist.'

I'm there, 'Yeah, you don't want to listen to him. He's full of shit.'

He goes, 'You seem to, um, rub a lot of people up the wrong way, don't you? Someone told me that you bought some sort of sex toy for that chap's wife for her birthday.'

I'm like, 'You don't want to believe everything you hear.'

'Well, that's quite true,' he goes.

I'm there, 'Firstly, she's his *ex*-wife? Secondly, I'd never even heard of anal beads before. And thirdly, someone else brought them and I just happened to steal them because I arrived without a present.'

The dude's face lights up like the kid on the *Late Late Toy Show* when – whatever he's called – Robbie focking Keane walked on. All his Christmases.

'Anyway,' I go, 'that's not even why he's pissed off with me. He's pissed off with me because I paid twenty grandingtons to some crowd of scammers who were sextorting his son for looking at gay porn online. And I did that to try to be a good godfather.'

Again, he just stares at me with his mouth wide open.

'Well,' he eventually goes, '*I* upset the other chap –'

I'm there, 'Which other chap?'

'Oh, the chap who invented the vertical bed.'

'Ah, you're talking about JP.'

'I mean, what a wonderful invention! What a fantastic example of British ingenuity!'

'Er, he's actually *Irish*?'

'Well, you know what I mean. Anyway, I just happened to turn to the lady standing beside him and I said, "You must be very proud of your son."'

I laugh. I'm there, 'That's his wife.'

He goes, 'Yes, I know that now! Well, she walked off in tears and he followed her.'

'It's an easy mistake to make,' I go. 'The girl I'm seeing at the moment said something similar. Although – to be honest – I don't know if I *am* still seeing her?'

He's like, 'What, trouble in paradise?'

I'm there, 'It's possible that she may have gone back to her ex-husband because I disappointed her in a sexual sense,' and I don't know why I'm suddenly telling him this shit. I just find it very easy to open up to him.

He's like, '*Amor et melle et felle est fecundissimus!* Your father said you know your Plautus.'

'Yeah, no, she invited me over,' I go, 'and she had Malaysian bulgogi.'

'Good Lord! Where did she catch that?'

'No, it's, like, a *dish*?'

'Oh, I see.'

'Anyway, she put it on the table, then we somehow managed to find ourselves having sex and I decided, not wanting the food to go cold – thinking of *her* feelings, because she did an Asian cooking course – to make it a really *quick* one?'

Suddenly, he puts a giant, meaty paw on my shoulder and goes, 'You know, if we'd known each other at Eton, I think you and I could have been dear, dear friends.'

Then the old man – again, making it about him – goes, 'Okay, it's almost midnight, everybody! The time has come – as it will for you, Boris, when you finally get rid of that wretched May woman! Let's go and talk to the real people of Ireland!'

And, with his orm around Boris Johnson's shoulder, he leads everyone outside onto the balcony. The crowd cheers and the old man ends up making a bit of a speech.

He's like, 'Ladies and gentlemen, we are about to make history! In a few moments' time, Ireland will celebrate its independence for the second time in a century!'

Sorcha's old man suddenly steps in front of me, blocking my view of the crowd. I'm like, 'What the fock are you doing?'

'Ninety-seven years ago,' the old man goes, 'it was freedom from Britain – no matter how ill-advised some of us believe that to have been in retrospect! This time, we celebrate our freedom from a real oppressor, a rules-loving, energy-sucking bureaucracy that forced you – the good people of Ireland – to carry the cost of bailing out the banks for their own greed and then did something that the British never did in all their years trying to improve us as a people! They burned our national porliament to the ground!'

I take a step to my right to try to see what's happening, but Sorcha's old man does the same thing.

I'm there, 'Are you trying to stop me from being in any of the footage?'

The old man goes, 'In less than one minute's time, we will be free – as our friends across the water will soon be free too! I want to thank you all for the courage to dream of a different kind of future for Ireland! And so – without further ado or a-don't! – I'm going to stort the countdown to what will henceforth become a public holiday in our country's calendar! Independence Day!'

I take a step to my left and Sorcha's old man does the same. I try to give him a nudge, but he stands firm.'

'Ten!' the old man goes. 'Nine! Eight! Seven! Six! Five! Four! Three! Two!'

And that's when I just happen to look to my right and I catch sight of my old dear, slowly undoing the buttons on her blouse.

Oisinn reminds me a lot of Boris Johnson in that I feel like I can talk to him about literally anything, including my old dear taking out her focking pinch pots in public.

'I was watching on TV,' he goes, 'and I didn't see anything.'

I'm like, 'Yeah, no, very few people did. Luckily, Sorcha's old dear saw what was happening and wrestled her to the ground before anyone in the crowd copped it.'

'So she's getting worse?' he goes.

I'm there, 'Some days she's fine. She needs, like, round-the-clock care, though. Astrid said she got one of the kids shit-faced. She thought she was out on the lash with Bláthnaid Ní Chofiagh.'

'Fock,' he goes.

I'm like, 'Fock is right.'

He's there, 'But I definitely didn't see any, well, you know –'

'Knocker,' I go.

He's like, 'Knocker, yeah. I suppose it would have been all over the internet, wouldn't it?'

I'm there, 'Yeah, no, when you think about some of the sick shit that *is* on there. People would look at anything when they're, well, you know –'

'Making stomach pancakes,' he goes.

I laugh. I'm there, 'Making stomach pancakes is a very good way to put it. God, I haven't heard that phrase in years. Playing air guitor naked was another one.'

He goes, 'God, I miss rugby – the dressing room, I mean.'

I'm there, 'Yeah, no, so do I. How did we get onto this subject again?'

'We were talking about your old dear's honey hams,' he goes.

Again, I laugh. I'm there, 'Honey hams. I love that one. Actually, let's stop, though, will we?'

He's like, 'Fair enough.'

This is us walking the beach in Brittas Bay, by the way. Oisinn wants to break in his new hiking boots before they head for, I don't know, whatever country the Camino happens to be in, and he asked me if I fancied joining him.

I'm there, 'So how are you feeling about it, by the way – as in, like, the walk?'

'A bit nervous,' he goes. 'I mean, out of all of us, I'm probably the least fit.'

I'm like, 'You're definitely the strongest, though – especially when you think about Fionn, the little focking weed with glasses.'

He goes, 'I wish you'd sort that out.'

'Who?'

'You and Fionn. You and Christian. It's focking ridiculous at this stage.'

'Hey, *they're* the ones who have the issue with *me*, remember? Saying I'm toxic.'

There's, like, silence between us then. It's, like, five o'clock in the evening and the beach is storting to empty for the day.

I'm there, 'I wish I was going with you, though. What country is it in again?'

He's like, 'It's in Spain – and a little bit in France.'

I'm there, 'Are Spain and France near each other? They don't sound like they are.'

'They're right next door to each other,' he goes.

I'm like, 'I did *not* know that. I must, like, improve my mind. I know I'm always saying that, but one day I'm going to actually mean it.'

We turn around and stort walking back to the gaff.

He goes, 'The other thing I'm nervous about is –'

I'm like, 'What?'

'What do you think?' he goes. 'This baby arriving.'

I'm there, 'I wouldn't sweat it, Dude. There's a very good chance that Sorcha's sister won't hand it over when the time comes. Like Sorcha said, she could decide to fock off back to Australia.'

'She's not going to do that. We have rights. One of us is the father.'

'Define *one of us*?'

'Well, me or Magnus, of course.'

'Of course.'

'I just worry, Ross, whether I'm cut out to be a parent.'

'Dude, I ask myself the same question constantly.'

'And?'

'Well, the answer I always come up with – believe it or not – is yes.'

'You don't ever worry that you're going to, I don't know, fock your kids up?'

'In my experience, there's very little you can do to affect how your kids turn out. It's a lottery, Dude.'

'Do you really think that?'

'You keep them alive, Oisinn. That's the job. And if you have a little bit of love to give them, well, that's good gravy. Or, as we say on our side of the city, *jus*.'

We're just arriving back at the gaff when Oisinn turns around to me and goes, 'Dude, can you do me a favour?'

I'm like, 'You name it – anything,' although obviously I don't mean that literally.

He goes, 'Can you keep an eye on our place in Dublin?'

He means their penthouse aportment in The Grange in Stillorgan.

I'm there, 'Yeah, no, not a problem.'

'It's just that our patients are due to stort arriving in the next few days,' he goes, 'and we're not going to be in a position to keep driving up and down.'

I'm like, 'Leave it to me, Dude,' taking the key from him. 'What's the alorm code?'

He's there, 'You need to ask?'

I'm like, '1, 9, 9, 9 – of course it is.'

We arrive back at Drayton Manor and Oisinn sits down on the doorstep to take off his hiking boots. And from inside the gaff – from the drawing room where I tried to get off with Andrea Roche the night Ireland lost the Six Nations decider to England in 2003 and she laughed in my face – we hear a woman pretty much groaning, going, 'Oh my God, that's nice . . . Oh my God, that's *so*, so nice . . .'

Me and Oisinn exchange looks.

I'm like, 'Who's here?'

And he goes, 'It was only Magnus when we left,' and we both head for the room at speed, half expecting to find the dude conkers-deep in some – like I said – woman.

It ends up not being that at all. Sorcha's sister is stretched out on the chaise longue from which Andrea Roche dismissed me with a simple but devastating, 'In your focking dreams!' and Magnus is – I shit you not – massaging her bare feet.

She sees us standing there.

'Oh my God,' she goes, 'this man has *the* most unbelievable hands!'

Oisinn's there, 'We, em, weren't expecting you.'

I notice her bags in the corner. I'm pretty sure Oisinn does as well.

'Yeah,' Magnus goes, 'she wash wondering if she could shtay here with ush – jusht until the baby arrivesh.'

Oisinn's like, 'Errr . . .' totally thrown by this development.

Sorcha's sister goes, 'It's just, I can't live with my parents any more. I just think the constant negative vibes will be bad for the baby's development.'

So Oisinn, of course, has no choice but to go, 'Oh, em, yeah, I suppose you could sleep in the nursery. I'll put one of the spare beds in there and push the cot up against the wall.'

She looks at *me* then and smiles. She's pure focking trouble, this girl.

She goes, 'How nice is this, Ross! Three daddies pampering their baby momma! Sorry, did I say three? I meant two.'

4.

Thunderballs

I ask the borman for two pints of the good stuff, but JP says he's not drinking and he'll just have a Ballygowan.

I'm there, 'Do *not* give him a Ballygowan. He'll have a pint of Heineken like normal people.'

Yeah, no, this is us in The Bridge 1859, doing our usual Friday night thing, except without Christian and Fionn, who hate me right now, and Oisinn and Magnus, who are down in Brittas Bay.

'Ross,' he tries to go, 'I want to be fit for the Camino. I haven't had a drink in, like, a month.'

I'm there, 'So, what, you're going to stand there all night watching me get shit-faced?'

'Yeah, no, that's the other thing,' he goes. 'I can only stay an hour.'

'An hour?'

'Delma has a restaurant booked. It's Belle's birthday.'

'This night is turning out to be a real cracker. How is she, by the way? I'm talking about Delma.'

'Did you hear what Boris Johnson said to her?'

'Dude, you can't blame Boris Johnson. The woman is, like, thirty years older than you.'

'Look, I don't care if people think she's my grandmother. But it's starting to really get her down – the age difference.'

'Has she ever considered –'

'What?'

'Well, having a bit of work done?'

'You mean plastic surgery?'

'Just a nip here and tuck there. She has horrendous crow's feet and I'm not saying that to be a dick.'

'They're laughter lines.'

'And her mouth is a bit – I'm just going to come out and say the word – *saggy*?'

'I love her mouth – *and* her eyes. I don't want her changing anything.'

'Fair enough, Dude. I still say she could make more of herself.'

All of a sudden, I notice a girl staring at me from the other side of the bor. If I had to say she looks like anyone, it would be Emmanuelle Chriqui. And she clearly has the hots for me because she smiles when I close one eye and pretend to shoot her with one of my finger guns.

'What are you doing?' JP goes. 'I thought you were all loved up these days?'

I'm there, 'Who, Roz? Yeah, no, I haven't heard from *her* in over a week. I think she's gone off me, if you can believe that.'

I pick up my pint and I'm like, 'See you later, Dude.'

He's there, 'What?'

'Dude,' I go, 'you're focking boring when you're not drinking. I'm going to go and talk to this gorgeous girl over here.'

She smiles as she watches me walk over to her.

'Did you really just pretend to shoot me?' she goes.

I'm there, 'Yeah, no, it's just a thing I do – break the ice. The name's Ross, by the way.'

She goes, 'Oh, I'm, em, Jane. Er, Jane *Murphy*?'

I'm there, 'Are you sure? You sounded like you had to think about it there.'

She cracks her hole laughing. I really am amazing at the whole chatting-up thing.

She goes, 'So are you, like, a rugby player?' at the same time checking out my shoulders and chest.

I'm there, 'Do I look like a rugby player to you?'

'You do actually.'

'The reason for that, Jane, is that I am – or used to be. Have you heard of Brian O'Driscoll?'

'Of course I've heard of Brian O'Driscoll!'

'Well, people used to say that I was better than him.'

'Wow!'

'Wow is right. Can I get you a drink?'

Jane's like, 'Er, no, thanks.'

I'm there, 'You're not here *with* someone, are you?'

She goes, 'Just my brother and his friends,' and she nods her head at a crew of dudes drinking pints in the corner. 'But I'm having a bit of a shit night. Okay, this is going to sound so forward – and I don't want you to think I'm a slut –'

I'm there, 'I'll be the judge of that, Jane. Keep going.'

She goes, 'Could we go back to your place?'

I'm like 'My place?' thinking, Shit, I don't have a focking place. I obviously can't bring her back to Erika and Helen's gaff – they'd have a shit-fit. But then I suddenly remember that I have the keys to Oisinn and Magnus's gaff in my pocket. 'Yeah, let's take this porty back to mine.'

She goes, 'Where is it? I probably should let my brother know where I'm going.'

I'm there, 'Yeah, no, it's called The Grange. They're, like, aport-ments on the Stillorgan dualler. The focking Spirit of Gracious Living, if you remember the famous sign.'

She focks off to tell her brother while I go outside to hail a taxi. Twenty minutes later, we're sitting in the back of the thing, wearing the face off each other like a couple of teenagers.

She goes, 'I want you to know that I don't usually do this kind of thing.'

And I'm there, 'Yeah, no, me neither,' which I suspect she *knows* is horseshit?

Twenty minutes later, I'm letting us into Oisinn and Magnus's aportment and Jane is going, 'Oh my God, you have a beautiful place! It's stunning!'

I'm like, 'Yeah, no, thanks,' because it's one of the penthouses.

She goes, 'That's, em, an unusual piece of art,' and I notice that she's looking at the giant photograph on the wall of two men kissing.

I'm there, 'Yeah, I don't know why I hung that there. I just thought it was a good picture.'

She's like, 'You're not –'

And I'm there, 'God, no – ask around if you're worried.'

She goes, 'Do you have anything to drink?'

I point her to the little tiki bor that I bought Oisinn and Magnus as a wedding present.

She's like, 'I am going to make you *the* most amazing cocktail. It's a speciality of mine.'

I'm there, 'What's in it?'

'I'm going to surprise you,' she goes. 'Sorry, what's with the penis theme here?'

I'm like, 'Excuse me?'

'The cocktail shaker is in the shape of a penis,' she goes. 'There's shot glasses shaped like penises. There's even penis straws.'

I'm like, 'Yeah, no, they were a jokey gift from a friend of mine, who happens to be gay. And so is his husband.'

'Oh,' she goes, bringing my cocktail over to me on the sofa. I take a sip from it and it's absolutely incredible.

I'm there, 'What do you call it?'

She goes, 'I've never actually given it a name. Why don't we call it Sex in Stillorgan?'

I offer her a toast.

I'm like, 'Sex in Stillorgan!' and then I knock back another mouthful.

She turns her head sideways then and storts looking at the DVDs. '*Brokeback Mountain*,' she goes. '*The Barbra Streisand Collection*.'

I'm there, 'You don't have to be . . . gaaay to enjoooy . . . *Brokeback Mooountain*,' and that's when I notice that I'm slurring my words. 'Jake . . . Gyllenhaaaal . . . has never been in a bad . . . mooovie . . .'

And those are the last words I remember saying before I end up suddenly falling asleep.

The only thing I remember about the hours that follow is being unable to open my eyes and hearing men's voices giving out instructions and the sound of things being dragged across the floor but not wanting to wake up because the feeling of being asleep was so, I want to say, blissful?

It's, like, three o'clock in the afternoon of the following day when

I finally wake up. It takes me a good, like, sixty seconds to become aware of my surroundings and remember where I am. I'm lying on the floor.

I'm like, 'Hello? Jane? Hello?' and my voice comes back at me as, like, a strange echo.

I push myself up onto my elbows and that's when I end up getting *the* biggest shock of my life. Oisinn and Magnus's aportment has been completely cleared out. They've taken everything. The TV. The oven. The fridge. The tiki bar. Jesus, even the picture of the two men kissing.

I'm just like, 'Fock!'

So it's, like, the following day and I'm flaked out on the sofa, trying to piece together the events of last night. Did the girl even like me or was it always her plan to clear out my gaff – along with, presumably, her brother and his mates? I remember her telling me that her name was Jane Murphy and how she seemed to be making it up on the spot. And I remember her mixing me that amazing cocktail – I'd still love the recipe – and how she must have slipped something into it to knock me out.

Erika comes pegging it into the room then, going, 'Ross! Ross! I have some amazing news!'

I'm there, 'Er, go on,' wondering is it worth sitting up for.

She goes, 'Sea-mon has agreed to apply for bail. And the State is no longer objecting to it.'

I'm like, 'Er, cool,' wondering – possibly selfishly – how this affects *me*?

She's there, 'It means she's being released, Ross – today!'

There's my answer. It doesn't affect me.

I'm like, 'That's, em, great,' trying to sound happy for the girl.

She goes, 'I'm just going to the prison to collect her.'

I'm there, 'Where's she going to stay – here?'

She's like, 'No, her parents have a holiday home in Roundstone. She's going to stay there with them until the trial.'

I'm there, 'Roundstone? I'm chuffed for the girl. Erika, can I ask you a question?'

She's like, 'What?'

I'm there, 'How do you know if you've been roofied?'

She's like, 'Roofied? Why the fock are you asking me?'

'I don't know.'

'Do you think *you've* been roofied?'

'God, no. I was just, em, having one of my deep-thinking moments. You know what my mind is like once it gets storted. It can go anywhere. Forget I said anything.'

At that exact moment, my phone beeps and I look at it. Oh, fock. It ends up being a message from Oisinn, asking me if I've checked on the aportment.

I decide that he deserves to know the truth, so I reply, going, 'Dude, I know you're going to laugh at this . . .' but then for some reason – quite possibly cowardice – I end up deleting it, then instead I write, 'Yeah, checked on it yesterday afternoon – everything seemed in order. Definitely nothing unusual to report,' and I send it to him, then ten seconds later he sends me back a thumbs-up emoji.

Erika goes, 'You look awful, by the way.'

I'm like, 'Yeah, no, thanks, I'm feeling a bit wrecked, in fairness to me.'

Honor walks in then, wearing – I shit you – a leather focking skirt that's about four inches long. This time I *do* sit up?

I'm like, 'What the fock? Where are you going dressed like that?'

She goes, 'Er, Dundrum *Town* Centre? What the fock business is it of yours?'

I'm there, 'Where did you get that so-called skirt?'

'From Erika,' she goes.

I'm like, 'Go and put something else on. You're not going out dressed like that. Jesus Christ, it's a shopping centre, Honor.'

She goes, 'This coming from the man who took his orse out in a pub full of people.'

I'm there, 'Yeah, that was rugby-related banter, Honor. Big, big difference,' and I hate that my daughter possibly respects me less for it.

Erika goes, 'Your father never had any objection to that skirt when I wore it.'

And that's when I suddenly recognize it.

I'm there, 'Whoa! Is that the skirt you wore to JP's eighteenth?'

'Yes,' she goes.

I'm there, '*And* to Hollywood Nights – the night we got our Leaving Cert results? *And* to the Wicked Wolf, the night before Sorcha went off on her J1-er?'

Erika and Honor are just, like, staring me out of it, like *I'm* the weirdo – which on balance I probably *am*?

The doorbell rings.

Honor's there, 'That'll be Sincerity. Erika, can she borrow something from your wardrobe as well?'

Erika goes, 'Of course she can, my love.'

'Hold on,' I go, 'how are you getting to Dundrum?'

Honor's there, 'Roz is going to drive us,' and then she goes out to open the door.

She invites Sincerity in. I hear her go, 'Okay, you are *not* wearing that,' presumably referring to Sincerity's mauve-coloured hoodie with 'Math Nerd' on the front. 'Erika's going to let you wear something of hers. She has – oh my God – *amazing* clothes!'

Honor brings her upstairs to dress her and I tip outside to hopefully have a word with Roz. She's sitting in the front seat of her X5 with the engine idling.

I walk up to the driver's window and go, 'Hey, how the hell are you?'

She's like, 'Oh, hi, Ross.'

I'm there, 'You haven't been –'

She goes, 'Returning your calls – yes, I'm sorry.'

'So what's the story? Are you, like, back with your husband?'

'Raymond?'

'Yeah, no, you were spotted together – in Cinnamon in Monkstown. He was having the something-something and you were having the something-else.'

'Ross, Raymond and I are still best friends. And, as it happens, his mother is dying at the moment.'

'Oh – em, bummer.'

'She's in a nursing home in Monkstown. We went to see her together.'

'But that doesn't explain why you've been giving me the cold shoulder ever since that night.'

'What night?'

'You know what night. The night we, you know, had sex.'

'You had sex, Ross. I didn't have sex.'

'Excuse me?'

'Jesus, Ross, is that what you call having sex with someone?'

'I know it was quick but you'd made a lovely meal.'

'Ross, you satisfied yourself and didn't give a damn about my pleasure at all.'

Jesus, she's obviously one of them – strong women.

I'm there, 'It's just that, well, it wasn't the first time we ever did it. I thought you knew what to expect.'

'Well,' she goes, 'I expect better than that. That's how teenage boys have sex, Ross, not grown men.'

'Give me another chance.'

'Ross –'

'Please, Roz. Look, we get on great, don't we?'

'Yes, we do,' she goes – and she smiles, which tells me that I'm still in with a shout here.

I'm like, 'There you are, then! So what do you say?'

She's just about to answer when all of a sudden a black Merc pulls right in front of us. It's, like, Sorcha's ministerial Merc and she gets out of the back of it, not looking happy. She totally ignores me and Roz, morches straight up to Erika's door and goes inside.

I'm there, 'I wonder what her issue is.'

Kennet gets out of the driver's seat, lights the little stub of a cig-arette clamped between his lips and goes, 'Howiya, Rosser. L . . . L . . . L . . . L . . . Lubbly day, wha'?'

I just blank him. The next thing I hear is, like, shouting coming from inside the gaff – we're talking Sorcha shouting, we're talking Honor shouting, we're talking Erika shouting.

I can't make out what's being said, but a second or two later they all emerge from the house, first Honor, then Sorcha, then Erika, then – Jesus Christ, wearing leather trousers and a black belly top – Sincerity.

Sorcha's going, 'You are *not* going to Dundrum Town Centre wearing that skirt!' and I'm thinking, How the fock did she know?

Honor is like, 'So this is how you parent now, is it – so-called *Mom*? You follow my Instagram posts and then react when you see something you don't like?'

'I'm a Government minister,' Sorcha goes. 'I don't want my daughter walking around a shopping centre dressed like a –'

She doesn't get to say the word because Erika puts her hand on her shoulder with the intention of calming her down.

She goes, 'Sorcha, don't say anything you'll regret.'

But Sorcha turns on her – they used to be, like, bezzy, bezzy mates, bear in mind.

Sorcha goes, 'And, what, you're encouraging this behaviour?'

The neighbours are certainly getting their money's worth today because Erika absolutely flips then.

She's there, 'Hey, you washed your focking hands of her, Sorcha. You told her you couldn't bear to look at her any more so she'd have to come and live with me – the same with your husband.'

I'm thinking, Shit, leave me out of it Erika.

Sorcha storts looking around her, going, 'What does Ross think of all this?' and that's when she spots me standing at the window of Roz's – like I said – X5.

I pretend that we're, like, locked in conversation. I'm there, 'So why don't I take you out to dinner on Friday night? I've heard good things about Sprezzatura, even though it's on Camden Street.'

But Sorcha doesn't give a shit. She morches straight up to me and goes, 'Your daughter is going to Dundrum – probably to meet boys – dressed like a prostitute.'

Whoa – *there* it is!

'They're called sex-workers now,' Honor goes, throwing open the back door of the X5. 'I thought you of all people would know that, being the Queen of Woke.'

Roz does something amazing then. She looks over her shoulder at Sincerity, sitting in the – again – leather pants with her entire midriff showing, and she goes, 'You look lovely, Sincerity.'

Of course, if there's one thing that Sorcha can't stand, it's not being the *cool* mom? She turns her anger on Roz then.

She goes, 'So you're perfectly fine with this as well? Two basically children, dressed up as –'

But she doesn't get to finish what she was going to say because Roz just smiles at me and goes, 'Dinner on Friday sounds lovely, Ross,' and then – a bit like my love-making technique – she's gone in a squeal of rubber.

So I'm driving through – believe it or not – Ranelagh and I'm passing the famous Taste of Décor, in other words Delma's interiors and soft-furnishings shop, when I decide to pop in and say hello.

Yeah, no, I haven't seen her since the day that Roz put her foot in it and I don't want things to be awks between us – well, any more awks than is natural between a man and a woman who rode each other in his mother's side passage.

I throw the cor into the wheelchair space outside and into the shop I walk.

Delma is on the phone, explaining to some randomer that their curtains won't be ready for another week, and she's very sorry, but they're coming from Italy and there's nothing she can do about it.

When she hangs up, I'm like, 'People are focking dicks, aren't they, Delma? Absolute focking dicks.'

She goes, 'What do *you* want?' although I think it's my language that she's more concerned about. There's, like, three or four other customers in the shop and two of them are elderly.

I walk to the counter and I go, 'How have you been?'

She's there, 'What do you mean, how have I *been*? What does it have to do with you?'

'Er, you're married to one of my best mates. I'm entitled to be concerned. Especially after Roz put her foot in it like she did – and then Boris Johnson, of course.'

She goes to open her order book, but I put my hand down firmly on the cover.

'Delma,' I go, 'you can talk to me.'

She's like, 'I don't want to talk to you.'

I'm there, 'Look, I know how hord it must be for you being married to a man who's, like, thirty years younger than you.'

'It's not thirty years.'

'It's very nearly, Delma. It's very nearly.'

One of the elderly ladies comes over and asks if she still has those pink taffeta cushions that were in the window during the summer and I turn around and go, 'Can you not focking see that she's serving someone?'

The woman's like, 'I *beg* your pordon?'

I'm there, 'Beg away, love – the focking ego of some people.'

She focks off and Delma is just, like, staring into space.

I'm there, 'JP is absolutely mad about you, Delma. I told you what he was like when he was a teenager, didn't I?'

She goes, 'I don't want to hear that story again.'

'When you came to see my old dear, he used to sniff the collar of your coat because it smelled of you. Then he stole your famous Hermès scorf and spent a month in Irish college wanking himself off every night with the thing balled up in his mouth.'

She roars at me then.

She's like, 'I told you I didn't want to hear that story!'

I'm there, 'Well, maybe you need to hear it. He's mad about you, Delma. He doesn't care what you look like.'

She goes, 'What do you mean, he doesn't care what I look like?'

I'm there, 'Okay, you're twisting my words now. All I'm saying is that he loves you for who you are – for what's on the inside. And what's on the outside isn't bad either. I can vouch for that!'

She goes, 'I'm really storting to age. I can see it in my face. And the older I get, the more like his mother I'm going to seem.'

I'm there, 'I'm not saying you couldn't, you know, do more with yourself.'

'What do you mean?'

'I'm just making the point that plastic surgery exists for a reason. Although my old dear is proof that you *can* go *too* far with it? She looks like a focking melted waxwork of Helena Bonham Corter.'

She storts touching her face with her hand then. She goes, 'Which bits are you talking about?'

I'm there, 'The wrinkles around your eyes, for storters. You can get them filled in. And then there's your mouth –'

'What about my mouth?'

'It's a bit –'

'What?'

'Okay, I'm trying to think of a nicer way of saying saggy.'

She looks, I don't know, devastated to hear this, even though all I'm doing is calling it, something I've never been afraid to do.

She goes, 'Did JP ask you to say something?'

I'm like, 'God, no. Like I said, JP loves you like that. Although –'

'What?' she goes.

I'm there, 'He's always had a thing for big lips.'

'Big lips?' she goes.

'Yeah, no, when I think about all of the girls he's been with over the years. We're talking Melanie Clorke. We're talking Emily Morley. We're talking Sally-Ann Delap. They all had the big mick–, I mean, the big lips.'

My phone all of a sudden rings. I can see that it's Oisinn. I'm thinking, Oh, fock – does he know?

Again, I try to just style it out. I'm like, 'Oisinn, how the hell are you? Have you broken those boots in yet?' and I give Delma a big wink – I don't actually *know* why?

He goes, 'What the fock, Ross? What the focking fock?'

I'm there, 'Okay, you're not making any sense there, Dude. Do you want to ring me back later?'

'It's been cleaned out,' he goes.

I'm like, 'What's been cleaned out?' playing dumb – the role I was born to play.

'Our focking aportment,' he goes. 'The aportment that *you* were supposedly looking after.'

I'm like, 'Hey, don't take it out on me. I said I'd keep an eye on the place and I did.'

'When were you here last?'

'I told you. On Saturday. It was, like, Saturday afternoon.'

'And, what, did you leave the door open when you left?'

'No, I distinctly remember locking it.'

'You didn't lose your key, did you? Or let it out of your sight for a time?'

'Dude, what's with the third degree you're giving me here?'

'Because, according to the Gords, there was no sign of forced entry, so whoever cleaned the place out used a key to get in.'

I'm like, 'Wait a minute, are you saying the Gords are involved?'

He's there, 'Of course the Gords are involved. They took everything we own, Ross. Jesus Christ, they even took the lightbulbs from the sockets.'

'That's, em, a shit one alright,' I go. 'It's a definite, definite shit one.'

He's there, 'Whoever did this better hope that the Gords catch up with them before I do – because I will focking kill them. And I mean that literally.'

Even, like, four days later, Honor hasn't calmed down. Yeah, no, we're in St Kilian's in Clonskeagh, watching the boys play hockey against St Brigid's Stillorgan, and she's got steam coming out of her pretty much ears.

'What focking business is it of *hers* how I dress?' she goes. 'She's not my focking mother.'

I'm like, 'Hey, I'm not defending her, but she kind of *is*?'

'No, she gave that up a focking long time ago. Making a focking show of me in front of Roz. Did she say anything?'

'In terms of?'

'Like, did *she* think I looked like a prostitute?'

'Er, if she did, it definitely wasn't mentioned. Look, again, I'm not defending your mother – I thought she lost her shit in a major way – but she's just a bit jealous that Erika is more of a mother figure to you now than *she* is, if that makes sense?'

'Well, she should have thought about that before she put her career ahead of her children and her marriage.'

I'm like, 'Very good way of looking at it. *Very* good way.'

'I'll get her back for that,' Honor goes. 'I will focking get her back.'

And she will. Honor holds grudges like a focking Lannister.

'Referee!' I suddenly shout because – yeah, no – the St Brigid's player who's morking Johnny – focking Morcus – keeps digging him in the ribs with the butt end of his hockey stick. And the worst thing is that Johnny is just *taking* it from him?

I'm like, 'Johnny, the next time he does that, smash him over the focking head with the business end of your stick.'

This doesn't go down well with the other parents, especially Morcus's old pair. His old man goes, 'That's our son you're referring to.'

And I'm there, 'Your son is a focking orsehole – and he was raised by a focking orsehole.'

The dude realizes he can't take me on physically, so he just tuts at me and Honor goes, 'Yeah, fock you, Tutty,' which makes me laugh a lot.

It's nice that she has my back.

When it carries on happening, I call Brian over to the sideline. I'm like, 'Brian, help your brother, will you?'

I swear to fock, he goes, 'Why?'

I'm like, 'Why? Because he's getting the piss taken out of him out there. Remember what I taught you? One in, all in. He does that to your brother again, I want you to crack him over the head like you're chopping focking logs.'

Word for word, he goes, 'But that's against the rules.'

This is what Sorcha's old man has done to them.

'Oh my God,' Honor goes, her nose stuck in her phone.

I'm like, 'What is it?'

She goes, 'Dad, can I go to the cinema tonight?'

I'm like, 'That depends – who with?'

She's there, 'MacDara.'

'Absolutely,' I go. 'One hundred per cent.'

I realize I know literally fock-all about this dude but I just get a good vibe from him.

'Oh my God,' she goes, 'it's, like, my first actual date!'

At least *she's* someone I can be proud of. She's got goys running around after her like fools, which is a serious achievement because – like I always say, with the greatest will in the world – she's not going to win many beauty contests in life.

Suddenly, Leo – in goals – ends up in a one-on-one situation with one of their players, who's at least six inches shorter than him. The little lad is running through on goal and Leo leaves his line and it's a fifty–fifty contest as to who gets to the ball first. As the bigger kid, Leo should focking plough him out of it – knock him into a twenty-year coma, if needs be – except he *doesn't*? Just before the point of impact – I shit you not – I watch him close his eyes and literally *wince*? The little kid flicks the ball around him, then rolls it into the empty net.

'Fock's sake,' I go. 'I'm ashamed of him. I'm ashamed of them all.'

Honor's there, 'Apparently, they're getting really good grades these days. We're talking, like, top of their *class*?'

I'm there, 'What use are good grades? Life is about winning the fifty–fifties, Honor.'

All of a sudden my phone rings. It's, like, JP, so I answer.

I'm there, 'I was just quoting Father Fehily there. There's hordly a day goes by when I don't. What's up?'

He's like, 'Yeah, no, Delma was saying you called into the shop to see her the other day.'

'Dude,' I go, 'I just said one or two things that I thought needed saying. If she took them the wrong way –'

He's there, 'She said you'd a great talk.'

I'm like, 'Did she? Jesus Christ – fair enough.'

He goes, 'She said you helped her get a lot of things straight in her head.'

I'm there, 'Fair play to me. I know I'm patting myself on the back here by saying that.'

'Anyway,' he goes, 'I just dropped her off at the airport.'

I'm like, 'Where's she headed?'

'She wouldn't say.'

'What do you mean?'

'She said she was going off to get me my Christmas present.'

'Dude, it's July.'

'An early Christmas present, then.'

I smile because the penny suddenly drops.

I'm like, 'That's, er, great news.'

He goes, 'Do you know what it is?'

I'm there, 'Let's just say that I might have had something to do with it.'

'Well, thanks,' he goes. 'She was in cracking form when she went off. By the way, any word from Roz, or is that still –'

I'm there, 'Yeah, no, like two orse cheeks, we're back together after a lot of shit. I'm seeing her on Friday night as a matter of fact. Actually, Dude, can I talk to you about something?' and I step away from Honor so that she can't hear me.

He's like, 'Yeah, no, what is it?'

'Okay, random one,' I go. 'Do you know the way some women are obsessed with, like, length?'

He's there, 'Are you seriously asking me about the size of your penis?'

I'm like, 'No, no, not size. When I say length, I mean duration – as in, some women like sex to last for ages, don't they?'

He goes, 'Jesus Christ, Ross, what are we, sixteen?'

'I'm just trying to have a conversation with you. You always hear people say that men should talk to each other more.'

'What's your definition of lasting for ages?'

'Well, longer than, say –'

'Go on.'

'Five *minutes*?'

'Five minutes? That's how long you usually last?'

'Not always. Sometimes it's longer.'

Sometimes it's shorter.

He's laughing his *head* off, by the way?

I'm like, 'Dude, I'm just wondering is there, like, a trick of the trade to stop yourself from, well, you know –'

'Yeah,' he goes, 'just don't be a selfish bastard.'

I'm like, 'Dude, I was thinking more in terms of, like, *practical* tips?'

He's there, 'Ross, you've had sex with, what, hundreds of women?'

I'm like, 'I don't want to be a dick about it but it's probably more like thousands. Obviously, don't mention that to Sorcha.'

He goes, 'And, what, this is the first time that anyone's ever told you that you're shit at it?'

I'm there, 'She didn't say I was shit at it. She said I have sex like a teenage boy, not a man.'

Again, he thinks this is hilarious.

I'm like, 'Fock sake, Dude.'

'Okay, I shouldn't laugh,' he goes. 'Look, all you have to do to, well, you know –'

'Keep the White Walkers from the gates.'

'– is think of something else at the crucial moment.'

'Like what?'

'Like anything.'

'I used to name old Leinster teams. The fifteen who storted against Leicester in 2009, the fifteen who storted against Northampton in 2011 –'

'So you *do* know how to do it?'

'Well, the only problem was that I had to say them out loud. Sorcha said it put her off her stroke, hearing me go, "Kearney, McFadden, O'Driscoll, D'Arcy . . ."'

'I can see how that might be an issue.'

I'm suddenly there, 'Listen, Dude, I have to go,' and I hang up on him because something is happening.

Yeah, no, Brian, Johnny *and* Leo – are being substituted!

I'm like, 'What the fock is going on?' directing my question at Mrs Kremers, the hockey coach.

Again, this doesn't go down well with the other mums and dads. They're a different breed here.

'I'm taking them off,' she goes. 'I want to give some of the other boys a chance.'

I'm there, 'But why are you subbing *my* focking kids off?' hoping at the same time that I'm not coming across as one of *those* parents.

'Because they're not playing very well,' she goes. 'They're playing very badly, in fact.'

It hits me like a kick in the crackers, especially when I notice quite a few of the other parents failing to – I think it's a word – *suppress* their laughter.

I'm there, 'Brian, Johnny, Leo – tell her you're not coming off. Tell her to go fock herself. Tell her you're staying on and you're going to turn it around.'

But they don't. They just walk off the pitch like focking sheep.

I don't care how much their behaviour or their grades have improved, Sorcha's old man has turned my children into losers. I'm actually tempted to let them get the focking bus home.

'Oh my God,' Honor suddenly goes, 'I know how I'm going to get my own back on that focking bitch!'

So – yeah, no – I'm standing on the doorstep having pressed the doorbell and I've got my features arranged into an expression that I call aloof yet persuadable. But then it ends up being Raymond, not Roz, who answers the door and the five minutes I spent in the cor pulling faces is for nothing.

He's there, 'Great to see you, Ross!' like he has absolutely no issue with me coming to his former home tonight to ride his ex-wife. 'How's it going?'

I'm like, 'Er, yeah, no, all good,' feeling like a kid who's been caught with his finger in the cake batter.

He goes, 'Jesus, look at you,' because I'm wearing my pink Abercrombie t-shirt, which has always done justice to my famous biceps. 'What the hell are you bench-pressing these days?'

I suddenly remember that it's impossible not to like Raymond.

I'm there, 'I can't put an actual figure on it for you. All I can tell you is that it's a lot.'

'My God, I can only imagine,' he goes. 'Anyway, come in. I'm just here to collect Sincerity. By the way, I have to thank you for, well, everything you've done for her. She's really come out of her shell.'

I'm like, 'Hey, it's all Honor. Don't thank me – and don't come running to me if it all goes wrong. Which, I'm warning you now, it *probably* will?'

He laughs like he thinks I'm joking.

He goes, 'Rosalind and I have always worried that Sincerity would end up as some highly educated, old spinster. She never had much of a sense of adventure. But in the past few weeks, that's all changed. You know she hasn't opened a schoolbook all summer?'

She can't. Honor focked them out of the window of the cor.

I'm like, 'That's, em, good news, isn't it?'

He's there, 'She's going to the beach. She's going to Dundrum Shopping Centre. She's doing the things that normal, fourteen-year-old girls do on their summer holidays.'

'Well, let's hope you're still happy when she fails her Leaving Cert and ends up addicted to drugs in a squat.'

He laughs. He gets a good kick out of me, in fairness to him.

Then he goes, 'I'm not sure if I'm supposed to tell you this, but she's been, em, asked out on a date.'

I'm like, 'A date? By who?'

He goes, 'Chap named *MacDara*,' and, like me, he can't help but smile when he says his name. 'That's his *first* name, believe it or not. Asked her to go to the cinema with him.'

I'm like, 'MacDara?'

He's there, 'I know! I said to Rosalind, "He sounds like *our* kind of people!" She knows I'm a terrible snob, you see.'

All of a sudden, Roz and Sincerity come down the stairs. Sincerity is carrying, like, an *overnight* bag?

She's like, 'Hi, Ross!'

And under my breath, I go, 'Yeah, no, whatever,' unable to even *look* at her? The treacherous bitch.

Roz sees them off, her daughter and her ex-husband, each with a hug and a kiss, then she closes the door, goes 'Hello, you!' and kisses me on the lips.

It's all *very* Goatstown – even though I'm not a hundred per cent sure what I *mean* by that?

She goes, 'The food's arrived,' leading me down to the kitchen. 'I ordered from that new sushi place in Mount Merrion. I hope you don't mind.'

I'm like, 'Yeah, no, I'm easy-breezy. So what's this about Sincerity going on a possibly date?'

She's there, 'Don't tell me Raymond told you. You know, I've honestly never seen him so proud. Although it's purely down to the fact that the boy's name is MacDara.'

I'm there, 'MacDara? I don't know, does he sound like someone who can be trusted to you?'

She's like, 'Oh, God, yeah! I mean, you don't hear of many boys named MacDara, do you? Anyway, he goes to Clongowes Wood, so he can't be all bad!'

I decide to let that one go.

She serves up her famous sushi. Everything is cold, so if we do end up suddenly going at each other again – we're talking pre- or even mid-meal – there's no fear of good food going to waste this time. I'm not sure if that's what was on her mind when she ordered the spicy seared albacore and lobster tacos, but I like a woman who thinks tactically.

I'm there, 'MacDara, though,' unable to let it go. 'I'm still not sure he's right for Sincerity.'

She's like, 'Oh, have you met him?'

'Only from far away,' I go. 'He was doing a cannonball down at the Forty Foot. Even from that glimpse, Roz, I'd have genuine concerns about him.'

She's like, 'Try the eel and avocado rolls, Ross.'

And – yeah, no – I *do*?

'By the way,' I go, 'I'm sorry again about Sorcha. She was bang out of order that day – and I *mean* bang?'

Roz is there, 'I understand what she's going through. I've been through a marriage break-up myself. I just decided that I didn't want to end up all angry and bitter like that. Raymond and I agreed that we loved each other too much as people to put each other through a bad divorce.'

'That's very Goatstown – if you don't mind me saying.'

'What do you mean by that?'

'I have absolutely no idea. Forget I even said it. I just think Sorcha – egged on by her old man, by the way – decided to put her career ahead of her marriage and her children and she's not one hundred per cent happy with her decision.'

'It's a tough life she's chosen for herself,' she goes, 'especially in this day and age, where you'd be terrified to open your mouth about anything. I mean, that stuff about her on the internet tonight –'

I'm like, 'What stuff about her on the internet tonight?'

'You haven't been on Twitter?'

'I'm not really *on* Twitter? Just the odd time to check that Honor hasn't broken the court order to stop trolling Holly Willoughby and, well, one or two others.'

'Someone's posted a video – from, like, fifteen years ago – when Sorcha owned, like, a *clothes* shop?'

'Yeah, no, it was in the Powerscourt Townhouse Centre. It never made a penny. It was, like, a tax write-off for her old man.'

She goes, 'Well, she did this video,' and she hands me her phone and there on the screen is the Sorcha I knew in my early twenties. I always thought she looked like Jennie Gorth.

She's going, 'Yes, gypsy dresses are going to be, like, *so* in this summer. What do I mean by gypsy dresses? By gypsy dresses, I mean loose t-shirt dresses. By gypsy dresses, I mean dresses with drawstring waists. By gypsy dresses, I mean lace dresses with fancy cuffs and statement buttons. By gypsy dresses, I mean Victorian-inspired sheer shifts.'

I'm like, 'Yeah, no, this is from *Off the Rails*. She used to do the odd bit on it. She was mates with Caroline Morahan – *and* Pamela Flood, if *mammary* serves.'

If mammary serves is just a funny thing I sometimes say – most people get the joke – but it seems to fly right over her head.

'No,' she goes, 'read the tweet *with* it, Ross.'

So I do.

It's like, *By g**sy dresses, I mean I'm a racist bitch!*

I'm there, 'Gypsy dresses? Okay, how is that racist?'

Then I notice that the tweet has come from the account that Honor used to use to troll – cords on the table here, even though the court case was heard in camera because of Honor's age – Michelle Obama.

Roz goes, 'Read the comments underneath.'

So I do, at the same time thinking, Oh, Honor, what the fock have you done now?

It's like, *She should resign but she won't.*

And it's, *Typical basic bitch behaviour telling us all how to lead our lives while guess what everyone I'm a f**king racist asshole.*

And it's, *Why aren't the MSM all over this? I've checked the Irish Times and Independent websites and there's literally nothing about it.*

And it's, *Er, because they're part of the Establishment.*

And it's, *G**sy dresses. G**sy dresses. G**sy dresses. She literally keeps on saying it. I can't believe people actually voted for this far-right f**king bitch.*

And it's, *They didn't. She was appointed to the Senate and then to the Cabinet because her father-in-law is the Taoiseach.*

And it's, *What do you have to say about one of your ministers being a f**king racist bitch @realcock @NewRepublic?*

And it's, *Am I being really stupid here wondering how this is actually racist?*

And it's, *If you don't know how it's racist to describe a dress as a g**sy dress, then you're a f**king racist too. #BeKind #BeBetter.*

And it's, *It's just that this clip is from 15 years ago when everyone called those dresses that.*

And it's, *Go and die of testicular cancer, you gammon bastard.*

And it's, *He's a f**king boomer as well. Die troll!*

And it's, *Why aren't the MSM covering this?*

And it's, *Typical Karen behaviour. Wants to tell me what to have for dinner and when I can drive my car but reserves the right to be a f**king racist.*

And it's, *Still no statement from her.*

And it's, *It's not only racist – it's also cultural appropriation surely?*

And it's, *It is cultural appropriation.*

And it's, *It's DEFINITELY cultural appropriation.*

And it's, *Why isn't the MSM covering this?*

And it's, *Typical white, privileged, cisgender behaviour. I bet she's a JK Rowling fan.*

And it's, *F**k JK Rowling. F**k TERFs.*

And it's, *Does anyone know any accounts I should follow on here that will help me better understand the g**sy experience? And also POC?*

And it's, *Good for you!*

And it's, *Good for you!*

And it's, *Thanks for being an ally!*

And it's, *If anyone out there knows this bitch, can they ask her to come on here to explain how this ISN'T the most f**king offensive thing ever?*

And it's, *She needs to engage.*

And it's, *Why isn't the MSM covering this?*

And it's, *Her husband is up in court next month for taking his mickey out in a pub – lovely people.*

I hand Roz back her phone. I'm there, 'It was my orse, by the way, not my mickey.'

She goes, 'People are just awful, aren't they?' and I'm thinking that there's probably no comeback for Honor and Sorcha after this.

I'm there, 'Like you said,' helping myself to the last California roll, 'you can't say anything these days.'

She's there, 'I hope Honor's not too upset.'

I'm like, 'About?'

'About all these horrible things being said about her mother,' she goes. 'She's not *on* Twitter, is she?'

And I'm there, 'Not as far as the law is concerned, no,' and I swallow the last piece of sushi and wash it down with a mouthful of the Malbec.

Roz cracks her hole laughing.

I'm there, 'What?'

She goes, 'You finish your dinner and you immediately stort looking at me like –'

I'm there, 'Like what?'

'Like I'm your dessert!' she goes.

I'm there, 'I didn't, did I?'

She goes, 'Yes, you did,' throwing her napkin in my face, but at the same time – thankfully – *laughing*?

I'm like, 'I'm sorry. It's just, after our last conversation, there's a lot of pressure on me here tonight.'

'Well,' she goes, 'I'm going to take the pressure off you by telling you that nothing is going to happen between us.'

Fock's sake.

She's like, 'Is that okay?'

I'm there, 'Yeah, no, that's cool. Have you got your, em –'

'No,' she goes, 'I don't have my period, although it's nice of you to ask. It's just that I don't feel . . . *in the mood.*'

I'm like, 'Fair enough.'

She goes, 'There must be times when you don't feel in the mood?'

Not focking once, not focking ever.

I'm there, 'Yeah, no, I'd have to rack my brains.'

'Anyway,' she goes, 'I'm enjoying just talking to you.'

Now, in normal circumstances, this would be the point at which I would fake a seafood allergy and get the fock out of there while The Goat is still serving. But I don't.

I go, 'I want to get better at it – as in, I want to be able to do it for longer. *If* that's what you're into.'

She's there, 'Have you ever heard of tantric sex?'

I'm like, 'Isn't that the one that, like, Sting is into? Banging his back out for hours?'

She laughs.

She goes upstairs to presumably her bedroom and comes down with a literally book in her hand. On the cover, it's like, *The Secrets of Tantra*.

I'm there, 'It sounds like something my old dear might have written.'

She goes, 'Come back to me when you've read that.'

I'm like, 'All of it?' because it's a focking big book.

She goes, 'Yes, all of it.'

Jesus Christ, I could end up being celibate for years.

I'm there, 'Is it available on Audible, do you know?'

'Ross,' she goes, 'just read it.'

So I'm showing Erika the video of Sorcha wearing the – I'm nearly scared to say the word myself now – but *gypsy* dress and I'm showing her the Twitter pile-on that it caused.

'Jesus,' she goes, reading the comments, 'poor Sorcha,' because there's, like, thousands more than there were last night.

It's, *Has anyone heard if she's apologized yet?*

And it's, *Fascists don't apologize.*

And it's, *Why aren't the MSM covering this?*

And it's, *Am I the only one who would LOVE to smash my fist into that stuck-up bitch's face?*

Erika just shakes her head. She's there, 'Look, I know she's not my favourite person in the world right now, but she doesn't deserve that.'

I'm there, 'Honor posted the video.'

Erika's like, 'What?' and she's surprised for some reason.

'Yeah, no,' I go, 'Honor posted it – presumably to get her back for making a show of her that day in the gorden.'

Erika's like, 'What are you going to do?'

I'm there, 'I was thinking we should maybe talk to her about it?'

'We?'

'Yeah.'

'Ross, I'm not her mother.'

'Yeah, no, but she listens to you.'

'Look, I told you that you were welcome to stay here with us, Ross, but that does not mean I'm going to parent your daughter. I have one of my own, remember?'

'Of course, the other option,' I go, 'is to say nothing.'

She's like, 'Nothing?'

'Like I said, Sorcha was a bitch to her, Erika. And she did say it was a *gypsy* dress – over and over again.'

'That was in 2003, Ross – years before the world lost its focking mind.'

Yeah, no, this is us sitting in the kitchen, by the way. Erika is just back from horse-riding and she's still wearing her usual jodhpurs and riding boots.

Outside, Helen and little Amelie are weeding the flowerbeds, even though Helen could easily afford to pay someone to do it. She did well out of divorcing my old man.

'Don't take this the wrong way,' I go, 'but I love when you come home smelling of dirt.'

She ends up giving me *the* most withering look – I possibly could have phrased it better – and that's when the doorbell thankfully rings.

'Ah,' I go, standing up and rubbing my two hands together, 'that'll be the famous MacDara.'

Erika's there, 'MacDara?'

'Yeah, no,' I go, 'isn't tonight the night he's bringing Honor to the flicks?'

She's like, 'Yeah, but he's already upstairs.'

I'm there, 'What? Since when?'

She goes, 'He called when you were outside, telling my mother that she should pay someone to pull up her weeds and that letting Amelie do manual labour was setting her on a slippery slope.'

The doorbell rings again.

'Well, you still should have told me,' I go. 'Me and MacDara need to have words.'

Erika's like, 'Go and have your words – but answer the door first.'

I'm there, 'And what the fock is he doing upstairs in her bedroom, can I just ask?'

The doorbell rings again.

'Ross,' she goes, 'answer the focking door.'

Which is what I end up doing. I have to admit, I'm surprised to find Ronan's daughter standing on the doorstep, with tears streaming down her face.

I'm like, 'Rihanna-Brogan – what the fock?'

She's there, 'Me ma's arthur thrunning me out.'

I'm like, 'She threw you out? Why?'

She goes, 'For robidden.'

I'm there, 'Robidden?'

'No,' she goes, '*robidden*!'

I'm there, 'You'd better come in – this could take a while.'

I step aside and in she walks. I notice her bag on the doorstep. It's a holdall, of course. The Tuites love a focking holdall. If the baby Jesus had been born to the Tuites, they'd have wrapped him in a holdall.

'Robbing!' I go, the penny suddenly dropping. 'You were focked out for robbing!'

She's like, 'That's what I said, idn't it?'

She has the exact same streak of defiance in her as her old man did at seven.

I'm there, 'What did you rob?'

She goes, 'Does it mathor what I robbed?'

Looking at the fortunes of our respective families, I would say that, yes, it matters *very* focking much indeed.

Erika hears the commotion and steps out into the hallway. She's like, 'What's going on?'

I'm there, 'Shadden focked her out – for, like, stealing.'

Erika's like, 'What did you steal?'

See, *she* knows. There's people behind bors for stealing baby formula to feed their children. Our old man has stolen more than the entire prison population of Ireland combined and he's the leader of the country. Of course it focking matters.

'Make-up,' Rihanna-Brogan goes. 'And untherweer.'

Erika's like, 'Why?'

'What do you mee-un why?' Rihanna-Brogan goes – and I've never seen this kind of 'tude from her before. 'Cos I was wanthon them, that's why!'

Erika's there, 'But you're not short of money. Ronan sends you money. I give you money.'

I keep my mouth shut. I've enough kids of my own to feed.

Helen steps out of the kitchen then with little Amelie.

She's like, 'What's going on?'

Erika's there, 'Rihanna-Brogan has been thrown out of home for, what, *shoplifting*?'

Rihanna-Brogan nods.

'In Penneys,' she goes.

I'm like, 'Jesus Christ,' and everyone looks at me. I'm there, 'Sorry, I don't know why I said that – continue.'

'Me ma said I've to foyunt somewheer edelese to lib,' Rihanna-Brogan goes. 'She said go and lib wit your fooken big-eared prick of a grandfadder.'

Yeah, no, for anyone struggling to keep up with our family's complicated family tree, she's referring to me.

Helen goes, 'I'll make up a bed for her in the, em, last spare room.'

Rihanna-Brogan's like, 'Tanks.'

And Helen's there, 'Come in, sweetheart – you must be hungry, are you?' and she puts her orm around her shoulder and brings her down to the kitchen.

Helen's always reminded me a lot of Devin Toner, in that you can't actually believe that another human being could be that nice while also possessing the springs to outjump any NBA player in history from a standing position – although that last bit obviously applies only to Devin Toner.

Erika stares me out of it. I know what she's thinking. She loves us all, but they can't keep taking in our family's waifs and strays.

I'm there, 'I'm, er, just going to pop upstairs and have a word with Justin focking Bieber.'

I'm telling you, it's all focking go here today.

So – yeah, no – up the stairs I tip. I don't even bother knocking. I just, like, burst into Honor's room. The two of them are, like, sitting on the end of Honor's bed. I don't know what I *expected* them to be doing but thankfully they're *not* doing it.

They're actually laughing at something on *her* phone, either a GIF or a TikTok or someone on Twitter calling her mother a *Nazi* or a *stooge of the patriarchy* or an *ugly, morbles-in-the-mouth slut*.

Honor ends up getting a fright. She goes, 'Oh my God, Dad, you can't just burst into my room like that?'

I'm there, 'Honor, you're wanted downstairs.'

She's like, 'Why?'

I'm there, 'Rihanna-Brogan has been focked out of home for stealing.'

Honor goes, 'Well, what did she steal?'

See? Even *she* knows.

I'm there, 'She was shoplifting, Honor – in focking Penneys.'

She's like, 'Jesus Christ,' then she goes running for the door, because she adores the little one. 'MacDara, I'll be back in a minute, okay?'

As soon as she's gone, I go, 'So . . . MacDara, huh?'

He's like, 'That's the one,' and the little focker – I swear to God – carries on looking at shit on Honor's phone.

I'm there, 'I'm Ross. I'm Honor's old man. Although you can call me Mr O'Carroll-Kelly.'

With a little focking smirk on his face, he taps his left temple with a finger and goes, 'I shall file that information away – in case I need it.'

I'm suddenly glowering at him like *I'm* Chris Robshaw and I've woken up in the middle of the night to find a complete stranger anally masturbating himself with my electric nose-hair trimmer.

I'm there, 'So you like Honor, do you?'

He goes, 'She's a cool girl.'

He hasn't looked at me once, by the way.

I'm like, 'And what about Sincerity? Do you like her too?'

He's there, 'Yeah, no, both cool girls.'

'If you had to choose between them,' I go, 'which one would you pick?'

He's there, 'Be hord.'

I'm like, 'I know it'd be hord – but if you absolutely *had* to choose one?'

'The point is,' he goes, 'that I *don't* have to choose?'

This sudden – I don't know – rage comes over me. I'm thinking, In a few weeks I'm quite possibly going to be in prison and I won't be able to protect my daughter from players like this dude.

I'm there, 'Yeah, maybe I'm not making myself understood here, MacDara,' and I suddenly grab him by the scruff of the shirt and drag him across the bedroom floor.

He's like, 'What the fock?' and he ends up dropping Honor's phone.

I throw open the window and I'm there, 'I want to show you something.'

Oh, *now* I have his undivided attention?

He's like, 'Wh . . . Wh . . . Wh . . . Wh . . . What?'

I'm there, 'Do you not see it?'

He goes, 'Wh . . . Wh . . . Wh . . . What am I looking at?'

And I'm like, 'A fall for twenty focking feet,' then I grab his two legs and literally shove him head-first out the window.

I make sure not to drop him, though. Yeah, no, I've experience in this area. We used to do this to the First Years in Castlerock just so they'd think better of us.

So I've got the dude tipped upside-down out the window and I'm clutching his knees to my chest.

He's going, 'FOOOCK! FOOOCK! FOOOCK!'

And I'm there, 'Dude, you keep screaming like that and I *will* drop you? Do you understand me?'

He nods – sensible lad.

I'm there, 'You asked my daughter to go to the cinema with you tonight?'

He's like, 'Yeah, I did.'

I'm there, 'To see what – as a matter of interest?'

'*Godzilla – King of the Monsters*,' he goes.

I'm like, 'I've heard good things. I wouldn't mind going to see that myself. But then you also asked Sincerity to go to the cinema with you as well, didn't you? And don't focking lie to me.'

'Yeah, I . . . d . . . d . . . d . . . *did*,' he goes.

'When?'

'Tomorrow night.'

'That's a nice little weekend you've got planned, MacDara. What movie?'

'*X-Men: Dork Phoenix*.'

'*X-Men: Dork Phoenix*? Jesus, I'd nearly go out with you myself. Except you're a dirty, two-timing bastard.'

He goes, 'Dude, please don't drop me. Please don't drop me.'

And I'm there, 'You see what I'm saying here, MacDara, don't you?'

He's like, 'No,' and I decide, fock that, it's time to *really* put the shits up him? So I drop him – but as he falls, I grab a hold of his ankles.

He storts babbling, going, 'Please don't drop me! I'm on the Leinster Schools Junior Cup team.'

I'm there, 'Being on the Leinster Schools Junior Cup team isn't an excuse for shitty behaviour.'

I obviously don't mean that.

I'm there, 'It's certainly not an excuse for messing girls around.'

I don't mean that either.

I'm there, 'You need to make a choice, Dude – is it going to be Honor or is it going to be Sincerity?'

'It's going to be neither,' he goes.

I'm there, 'Excuse me?' because it's not the answer I was *expecting* to hear?

He goes, 'Sincerity knocked me back. She said she wouldn't go out with me because she knows how much Honor likes me.'

I'm like, 'That's called loyalty. So what's the deal with you and Honor?'

'There's no deal. She's just a mate of mine.'

'A *mate*?'

'Yeah, I think she's a legend – *all* the goys do?'

'A legend for what?'

'For what she did to Reese!'

'What, you only like her because she locked a Michael's boy in the boot of a cor and drove him up the mountains so that he'd miss the Leinster Schools Senior Cup final?'

'Yeah, she focking rocks, man! Every goy in Dublin wants to be friends with her.'

'But *just* friends?'

'Well, yeah.'

'But why not more than that?'

'Dude, can you please pull me up. All the blood is running to my head.'

I go, 'Answer me, you little focker!' and I give him a good shake by the ankles.

He's there, 'Look, no offence, but she wouldn't be my cup of tea – in, like, *that* way.'

'Why not?'

'I just don't think she's great – in terms of looks.'

All of a sudden, I hear a voice behind me go, 'What the fock is going on? Where's MacDara?' and I get such a fright that I end up actually dropping the little focker.

He falls, like, twenty feet to the ground and lands on his back with a loud splat.

He's fine, though. I actually hear him mutter, 'You focking . . . wanker . . .' but by that stage I'm already closing the window and I'm going, 'Sorry, Honor, what was what?'

She goes, 'Where's MacDara? Oh my God, you haven't frightened him off, have you?'

I'm there, 'No, I didn't frighten him off. He said he had to head off.'

'But we're supposed to be going to see *Godzilla*,' she goes.

I'm there, 'Something must have come up.'

She goes, 'Why are you holding his Dubes?'

Yeah, no, I forgot to mention, I was still holding his Dubes when I dropped him.

I'm there, 'He, em, asked me to *give* you these?'

She's like, 'Er, why?'

I'm there, 'I don't know. Back in the day, the girls from Holy Child Killiney used to give their scorves to boys they'd scored. I'd thirty or forty of the things. This might be the Clongowes equivalent? It's a weird school.'

She doesn't buy this shit for a minute. She rushes to the window, shoving me out of the way, pushes the thing open and looks out.

'Oh my God,' she goes, 'you threw him out of the window!' and bear in mind, it takes a lot to shock Honor. 'MacDara, are you okay? Why did you throw him out of the window?'

I'm there, 'Just a misunderstanding, Honor. Enjoy *Godzilla*,' and then I raise my voice and go, 'You too, MacDara.'

I know she's my technically daughter-in-law, but Shadden's voice still gets on my nerves like driving a stick-shift cor with a focked fanbelt. It's just as loud as well and I end up having to hold the phone away from my ear.

She's going, 'You can bleaten keep her! I doatunt wanth her hee-or!'

I really don't need this hassle in my life right now. I haven't even opened *The Secrets of Tantra* and I'm supposedly meeting Roz for a drink tomorrow night.

I'm there, 'Shadden, she's your daughter.'

I'm stopped at the traffic lights outside Donnybrook Gordaí Station.

'She's no thaughter of moyen,' she goes. 'She's a bleaten robber. That's not how she was rayuzed.'

I'm like, 'What the fock are you talking about?' suddenly losing it with her. 'That's *exactly* how she was raised!'

She's there, 'Soddy?'

I'm like, 'The first time I ever met your old man, he whipped the focking wheels off my cor – because I wouldn't pay him, I don't know, whatever the going rate is in protection money to pork near Croke Pork. Your brother Dadden sawed off one of his fingers with a focking bread knife for an insurance claim. Your old dear got caught claiming children's allowance for thirty-focking-eight of you. The *Sunday Wurdled* nicknamed her The Old Woman Who Lived in a Shoe. Is any of this ringing any bells?'

'That's difford to robbing,' she goes. 'I was bleaten mortified, so I was, when I got the calt to say me thaughter was arthur been lifted by securitoddy. If it wadn't for Heddessy, thee would have calt the Geerds.'

I'm like, 'Hennessy?' suddenly wondering how he fits into this. 'What the fock?'

She goes, 'I ditn't know who else to calt. So I reng him up and he came straight away.'

I'm there, 'What, to Penneys? On O'Connell Street?'

'No,' she goes, 'it was the wooden on Meerdy Street.'

I'm there, 'What, and the Attorney focking General showed up?'

'He had a woord with the securitoddy geerd,' she goes, 'and he agreeyut to lerrer off wit a warden.'

I'm like, 'And let me guess,' because it's all storting to make sudden sense to me, 'it was Hennessy who suggested you throw her out of the gaff?'

'Alls he said was a showurt, sheerp shock was what she needed.'

'Shadden, can you not see that you're being used here? The reason he told you to fock her out was so that it would get back to Ronan.'

'It's your doorty, lying bastard sudden's fault that she's robbing in the foorst place. Heddessy said the oatenly reason she's acting out is because she's been abandoned by her fadder.'

'Yeah, that's what he wants you think, Shadden. He wants Ronan to hear that his daughter's out of control so that he'll come home. And I'm begging you, Shadden, not to tell him.'

She goes, 'I toawult him altreddy.'

I'm there, 'When?'

She's like, 'Bout twedenty midutes ago. I seddent him a message saying he's thaughter was a robben bitch and if that wadn't he's foddelt, then I doatunt know whose foddelt it is.'

'Shadden,' I go, 'you have to take her back.'

She's like, 'Ine soddy, Ine acton on the advice of me solicitodder.'

I'm there, 'Fock's sake,' and I hang up on her.

I call Hennessy's number, except he doesn't answer. Of course he doesn't. He's the Attorney focking General. So I decide to go and see him in person and I point the cor in the direction of the Áras.

I'm flying along the quays when my phone all of a sudden rings. I can see from the number that it's, like, Ronan. The only reason I answer is because I'm scared he's going to be on the next flight home.

He's like, 'Rosser –'

But I'm there, 'Ro, it's nothing to worry about – okay?'

'Nuttin to woody about?' he goes. 'Me thaughter – out robben? Wheer's this cubben from, Rosser?'

Jesus – and I thought *my* old pair were in denial.

I'm there, 'Who knows, Ro? It's a real focking mystery.'

He goes, 'Ine steerting to think it's mebbe *my* foddelt.'

I'm like, 'Your fault? Why would you say that?'

'Because I walked out on her and her mammy,' he goes. 'Ine thinking mebbe that's why she's actodden out.'

'Ro, she's the offspring of two of Ireland's most notorious criminal families. Trust me – some make-up and a pair of knickers is small change compared to what the Tuites and the O'Carroll-Kellys have got up to over the years. This is probably only the stort of it for her.'

'Ine cubben howum.'

'Ro, please don't come home. This is exactly what Hennessy wants – he's stirring the shit.'

'Me thaughter needs me, Rosser.'

'Ro, me and Erika have got this, okay? She's going to stay with us for a few weeks. Erika's taken her horse-riding today with Honor and Amelie. It's all good.'

'Rosser –'

'Just let me have a word with Hennessy, okay?'

Ten minutes later, I'm taking the turn into the Áras and that's when I see the massive crowd of people gathered – yeah, no – in the front gorden, staring up at the balcony, where the old dear – holy shit on a cracker – is standing there in a fur coat, making a speech to the crowd.

I pork the cor and get out. As I approach the house, I can suddenly hear what the old dear is saying.

She's going, 'Good manners cost nothing. We are living in an age where the importance of civility has been forgotten. However, to put it simply, good people have good manners – and this is how it's been since time began. Always say "please" and – provided, of course, that you've received good service – "thank you". If you haven't, then you should deliver a frosty look, followed by a curt request to speak to a manager or other senior member of staff.'

All around me, people are laughing at her.

She's there, 'Don't be afraid to wear fab-a-lous clothes. Every morning for the past forty years, I've looked myself in the mirror and I've said, "Fionnuala, do that gorgeous figure of yours justice by looking your very, very best today." Of course, not everyone is lucky enough to have a figure like mine, in which case fab-a-lous clothes are wasted on you. As I once said on *The Oprah Winfrey Show* – even though it got me into a lot of trouble at the time – a pig is still a pig, even if that pig is dressed by Diane von Furstenberg.'

I push my way through the crowds to the front door, where a dude from the old man's security detail, who knows me, lets me past.

I hear her go, 'Try to spend at least port of the year in French Polynesia or some similar paradise.'

I'm there, 'Why isn't someone stopping this?'

The dude just shrugs and goes, 'Orders,' like that's *any* kind of excuse?

I take the stairs like I'd take the Kordashians – three by three and without even pausing for breath. When I reach the top, I walk through the crèche and head for the French doors that lead out onto the balcony. But there I end up being stopped by two other security dudes.

They're like, 'I'm sorry, we can't let you out there. She said she's not to be disturbed while she's talking to her people.'

I'm there, 'She's making a focking orse of herself – that's what she's doing. Someone needs to drag her in here.'

'I'm sorry,' he goes, 'those are our instructions.'

I'm there, 'Yeah, we'll focking see about that,' and I've suddenly forgotten the reason I came here in the first place. I storm up another flight of stairs to my old man's office and I end up bumping into Sorcha on her way out.

She looks like she's been crying.

I'm there, 'Hey, how the hell are you?'

I swear to fock, she looks around – presumably to make sure no one sees us talking to each other.

She goes, 'I know it was Honor, Ross.'

I'm there, 'Honor?' because I want to protect her. 'I've no idea what you're talking about?'

'She posted that video of me talking about the gypsy dress. It wasn't racist, Ross – not at the time.'

'Who's to say what's racist and isn't any more?'

'If she thinks this is going to deflect me from my commitment to deliver on my zero corbon torgets in the short-to-medium term –'

'I'm not sure that was her intention, Sorcha.'

She looks sad. She just shakes her head. She goes, 'She hates me.'

I'm there, 'You embarrassed her in front of people.'

She goes, 'I just can't believe she's the same girl who at five years of age said to me, "Is the company called Amazon because of all the trees they cut down for their packaging?" I cried that day, Ross.'

I'm like, 'I remember you crying.'

In fairness, at the time, she was on a course of corticosteroids for her allergic rhinitis that sent her bat-shit crazy.

'The Taoiseach has offered me his full support,' she goes. 'But Hennessy wants me to issue one of those apologies – different times, anyone who knows me knows that it doesn't reflect the kind of person that I am or the values I hold dear, get on with the job of delivering on the commitments we made to voters, blah, blah, blah.'

'Are you going to?'

'No, but I think they're playing good cop, bad cop with me.'

I'm there, 'Yeah, no, they do that.'

'Anyway,' she goes, 'I have to go,' and off she focks.

I morch past the old man's secretary into his office.

He goes, 'Kicker!' pretending that he's pleased to see me. 'How the hell are you? I was talking to your pal Boris earlier! It's looking increasingly likely that he's going to be the next PM!'

I'm there, 'What the fock is going on with the old dear?'

He's like, 'What do you mean?'

'She's out on the balcony,' I go, 'ranting and raving like a focking crazy person.'

He's there, 'Oh, she's just connecting with her public!'

'They're laughing at her. Dude, she's not well – in the head.'

'I've told the chaps that if they think she's crossing a line into, well, madness – or taking her clothes off – they're to intervene immediately! Don't worry, Kicker!'

Hennessy steps into the room then. He's got, like, a big smirk on his face.

I'm there, 'How are things, Hennessy?'

He goes, 'Busy – too busy to waste time talking to you.'

I'm like, 'But not too busy that you can take on a juvenile shop-lifting case.'

The old man's there, 'Oh, yes, I heard about Rihanna-Brogan! The poor child is obviously missing her father!'

Hennessy whips out his phone, presses a button, then holds it to his ear.

I'm there, 'I know your game. Both of you. And I'm here to tell you that it's not going to work. Ronan isn't coming home – ever.'

And into his phone, Hennessy goes, 'Can you send someone from security up to the Taoiseach's office to throw a man down the stairs, please?'

The old man laughs and goes, 'Oh, Hennessy! You'd humour a dying man!'

But I can tell from Hennessy's face that he's not joking – he's not joking at all.

Roz looks incredible tonight. Yeah, no, we're in The Goat and I'm on my best behaviour, which means actually listening to what the girl has to say – she's describing some boring dream she had two nights ago – while trying *not* to stare at her Julius Squeezers, which look tremendous, by the way, from the two or three accidental glimpses that I've had of them.

She goes, 'So how have you been?' just as I'm sinking a mouthful of the golden wonder.

I'm there, 'Yeah, no, things have been quiet – the way I like it!'

She goes, 'I heard you threw MacDara out of an upstairs window,' but she's laughing as she says it.

I'm there, 'It's true what they say – nothing stays a secret for long in South Dublin. Although, as I keep pointing out to Honor, I accidentally dropped him in the course of trying to put the *frighteners* on him?'

She goes, 'Sincerity said he had it coming to him.'

I'm there, 'She didn't go to the flicks with him in the end?'

She's like, 'No – because she knew how much Honor likes him. Anyway, she's keen on this other boy now. His name's, like, *Jonah*?'

I'm there, '*Jonah*?' trying to remember if Honor has ever mentioned him before. 'Yeah, no, that's a new one on me. I like the sound of him, though.'

'He's a boy she met in Dundrum with Honor. They've been texting.'

'She's certainly getting around – and that's not me, I don't know, slut-shaming the girl. And can I ask the all-important –'

'High School Rathgor,' she goes.

I'm there, 'Fair focks. Fair focking focks.'

'So,' she suddenly goes out of absolutely nowhere, 'did you read the book?'

I'm like, 'The which?'

She's there, 'Ross –'

I'm like, 'I honestly *meant* to? But there's just been so much shit going on.'

She goes, 'Did you even open it?'

I'm there, 'You have to understand, Roz, that I've never read a book that wasn't by either Brian O'Driscoll, Ronan O'Gara or Johnny Sexton. Could you even maybe give me the gist of it?'

She shakes her head, but at the same time she's *smiling*? I think she's genuinely very fond of me.

'Okay,' she goes, 'tantra is an Indian form of meditation that can be used to make sex slower and more satisfying. The whole goal is to make it a long, sensual experience, to enjoy the closeness and intimacy and to put off orgasm for as long as possible.'

I'm like, 'Sting –'

She's there, 'Forget about Sting, Ross. It isn't about setting a stop-watch. It's about feeling a heightened sense of sensuality and connection. It's about becoming aware of each other's breathing, sounds, movements.'

I'm like, 'This actually reminds me of –'

She goes, 'What?'

'No, it's going to come out all wrong.'

'No, Ross, tell me.'

'Yeah, no, back in my famous rugby-playing days, I used to use, like, visualization exercises as port of my kicking technique. I was able to, like, blank out the crowd – the haters, let's be honest.'

'That's exactly what tantra is, Ross. It's mindfulness.'

'So you're saying I could use, like, similar mind tricks to, er, keep the cork in the bottle?'

She goes, 'Let's not talk about it,' and she stands up. 'Let's go back to mine, will we?'

I'm like, 'Er, yeah,' trying not to sound too keen, but then my orse is already up off the stool. 'Where's Sincerity tonight?'

She goes, 'She's staying over at Raymond's.'

So I knock back the rest of my pint, then off we head. I've got a big dopey grin on my face, like someone who's been handed a giant novelty cheque and been told to smile for the camera, as I follow her outside.

We go into the gaff and head straight upstairs. I try to throw the lips on her, but she pushes me backwards onto the bed and goes, 'It's all about *delaying* gratification. We're going to meditate together.'

I'm like, 'Er, cool.'

She kicks off her white Converse and lies down on the bed next to me. She goes, 'Close your eyes. Now, slowly, become aware of your surroundings. Use your five senses to absorb everything that's going on around you.'

I'm there, 'This is literally what I did to improve my kicking. Are there definitely five, by the way?'

She goes, 'Just concentrate, Ross. Now, inhale deeply and slowly, then exhale and empty your lungs – like you're blowing out a candle. Do it with me. Let's do it together. Let's sync our breathing.'

We do that for a good – I shit you not – twenty minutes.

She goes, 'Okay, as you breathe, arch your back and lift your pelvis.'

I'm like, 'My –'

'Pelvis.'

'I thought that's what you said.'

'Now, start doing it rhythmically. Up and down. Up and down. Feel yourself letting go of your stress. You're connecting with your body and your emotions.'

Jesus Christ, I've a boner on me like a policeman's torch.

'Now,' she goes, 'open your eyes and look into mine.'

Yeah, no, we're suddenly lying side by side.

She goes, 'Try to maintain eye contact for as long as possible.'

I do. I end up totally losing myself in her eyes, which I've noticed for the first are, like, *blue*?

'Keep focusing on your breathing. Now, touch my body – slowly. Remember, we're not in any rush here.'

Typical of me, I go straight for the old blouse clowns. I slip my hand into her bra and have a good rummage around.

'Slowly,' she keeps going.

She takes off my t-shirt and storts tracing her fingers over the rough terrain of my abs.

'I can hear your breathing,' she goes.

I'm like, 'Yeah, no, I can hear yours.'

We spend a good – I'm not making this up – forty minutes, feeling each other up and taking off each other's clothes item by item – my Dubes, her cut-off jeans and her knickers with them, my chinos and my boxers, her white camisole top.

Then finally, once we're naked, she throws the lips on me. Her mouth tastes of Pinot Grigio and bacon fries – yeah, no, she had one or two of my bacon fries, although in fairness I did offer to buy them for her. We kiss – just kiss – for, like, half an hour, then things go up a gear.

She burps the old worm for a bit, then she tells me to stand up, which I do. I pick her up and she wraps her legs around my waist and her orms around my shoulders. Again, there's more kissing and every time we pause to take a breath she goes, 'Remember – it's about connection, okay?'

At this stage, in normal circumstances, I'd be finishing off, then making my apologies around about now. But I feel weirdly in the zone tonight, my eyes lock on hers, listening to my breathing and her groans, while using all of my famous focus to *not* come.

We keep on kissing with her still clinging to me like a human papoose and it's not long before I stort to feel it in my lower back. I picked up a lumbar strain playing for Seapoint against Cork Con back in the day and Roz is the kind of woman who enjoys her food, not that there's anything wrong with that. But – again – I use the same visual exercises I used back in my rugby-playing days to stop myself from dropping her on her orse.

Eventually, though, it becomes too much – like I said, she's no stranger to a spice bag – and I lie her down on the bed. She grabs me by the hair and sort of, like, pushes my head down and I know what's required of me. Again, using one or two old tricks to help me with my focus, I spend literally twenty minutes – I don't know, I'm trying to think of a nice way of putting it – licking bisque off the proverbial borbershop floor, while she screams like she's being murdered.

When she's had her fill of that, she taps out and that's when the dirty talk starts. She looks deep into my eyes and tells me that she's going to fock me to death tonight and she hopes I've made a will because she's going to make orphans of every single one of my focking children.

And there I'm going to fade the scene to black, out of fear of the story sounding like a cheap porn movie. All I will say – not to hammer the point home – is that the proceedings continue long into the night, so long that I end up losing track of time – although it's definitely *hours*? – the two of us throwing each other around the room like focking circus performers, me following her very specific instructions to lick, bite, kiss and fiddle with her various bits, and her making all sorts of sweary threats – me dying intestate seems to be a bit of an obsession with her – until she announces, as if addressing a crowd of thousands, that she's about to come, then makes a mournful mooing sound like a cow that's been separated from its calf.

Afterwards, we lie there for a few minutes, me on top of her, her staring at the ceiling as if she's witnessed some traumatic event.

I'm like, 'Was that okay?' and at the same time I realize that I actually didn't finish up myself.

'Okay?' she goes – then she laughs and says something that no one has ever said to me in my life.

She's like, 'That was the best I've ever had.'

I tell Honor that I saw her old dear and she ignores me and carries on looking for whatever she's looking for.

I'm there, 'Don't go mad, but she thinks it was possibly you who

posted the video of her talking about the – sorry for being racist –
but *gypsy* dress?'

She goes, 'It *was* me,' and she carries on turning the kitchen over.
'Have you seen my Chorlotte Tilbury lipliner?'

I'm there, 'Yeah, no, Hennessy is telling her that she should, like,
apologize.'

'She *should* apologize,' Honor goes. 'She's a focking racist bitch.'

I'm there, 'I've said my piece. So where are you and Sincerity
heading today?'

She goes, 'We're just going to, like, Herbert *Pork*?'

'And can I ask who you're meeting there?'

'Why, do you want to throw them out the window as well?'

'Honor, I told you, it was an accident.'

'I don't care. I'm actually *glad* you did it?'

'Really?'

'Yeah, MacDara is a bit of an orsehole.'

'Yeah, no, I didn't get a good vibe off him.'

'Can you believe he actually, like, *friend*-zoned me?'

'Fock off!'

'He liked Sincerity. He asked her to go to the cinema with him.'

I'm there, 'MacDara?' because I still love saying his name.
'MacDara did that? MacDara?'

'Sincerity said no,' she goes, 'because she's loyal to me.'

I'm there, 'I had high hopes for MacDara – although that was
mainly based on him being called MacDara. I'm sorry it didn't work
out. With MacDara.'

She goes, 'It doesn't matter. I like this *other* boy now? His name's,
like, *Jonah*?'

Oh, fock.

I'm like, 'Jonah? As in, like, Jonah from High School Rathgor?'

She looks at me with her mouth open.

She's there, 'How do you know he goes to High School
Rathgor?'

I'm like, 'Er, I don't know. It's, em, a real High School Rathgor
name, isn't it? Like the way half the kids in Gonzaga are called
Hugo.'

All of a sudden, I hear a voice out in the hallway go, 'Honor, I found your lipliner,' and – yeah, no – it ends up being the famous Sincerity. A second later, she's standing in the doorway and I end up having to do a *double*-take? Yeah, no, the girl is done up like a focking catwalk model. My hort immediately breaks for Honor.

I'm there, 'Sincerity, would you mind if I had just a quick word with my daughter in private?' and I walk over and close the kitchen door in her face.

Honor's there, 'Oh my God, Dad, that's *so* rude!'

I'm like, 'Is that your top and skirt she's wearing?' because I hate seeing the girl being taken for a mug.

She's there, 'Yeah – so what?'

'I'm wondering would she not be more comfortable in her focking nerd clothes?'

'What?'

'Yeah, no, put her back in the hoodies and the combats. Wash that focking make-up off her face.'

'Why?'

Oh my God, this is so hord. How can I tell my daughter that she's basically the Ugly Best Friend in this relationship?

I'm there, 'You're going to Herbert Pork, Honor, presumably to watch boys throw a rugby ball around. She's taking the focking piss.'

She goes, 'You were the one who asked me to be friends with her? I'm doing this as a favour to you – because I want it to work out with you and her mom.'

'I know that. And it's going well, by the way.'

'Is it?'

'*Very* focking well. Although I won't go into the nitty-gritty because Sincerity can probably hear us through that door. And because obviously you're my daughter.'

That's when the kitchen door is thrown open and Erika walks in, going, 'What are you doing standing outside the door, Sincerity? Come in,' so she does.

Amelie is there. Erika was bringing her to the dentist for, like, a

check-up. The kid goes, 'Sincerity, you look really pretty,' and then –
yeah, no – she says fock-all to Honor.

I'm there, 'I'm wondering is it not a bit OTT for Herbert Pork,
though? Should she not be back in her focking hoodies and her
focking combats?'

Everyone ignores this basic point.

Erika goes, 'How did you get here, Sincerity? Did your mum
drop you?'

Sincerity's like, 'No, I got the bus. My mom is very tired today.'

I'm thinking, Yeah, no, she would be.

She goes, 'And her back is sore. She thinks she might have over-
done it in her spin class.'

Again, I'm saying nothing.

Erika's like, 'What was that, Ross?'

I'm there, 'I don't think I spoke, did I?'

She goes, 'You sort of, like, guffawed.'

I'm there, 'I'm not sure I did, Erika,' and then the doorbell ends
up saving me.

Honor's like, 'That'll be our Uber,' and I'm thinking, A focking
taxi? To Herbert Pork? You wouldn't blame them! But then Sincerity can barely walk in those four-inch heels. She staggers up the
hallway after Honor and I turn to Erika and go, 'A focking Uber? To
Herbert Pork? You wouldn't blame them!'

All of a sudden, I hear shouting in the hallway. It's, like, a dude's
voice going, 'Where is he? Where's your dad?'

Erika's like, 'Is that JP?'

I'm there, 'It certainly sounds like him.'

And then into the kitchen he morches, looking like a man who
wants to murder someone. And that someone just so happens to
be me.

He points at me and goes, 'I am going focking kill you!'

Erika's like, 'JP, whatever he's done, can I just remind you that
there are children in this house? Amelie, go upstairs.'

JP storts walking towards me and I back away from him to the
other side of the island.

I'm like, 'Dude,' with my two hands raised, 'whatever you think I've done, I didn't do it.'

He goes, 'You told Delma to have her lips done.'

I'm there, 'I didn't. I just mentioned that you happened to like mickey –. Amelie, your old dear told you to go upstairs.'

'Well, she *had* them done,' he goes. 'She went to focking Turkey to have them done.'

I'm like, 'Oh, right – this was the famous early Christmas present she was talking about?' just trying to calm the situation, because he's, like, following me around and around the island.

Erika goes, 'JP, what happened?'

He's like, 'What happened? I'll tell you what happened. She's destroyed herself.'

I'm there, 'In terms of?' still backing away, keen to stay out of punching range.

He goes, 'She looks focking hideous!'

I'm there, 'Dude, I'm sure she doesn't look hideous.'

At that exact moment, the woman herself steps into the kitchen. And – yeah, no – let's just say that it's a day for double-takes.

'Jesus focking Christ!' I go. 'Jesus focking Christ!'

I'm thinking, Okay, stop saying Jesus focking Christ!

I'm there, 'Jesus focking Christ!'

He wasn't exaggerating. Delma has – oh my God – *the* most enormous trout pout I've ever seen. She looks like an actual sex doll.

Amelie screams at the sight of her – a proper, full-on scream.

Delma goes, 'JP, let's go,' but her lips are so swollen that she can barely speak. 'I don't want this.'

But JP is just, like, glowering at me, going, 'Look at her! Take a focking look at her!'

I'm there, 'I can't! I can't!' because it actually *hurts* to look at her?

Honor and Sincerity are back in the kitchen and they're just, like, staring at the woman like she's a circus freak.

Sincerity is going, 'Oh my God, your poor face! Oh my God, your poor face!'

And I'm like, 'Yeah, you're not exactly *helping* here, Sincerity?'

Delma goes, 'JP, please! Let's go home!'

And I'm like, 'Dude, I'm sure it won't look as bad after a few –'
but I don't get to say the word 'beers' because JP has suddenly
thrown a punch at me. It lands right on my chin and I go down like
a detonated building.

Erika goes, 'Amelie – upstairs! Girls, go outside and wait for your
taxi!'

I'm lying on the deck with JP standing over me. He jabs his finger
in my pretty much face and goes, 'You and me are focking done.'

5.

Live and Let Tie

So it's, like, Wednesday night and Roz invites me over for dinner. Sincerity is staying with her old man tonight and she's doing a spag bol – her old dear's recipe, she says, although she doesn't have any Pormigiano Reggiano.

I laugh as I kiss her and hand her a bottle of red. It's none of your Châteauneuf-du-Crap either. It cost me, like, twenty-something sheets, although I decide not to make an issue of it, which is the classy thing to do.

I'm there, 'No Pormigiano Reggiano? Talk about First World problems!'

'Apparently, it's because of Irexit,' she goes. 'The shelves in Donnybrook Fair were half empty today.'

I'm there, 'Fock!' at the same time realizing that I have a massive horn on me just looking at her.

'Apparently, imports from Europe have completely stopped,' she goes. 'You can't buy Iberico ham in this country now for love nor money.'

I'm there, 'Did you try Thomas's in Foxrock? He has everything.'

'I did,' she goes. 'He was the one who was telling me he can't get Kalamata olives or even black pumpernickel.'

I'm there, 'Jesus, I'm sorry for making light of it a second ago. That's, em, a *good* bottle of wine, by the way? I drove all the way to Mitchell's for it.'

She goes, 'I wouldn't know,' barely even glancing at the label. 'I'm not exactly a connoisseur.'

Oh, for fock's sake.

I'm there, 'Maybe you should just open a bottle of Dadá then and I'll hang onto this. I'm only mentioning it because it cost, like, twenty-something sheets and I was under the impression that you *knew* your wine?'

She goes, 'No, I'm sure it's lovely, though,' totally missing the point that it's possibly wasted on her.

I'm there, 'So, er, I really enjoyed the old tartare –'

She's like, 'Tantric.'

'– the old tantric sex.'

She kisses me on the lips. I'm getting the impression that it might be on the old menu again tonight.

She goes, 'You see how good it can be when you take your time and remember to breathe?'

I'm there, 'It's *exactly* the same as kicking. Who knew?'

She opens the bottle and pours us each a glass. Then she serves up the spag and we both sit down at the table.

'So how have you been?' she goes.

She looks fantastic and I'm only mentioning that for colour. I can't stop staring at the outline of her shirt potatoes and I couldn't be a hundred per cent sure that she's even wearing a bra.

I'm there, 'Yeah, no, not bad – although JP's still pissed off with me.'

She goes, 'Is her face really that bad?'

I'm there, 'It looks like someone smashed her in the mouth with a snow shovel. And of course I'm the one being blamed – not the surgeon who actually *did* it to her, by the way?'

'That seems very unfair.'

'Yeah, no, he butchered her face. But it's apparently my fault – because I just so happened to mention that JP was a lips man.'

'Is it really awful – her mouth, I mean?'

'I'm not going to lie to you, Roz, she looks like something you'd catch off Dún Laoghaire Pier using lugworms.'

'Poor her.'

'Er, poor me as well, Roz. I'm more of a victim than *she* is in all of this? I mean, she did that to herself. I've lost another mate – again, through no fault of my own.'

She goes, 'I'm sure JP will come around.'

But I'm there, 'I'm not sure he will, Roz. I've phoned the dude four or five times now and he just keeps putting the phone down on me.'

As I'm saying it, I find myself getting, I don't know, *emotional*?

She reaches across the table and puts her hand on top of mine.

I'm there, 'I'm sorry, I just thought that me and the goys would always be friends. I mean, we played rugby together. That used to mean something.'

She goes, 'They won't stay angry forever.'

I'm there, 'I wouldn't count on it. You'd want to see Delma's face. Swing into that interiors shop of hers if you're passing through Ranelagh and have a sneaky look. It's pure focking comical.'

'Even so, I'm sure he's not going to let it destroy a perfectly good friendship.'

'This is all good stuff for me to hear, Roz. You're talking about a bunch of goys who wouldn't have a Leinster Schools Senior Cup medal between them if it wasn't for me. And yet Oisinn is the only one who's talking to me at this precise moment in time.'

'It must be awful for you.'

'He wants us to go on a double date, by the way, with him and Magnus.'

'Okay.'

I'm there, 'It's the night before my – I suppose – *trial*? It's also the night before the goys head off to do the Camino. He's thinking in terms of Volpe Nera in Blackrock.'

'How do you feel about that?' she goes.

I'm there, 'Yeah, no, I've heard good things. They've got, like, a Michelin stor.'

She's like, 'I was talking about your friends doing the Camino – without you.'

'Fock them,' I go. 'They're not my friends any more,' but she can tell that I don't mean it. 'I saw Fionn, JP and Christian out training the other night, walking up Ballinclea Road with all their North Face clobber on them. I wound down the window and shouted, "Eat, Pray, Love!" at them, then gave them the finger.'

She smiles at me sadly. Her hort is broken for me.

'Speaking of dates,' she – out of nowhere – goes, 'that boy Jonah asked Sincerity out.'

I end up nearly choking on a mouthful of the far-from-cheap wine.

I'm there, 'I'm presuming she told him to fock off?'

She goes, 'No, she didn't.'

I'm like, 'Er, she does know that Honor's keen on him, doesn't she?'

'Well, that's why she said no to him originally. But I had a chat with her last night. I hope you don't mind.'

'A chat? Er – in terms of *what* exactly?'

'I just told her that she shouldn't keep turning boys down just because Honor happens to like them.'

'Er, shouldn't she?'

'Well, no. If a boy likes her and she likes him, then she should be free to go out with him if she wants.'

I'm there, 'That's one way of looking at it, I suppose.'

I doubt if that's the way Honor will see it. This is a girl, bear in mind, who she dragged from the slums of Dweebsville. She dressed her up and slapped make-up on her and this is how the girl repays her.

Roz goes, 'I told Sincerity that she should text him back and tell him that she will go out with him after all.'

There's a name for girls like that and it begins with a B. I should point out to her that her daughter is in danger of getting a reputation, except I don't get the chance because my phone all of a sudden rings. I can see the name on the screen.

I'm there, 'It's Astrid.'

Roz goes, 'Who's Astrid?' and she says it in a sort of, like, *jealous* way?

I'm there, 'Hey, if you saw her, you wouldn't be worried. A focking hitman wouldn't take her out. Yeah, no, she's my old dear's nanny. She's German, if that doesn't sound too racist.'

She goes, 'You should answer it,' because I've obviously put her mind at ease. 'It might be important.'

So that's what I end up doing. I can hear the panic in the woman's voice straight away.

She goes, 'Ross, I did not know who else to call.'

I'm there, 'What's wrong?'

She's like, 'I'm at the hospital.'

'The hospital?' I go. 'Which hospital?'

She's there, 'Blanchardstown Hospital.'

I'm like, 'Jesus focking Christ!' then I suddenly realize that I haven't even asked her *why* she's in Blanchardstown Hospital. But, deep down, I probably *already* know?

'It's your mother,' she goes.

I'm there, 'My old dear?' and Roz immediately stands up. 'What happened?'

Astrid goes, 'She fell down the stairs.'

I'm like, 'Fock! Is she okay?'

She's there, 'She has fractured her collarbone.'

I'm suddenly up off the chair. Roz – in fairness to her – goes, 'I'll drive. I only had a sip of the wine,' and she grabs her cor keys.

We take the M50 to – again, I'm saying it – Blanchardstown, driving mostly in silence. Some dude on the radio says that Boris Johnson is the new Prime Minister of Britain and I actually laugh, even though I've no idea why. It's possibly nerves.

We reach the hospital and we find the ward. Astrid is standing outside in the corridor, with Cassiopeia, Diana, Mellicent, Louisa May, Emily and Hugo. She's trying to stop them from wandering off but it's like herding cats. I've never seen a woman look so stressed. I'm sure it's a relief to Roz to see how bet-down the woman is in real life.

I'm there, 'Astrid?'

She looks at me and goes, 'Ross! I cannot do this any more! I am paid to look after these children – not this crazy old woman!'

I'm there, 'Where's my old man?'

She's like, 'He is gone to London.'

I'm there, 'What the fock is he doing in London?'

She's like, 'He goes to see Boris Johnson, who is new Prime Minister. I phone him and I say, "Your wife has fallen down stairs." He says to me, "I am away on Government business! You are paid to deal with problems, not bring them to me!" I'm sorry, Ross, I quit.'

I'm there, 'You can't just quit. Who's going to look after the kids?'

'Perhaps you,' she goes.

I'm like, 'I can't. I'm quite possibly going to prison soon.'

176

'It is not my problem,' she goes.

I'm there, 'Please don't quit. Look, I'll be having serious words with the old man when he gets home. Just let me go in and see the old dear first.'

So into the ward I go. The old dear is sitting up in the bed with her shoulder heavily bandaged and strapped.

She goes, 'Oh, hello, Ross,' as casually as if she were sitting in the bor in Foxrock Golf Club with four fingers of Tanqueray inside her. 'How are you, Dorling?'

I'm like, 'How am *I*? How are *you* is more like it?'

'Oh, there's nothing wrong with me,' she goes. 'I don't even understand why I've been committed?'

I'm there, 'Committed? What are you shitting on about?'

'I keep telling them there's nothing wrong with my mind. But they're insisting on cutting my head open – looking for God knows what!'

She cops Roz standing in the doorway. She goes, 'Oh, hello, Sorcha, Dorling. I love what you've done to your hair.'

I'm there, 'It's not Sorcha. It's a woman from Goatstown that I'm seeing called Roz.'

'Hello,' Roz goes – obviously figuring that it's nice to be nice.

The old dear squints her eyes and goes, 'Don't be absurd. I know my own daughter-in-law, thank you very much. Why isn't she wearing a bra, Ross?'

I'm there, 'Jesus Christ! Seriously?'

'Well, anyway,' the woman goes, throwing back her bedsheets then with her one good orm, 'I'm going home. I think it should be perfectly obvious to everyone by now that I don't belong in a mental institution.'

I'm there, 'You're not *in* a mental institution. You're in hospital. You fell down the stairs and broke your collarbone.'

'Oh, that's just what they want you to think,' she goes. 'I know their real interest is in cutting up my brain. They're not going to make a guinea pig out of me, Ross. I've sent Delma a text message and asked her to come and get me.'

I'm there, 'You're not going anywhere. You belong in hospital.'

'I belong at home,' she goes. 'I have important work to do. I have speeches to write. I have my public who depend on hearing from me.'

It's at that exact moment that I hear Roz behind me go, 'Oh my God! Oh, Jesus Christ!'

I look over my shoulder. It turns out that Delma has arrived on the scene and Roz is suddenly confronted with the true meaning of the phrase 'smashed in the mouth with a snow shovel'.

'Oh my God!' she keeps going, unable to stop herself. She's staring at the woman with her hand clasped over her mouth. 'Oh, Jesus! Oh, Jesus Christ!'

It's not exactly helping *my* cause, by the way?

The old dear is out of the bed now. She's down on her hunkers, trying to stuff her clothes into her overnight bag, getting ready to flee. Her hospital gown is untied at the back. It gives me no pleasure to say that I can see her orse and she looks like a focking warthog at a feeding hole.

I'm like, 'Get back in that bed! Seriously, get back in that actual bed!'

She turns to look at me. She goes, 'They want to remove my brain to steal my DNA. Why can't you and Astrid see –'

And then she suddenly cops Delma standing behind me. One of her oldest friends in the world and she doesn't even recognize her with the humungous, sink-plunger lips. This look of, like, terror comes over her face, then she storts screaming in a pitch that sounds barely even human.

She's like, 'AAAGGGHHH!' and it reminds me of the time I told her for the craic that the Guinness Gallery in Foxrock Village was being turned into a vape shop. 'AAAGGGHHH!!! AAAGGGHHH!!! AAAGGGHHH!!!'

I ring the old man and I tell him that I need to talk to him – as in, like, *urgently*?

He goes, 'I've just arrived back from London, Ross! Government jet and so forth! The Prime Minister was asking for you! I think you've got a bit of a fan there! He asked me for your number! Wants to ring you to wish you all the best with this famous court date of yours!'

I'm like, 'Dude, we need to talk – about the *old* dear?'

He goes, 'Yes, it'd be wonderful to have one of our famous tête-à-têtes! Like the old days, eh, Kicker? Why don't you call into Kildare Street this morning! They're about to stort digging the foundations for the – inverted commas – *new* Leinster House! I'm hosting a press conference.'

So – yeah, no – it's, like, half eleven in the morning when I show my pretty face on Kildare Street. The dude is already mid-speech, surrounded by the usual heads from RTÉ, Virgin Media, Newstalk and whoever else.

He's going, 'It is my sincere hope that the work that has commenced here this morning will lay to rest the opposition's frankly scurrilous claims that this Government is not committed to porliamentary democracy! Exclamation mork!'

The famous Fionnán Sheahan from the *Indo* goes, 'We've been told that it's going to take up to four years to rebuild Leinster House. Are there any plans for either house of the Oireachtas to sit in an alternative venue in the meantime? I know the National Convention Centre has been mentioned by Micheál Martin as a possible –'

The old man exchanges a look with Hennessy, who's standing off to the side. He goes, 'We're still, em, investigating that possibility – isn't that right, Hennessy?'

Hennessy just shrugs like a dude with zero focks to give.

'Yes,' the old man goes, 'as the Attorney General said, we are, of course, keen to reconvene both the Dáil and – why the hell not? – even the Seanad, provided we can identify a suitable temporary location! Now, does anybody have any questions about my visit to London yesterday and my talks with the Prime Minister, who I'm very excited to tell you is absolutely determined to deliver on the electorally expressed wish of the people of the United Kingdom to secede, like us, from the failed European Über Staat!'

Some other dude – I'm pretty sure it's Pat Leahy – goes, 'Taoiseach, are you aware of reports this morning that many shops in the

Republic are experiencing supply problems with respect to vital foodstuffs?'

I laugh. I wonder is Roz listening to this?

The old man goes, 'I am aware of some anecdotal *evidence* – and I wish to italicize that last word – that, yes, people are experiencing some temporary difficulties in sourcing several EU-manufactured products! We are – if nothing else – an adaptable race! There are always alternatives to these products! And this is the price that I believe the people of Ireland are prepared to pay to guarantee their sovereignty and their independence!'

'When you mention alternatives,' the famous Miriam Lord goes, rooting around in her handbag for something, then whipping out – believe it or not – a block of cheese, 'do you mean this non-PDO Roquefort that I bought in Fallon & Byrne this morning? There's some Chinese writing on it that literally means Cheese Product Number 12.'

The old man goes, 'The people of China are as capable of making delicious blue cheese as the French – regordless of what Jean-Claude Juncker and his ilk would have you believe!'

'Maybe you should try some!' Pat Leahy shouts.

The old man chuckles. He goes, 'I shan't dignify that with a response!'

All of a sudden, I spot Sorcha standing a few feet to my left. She's in, like, deep conversation with her old man, which is the reason I decide to tip over to them. I know I make his skin crawl.

I go, 'Sorcha!' full of the joys. 'How the hell *are* you? Chinese Roquefort, huh? I wouldn't say *you'd* be a fan.'

Her old man goes, 'Can't you see that we're having a private discussion?'

I'm like, 'Yeah?' with a big smirk on my face. 'What about?'

Sorcha goes, 'I've decided to apologize – for using the G word.'

I'm there, 'Hennessy always gets his way in the end, doesn't he?'

She goes, 'I was the one who offered to do it, Ross, because I felt it was distracting everyone from the vital work of Government.'

'Sorcha, it's just an empty formula of words,' her old man tries to go, 'that will allow you to get on with the job of safegording the future of this planet for your children and your children's children.'

I laugh – can't help it.

I'm there, 'Yeah, focking spare me, would you?'

Sorcha goes, 'Ross, I will never, *ever* forgive Honor for putting me through this humiliation.'

A big roar goes up from the crowd of, like, reporters. Yeah, no, the old man has been persuaded to try the Chinese Roquefort. He's, like, peeling off the wrapper with the funny writing on it and the press are all, I don't know, cheering him on.

He goes, 'I have absolutely no issue with eating it!'

He's right. He'd eat anything. He told me once that he ate panda when he was on a jolly to Tokyo with Hennessy and a few of their Anglo Irish Bank mates. I wonder has he ever told Sorcha that hilarious anecdote?

He takes a humungous bite, then he storts chewing it and eventually goes, 'Tastes exactly the same as the real thing!' which seems to disappoint *everyone*? 'Now, if you have nothing further to ask, the Minister for Climate Action would like to make a personal statement.'

He steps away from the podium just as Sorcha steps up to it.

She goes, 'As you may be aware, a video is circulating on social media showing me using a word that was in common usage in 2003 to describe a particular style of dress but which I now realize was wrong and deeply hurtful to a great many people.'

I walk over to the old man. He's like, 'Look at her, Ross! She's a born politician! A future Taoiseach – as I told her father this morning!'

He reaches into his jacket pocket and whips out a handkerchief, then uses his tongue to dislodge the giant piece of Chinese Roquefort that he's stashed in his jowls. He spits it into the handkerchief, then goes, 'Absolutely vile!'

I'm there, 'Dude, what's the story with the old dear?'

He's like, 'Your mother?' balling up the handkerchief and putting it back in his pocket. 'There's nothing wrong with her! I spoke to her an hour ago!'

I'm there, 'Er, she fell down the focking stairs yesterday and fractured her actual *collarbone*?'

'Oh, it's that bloody corpet, don't you know! I think Michael D. must have had it fitted! I've had one or two very near spills myself!'

'Dude, she's not well.'

'Oh, she's perfectly fine, Ross! As a matter of fact, she's being dischorged this morning!'

'She needs round-the-clock care.'

'She's got Astrid!'

'Astrid is there to look after the kids – which you decided to bring into the world, by the way, without a thought about who was going to actually raise them.'

I can't believe how suddenly emotional I'm getting.

'Look,' he goes, 'I had a word with Astrid last night! I've promised to double her pay and get her some extra help!'

'Dude, the old dear should be in, like, a home.'

'Oh, nonsense! She's not always like that! She just has the occasional bad day! I'm more interested in discussing what we're going to do about *your* situation!'

'*My* situation?'

'Yes, your impending appearance in front of one of our learned friends of the bench! Quote-unquote!'

'I've told you before – it's fock-all to do with you.'

'Hennessy knows him, you know!'

'Who?'

'The judge who is to decide your fate next week! They played rugby together for Lansdowne! Hennessy at loosehead and this chap at inside-centre! What a wonderful country, eh, Ross?'

'I don't want Hennessy's help.'

'But why? You don't actually *wish* to go to prison, do you?'

'Not if I can help it – but I'm not prepared to pay the price of Hennessy's help.'

'Please yourself!'

Up at the podium, Sorcha is going, 'My use of that racial slur in the video does not reflect the person that I am today or the values that I hold dear. I wish to apologize to anyone who may have been offended and I hope now to get on with delivering on my commitment to achieve corbon neutrality for Ireland in the medium term.'

All of a sudden, my phone beeps in my pocket. I whip it out and it ends up being – yeah, no – a message from Sorcha's sister. It's, like, a photograph and I end up staring at it for a good, like, twenty seconds before I realize that it's an x-ray of her – I want to say – *womb*? Or, more pacifically, it's an x-ray of her womb with an actual baby inside.

The message with it is like, 'Had my three-month scan!!! Oh my God, this baby is the actual IMAGE of you!!!'

Five hours later and I still can't stop *looking* at it? And the more I look at it, the more like me the baby looks, even though the thing is, like, tiny? I'm looking at the shape of its head and even the way its tiny little hands seem to be giving the guns, although that could just be my imagination. I've been staring at the screen for so long now that it's possible I'm storting to hallucinate.

Helen goes, 'What little baby is that?'

Yeah, no, she's just walked into the kitchen. I quickly put my phone face-down on the table.

I'm there, 'Sorry, Helen?'

'You were muttering the words "Little baby!"'

'Was I? Oh, yeah, no, it was just a funny video that, em, someone sent me.'

'Will you have a cup of coffee?'

Like I said – *so* like Devin Toner.

I'm there, 'Yeah, if you're making one.'

She goes, 'How's your mum doing? Erika said she's in hospital.'

I'm like, 'Yeah, no, they dischorged her this morning. Broke her collarbone. She shouldn't be on her own.'

She's there, 'Poor Fionnuala.'

'It's so random to hear you say that – you know, after everything that's happened.'

In other words, the old dear stealing the old man *from* her? Not once, but twice.

She goes, 'I was always very fond of Fionnuala.'

I'm there, 'The old man is in total denial about what's happening with her.'

She's like, 'It must be so difficult for him.'

I'm there, 'I hope you don't mind me saying this, Helen, but you remind me a lot of big Devin Toner.'

She goes, 'Who's big Devin Toner?'

And I think, Jesus Christ, I'm glad the dude isn't sitting within earshot of us, because that'd break his focking hort in two.

I'm there, 'Leinster and Ireland second-row, Helen. Four Heineken Cups. Three Six Nations Championships, including a Grand Slam. Take it as a compliment.'

'Oh,' she goes, smiling to herself, 'I will.'

It's at that exact moment that the kitchen door opens and the expression on Helen's face suddenly changes.

'Oh my God!' she goes, her face – I swear to fock – visibly whitening. 'What have you done?'

I turn around and it ends up being – yeah, no – Rihanna-Brogan. It takes me about ten seconds to notice what it is that's caused Helen to lose her world-famous composure and big-match temperament. Rihanna-Brogan has a humungous Indian ink spot on her right cheek below her eye.

I end up flying off the handle. I'm like, 'What the fock? What the focking fock is that?'

Rihanna-Brogan goes, 'It's a borstoddle meerk,' and she sort of, like, casually throws open the fridge.

I'm there, 'It's a what?'

She goes, 'A borstoddle meerk. People get them when thee do their foorst stint in jayult.'

I'm there, 'I know what a focking borstal mork is. I went to enough parents' evenings at Ronan's so-called school. I'm asking why have you got one?'

She goes, 'I think thee look nice,' slamming the fridge door, having decided there's nothing in there that interests her. 'And so do alt me freddens on Instagraddam.'

I'm there, 'Instagram? You put it up on Instagram? What if

Ronan –' and then I stop, because I suddenly realize that that's the reason she actually did it.

The front door slams then. I'm there, 'Oh, I can't wait to hear what Honor has to say about this!'

Except Honor doesn't come down to the kitchen. She just tramps up the stairs and I'm pretty sure I can hear crying.

Helen's there, 'It sounds like she's upset about something.'

I roll my eyes and go, 'Yeah, best leave her to cool off for a few hours – and I'm saying that from past experience. She tends to say hurtful things when she's upset, especially about my rugby career – or lack thereof.'

'Or,' Helen goes, 'you could go upstairs and find out what's upset her.'

I just stare back at her. It's exactly the kind of thing that Dev would say and I know she's right.

I'm there, 'That's what I'll do so,' and I toddle up the stairs after her.

She's sitting on the end of her bed with her head in her hands, sobbing her little hort out.

I'm there, 'Honor? Are you okay?'

'Fock off,' she goes. 'You're a shit dad – just like you were a shit rugby player.'

I'm like, 'Er, okay – at least I tried,' and I turn to leave.

She goes, 'She's a focking slut, Dad.'

I love that she calls me Dad. I walk back over to her and I sit down beside her.

I'm there, 'Who?'

'Focking Sincerity,' she goes. 'She's a focking slut – and a focking bitch.'

I'm like, 'What happened?' even though I'm pretty sure I already *know* the answer?

'She's going out with Jonah,' she goes, 'to the cinema.'

I'm there, 'What are they going to see? Just as a matter of interest.'

'I don't focking know,' she goes, suddenly looking at me. Her eyes are red like she's been crying for an hour. 'Why is that important?'

I'm there, 'I don't know. I'm just trying to think of the right thing to say. There's a new Quentin Tarantino, although it might be 18s.'

She's there, 'She focking knew I liked him. That should mean he's not an option for her.'

'I agree with you – one hundred per cent.'

'You should have seen her flirting with him on the beach today. She asked him to put suntan lotion on her back – the focking slut.'

'It certainly *sounds* like slutty behaviour?'

'Do you know what she *actually* said to me? She said if I was a real friend, I'd be happy for her.'

'The focking nerve of her.'

'Focking bitch.'

'I mean, this is a girl you – again – dragged out of Dweebsville and made something out of her.'

'I focking hate her.'

'You were too good to her, Honor. You should have left her in her nerdy clothes. No one fancied her when she was a plain Jane.'

There's, like, silence between us then. She puts her head on my shoulder. After maybe thirty seconds, she goes, 'Dad, why don't boys like me?'

I'm there, 'What do you mean? They're all over you like flies on, you know – I hate to say it, Honor, but *shit*?'

'That's just because of what I did to Reese. They all think I'm a legend.'

'And what the hell is wrong with that? Speaking as one myself, of course!'

'None of them wants to *be* with me, though. They all want to be with her. Focking slapper. Focking bitch. Focking whore.'

Again, there's, like, more silence. She's so upset that it's hord to know what to say.

She goes, 'Dad, I wish I was good-looking.'

I'm there, 'You are good-looking, Honor.'

I hate lying to her, but what's the alternative?

She goes, 'I bet I end up marrying someone really, really ugly.'

I'm there, 'Looks aren't everything, Honor. You always hear people say that.'

Then, totally out of left field, she goes, 'Dad, I don't want you to go to prison.'

I'm there, 'I'm not going to prison, Honor.'

Again, it's a day for lies.

She goes, 'You're my only real friend. I don't know what I'd do if I didn't have you.'

In that moment, my hort breaks like a focking egg. *I* actually stort to cry then? But then I wipe the tears from my face and I go, 'Hey, I'll tell you something that'll hopefully make you laugh! Rihanna-Brogan got a borstal mork on her face!'

Someone has written 'Irexit = I Wrecked Shit!' on a wall in Herbert Pork and it's obvious that the shortage of things like prosciutto and – Roz mentioned yesterday – pomegranates is really storting to bite in this port of the world.

Yeah, no, it's one of my famous unsupervised access days with the boys and I'm sitting on a bench with Honor, who's got her nose buried in her phone as usual.

She goes, 'Sincerity texted me.'

I'm there, 'I'll say it again. Where does she get the focking ego?'

'She says that she still considers me a friend and she doesn't want her relationship with Jonah to come between us.'

'Oh, she's in a *relationship* with him, is she? I can't believe I'm saying this about someone but I liked her more as a dork.'

'I'm not even going to bother replying. I'm going to focking ghost her. It'll drive her mad.'

I'm watching Brian, Johnny and Leo through the railings of the playground. They're waiting for their turn on the swings. That's actually worth repeating. They're waiting for their turn.

'God,' I go, 'do you remember the days when they had everyone in that playground terrorized?'

Honor looks up from her phone and smiles.

'Yeah,' she goes, 'do you remember they tried to waterboard that older boy in the duck pond?'

I laugh. Can't help it.

I'm there, 'At least there was a bit of craic out of them. Yeah, no,

I think I'll get them some ice cream – hopefully the sugar rush will send them over the edge.'

I call them over. I'm like, 'Johnny! Brian! Leo!' and the three of them come running. They don't tell me to fock off or give me the finger – they literally come running.

Brian goes, 'What is it, Dad?'

I'm thinking, Who the fock *are* these children?

I hand him a fifty and I go, 'Here, get yourselves an ice-cream – syrup, a flake, the focking works.'

'We're not allowed to have sugar,' Leo goes – word for word. 'Granddad Lalor said it sends us loopy.'

I'm there, 'Well, you're not with your Granddad Lalor today. You're with your dad. And I'm telling you to have an ice cream. And a fizzy drink. A Coke. Something with caffeine in it.'

The three of them just stand there looking at me with their mouths wide open.

I'm there, 'Take the focking money and go to the ice-cream van. That's a focking order.'

They do what they're told.

I turn around to Honor and I'm like, 'Can you focking *believe* Sorcha's old man? Not allowed to have sugar because it sends them loopy?'

'He's such a wanker,' Honor goes.

I'm there, 'Wanker is the word. You know he used to give Sorcha grapes and carrot batons as treats when she was a kid? She didn't taste chocolate until she was, like, seventeen.'

'Explains a lot,' Honor goes.

My phone all of a sudden rings. I check the screen.

'Fock,' I go. 'It's Ronan.'

She's like, 'Answer it.'

I'm there, 'I can't. What if he's been on Instagram and he's ringing to find out why his daughter has a focking borstal mork?'

'Dad,' she goes, 'answer the focking phone.'

So that's what I end *up* doing?

I'm there, 'Ronan, how the hell are you? I can't talk right now. I'm at a funeral.'

He goes, 'Would you ebber ast me boddicks – at a funerdoddle, you bleaten spoofer! Amn't I looking sthraight at you!'

I look up and I spot him standing literally twenty feet away from where we're sitting. Me and Honor are up off the bench like the thing is on fire. We run towards him and throw our orms around him.

He's like, 'Howiya, Rosser? Howiya, Hodor?'

I'm there, 'What the fock are you doing home?' and as I pull away from him I notice that Avery and the famous Rihanna-Brogan are standing behind him.

He goes, 'Ah, you know yisser self, Rosser. Some wooden tells you not to woody, thee'll look arthur your thaughter. Then your thaughter turdens up on Instgraddem with a tattoo on her bleaten face – which she's habbon removed by lasor surgerdoddy. Am I reet, Ri?'

Rihanna-Brogan smiles and nods her little head. She's just delighted to have her old man home.

I give Avery a hug then. I'm there, 'It's nice to finally meet you in person.'

She goes, 'You too. Ronan talks about you – oh my God – *all* the time?'

'I wouldn't say *all* the toyum,' Ronan goes, obviously embarrassed.

'*All* the time,' she goes. 'And when he's not talking about Rosser or Ri, he's talking about his stunning sister.'

To my great shame, I end up looking around me, wondering who the fock she could be talking about. It turns out she's talking about Honor.

'Oh my God,' Honor goes, just staring at her, 'you are *so* pretty!'

Avery's there, 'So are you!' moving in for the hug. 'You're absolutely gorgeous,' and I have to admit that I'd have one or two concerns about my son being with a girl who can lie without even looking even remotely embarrassed about it.

I'm like, 'So how long are you goys staying? When is Rihanna-Brogan having a tattoo removed again?'

Ronan goes, 'Ine not hee-or to see Ri hab lasor surgerdoddy, Rosser. Ine hee-or for your thrial.'

I'm there, 'My trial?' and I can feel my eyes storting to fill up.

He goes, 'You didn't think I'd let you go through that on yisser owen, did you?'

I'm like, 'Jesus, Ro.'

'Plus,' he goes, 'I know one or two heads – including Gull and Buckets – who can teddle you what to expect in prison.'

I'm there, 'Er, great.'

'Hee-or,' he goes, suddenly looking around him, 'where's the boyuz?'

I'm there, 'They're playing on the, em –' and, as I turn around to look at the playground, I notice that the three of them are queuing for the swings again – and there's no sign of ice creams or fizzy drinks in their hands.

I end up losing it.

I'm there, 'Brian! Johnny! Leo! Get the fock over here now!'

Again, they come running. They spot Ronan first and it's all hugs and kisses and blah, blah, blah.

I'm like, 'Never mind all that. I told you to have ice creams and fizzy drinks.'

Avery – meaning well – goes, 'Oh my God, do you know how bad that much sugar is for children?'

I feel like nearly telling her to stay the fock out of it.

Leo goes, 'A boy took our money.'

I'm there, 'What boy?'

Brian goes, 'I don't want to say. I don't want to be a tout,' at the same time sneaking a look at Ronan.

I'm there, 'Tell me what boy took my fifty focking notes.'

Eventually, it's Johnny who points to this big-boned kid with a skinhead, who just so happens to be pushing his way to the front of the queue for the swings, shoving kids out of his way.

I'm there, 'Do you remember when that used to be you? Okay, the three of you, go and tell him that you want my fifty back.'

None of them moves.

Leo goes, 'I didn't want an ice cream or a drink anyway.'

I've never been more ashamed of my children – and that's saying something, given that Johnny used the C word on the *Late Late Toy Show*.

I'm there, 'That's not the focking point. He took fifty snots off you and you all just stood there and let him.'

Again, they don't seem in any way *embarrassed* by this?

Honor goes, '*I'll* get it back!' and then she morches off in the direction of the playground.

She walks up to this dude just as he's climbing onto the swing. She says something to him, which I don't hear, then he says something back to her, which I do. Well, I hear the end of it. It's like, 'Something, something, something – you ugly focking bitch.'

Then – I shit you not – the dude spits in Honor's face.

What happens next happens in the blink of an eye. Honor suddenly kicks the legs from under him and the dude hits the deck with a heavy thump. Then she grabs him by the legs and she drags him all the way to the edge of the duck pond. She picks him up by the ankles and she sticks his head into the water, then pulls it out again, like she's dunking a Hobnob.

The kid, by the way, is screaming.

'Oh my God,' Avery goes, 'she's going to drown him.'

I'm there, 'She's only waterboarding him. Don't stop her. These boys need to remember how the real world works.'

Honor sticks his head in the water three times before the boy apologizes to her and agrees to give up the money. She drops him face-first on the ground, rolls him over and takes the fifty from his pocket.

I feel suddenly sad, thinking about the day when I might not be here to help them deal with this kind of situation.

'And that,' I go, 'is how we deal with pricks.'

'You sicken me – you privileged, South Dublin thug.'

Yeah, no, it'd be fair to say that Frankie de Felice still hasn't warmed to me. I turn to Ronan – who's studying the famous chisel in the glass case – and I go, 'He does this, by the way, throwing out insults, to try to push the meeting into a second billable hour.'

Frankie keeps glowering at me across his desk. 'You worthless, entitled piece of new-money filth,' he goes.

I'm there, 'I'll tell you what, why don't we agree now that I'll pay for a second hour, then you won't have to keep coming up with new ways to insult me and we can all be out of here in fifteen minutes?'

He goes, 'You brain-damaged streak of human urine.'

Ronan sits down beside me. He's there, 'So what are he's chaddences, Frankie?'

Frankie goes, 'Chances? Chances of what?'

'He's chaddences of staying ourra jayult?'

Frankie sort of, like, laughs to himself.

'I'd say he has two hopes,' he goes. 'Slim and none. And slim just left town.'

I'm there, 'People from my background have walked away from worse shit than this. They do it all the time. And you're supposed to be good at getting people off. Or do all those tabloid front pages out there mean nothing?'

'The facts,' he goes, drumming the table with his index finger, 'are these. You performed an act of indecent exposure in a pub where women and children were present.'

I'm there, 'It's called a mooner – but continue.'

He goes, 'You gave someone else's name and address when arrested. Then you appeared in court and allowed someone else to be convicted of a crime of which they knew nothing.'

I notice Ronan beside me nodding along – my own focking son, bear in mind.

Frankie goes, 'Those people in those tabloid stories you mentioned – you know what they all had in common? They had charm. They had likeability. How the hell am I going to get a jury to like you?'

Ronan offers absolutely zilch on this question, by the way.

I go, 'Okay, can I mention a word that no one seems to be bringing up here? And that word is rugby.'

The dude looks at me like I've just storted picking my teeth with his letter opener.

'That's your legal strategy?' he goes. 'You want me to walk in there and announce that you played rugby?'

I'm there, 'No, I could get one or two famous ex-players to show up and say that I'm a good goy and that people just didn't get the joke.'

Ronan goes, 'Rosser, I doatunt think that's godda woork in this case.'

I'm there, 'So what *are* we suggesting – given that the trial opens the day after tomorrow.'

'Plead guilty,' Frankie goes.

I'm there, 'On what basis?'

'On the basis that you *are* guilty. If we spare the legal system the expense of a trial, you could end up with a more lenient sentence.'

'Who's the finger of Fudge?' Ronan goes.

Frankie's there, 'It's Justice Bryan Hickson,' and Ronan's mouth immediately forms a little O, suggesting that I'm focked here.

I'm there, 'I happen to know that he played for Lansdowne at inside-centre. Surely that's going to stand to me?'

Frankie ends up suddenly losing his shit with me. He goes, 'You bring up rugby one more time,' pointing his finger at me, 'and you can find yourself another barrister. I have a reputation and I would like to keep it.'

Ronan's there, 'If he pleads giddlety, Frankie, what's he looking at in teerms of jayult toyum?'

'Three years,' Frankie goes and I feel my hort suddenly quicken. 'With eighteen months suspended. Throw in time off for good behaviour and he'll be out in a year.'

'A yee-or,' Ro goes, looking at me. 'That'd be a resuddult, wouldn't it, Rosser?'

I'm like, 'Er, yeah, no, definitely,' but the reality of what's about to happen to me is only really *hitting* me now?

'So you're going to switch your plea to guilty?' Frankie goes.

And I'm there, 'No, yeah, let's do it.'

'Okay,' he goes, 'now get the hell out of here – just the sight of you makes my skin crawl.'

Me and Ronan tip downstairs, then through the bookies and out onto the street. Ro tries to put a positive *spin* on shit?

He's like, 'A yee-or? Could be woorse, Rosser – a heddov a lot woorse.'

I'm there, 'Yeah, no, I'm sure the time will fly.'

'I toawult you, me mate Gull has two brutters who are screws in The Joy – thee'll make shewer you'll do yisser poddidge on a piddow.'

'My what on a what?'

'Yisser poddidge on a piddow.'

'My porridge on a pillow?'

'Mee-uns you'll hab it easy –'

'Yeah, no, I think I can guess what it means.'

'Addyhow, let's go. I toawult Avody we'd meet her for luddench. Ine dying for her to see The Broken Eerms.'

That's when, all of sudden, out of nowhere, I end up just bursting into tears.

Ronan goes, 'Jaysus sakes, Rosser,' looking around, worried, 'do you know where you bleaten are?'

I'm there, 'Cabra,' through my snot and tears.

'Cabberda is reet,' he goes. 'And you caddent be stanton around Cabberda crying yisser bleaten eyes out.'

I'm there, 'I don't want to go to prison, Ro. Not for a year. Not even for one focking day.'

He's like, 'Rosser –'

'Ro, I don't give a fock how many screws Gull knows.'

'Rosser, people are looking.'

'One of the first things you ever said to me, Ro – you couldn't have been much older than seven at the time – you told me that when you're in prison, it's not where you are that kills you, it's where you're not.'

'Rosser, I was a choyult, just paddoting the things I heerd other shams arowunt Finglas saying.'

'What you said is true, Ro. I belong out here. Well, not literally – the other side of the river. I'm seeing someone. Her name is Roz.'

'If she's woort it, she'll wait for you, Rosser.'

'I don't want her to have to wait for me. And then there's Honor. She's going through a tough time. She's realizing that she's not great in terms of looks and I need to be here for her. And Brian, Johnny and Leo – they've already turned soft without my influence. They're being bullied. And then there's my old dear. Who's going to look after her? The old man has literally zero interest.'

As I'm saying all of this, I'm, like, sobbing my focking hort out. And, like Ronan said, people are staring and they don't look like the kind of crowd who'd be sensitive to a man's feelings. And that *includes* Ronan, by the way?

He looks at me – I *think* it's a word? – *disparagingly* and he goes, 'Rosser, you're godda have to madden up.'

I'm there, 'I'm going to have to what?'

'Madden up.'

'Again?'

'Madden up.'

'Again?'

'Madden. Fooken. Up.'

'Sho will you wait for him,' Magnus goes, 'if he ish shent to prishon tomorrow?'

I end up nearly spitting a smoked Jerusalem ortichoke across the table. It's something that me and Roz have, like, never even *discussed*?

I'm there, 'There's a very good chance that I *won't* go to prison?' even though I'm lying to myself.

Roz puts her hand on my knee under the table and goes, 'Yes, I'll wait for him,' which is an incredible thing for me to hear.

This is us in, like, Volpe Nera in Blackrock for what Oisinn is very sensitively calling The Last Supper.

I'm there, 'I'm actually serious about hopefully getting off. The dude who's going to be sentencing me played for Lansdowne. I doubt if he's going to be shocked at the idea of someone flashing their hole in a pub.'

Oisinn goes, 'Well, I'm sorry I won't be in court to, you know, support you. I can't believe we're flying out on the same day.'

I'm like, 'Hey, ain't no thing but a Stephen Bing,' even though I'm pissed off with him – with *all* of them – for not putting it off to be there to support me.

Father Fehily would be ashamed of them.

Roz goes, 'It would be nice – if his friends were there for him,' because she's one hundred per cent on my side.

I think I'm actually storting to fall in love with this woman.

In fairness to Magnus, he goes, 'You have all been friendsh for shuch a long time. It musht be difficult for Rosh to have Fionn, then Chrishtian, then JP turn their backsh on him.'

I'm there, 'That's great stuff for me to hear, Magnus. Thanks, Dude.'

'So,' Oisinn goes, quickly changing the subject, 'Ross tells me that you've a daughter in Honor's class in school.'

Roz smiles. God, I love her smile.

She's like, 'Yes, her name is Sincerity. And she and Honor have become really good friends this summer, haven't they, Ross?'

I'm there, 'Hmmm,' not wanting to commit myself here.

She goes, 'Although I think they may have had a little falling-out over this boy they both liked.'

Again, I'm like, 'Hmmm.'

'But that's teenage girls for you. Honor will get over it, won't she, Ross?'

Now it's, like, *my* turn to change the subject.

I'm there, 'So, goys, how are things down in Brittas? I don't know if I told you, Roz, but Oisinn and Magnus are renting Gerald Kean's old gaff. They've turned it into, like, a treatment centre for people who used to work for big American tech and fintech companies and are struggling to recover.'

'Oh, wow, that's *so* needed!' Roz goes. 'There's a woman in my spin class who was made redundant by LinkedIn and she kept turning up at the office for, like, a year afterwards.'

Magnus is there, 'Thish ish shadly very common. We have one man who ish an in-patient with us at the moment and he wash let go by Google lasht year. He keepsh shinging the company shong, over and over again, all day, every day. We have had to shoundproof hish room.'

I'm like, 'Fock!' and I mean it.

The waiter comes and clears away our storters. I'm thinking, Jesus, this might *well* be the last decent meal I have in a long time. I should have ordered the venison instead of the salt-aged Delmonico beef.

'So,' Roz goes, again turning over the play, 'I believe you're about to become parents.'

I feel my face instantly redden.

'Yeah, no,' Oisinn goes, whipping out his phone, 'did I show you the scan, Ross?'

I'm there, 'Er, no need, Dude, if you don't have it handy. I've seen a lot of scans in my time.'

He hands it Roz, who goes, 'Oh my God! Do you know if it's a boy or a girl yet?'

Oisinn's like, 'No, we don't care as long as it's healthy – and *ours*, of course!'

He and Magnus exchange a smile. I'm thinking, Oh, fock.

Our main courses suddenly arrive.

'I'm so sorry,' the waiter goes, 'I forgot to mention that the halibut comes *without* the chorizo. We just can't get it at the moment because of –'

'Irexit!' everyone at the table goes.

The dude's like, 'Exactly. Anyway, enjoy your meal,' and he focks off.

'Ross,' Oisinn goes, trying to shove his phone in my face, 'have a look at the scan.'

I'm like, 'Dude, I'm about to eat here,' because the steak comes with a confit egg yolk.

He's like, 'Ross, just look at it! It's our baby!' and I end up having no choice but to – I suppose – *comply*?

'Yeah, no, very nice,' I go, as I look at the same photo that Sorcha's sister sent me. 'Very nice indeed.'

'Shorcha's shishter joked with ush,' Magnus goes. 'She shaid the baby wash the image of you, Rosh – eshpeshially itsh fat head!'

They all laugh and of course I have no option than to laugh along with them.

'Looks like me!' I go. 'That's hilarious!'

I can feel my cheeks burning now and I have to admit that it's a massive relief when my *phone* all of a sudden rings. I check the screen.

I'm there, 'It's Boris Johnson.'

The three of them all exchange looks.

'Borish Johnshon?' Magnus goes. 'The British Prime Minishter?'

I'm there, 'Yeah, no, the old man said he was going to ring me to wish me luck ahead of tomorrow.'

I stand up from the table and I go, 'I'm going to take this outside.'

So I step out onto the road and I answer the phone. I'm there, 'Hello?'

And Boris Johnson goes, 'Ah, Ross! *Da Deus fortunae! Dominus vobiscum* and so forth!'

I'm like, 'Er, yeah, no, whatever.'

'I'm just phoning to, you know, wish you the best of British for tomorrow. *Fiat iustitia er pereat mundus!*'

'Er, fair enough.'

'Let justice be done, though the world shall perish! How are you feeling?'

'Not great actually. My so-called barrister reckons I'm going to do about a year in jail.'

'*Auctoritas non veritas facit legem!* As your father said to me this very afternoon!'

'Whatever.'

'Well, at least you've got good people around you. I'm presuming your friends have all rallied around?'

I'm there, 'You're presuming wrong, then. They all hate me. Including JP, who's not talking to me just because I told his wife, who's old enough to be his mother, that he liked mickey lips, then she went off to Turkey to have them done and she's ended up look-ing like – I'm not being a wanker here – but a bloodhound with its head stuck out the window of a moving cor.'

He laughs. He seems to find my life very amusing.

I'm there, 'As a matter of fact, the only friend of mine who's still talking to me is the dude whose surrogate I secretly rode – you met her in the jacks that time – and he has no idea that the baby is potentially –'

As I'm talking to him, I'm looking through the window of the restaurant. I notice that Oisinn has his phone to his ear and he looks like he's in shock. Roz and Magnus look like they're in shock too.

I'm there, 'Oh, fock! I think they know!'

Back into the restaurant I go. Oisinn takes the phone away from his ear. He's just, like, staring at me, ashen-faced, shaking his head from side to side, like he can't believe what he's just heard.

I'm thinking, She's told him. Sorcha's sister has focking told him.

I'm there, 'Dude, don't overreact! I still think the baby is hopefully yours – yours or Magnus's.'

He's like, 'What?'

I'm there, 'Er, I'm just presuming that's why you look so pissed *off*?'

He goes, 'That was the Gords in Blackrock, Ross.'

I'm like, 'Oh!' suddenly relieved to be off the hook. 'What were they ringing in relation to?'

'They found our shtuff,' Magnus goes.

I'm like, 'Your shtuff? What shtuff?'

He goes, 'The shtuff that wash shtolen when our apartment wash cleaned out.'

Oh, fock.

I'm like, 'Oh, yeah?' trying to act all casual.

'They arrested a woman,' Oisinn goes.

I'm there, 'Thank God for that.'

'And she had a shtory to tell,' Magnus goes.

I'm like, 'Oh, really?'

'She said that she and her brothers trawl the pubs of Dublin,' Oisinn goes, 'looking for gullible men, drinking on their own, who'll invite her back to their place. Once there, she roofies them, then she rings her brothers and they arrive in a van to clear out the property.'

I'm there, 'Dicks. Did she, em, give a good description of the dude who invited her back to your gaff?'

'Fat head,' Oisinn goes. 'Big nose. Rugby ears.'

I'm there, 'That could be thousands of people on this side of the city.'

Magnus reaches across the table and shoves me hord in the chest – to the point where I end up having to take a step backwards.

'We fucking trushted you!' he goes. 'We trushted you and thish ish how you treat ush!'

Oisinn's there, 'Come on, Magnus, we're leaving.'

I'm like, 'Dudes, let's talk about this!'

But Oisinn goes, 'I actually feel sorry for you, Ross,' and then the two of them morch straight past me and out the door.

Roz looks seriously pissed off and I'm trying to subtly figure out whether she's pissed off at me or them. I soon have my answer.

She goes, 'You and I were going out together when that happened, Ross.'

And I end up using a line that I thought I'd never end up using on her – certainly not this soon into the relationship.

I'm there, 'Yeah, no, we were on a break. Remember?'

She goes, 'You expect me to wait a year for you – and you wouldn't even wait a few days for me?'

She just shakes her head at me – again, like she pities me. Then she walks out, leaving me to pay the bill.

And what I've forgotten, of course, is to hang up on Boris Johnson. I can hear him on the other end of my phone, going, 'Hello? Ross? Good Lord! Ross! Hello? Oh my!'

The day has finally come. The day that will decide my fate. By the end of it, I'll either be a free man, or – more likely – making a new home for myself in a cell no bigger than a Homedrobe. It's no wonder I'm sitting on the jacks shitting wallpaper paste.

I pick up my phone to find out if there's any good luck messages. There isn't one. There's nothing from Roz. Nothing from Sorcha. Nothing from the goys. It looks like I'm very much on my Tobler.

I go onto Instagram and the first photo that pops up is from Christian's account. Yeah, no, it's him, JP, Fionn and Oisinn, standing at the departures gate in the airport, with their rucksacks on their backs and their walking boots dangling from them. Oisinn is wearing a t-shirt that says, 'Castlerock College Dream Team – Camino Walk 2019!'

Underneath, there's, like, loads of replies, going, 'Where's Ross?' and 'Is the Rossmeister General not with you?' and 'Where's THE MAN himself?'

Which is nice for me to read, but I end up feeling suddenly sad, then I have to get out of Instagram altogether.

I finish up in the jacks, then I find myself doing *the* most random thing. I kneel down beside my bed and I pray – not to God, because I always have this sense that if there is a God – as in, if the dude actually exists – He's always slightly pissed off with me. No, I pray to Father Fehily.

I'm like, 'Father, you told us back in the day that, even after death, you would continue to look over us. Well, I really need you today, Dude, because I'm in serious shit, even worse than the time that I egged that girl from Sion Hill and she turned out to be allergic to the things and her head blew up like a focking medicine ball and you persuaded the Gordaí not to press chorges. Well, I need a similar kind of help today. People like me – meaning people from my background – don't belong in jail. Please let the judge realize that. Please let the judge look at me and see someone who could have been an amazing rugby player if it wasn't for bad luck and injuries. And please let him see that, on balance, what I did was pretty focking hilarious. Amen.'

I stand up and I throw on my suit, including my old Castlerock College tie, hoping it will jog something in the judge's mind.

My phone beeps. It's, like, a text from the old man. He's like, 'Best of luck today, Kicker!' like I'm about to sit my driving test for the – I don't know, whatever we're up to now – *seventeenth* time? 'Sorry I can't be there! Doing the business of Government and so forth! Fingers crossed for the right result!'

What a focking knob-end.

I step out onto the landing and I knock on Honor's door. I'm there, 'Honor, if you're coming to court with me, you better stort getting ready now.'

There's, like, no answer from her. I push the door and I stick my head around it. She's not in her bed.

I tip down the stairs and I walk into the kitchen to be greeted by a sight that moves me to pretty much tears. The kitchen is full of people – we're talking Honor, we're talking Erika, we're talking Helen, we're talking Ronan, we're talking Avery, we're talking Rihanna-Brogan and we're talking Amelie.

When I walk in, they all shout, 'Surprise!'

There's, like, balloons everywhere and a giant banner hanging from one side of the kitchen to the other, saying, 'Good Luck, Ross!'

Honor walks up to me and hugs me and goes, 'I made you your favourite breakfast. Smashed avocado on sourdough with a poached egg on top.'

I kiss the top of her head and I laugh. I'm there, 'This could be the last time I taste avocado for a while.'

'Actually,' Honor goes, 'I had to make it *without* avocado? You can't get them anywhere at the moment.'

'Because of Irexit,' everyone – at the same time – goes.

No avocados? Jesus, it won't be long before there's riots on the streets of Ranelagh.

I sit down at the table. I notice that Honor has substituted mushy peas for the avocado. I horse into it, even though it's absolutely vile. Everyone is being unbelievably nice to me, which just makes me realize how utterly focked they think I am.

'Rosser,' Rihanna-Brogan goes, 'my daddy and Avody are brigging me to Disneyladdend Paddis!'

I'm like, 'Wow!'

Ronan goes, 'Yeah, we're heading off tomoddow to do a birrof a tewer of Eurdope. Paddis, Rowum, Athiddens. Avody's wanthon to see the sights.'

She's like, 'I can't wait!'

I'm thinking, If they're taking off tomorrow, it's obvious they're not expecting me to be around.

I'm there, 'Fair focks to you. I mean it.'

The doorbell rings and Helen goes to answer it, while Erika puts a cup of coffee down in front of me.

'I made you a vanilla latte,' she goes. 'Your favourite.'

I'm like, 'Goys, thanks for this. I'm, like, really bowled over here.'

A second or two later, Helen arrives back and tells me that there's someone at the door for me, although she doesn't say who.

I tip outside and – yeah, no – it ends up being Roz, dressed to the focking nines. I'm in, like, shock. I'm, like, totally speechless.

I just blurt out, 'I didn't ride the girl. She roofied me before anything could happen.'

She doesn't even acknowledge this. She just goes, 'Ross, I really like you.'

And I'm there, 'Er,' a little bit thrown by this, 'yeah, no, I really like you too.'

She goes, 'I don't want to be messed about, okay? I don't want you to treat me the way, I gather, you've treated other women.'

I'm there, 'I won't. That was the old Rossmeis–. The old me.'

'Just tell me,' she goes, 'is there anything else I need to know?'

Of course, I possibly should mention that the unborn baby she was looking at on Oisinn's phone last night is potentially the fruit of my overactive loins. But I don't.

I'm there, 'You know everything now. I'm, like, an open book.'

She smiles at me and goes, 'You look very smort.'

I'm there, 'You do too. Where are you off to?'

She laughs like she can't believe anyone could be so thick.

She goes, 'I'm going to court, Ross, with you.'

My hort skips a literally beat.

I'm there, 'Do you want to come in? We're having my farewell breakfast. It's smashed avocado – without the avocado.'

'You can't get them anywhere,' Roz goes, stepping into the hallway. 'There's real anger building out there, especially in Rane–'

I kiss her on the lips, then we end up wearing the face off each other for a minute or two, both of us knowing that this could be the last time in a long time that we get to spend a moment together like this.

I'm there, 'I –' and I swear to fock, I very nearly tell her that I love her, but then I think better of it, because it'd be unfair to lay that one on her just before I'm sent down.

She's like, 'What was that you were going to say?'

And I'm there, 'I, er, wouldn't recommend Honor's smashed avocado substitute.'

'Mr O'Carroll-Kelly is a privileged, obnoxious yob,' the dude representing the State goes, 'who believes that his family's wealth and status place him above the law. Not only did he indecently expose himself in a public place, where women and children were present –'

I end up suddenly losing it – there in the middle of the courtroom.

I'm like, 'How many times do I have to repeat myself? It was a mooner!'

Justice Bryan Hickson looks at me over the top of his glasses.

He goes, 'Can I remind you that you have pleaded guilty to these charges and the court does not wish to hear from you.'

I'm there, 'Fair enough.'

Out of the corner of his mouth, Frankie de Felice goes, 'You've just added another year onto your sentence – congratulations.'

He really hates me, this dude.

'As I was saying,' the State's dude goes, 'Mr O'Carroll-Kelly believes that the laws that govern civil society should not apply to him. Thus, when he's caught in the act of doing something illegal, his first instinct is to try to pin the blame on an entirely innocent third party. The court needs to send out a very strong message that this kind of contempt for the rule of law is unacceptable, even more so given that his father is the Taoiseach of this country. To show lenience would create the impression that wealthy and well-connected people can do whatever the hell they want without any fear of the repercussions.'

I look over at the press box, which is, like, packed with reporters and they're lapping up every focking word.

'That is why I would urge you to make a strong statement by giving him the maximum sentence allowed under the law, which is five years imprisonment.'

'Fock you!' a voice from the public gallery shouts. It's Honor – she's such a daddy's girl. 'I hope you have a focking hort attack, you fat focking prick!'

Justice Hickson goes, 'I will have order in this courtroom or I will clear the public gallery!'

I turn around and give her a big smile.

'That's going to be another year,' Frankie mutters under his breath.

Justice Hickson goes, 'Mr de Felice. Do you have anything you wish to say on behalf of your client?'

Frankie stands up.

He's like, 'I will be very brief, Judge, as I have another case in a different court in less than an hour's time.'

Seriously? For fock's sake!

He goes, 'My client's actions were inexcusable and I can offer very little by way of mitigation, other than to say he is a man of very low intelligence. Intellectually, I would place him in the bottom five per cent of the adult population, while he has the emotional age of a child.'

Jesus Christ, you wouldn't want to be sensitive.

'He took his bottom out in the pub,' he goes, 'in the mistaken belief that this was a funny prank, fuelled by the seventeen pints of lager that my client estimates he consumed in the hours preceding the incident. Indeed, he was so inebriated when he was arrested that he has no memory of giving a false name and address to the Gardaí. He should have corrected the record when the error became apparent to him in court, but he failed to do so out of fear of embarrassing his father, who was very much a public figure at the time.'

Again, the press are writing all of this shit down.

'Also,' he goes, 'my client has –' and then he turns to me and goes, 'how many children?'

I'm like 'Five – as far as I know.'

Everyone in the courtroom laughs.

'Five children,' he goes. 'And while he doesn't actually work to support any of them, I do not believe it would be in their best interests to place their father in prison. Visiting him would no doubt be a traumatic experience for all five.'

I'd say four. Ronan's seen more of that prison than all of D Wing put together.

'In summary, Judge,' Frankie goes, 'I would say that, while my client is an imbecile, it would serve no purpose in sending him to prison. He has pleaded guilty, thus saving the State the expense of a lengthy trial. And so I would submit that some form of community service would be a suitable punishment in this case.'

Justice Hickson takes off his glasses and pinches the bridge of his nose. He sits back in his seat, makes a steeple of his fingers and exhales deeply. Then he sits forward and puts his glasses back on.

'Mr O'Carroll-Kelly,' he goes, sounding cross, 'can you stand up, please?'

I do – even though I have to admit that my legs are a bit on the shaky side.

He's there, 'Giving a false name and address to the Gardaí, then representing yourself as someone else in a court of law is a matter of the utmost gravity. It demonstrates a contempt for the law that I find inexcusable.'

I'm staring at the ground, trying to look ashamed of myself.

'However,' he goes, 'there is one word that hasn't been mentioned here in court today – and that word is rugby.'

I suddenly look up. I'm thinking, Holy focking shit!

He's like, 'That tie you're wearing – what school is that from?'

I'm there, 'It's, er, Castlerock College.'

'Yes, I thought so. I went to Terenure College.'

A school for focking dicks, I think.

He goes, 'Our battles with Castlerock College were legendary,' and then he sort of, like, chuckles to himself at some – I don't know if it's a word – but *reminiscery*?

He goes, 'Coming from a rugby background, I'm aware that exposing one's bottom in public is all part of the colour and pageantry surrounding the game.'

I'm there, 'I'm blue in the face trying to explain that to people.'

'Notwithstanding your guilty plea, I am going to dismiss the charge of indecent exposure. However, the remaining charges of which you are by your admission guilty are very, very serious indeed. It is, of course, incumbent on me to weigh up these crimes with the fact that you come from a good background and attended a highly respected school.'

He goes quiet for a good, I don't know, thirty seconds, except it feels like thirty minutes. My mouth feels suddenly dry and I think my hort is going to beat right out of my chest.

'Mr O'Carroll-Kelly,' he eventually goes, 'I am sentencing you . . . to two years in prison.'

Oh, shit. There's, like, gasps in the courtroom. I feel my knees nearly buckle.

'You focking big-eared bastard,' Honor shouts.

'But,' the dude goes, 'I am going to suspend the sentence – on condition that you stay out of trouble for that period.'

I can't even begin to explain the feeling of joy that washes over me in that moment. I look up and I go, 'Thank you! Thank you! Thank you!' to Father Fehily, because I know he's answered my prayers here today.

I turn around and I hug Frankie, who tells me to take my filthy hands off him. Honor comes chorging up the middle aisle of the court and she throws her orms around me. She's bawling her eyes out.

Next comes Ronan and Avery, then Erika and Helen, then Rihanna-Brogan and Amelie. They're all hugging me and telling me that they were convinced I was going to go down and they're so happy for me. The relief is something I couldn't even put into words.

The reporters are all shouting at me, 'Ross, how do you feel?' and 'Do you think the Taoiseach will be pleased?' and 'Does the dismissal of the indecent exposure charge open up the possibility of you returning as the coach of the Ireland women's team?'

I'm there, 'Those are all questions for another day, goys. Right now, I just want to spend some time with the people who supported me throughout this entire, I don't know, *thing*?'

I spot Roz standing at the back of the court with a humungous smile on her face. The woman who stood up for me when Lychee and the rest of them were dissing me at the borbecue. The woman who came to the hospital with me when my old dear fell down the stairs. The woman who forgave me for very nearly riding the woman who roofied me. The woman who promised to wait for me if I was sent down.

I walk up to her and I kiss her and I go, 'Thank you for believing in me. I honestly wouldn't have got through these last few weeks if it wasn't for you.'

'I've got something for you,' she whispers to me. 'Do you want to come outside?'

I'm like, 'Er, yeah, no, whatever,' and I follow her out onto the steps of the court.

She reaches into her handbag and she whips out an envelope, which she hands to me.

I'm there, 'What's this?'

She goes, 'It's a flight – to Biarritz.'

Of course, my first thought is, Biarritz? The rugby season doesn't stort for another month.

I'm there, 'I don't understand.'

She goes, 'You're going there – tonight.'

I'm there, 'But the rugby season doesn't stort for another month.'

'You're not going there to watch a rugby match,' she goes. 'You're going to take a bus from Biarritz to St Jean Pied de Port. The full itinerary is in the envelope.'

I'm there, 'But, like, why am going to, whatever you said – Peddaporpa?'

And she goes, 'You're going to walk the Camino.'

'Oh my God,' I go, before I even know what I'm saying, 'I focking love you.'

She doesn't respond. She just smiles at me and she's like, 'Go and see if you can fix things with your friends.'

And I must have genuine feelings for this woman because in that moment I make a solemn promise to myself that I hopefully won't ride anyone else while I'm away from home.

6.

On Fr Fehily's Secret Service

It's, like, just before ten o'clock at night when the bus pulls into St Jean Pied de Port. The dude in the seat behind me – some Australian randomer – nudges me awake.

He goes, 'Mate, we're here!'

I'm like, 'Stringer, I'm in the pocket! I'm in the pocket!' for a moment forgetting where I even *am*?

He goes, 'This is the staaht of the Camoynoy, mate,' and I realize that I've slept pretty much the entire way from Biarritz.

I get off the bus, still half asleep, in fairness to me. The driver has opened the door of the, I don't know, baggage comportment and he's pulling out rucksack after rucksack.

'Where's your shit?' the Australian dude goes.

I find Australians very annoying – aport from obviously Matt Williams and Michael Cheika – and I hope that doesn't come across as racist.

I'm there, 'I don't have any.'

'Are you actually planning to walk the Camoynoy?'

'Yeah.'

'What,' he goes, looking down at my feet, 'in thoyse facking shoys?'

Those focking shoes happen to be my Dubes.

I'm like, 'Dude, I don't want to be rude but I'm not really a fan of the whole Australia thing – with certain exceptions, including obviously Matt Williams and Michael Cheika – so I'm going to stop talking to you now.'

I head off up the street, even though I've no idea where I'm actually going. I could text the goys and ask them where they're staying, but I doubt if they'd tell me. In fact, they'd probably skip town straight away.

So instead I walk the streets for, like, half an hour, looking at the crowds of people sitting outside the pubs and restaurants, drinking glasses of wine or pints of beer in the warm evening air.

There's no sign of them anywhere.

A gang of dudes walk past me – shit-faced – and I can tell from their accents that they're Irish.

I'm like, 'Hey, goys – where are you from?'

'From the taown,' one of them goes.

I'm like, 'Where?'

'From the taown,' one of the others goes. 'Draawda.'

I'm there, 'Drogheda! A lovely port of the country.'

It's not. It's a focking pigsty. I sold houses there and it still troubles my conscience to this day.

I'm like, 'You haven't seen any other Irish around, have you? I'm looking for a group of, like, four goys – one of them is, like, a fat dude with curly, blond hair, another one is a real dork with glasses –'

'That's them dray shates we met in Club Luis,' one of them goes. 'They weren't even thrinking, so they weren't.'

I'm like, 'Yeah, no, that sounds like them alright. Where's this, I don't know, Club Luis?'

'It's up there on the left,' the same dude goes.

I'm like, 'Thanks, goys.'

'*Buen Camino*,' one of them goes.

Drogheda. Jesus Christ.

I find Club Luis easily enough. I stick my head around the door and – yeah, no – there they are, we're talking Christian, we're talking Oisinn, we're talking JP, we're talking Fionn. They're sitting there with four glasses of water in front of them, having zero craic. I notice that Fionn is – I shit you not – reading to them from a Lonely Planet guidebook.

They don't see me. I think they might have all slipped into a focking trance listening to *him* bang on about, I don't know, churches and museums that they might visit along the way.

To my right, I spot a jukebox. I walk over to it and I stort flicking through the albums until I reach the Q's. I slip a yoyo into the slot and I press 87 for *Queen's Greatest Hits*, then 16 for *We Will Rock You*, which was *our* song back in the day. We used to sing it in the dressing room before and after matches. It was like, 'We will, we will, rock you – fock you, any way you want to!'

Five seconds later, the song comes on and I watch their reaction from the other side of the bor. It's, like, a happy surprise at first – they're obviously thinking, Wow, what a coincidence, that here we are, four Rock boys, about to walk the Camino because it was our former coach's dying wish, and that song – it was, like, a Rock anthem – just happens to come on. Then I watch their four smiles disappear at exactly the same time because they're suddenly thinking, what if it's not a coincidence? What if –

They all look up together to see the Rossmeister General standing there with a big, superhero grin on his – let's be honest – gorgeous face.

I go, 'This looks like a fun night!'

It's a cracking opening line – to which they have no answer.

Fionn's there, 'I thought you were –'

I'm like, 'Dead?'

He's there, 'No.'

'In prison?' I go.

He's like, 'Well – let's be honest, yeah.'

I'm there, 'No, sorry to disappoint you, Fionn, but I got a little thing known as a suspended *sentence*?'

I'm actually hurt that they didn't bother their holes checking the internet to see what happened to me.

I'm like, 'Thanks for all the good luck messages, by the way. They meant a lot to me.'

Fionn's still struggling with it – as in, like, the *verdict*?

'How?' he goes. 'As in, like, how the fock did you get a suspended sentence?'

I'm there, 'Rugby, Fionn. That's how.'

I catch the borman's eye and I go, 'Hola! Pint of Heineken, por favor.'

Fionn's there, 'We're in France, Ross.'

Which is *such* a Fionn thing to say.

Oisinn goes, 'Dude, what the fock are you doing here?'

I'm there, 'Same as you, Big O. I'm walking the Camino – just like Father Fehily wanted me to do.'

'Where's your gear?' JP goes.

I'm there, 'Don't have any. Came here straight from court,' because – yeah, no – I'm still in my navy Hugo Boss suit.

'You're not walking with us,' Fionn goes.

I'm there, 'Why not?'

'Because you're a focking wanker,' Christian goes, 'and none of us ever wants to see you again.'

I'm like, 'Okay, let's put that to a vote, shall we? Who here wants to walk with me? Raise your hand.'

No one raises their hand. I don't know why I thought they *might*?

'You got me put on the sex offenders' register,' Fionn goes, 'and you nearly cost me my focking job.'

I'm there, 'Well, the good news is that you're off it now and you're back at work.'

JP's there, 'You persuaded my wife to have plastic surgery and she's destroyed her face.'

'Dude, you'll get used to it,' I go. 'It's like when someone gets a really drastic haircut. A week or two later, you can't even remember what they looked like before.'

Oisinn's like, 'You let someone into our home and they stole everything we owned in the world. And you lied about it.'

'You got your shit back,' I go. 'Most of it.'

Christian's there, 'And you knew my son was being sextorted – and you didn't tell me.'

I'm like, 'Hey, he was the one who was looking at gay porn, not me. But, as his godfather, I tried to protect him. I paid the bastards off – and you've never offered to give me my money back, by the way.'

Fionn stands up and the other three do the same.

He's like, 'I'm going back to the hostel. We've an early stort tomorrow.'

I'm like, 'Which hostel is it, just as a matter of interest? And will you wait five minutes? I've just ordered a pint.'

Fionn goes, 'I know you're famously slow on the uptake,' which

I think is a bit uncalled for, 'but get this through your thick skull, Ross. We don't! Focking! Want you here!'

Then off they trot, just as the borman hands me my pint. I knock it back in one – an old porty-piece of mine – and then I tip outside and I follow them up the road to their hostel, which turns out to be called La Villa, I don't know, something-or-other.

Oisinn looks over his shoulder at me and goes, 'The place is full, Ross. We got the last four beds.'

I'm like, 'I'll just have to use my famous chorm on the owner – provided it's a woman. *Is* it a woman?'

No one says shit to me.

I actually feel quite light-headed. I think it's from skulling that beer. I'm not in my twenties any more.

Into the place we go. The four goys head upstairs to bed without so much as a goodnight. I tip over to the reception desk and I press the bell. A few seconds later, a woman – thank focking God – comes out and goes, 'Bonjour!'

She's not great. If I had to say she looked like anyone, it'd be Russell Crowe.

I'm there, 'Absolutely bonjour! How the hell are you?' giving her one of my special smiles – the same one that Kathryn Thomas could never resist.

'I am good,' she goes – yeah, no – *blushing*? 'There is something I can help?'

I'm there, 'There is something you can help alright. I'm looking for a bed. And that's not a come-on. Although if you were a few years older. What are you, twenty?'

I'm ripping the piss. She's focking fifty if she's a day.

She goes, 'You are flattery man. Very charm. You have luck. I have one bed left.'

I'm there, 'I'll take it.'

'Is fifty euros,' she goes. 'And you pay now.'

I whip out a roll of notes and I peel a fifty off it, before slapping it down on the counter.

'Upstairs,' she goes. 'Bed is number twenty-five.'

I tell her goodnight, then I give her a kissy face and head up the stairs into this humungous dorm with, like, forty or fifty sets of bunkbeds in it. Even in the dorkness of the room, I can sense the four goys rolling their eyes when they see the Rossmeister walk in.

I'm there, 'Look at this, dudes! It's just like the year we all boarded in Castlerock, isn't it? I can't wait for the next four weeks of this.'

Bed number twenty-five, it turns out, is the bottom bunk below JP's. I lie down on it, then I swing my legs into the air, placing the soles of my Dubes against the underside of his mattress. Then I give it a good kick, sending the dude about three feet into the air.

'Fock's sake!' he goes.

And I'm there, 'Yeah, no, just like old times.'

I end up having the best night's sleep I've had since, well, that bird roofied me and stole all of Oisinn and Magnus's shit. I open my eyes and I wait for my brain to engage, which usually takes a minute or two. As it does, I slowly become aware that I'm, like, alone in the room.

I sit up in the bed and – yeah, no – everyone has gone, including Christian, Oisinn, JP and Fionn. I throw my legs out of the bed and I go to grab my clothes. Except *they're* gone as *well*? The absolute fockers. They've stolen my good tin of fruit – presumably to stop me from following them.

I look under the bed. They've left me my Dubes. At least there's *some* focking humanity left in them. I step into them and I tip downstairs to the reception desk. The woman from last night – focking Russell Crowe – is still on. She puts her hand over her mouth and gasps – either at the sight of my six-pack or simply because I'm standing there in just my Dubes and a very tight pair of jockeys that leave nothing to the imagination.

'I'm sorry,' I go. 'My friends – so-called – have stolen my clothes and focked off without me.'

'You cannot stand here,' the poor woman goes, 'with no clothes.'

I'm there, 'That's what I'm trying to explain to you. They've been stolen. Can you give me something to wear?'

She's like, 'Perhaps in Lost and Found. Come. I cannot let people see you in this naked way.'

So she leads me through to the back office and she pulls a cord-board box from a shelf. On the side of it someone has written 'Lost Property' in black morker. She puts the box on a table, reaches into it and whips out a t-shirt, which she hands to me.

Hilariously, it's one of those, like, novelty t-shirts, with a tuxedo jacket, shirt and bow-tie printed on it. On the back it says, 'Desmond's Stag – Camino 2019!'

I throw it on. It fits perfectly.

Next from the box, she whips out a pair of black jeans. The legs have been cut off just below the knee to turn them into shorts. I step into them and – yeah, no – they fit as well.

I'm like, 'Thanks. I really appreciate it.'

She's there, 'Now, you go.'

I'm like, 'Just before I do, can you tell me how long ago my friends checked out?'

'They go early.'

'As in, like, how early?'

'Perhaps two hours. Is long walk to Roncesvalles.'

'How long are we talking in terms of?'

'Perhaps six hours.'

Six hours? For fock's sake – they'll be long gone, I think. I've no chance of catching up with them. Then I think, why the fock would I even bother? Leave them to it. I'm not going to beg for their forgiveness. Fock them.

I decide to grab a bit of breakfast, then take the old Bualadh back to Biarritz for the next flight home. I sit down outside this, like, café and I order a cappuccino and a *pain au chocolat*. As I'm horsing into them, I hear a woman's voice go, 'Deshmond! Deshmond! Deshmond!'

That's when I remember that Desmond is the name on the back of my t-shirt. I turn around and there's, like, three birds sitting at the table behind me. One of them is a ringer for Beba Suki and the other two – not being a wanker or anything – don't really look like anyone at all.

'How are you enjoying your shtag party?' the one who looks like Beba Suki goes.

She sounds like she's, I don't know, Dutch?

I'm there, 'Yeah, no, it's a bit of a disaster. As a matter of fact, I'm going home.'

'From your own shtag?' one of the two not-so-good-looking ones goes. 'What ish wrong?'

I'm there, 'I had a row with my friends. Well, not so much a row – they just, like, focked off without me.'

'Thish ish terrible,' Beba Suki goes. 'Come and shit with ush.'

I'm there, 'Come and what? Oh, *sit* with you.'

So – yeah, no – I join them at their table and they introduce themselves. The looker's name is Merrel and the other two are Esmee and Katja.

'And you are Deshmond?' Merrel goes.

I'm like, 'Yeah, no, that's my name alright – Deshmond,' because it can be a bit of a thrill sometimes to pretend to be someone else – like when I used to ride Sorcha as a Deliveroo courier, or a UPS delivery man, which was another one we tried out, although she wasn't *as* into it. 'Deshmond. Deshmond something is my name. Deshmond Sexton.'

Merrel goes, 'It ish lovely to meet you, Deshmond Shexton.'

I think she's taken a genuine shine to me. They're all dressed in – believe it or not – leather gear and they tell me they're doing the Camino on, like, motorbikes?

I'm like, 'That's cool. Just the three of you, is it?'

'No,' Esmee goes, 'altogether, there ish twenty-five of ush. The othersh have already shet off thish morning.'

Merrel's like, 'It ish very wrong that you have to go home alone from your shtag. Perhapsh, Deshmond, you can fixsh thish thing with your friendsh?'

'We can bring you to Ronceshvallesh,' Katja goes, 'if that ish where your friendsh are going.'

I'm there, 'Are you serious?'

She's like, 'Of coursh. It ish not a problem.'

So – yeah, no – twenty minutes later I'm pulling on a motorcycle helmet and throwing my leg over Merrel's Kawasaki something-or-other. Over her shoulder, Merrel goes, 'Hold on to me, Deshmond,' so I put my orms around her waist, locking my fingers together at the front.

We take off like the absolute clappers, with me and Merrel at the front. Pretty soon we're out in the wilds, driving up this, like, seriously steep mountain. Every few seconds we pass little groups of walkers, who look absolutely wrecked, and I think how happy I am that I'm not walking like these other focking mugs.

Merrel looks over her shoulder and at the top of her voice goes, 'Are you okay back there, Deshmond?'

And I'm there, 'Yeah, no, all good, Merrel, thanks.'

The scenery, I'm sure, is stunning, if you're into that kind of thing, which fortunately I'm not. But there's, like, mountains and valleys and forests and whatever else you're into if you don't find nature boring like I do.

All of a sudden, I see them up ahead – we're talking Christian, JP, Oisinn and Fionn. They're, like, sitting on a wall, looking absolutely focking flogged and they're probably not even halfway to where they're even *going* yet?

I'm just about to go, 'Hey, that's them!' but then I think, no, fock it, leave them to it, them and their focking walk.

We arrive in Roncesvalles within about, I don't know, forty focking minutes or something. The girls are meeting the rest of their porty in a pizza restaurant called Lambretta and they ask me to join them. Being very much a social animal, I say yes.

Of course, it turns out that they're all women – all twenty-focking-five of them – and a very high percentage of them, I just so happen to notice, are gorgeous. They're sitting outside on this, like, terrace in front of the restaurant.

'Thish ish Deshmond,' Merrel goes, introducing me to her crew. 'He ish on hish shtag but hish ash-hole friendsh abandoned him after an argument. Sho we gave him a lift here.'

All the women are like, 'Hi, Deshmond!' and you can see that they're all very, very fond of me.

I'm there, 'Let's get some wine,' because I am focking gagging for a drink.

So we order, like, five bottles, which turns into another five, then another five, then another five. The restaurant is playing ABBA's greatest hits and it's not long before we're all up dancing on the tables and singing 'Mama Mia' and 'Dancing Queen' and whatever else at the top of our lungs.

All the girls are, like, hugging me and telling me that they love my Irish accent.

The entire afternoon ends up passing in a flash. Then, just before the sun goes down, I spot them, we're talking Christian, we're talking JP, we're talking Oisinn and we're talking Fionn, walking into the village, looking absolutely bolloxed.

This is after, like, one day of walking?

I can't even begin to describe the look on their faces when they see me, the Rossmeister himself, standing on a table, dressed in my tuxedo t-shirt, a bottle of wine in one hand and my orm around Merrel's shoulder, surrounded by beautiful – with the exception of one or two – Dutch women.

Oisinn ends up having to do a double-take and I see JP mouth the words, 'What the fock?'

They probably thought – yeah, no – I'd be on the flight back to Dublin by now. Instead, I'm at the centre of this wild porty with, like, twenty-five women, many of them good-looking.

I jump down off the table and I walk up to them. I'm there, 'Come and join us for a drink,' because I'm prepared to let the past be the past.

In my defence, I'm completely focking shit-faced.

Fionn goes, 'No, thanks. Goys, we've got an early stort tomorrow. I'd suggest a light dinner and an early night.'

I'm like, 'Yeah, that's you every focking night, Fionn. Come on, goys, you're on your holliers.'

'No, thanks,' Oisinn goes. 'I'm picky about who I drink with.'

I can see Christian and JP stalling, though. They can see that it's kicking off here – and in a major, major way.

Fionn – in a focking sulk – goes, 'Fine, but I'm leaving at six a.m., goys, whether you're up or not.'

Him and Oisinn fock off to whatever little grief hole they've booked themselves into for the night.

I'm like, 'JP, get some of this wine into you. Oh, the girls think my name is Deshmond, by the way – just go along with it.'

Christian's like, 'How the – Like, how did –' still unable to get his head around the scene.

Merrel and Katja tip over to us and Merrel's like, 'Sho you are Deshmond'sh friendsh who abandoned him, yesh?'

The goys are like, 'Errrr.'

'Which one of you shtole hish clothesh?' Katja goes.

JP's there, 'It was Fionn. He put them in a bin. But, in fairness, he ended up on a sex offenders' register because of –'

I'm like, 'Okay, can we just forget about the who's, the what's, the why's and the wherefore's – and just, like, *porty*?'

Which is what we do. There's, like, dancing, drinking, laughter, the whole bit. It ends up being one of the best nights out ever. I teach the girls a drinking game that, I don't know, either I taught Fergus McFadden or Fergus McFadden taught me. It's the subject of ongoing orgument between us. It's called Fuzzy Duck and it involves ordering, like, a hundred shots of tequila, which are placed in the middle of the table. Then everyone around the table, in turn, goes, 'Fuzzy duck!', 'Fuzzy duck!', 'Fuzzy duck!', until someone randomly goes, 'Does he fock?' and then the direction suddenly reverses and everyone suddenly has to go, 'Does he fock?' and 'Does he fock?' and 'Does he fock?'

But if someone accidentally goes, 'Fuzzy duck?' instead of 'Does he fock?' then they have to drink a shot of tequila.

It's an amazing, amazing game, which the girls all love. And after, like, an hour of it, they're all off their pretty much tits.

At some point, very, very late into the evening, Merrel makes a bit of a drunken move on me. She goes, 'What ish the name of thish girl you are marrying?'

I'm there, 'It's, em, Roz,' and I don't know *why* I use her name?

'She ish very lucky lady,' Merrel goes, grabbing a hold of my hand. 'Do you think before you are married you would like to have perhapsh one lasht . . . hurrah?'

I smile at her. I'm there, 'Six months ago, Merrel, I'd have been all over you like a dog on a dropped pie. But I'm going to try and do things *right* this time?'

She lets go of my hand and she's like, 'Thank you for being sho honesht with me, Deshmond.'

I notice Christian – oh, fock it – absolutely necking a glass of red wine. The dude is supposedly in recovery, but then I'm thinking, Is wine allowed? Is it just, like, spirits that are off limits for alcoholics?

'Dancing Queen' comes on for, like, the twentieth time. Merrel grabs my hand again – she really is one smitten kitten – and goes, 'Come on, Deshmond, dansh with me,' and she drags me out into the middle of the terrace.

And as we're showing each other one or two moves, I can't help but notice JP and Katja kissing each other, then disappearing, hand in hand, off into the night.

I'm like, 'Goys, slow the fock down, will you?' and I end up having to shout because they're walking way ahead of me on the road.

I'm hungover to fock and I've only had, like, three hours' sleep and that was on the floor of the hostel where the Dutch birds were staying. And – yeah, no – I'm also walking in, like, Dubes?

I'm there, 'What's the focking rush?' except there's not a word out of any of them.

Fionn is walking at the front. He's pissed off because we set off three hours later than he planned. Oisinn is walking twenty or thirty feet behind him. Then it's, like, JP, then Christian, then the Rossmeister himself bringing up the rear.

I break into a bit of a jog to catch up with Christian. He's, like, seriously hanging – worse than even me.

I'm there, 'That was some focking session last night, wasn't it?'

He stops, turns around and in pretty much the same movement grabs me by the scruff of my famous tuxedo t-shirt.

I'm like, 'Dude, what the fock?'

He goes, 'I fell off the focking wagon last night.'

'It was only wine. I thought you were allowed to drink wine.'

'I'm a focking alcoholic. I'm not supposed to drink alcohol of any kind.'

'Dude, I didn't exactly pour it down your throat.'

'You put temptation in my way. You were the one who said, "Join us for a drink."'

'You could have said no and then had an early night like focking, I don't know, Glasses Face up there.'

'Things like this happen when you're around, because you're focking toxic.'

He lets go of my t-shirt and shoves me in the chest. Then he turns around and storts walking again.

I'm there, 'You drank because you wanted to drink. Don't focking blame me.'

We walk on in, like, silence for another maybe half an hour, then Fionn decides that it's time to stop. When I catch up with them, the four of them are sitting on the – I want to say – *parapet* of a bridge over this little stream, having their lunch. Oisinn is horsing into a big lump of chicken, Fionn and Christian are eating cheese sandwiches and JP is munching on a Tracker bor.

The fockers never mentioned that they were bringing a packed lunch.

I'm there, 'Is there any of those sandwiches going spare, goys?'

Fionn's like, 'No.'

I'm there, 'Fair enough. Could I even have a sip of your water?' because they've all got, like, flasks with them and it's absolutely focking roasting this morning.

'Why didn't you bring water?' Christian goes.

I'm there, 'Dude, I didn't have time to plan this trip. I thought I was going to be in prison.'

'You *should* be in prison,' Fionn goes.

Several groups of people pass. They go, *'Buen Camino!'* and the goys are all like, *'Buen Camino!'* and I've literally no idea what they're saying.

I watch JP finish his Tracker, then I go, 'What about you last night, huh?' at the same time laughing. 'You focking dirtbag!'

Fionn, Oisinn and Christian all look at him – not a clue what I'm on about.

JP has the actual balls to go, 'What do you mean?'

I'm there, 'Er, I saw you with – what was her name? – Katja?'

He goes, 'No, you didn't,' but at the same time his face turns red.

I'm like, 'Dude, I saw you kissing her, then you headed off into the night, hand in hand. Very romantic.'

Yeah, no, it's definitely news to the others, judging from their faces.

JP goes, 'I'm a married man, Ross,' like that somehow proves that it didn't happen.

I'm there, 'Dude, I'm not going to say shit to Delma. What goes on tour – and blah, blah, blah.'

He ends up suddenly losing it with me. He goes, 'I said nothing *focking* happened, alright?'

I'm like, 'Fair enough, Dude. Whatever you say.'

Oisinn goes, 'How far are we from this monastery?'

Fionn's there, 'It's about a ten-minute walk.'

I'm like, 'What monastery is this?'

No one answers me.

I'm there, 'Goys, I know you all hate me right now – and maybe one or two of you have good reason to – but I'm going to be with you for the next, like, month. You can't keep ignoring me.'

Oisinn rolls his eyes – the focking gall of him – and goes, 'Father Fehily left us a list of addresses. Four of them. Apparently, he left letters for us in each of them.'

I'm like, 'What kind of letters?'

'We don't know,' Fionn goes – then he pushes his glasses up onto the bridge of his nose. 'Let's go and find out.'

So we all set off again, Fionn leading, following the route on his Google Maps. After maybe ten or fifteen minutes of walking, we come to this small, churchy building with grey stone walls and, like, a tan-coloured roof.

'Saint Felix,' Fionn goes. 'This is the place.'

In front of us, there's, like, a black, wooden door, with a heavy knocker on it. Oisinn steps forward and – like JP with Katja last night – he gives the thing a seriously good hammering.

Thirty seconds later, the door opens slowly and we find ourselves staring at this, like, ancient dude in monk's robes, who's bent double, like he's searching the floor for a dropped contact lens.

He goes, 'If you're pilgrims on the way to Zubiri, you're on the wrong road.'

I could be wrong, but the dude sounds Irish.

'No, we're not lost,' Fionn goes. 'We are on our way to Zubiri, but we took a detour. Are you Brother Placidus?'

He's there, 'I am – and who might you be?'

Yeah, no, he's *definitely* Irish?

'We're friends of Father Fehily,' Oisinn goes. 'Well, he was our school principal.'

I'm there, 'And rugby coach.'

'Ah,' he goes, 'you're the famous boys he talked about all the time.'

We all smile.

He's there, 'Come in, come in. Will you have some wine?'

Fionn goes, 'No, it's a bit early for –'

But Christian is like, 'Yes, we will,' and he's obviously decided to just go for it in a big-time way.

The dude leads us into this – I think it's a word – *sporse* kitchen with whitewashed walls and a long, black table with two benches on either side. He tells us to sit down, which we do, then he pro-duces a carafe of – I shit you not – *pink* wine and six glasses.

'So how did you know Father Fehily?' Christian goes.

The dude's like, 'Who, Denis?' while he pours us each what my old dear would consider a measure – in other words, three focking measures. 'Oh, we met in Lourdes back in – what was it? – must have been nineteen-sixty-something-or-other.'

I'm like, 'Are you talking about Lourdes in, em –'

I have literally no idea what country Lourdes is in. I'm thicker than camel shit.

'France,' Fionn goes.

Again, it's *such* a Fionn thing to say.

'Yes,' Brother Placidus goes, 'we used to volunteer there for two or three months every summer – pushing old ladies around in wheelchairs!' and he sort of, like, chuckles to himself.

Fionn's there, 'I remember that's what he used to do when the school year ended.'

I take a sip of the wine. It's focking revolting. Monks make shit wine – note to self. I'd honestly rather drink the sweat from Oisinn's hiking socks. Christian knocks it back, though. He's well and truly off the wagon.

JP's there, 'Father Fehily was a huge influence on us. He was a brilliant man.'

'Yes,' Brother Placidus goes, 'he was also a Nazi, of course.'

Oisinn's there, 'But he wasn't a Nazi like the Nazis of today. He was just a big fan of, well, Hitler.'

I'm like, 'He used to play his speeches to us before we went out to play for the school,' and I end up getting a bit emotional about it.

Christian grabs my glass and goes, 'Are you not drinking that?' and he knocks it back in one.

Rather him than me, I think.

Fionn goes, 'So, anyway, Father Fehily left us some money in his will. He said when the first of us turned forty years of age, he wanted us to walk the Camino, just like he did at our age.'

'Yes,' Brother Placidus goes, 'he told me all about his plan before he died.'

Fionn's there, 'He told us we were to collect an envelope here on our way to Zubiri. Do you know anything about it?'

'It's been sitting in my desk drawer for nearly ten years now,' Brother Placidus goes. 'Wait here.'

Off the dude focks – again, bent double. His back must be in rag order. I suddenly realize that I haven't even had a good look at his boat race.

Christian grabs Oisinn's glass of wine and knocks it back.

JP goes, 'For fock's sake, Christian, what are you doing?'

Christian's there, 'It's rude not to drink the wine the nice man poured out for us,' and he's already well on the road to Shitfocked, Illinois.

A minute or two later, Brother Placidus returns, holding a little white envelope, which he hands to Fionn. The dude asks us to stay for dinner. I say yes because I'm focking storving, but Fionn says we have to be in the albergue – that's a hostel to normal people – by half three, otherwise they'll give our beds to someone else.

So – yeah, no – off we fock, with Brother Placidus waving us off, again bent double, at the door.

We're, like, fifty yords down the road when JP goes, 'Are you not going to open it?' meaning the envelope.

Fionn's there, 'I thought I'd wait until we reached the hostel.'

JP goes, 'For fock's sake, Fionn, this is a letter from Father Fehily, who died over ten years ago. This is, like, the closest thing we're going to get to a message from beyond the grave.'

Oisinn's like, 'Yeah, no, I say we open it now.'

So we all stop and Fionn whips out the envelope and tears it open and we all gather around to hear the great man's words of wisdom. Fionn pulls out a single sheet of A4 paper, which has been folded in three. He opens it out. It ends up not being a letter at all. It's, like, a quote from the Bible, printed out.

'It's from the Book of Proverbs,' Fionn goes, unable to hide his disappointment. 'I thought it was going to be a note from Father Fehily himself.'

JP's like, 'Show me that,' because he's still the most religious of us all. First, he reads it to himself, then I go, 'What does it say?'

Then he reads it to *us*? He's like, '*Drink water from your own cistern, running water from your own well. Should your springs overflow in the streets, your streams of water in the public square? Let them be yours alone, never to be shared with strangers.*'

I'm there, 'That sounds like gobbledygook to me. Are you sure that's in the Bible?'

He goes, '*May your fountain be blessed, and may you rejoice in the wife of your youth. A loving doe, a graceful deer – may her breasts . . . satisfy you always.*'

I crack up laughing. I'm like, 'There's no way that's from the Bible.'

'*May you ever be intoxicated with her love,*' JP goes. '*Why, my son, be intoxicated with . . . another man's wife? Why embrace . . . the bosom of a wayward woman?*'

Fionn goes, 'JP, you don't have to read any more.'

But he carries on. He's like, 'For your ways are in full view of the Lord, and he examines all your paths. The evil deeds of the wicked ensnare them; the cords of their sins hold them fast. For lack of discipline . . . they will die. Led astray by their own great . . . folly.'

I'm there, 'Well, you lost me a long focking time ago. Couldn't follow a word of it.'

Oisinn goes, 'Is it supposed to be some kind of clue? As in, like, a puzzle for us to solve?'

Fionn's there, 'Let's just walk. It's going to be another two hours before we reach Zubiri.'

As we set off again, I feel someone give me a nudge on the shoulder. When I turn around, Oisinn is offering me a drink from his water bottle.

Roz asks me how the walk is going and I laugh and tell her I'm already focked.

I'm there, 'It's, like, five hundred miles – and we have to do it in, like, a *month*?'

She goes, 'I meant your friends. Have you patched things up?'

I'm like, 'Not exactly. They tried to abandon me on day one. Fionn focked my good suit in a bin. But I'm sure they'll come round. I can be very chorming.'

She laughs and goes, 'Yes, I know that!'

God, I'd love to ride her right now, if I wasn't on – quite possibly – the other side of the world.

I'm there, 'So – yeah, no – how are things at home?'

She's like, 'Oh, you know, same old, same old. Sincerity brought Jonah over today.'

The dude she stole from my daughter. I don't say shit, though.

I go, 'Sounds like that's getting serious.'

She's there, 'He's such a sweet boy. He has lovely manners.'

I'm like, 'High School Rathgor. Why wouldn't he? Yeah, no, I'm delighted for all porties concerned.'

'Honor's still not talking to her, though. She's very upset. I told her that she'd eventually come round.'

She focking won't.

I'm there, 'Yeah, no, I'm sure she will.'

Honestly, there's more chance of Ronan O'Gara coaching Leinster.

'So where are you off to next?' Roz goes. 'What's tomorrow?'

'According to JP,' I go, 'it's, like, a four-hour walk to, I don't know, Pompa Pompa or something like that?'

'Do you mean Pamplona?'

'Er, yeah, no, quite *possibly*?'

'That's where they do the running of the bulls every year.'

'Oh, yeah, I've seen that on TV.'

'It's supposed to be beautiful. Please don't get chased by any bulls, okay? I want you back in one piece.'

I laugh, then I tell her that I'd better hit the sack.

She goes, 'It's only ten o'clock!'

I'm like, 'Yeah, no, this hostel we're staying in has a strict nine p.m. lights-out policy. Plus, Fionn wants us all up and on the road by six a.m. I miss you.'

'I miss you too.'

'I can't wait to have tantric sex with you again.'

She laughs and goes, 'You can just call it sex, Ross.'

'Sex, then. I can't wait to have sex with you again. By the way, I haven't done the dirt on you – just to let you know.'

'You've only been away three days.'

'That's still a record for me, Roz – believe me.'

She laughs again. She really is the coolest girl I've ever met.

She's like, 'Goodnight, Ross.'

And I'm there, 'Goodnight, Roz.'

I tip back into the dorm. It's, like, a humungous room with, like, thirty sets of bunkbeds in it. The smell of B.O. and feet would stop a herd of elephants in its tracks.

I'm there, 'Tremendous chat with Roz, goys!' a little too loudly for some people. It ends up being greeted by a chorus of shushing and randomers going, 'Will you keep your voice down!' and 'Lights out was an hour ago!'

I'm there, 'Go to focking sleep, then – you pack of focking tossers.'

I use the torch on my iPhone to find my bed. I'm sleeping in the bunk above Fionn. He's fast asleep and he's wearing a – believe it or not – eye mask. I notice his orm hanging over the side of his mattress. As I'm climbing up, I make sure to stand on it, just to get him back for focking my suit in a bin.

He lets a big roar out of him. He's like, 'AAARRRGGGHHH!!!' like the focking drama queen that he is.

Again, there's more shouts of, 'I'm trying to sleep here!' and I'm like, 'Yeah, get a focking life – you focking orsehole.'

I get into the bed and I lie there for, like, ten minutes, thinking happy thoughts about Roz.

Eventually, Fionn goes, 'Are you focking kidding me?' and he sounds *seriously* pissed off?

I'm like, 'What?'

'Are you having a wank?' he goes.

I'm like, 'Yeah – so?'

He's there, 'Can you maybe *not*?'

In fairness to him, the bed is a bit of a squeaker.

I'm there, 'I have to wank off – otherwise, I won't sleep.'

'For fock's sake,' he goes.

Yeah, no, all anyone can hear is the bed going, *wank-wank, wank-wank, wank-wank* . . .

Oisinn – in the next bed – goes, 'Ross, can you maybe find a toilet in which to do it.'

I'm there, 'I'll be finished in a minute. Jesus Christ, you'd swear you never boarded – any of you.'

Wank-wank, wank-wank, wank-wank . . .

Oisinn goes, 'I can't believe I'm focking listening to this.'

I'm there, 'Yeah, says the man who spent a whole J1 summer holding the sausage hostage with me having to listen to you. Anyway, let me concentrate here. The more you keep talking to me, the longer I'm going to take.'

Wank-wank, wank-wank, wank-wank . . .

Suddenly, out of nowhere, JP goes, 'He's thinking about me.'

Instantly, of course, I lose my stroke.

It's like, *wank-wank, wank –*.

I'm there, 'I was in my focking hole thinking about you. I was

228

thinking about Roz – and maybe a little bit about Dua Lipa and Jasmine Tookes.'

'I meant Father Fehily,' JP goes.

Again, there's more shouts of, 'Can you *please* stop talking!' and 'We're getting up in six hours!'

Oisinn's there, 'What about Father Fehily?'

'That quote,' JP goes, 'from the Book of Proverbs. It was aimed at me.'

I'm like, 'What are you talking about?'

'It was all about adultery,' he goes. *'Why, my son, be intoxicated with another man's wife? Why embrace the bosom of a wayward woman?'*

I'm there, 'Are you talking about Katja? She wasn't another man's wife. She told me she's been single for a year. She caught her ex riding his driving instructor – or possibly his *diving* instructor?'

All of a sudden, I hear Christian gagging. I jump out of my bunk, go over to his bed and roll him onto his side.

I'm there, 'Jesus Christ, how much did he have to drink tonight?' No one answers me.

'Father Fehily is sending me a message,' JP goes, 'from Heaven.'

Fionn, who doesn't believe in God or ghosts or any of that stuff, goes, 'JP, Father Fehily has been dead for ten years. It's just a quote that he pulled from the Bible.'

I'm like, 'Exactly,' as I climb into my bunk again, 'he didn't know you were going to cheat on your wife with some random Dutch bird.'

But JP goes, 'Trust me. He's talking to me from the other side.'

I yawn.

I'm there, 'Just to warn you, I'm going back to destroying my eyesight here.'

Wank-wank, wank-wank, wank-wank . . .

We've been walking for, like, two hours and I am focking storving. I mention it as well, but I get no sympathy slash offers of food from the others.

Fionn's there, 'You should have had breakfast before we left Zubiri.'

And I'm like, 'There wasn't focking time.'

'Then you should have got up earlier,' he goes.

I thought there'd be, like, a Buckys or a Costa somewhere along the way, but again it's just more fields and hills and whatever the fock else.

Oisinn's there, 'It's no wonder he's hungry – the amount of energy he expended last night.'

Yeah, no, he's talking about me being up until nearly two, roughing up the hostage.

I'm like, 'Fionn, just stop acting the dick and give me something to eat, will you?'

He's there, 'I don't have anything for you.'

'Yes, you do,' I go. 'I saw you putting bread rolls into your rucksack. And cheese.'

'I said I don't have anything – for *you*.'

'Dude, how long are you going to keep this up?'

'Keep what up?'

'This horseshit. You being a dick to me. Dude, I went to court and I faced the music. I've repaid my debt to society.'

'No, you didn't. You got off – without any punishment whatsoever.'

'Hey, it's not my fault that the judge was a rugby fan. That's how Ireland works.'

'And, what, you think I should just forgive and forget everything you did?'

'That's what Father Fehily would want you to do.'

'Don't use his name against me!'

'And he'd want you to give me a bread roll and a bit of focking cheese as well.'

'Like I said to JP last night, Father Fehily is dead.'

I turn around to the others.

I'm there, 'What about you lot? Are you happy to watch me go hungry?'

'You shouldn't even be here,' JP – under his breath – goes.

I'm there, 'Well, I'm not going to storve, goys. If I have to rely on my wits to feed myself, that's what I'm going to do.'

It's at that exact point that a woman passes me, walking with a stick, and goes, *'Buen Camino!'*

I'm not going to describe her because I don't want to come across as a complete orsehole. But she's not great. She's not great at all. She's, like, late forties and she has, like, Cleopatra hair, except it's dyed bright purple, the object of the exercise being to draw attention away from her face and – not being a dick – but, body.

I'm like, '*Buen Camino!*' quickly separating myself from the others. 'What's that accent? I'm trying to place it.'

'Oh,' she goes, turning around with a big smile on her face, 'I'm from, like, Tennessee!' like she's expecting a round of applause.

I'm there, 'Tennessee, huh? The Lone Stor State!'

She goes, 'No, the Lone Star State is Texas. Tennessee is the Volunteer State.'

I'm like, 'Either way, it's a beautiful port of the world.'

It could be some backwards shithole where people have sex with chickens and drink their own piss for all I know. But American women are, like, low-lying fruit to me. Easy pickings.

She goes, 'So where are you from?'

I'm like, 'Ireland.'

'Oh my God, my great-, great-, great-grandmother came from Bunclody, County Wexford.'

'Bunclody. Stunning.'

Again, I haven't a clue about the place or what goes on there.

She goes, 'So are you walking all the way to Santiago de Compostela?'

I'm there, 'Is that, like, the *end*?'

'Well, yes.'

'Yeah, no, that's the plan alright.'

She introduces herself to me then.

'I'm Vivica,' she goes.

She's no Vivica, by the way. Although with that name, I'd say she's suckered quite a few dudes into going on blind dates with her.

I'm there, 'I'm Neville. Neville Archeson . . . ston.'

She's like, 'Neville Archeson . . . ston?'

'That's right – Neville Archeson . . . ston.'

'Okay,' she goes, 'I'm going to struggle to remember that name.'

You're not the only one, I think.

'Wait a minute,' she goes, 'where's all your stuff, Neville?'

I'm like, 'My *stuff*?'

'Don't you have, like, a rucksack?'

'Yeah, no, it was stolen – along with everything else I own.'

'Stolen?'

'Yeah, no, they took everything. I haven't eaten in literally days.'

'I have food. I can give you food.'

The goys are looking back at me with the usual mixture of disgust and admiration.

I'm there, 'Are you sure? You don't have to. I'm sure I'll come across a bush with berries on it.'

'Neville, you can't walk the Camino on berries,' she goes, then she spots this random picnic bench on the side of the road just up ahead. 'Let's go and sit down. I'm pretty hungry myself.'

And I think, for fock's sake. I just wanted her to *give* me food. I didn't want to have to sit down for a focking meal with her, but suddenly she's setting the actual table, pulling paper plates and plastic cutlery from her rucksack, then Tupperware containers and Ziploc bags with, like, all sorts of shit in them – we're talking turkey drumsticks and pasta salad and avocado and Swiss cheese and Porma ham and sourdough and tomatoes and pesto. She basically lays out a feast for me and I mill into it like I've been rescued from a capsized boat after fifteen days lost at sea.

I make an absolute pig of myself, to the point where she eventually storts putting the lids back on containers, obviously scared that I'll horse the lot. She packs everything back in her rucksack and of course now that I've satisfied my appetite, I'm left with the age-old dilemma of how to get rid of the woman without coming across as a dick.

I'm there, 'So, anyway, it was nice to meet you,' standing up from the table, 'em –'

Jesus Christ, I've forgotten her name already.

'Vivica,' I suddenly remember. 'Thanks for the, er, nosebag.'

She goes, 'Hey, we can walk together if you like.'

'Er, yeah, no, the thing is, Vivica, I'm a lot more unfit than I *look*? I'd only hold you up.'

'Hey, I'm pretty slow myself – especially since I had my gall bladder removed in April.'

I don't even know what that is, but Jesus Christ I feel sick.

She goes, 'We'll find a pace that suits us both. It'll be nice to have company on the walk to Pamplona.'

Fock's sake, I think. I didn't agree to this.

'Neville,' she goes to herself. 'And what did you say your second name was? Archeson . . . ston?'

I'm there, 'Yeah, no, that sounds about right.'

We stort walking. And, of course, the goys – who love seeing the Rossmeister with his back to the wall – have decided to wait up the road for me.

She sees them standing there on the side of the road smiling in our general postcode and she goes, 'Hey! Are you Neville's friends?'

Neville – oh, they all love that one.

Oisinn's like, 'Ah, there you are, Neville! We thought we'd lost you!'

I'm thinking, Hey, at least they're smiling again – even Fionn.

So we end up walking with Vivica the entire way to Pamplona and she fills us in on every focking boring detail of her summer trip to Europe so far. She's been all over France, apparently, and to Italy and – yeah, no – to five or six of the Greek islands and I'm thinking, This is like reading Fionn's blog the time he travelled around South America. Except I *didn't* read it. No one did.

'So why did you want to do the Camino?' Oisinn goes.

Vivica's there, 'It was a promise I made to my sister. My late sister.'

Fionn's there, 'Oh, I'm so sorry for your loss.'

She's like, 'Yeah, her name was Anka. She died in January.'

I'm there, 'Er, shit one,' because it's one of those times when you feel like you *should* say something?

'Anyway, Anka did the Camino five years ago,' she goes, 'and she always said it was the happiest time of her life. So I'm sort of, like, following in her footsteps – to keep a promise that I made to her.'

I'm like, 'Er, yeah, no, fair focks.'

It's, like, midday when we finally reach Pamplona and I'm thinking, Okay, now it's finally time to say goodbye and good riddance to the girl and I don't care if she thinks I'm rude.

I'm there, 'Anyway, Vivica, I've loved listening to the stories of your travels and blah, blah, blah –'

But before I can give her the big kiss-off, Oisinn goes, 'Where are you staying, Vivica?'

She goes, 'The Municipal Albergue Jesús y María.'

'That's where *we're* staying!' Fionn goes – focking delighted with himself.

Oh, they're loving watching me squirm.

Fionn's there, 'Why don't we all get ourselves checked in and then we can explore Pamplona together. Neville, you were saying how much you were looking forward to seeing the cathedral and the Museum of Navarra and the Plaza del Castillo. We could do it together.'

'That would be *so* good,' Vivica goes.

I'm thinking, Fock's sake – all this for a bit of Swiss cheese and some Porma focking ham. I get myself into some situations.

But – yeah, no – that's what ends up happening. We end up spending the entire day walking around – I shit you not – museums and churches and other boring places to the point where I'm nearly praying that a bull would come chorging down the street to gore me and put me out of my literally misery.

The whole time we're walking around, I can hear Oisinn and Christian trying to basically sic the girl on me.

She's going, 'So what's Neville's situation? Is he, like, married or –'

And Christian – who's been knocking back wine all afternoon – goes, 'He's actually widowed. And I'm not being funny but his late wife looked a lot like you.'

This is what I'm having to listen to while Fionn is reading shit out of his guidebook about the burial place of some saint or other.

Oisinn goes, 'Neville has been very lonely since, em, Shoshanna died. It's funny, you're the first girl we've seen him really open up to since then.'

I'm looking at her face out of the corner of my eye. It's like all of her focking Christmases have come at once.

It's one of those days that you think will never focking end. We all end up having dinner together that night outside this, like, tavern called Ibarrola, which was a spot that her sister apparently loved.

We end up eating Pintxos, which are basically small slices of bread with bits of fish, meat and peppers skewered to them with a toothpick and drinking white wine of some kind in the warm evening sun. Some random local dude is standing a few feet away playing 'Volare' on the accordion.

Vivica goes, 'Anka said this was the place she actually felt *the* most centred she ever felt.'

I think Vivica is as pissed as the rest of us. I'm certainly throwing the wine into me, wishing – as you do sometimes – that the sun would just fock the fock off and the nightmare of this day would end.

Anyway, night eventually comes, as it always does. I do a big theatrical yawn and announce that I'm heading back to the hostel to get some kip.

Vivica goes, 'Yeah, I'm kind of tired too.'

I'm like, 'Goys, are you coming?' and I can hear the desperation in my voice.

But they're all there, 'No, I think I might stay out for one or two more.'

Fock's sake. So – yeah, no – I end up having to go back to the hostel with just Vivica.

'So what was she like?' she goes.

I'm like, 'Who?'

She's there, 'Shoshanna,' and I'm thinking, I can't believe I'm having to invent a dead wife for a woman I have literally no interest in.

I'm there, 'I don't know. She was, like, five foot six,' totally saying shit off the top of my head now. 'Black hair. Big lips. Big chest.'

I don't know why but I'm describing Dua Lipa.

She goes, 'But tell me about *her*. What did she do?'

I'm there, 'She was, em, a paediatrician,' even though I'm not a hundred per cent sure what that even is. 'That was her job and, well, her main passion in life.'

She's like, 'She loved children?'

I'm there, 'No, feet – I'm pretty sure.'

I get into my bunk and I go, 'Anyway, I'm pretty wrecked, it has to be said. I'm going to get my head down now.'

I get into the sack and I lie there with my eyes closed, listening out to hear if she's asleep so that I can maybe badger the witness some more, but then all of a sudden I hear her standing beside my bed. She grabs the covers and she throws them back.

She goes, 'I hope you don't consider this inappropriate. I don't know about you, but after the months and months of grief that I've been through, I just need to feel the consolation of a warm body against me tonight.'

She gets into the bed beside me and pulls me close to her, then after a few seconds she storts sniffing the air and she goes, 'I think that t-shirt you're wearing could do with a wash.'

I wake up at, like, five o'clock in the morning and I manage to, like, prise myself from Vivica's lobster-like grip. Luckily, she's a heavy sleeper and doesn't wake up.

I walk across the floor of the dorm and I give Fionn, then JP, a shove.

I'm like, 'Come on,' in, like, an urgent whisper, 'wake up, let's go.'

Fionn puts on his glasses. He's like, 'What time is it?'

I'm there, 'It's a quarter to seven.'

'Oh, no,' he goes, sitting bolt upright in the bed, 'we've overslept. I wanted to be on the road by six.'

I'm there, 'Get your shit together, then,' and he hops out of the bed and storts throwing on his green t-shirt, shorts and hiking boots. I walk over to Christian and Oisinn's beds and I shake them awake too.

I'm like, 'Come on, goys, let's get the show on the road.'

Oisinn goes, 'Do I have time for a shower?'

Fionn's there, 'Let's all have one when we get to Puente la Reina. It's a pretty much five-hour walk and we're already –' and that's when he looks at his phone. 'Ross, it's not a quarter to seven – it's focking five o'clock in the morning.'

I'm there, 'Dude, I have to get the fock out of here before *she* wakes up.'

Oisinn's like, 'Dude, you were the one who led her on.'

'I didn't know she was a focking Klingon,' I go. 'Seriously, I need to put some road between me and her.'

JP's there, 'Did you ride her?' as he sits down to pull on his hiking boots.

'No, I focking didn't ride her. She just held onto me all night and cried about her dead sister.'

They all find this hilarious.

I'm like, 'Come on, let's go,' and that's when I notice her rucksack leaning against the wall. I tip over to it.

'What are you doing?' Fionn goes.

I'm there, 'I'm getting myself a bit of brekky.'

'Ross,' Oisinn goes, 'that's crossing a line – seriously.'

I'm like, 'What, and *she* wasn't crossing a line when she hopped into the focking bed beside me last night and I had to listen to her banging on all night about how the universe had brought us together because it recognized that we were two grieving souls?'

I whip out two or three Tupperware boxes and a couple of Ziploc bags.

I'm there, 'Don't worry, I'm not going to take it all. I'll leave her the zucchini. I wasn't mad about it. And, to be honest, I can take or leave sourdough. Actually, I'll take it – it definitely fills a gap – but I'll leave her a slice or two.'

I find a plastic bag at the bottom of her rucksack and I put my stash into that, then I go, 'Okay, dudes, let's hit the road.'

So we set off for – what did Fionn say? – Puente la Reine? It's, like, pitch-dork outside, but they all have, like, head torches, which light the road ahead for us.

Christian is quiet. He's absolutely hanging.

I'm there, 'Dude, maybe you should lay off the sauce today – what do you think?'

He's like, 'What are you, my focking mother?'

Oisinn goes, 'Jesus Christ, Ross, that t-shirt of yours is really storting to stink.'

I'm like, 'I'll wash it when we get to, I don't know, wherever,' and I'm walking along, happily swinging my little plastic nosebag by my side.

'Stealing food from a sleeping woman,' Fionn goes. 'Are there any depths to which you won't stoop?'

But it's nice because at least they're, like, *talking* to me again?

We walk for a couple of hours before the sun storts to come up. It's, like, deathly quiet and we seem to be the only people on the road this early. My feet are storting to get sore. I've worn nothing but Dubes since I was, like, ten years of age, but they're definitely not a walking shoe and I've already got, like, blisters on the balls of both feet.

I don't know if it's because the mood between me and the goys is improving, but I'm storting to actually appreciate the scenery, which is highly unusual for me. I'm looking at, like, fields of wheat, stretching off as far as the eye can see, then fields full of sunflowers, we're talking thousands and thousands of them, and I'm thinking how beautiful everything looks.

I must be still shit-faced from last night.

I decide to ring Honor to find out how she's getting on. She answers on, like, the seventh ring, which means she was obviously sleeping.

She goes, 'Why the fock are you ringing me at – oh! my God! – not even nine o'clock in the *morning?*'

I'm there, 'I was just thinking about you – wondering how you were.'

She's like, 'Er, can you not just send me a WhatsApp like normal people?'

I'm there, 'I suppose that's one way of looking at it.'

'How is the Camino?'

'I'm going to be honest, there's a lot more walking involved than I expected.'

'And what about your friends? Are they talking to you again?'

'Yeah, no, a few bumps along the road, Honor, but we're getting on like a house on fire now. We're pretty much back to the way we used to be.'

I notice Fionn, just in front of me, shaking his head at that line.

Honor goes, 'So have you done the dirt on Roz yet?'

Seriously, why does everyone have such low expectations of me?

I'm there, 'No, I haven't done the dirt on Roz, Honor, even

though I've had plenty of opportunities – one with a Dutch girl who was an absolute lasher and then one with an American girl who, well, wasn't. But it was there on a plate for me if I'd wanted it.'

'Dad,' Honor goes, 'what have I told you before about boundaries?'

I'm like, 'Yeah, no, sorry. I was actually talking to Roz, by the way. She said that Sincerity and that Jonah dude are still doing a line.'

'Oh my God,' Honor goes, 'they're doing, like, TikTok dances together now. The stupid focking bitch. She was, like, no one until she storted hanging around with me. I turned her from a weed into a flower.'

'Maybe it's time you, em, reversed the process. Send her back to Nerdsville.'

'What do you mean?'

'Like, does she still have any of your clothes?'

'She has loads of my clothes – and my make-up.'

'Well, send her a text message and tell her you want all your shit back. You owe this girl nothing, Honor. She's not your friend any more – as a matter of fact, she never was. See how this Jonah dude likes her when she's back in her shit clothes.'

She goes, 'Oh my God, I'm going to do that right now. Thanks, Dad!' and she hangs up on me.

I get the impression that the goys have been listening to every word of the conversation and I sense a bit of, I don't know, shock slash disapproval at my call-it-like-it-is approach to parenting.

I go, 'That, my friends, is how you stop your children being taken for focking mugs.'

We walk on for another good bit until Fionn eventually goes, 'El Alto del Perdón isn't too far away. But get ready for a bit of a climb.'

I've no idea what El Alto whatever-the-fock even is, but he's not wrong about the climb. The route ends up being pretty steep and rocky and suddenly the blisters on my feet are hurting like fock.

We finally reach the top of this, like, hill and El Alto whatever turns out to be this, like, sculpture of all these, I suppose, pilgrims doing the walk with, like, horses and dogs and donkeys.

239

'It's one of the most photographed features on the Camino,' Fionn goes – to which there's no real response, so I don't offer one.

Christian's there, 'I told Lychee I'd send her a selfie when we got here,' and he whips out his phone and storts taking a picture of himself standing next to one of the dudes on horseback.

He looks like shit, by the way. I'm talking about Christian, not the dude on the horse. His eyes are, like, seriously bloodshot and he's obviously decided to let his goatee become, like, a full beard, which is all scraggly and filthy-looking.

'Let's get a selfie of the whole group,' Oisinn goes and they all huddle together and there's this, like, awkward moment when everyone's wondering does that include me, until JP finally goes, 'Ross, get in the photo, will you?' so that's what ends up happening.

'Here's to Father Fehily!' Oisinn goes.

And I'm there, 'Castlerock Über Alles!'

The others all shout it as well. They're like, 'Castlerock Über Alles!'

It's a definite moment – the first we've shared in a long, long time.

We stort making our way down the hill then. It's pretty hord-going, especially on the fronts of our thighs, but the months of training are obviously standing to the goys because they're, like, basically the length of a rugby pitch in front of me. I'm in, like, agony with the blisters.

They eventually stop to let me catch up with them.

I'm there, 'I need to sit down,' because on top of everything else the sun is beating down on us and I can feel the back of my neck getting burned.

Fionn goes, 'According to the map, there's a picnic area about five minutes ahead,' so we walk to that, then we all sit down to take a load off.

I'm, like, wrecked. We *all* are? I slip off my Dubes and tear off my socks to check out my feet.

'Jesus Christ,' Oisinn goes when he sees my blisters. Yeah, no, they're the size of, like, two-euro coins and they're sort of, like, an angry shade of red. 'How are you even able to walk like that?'

I'm there, 'I suppose I've always had a serious, serious pain tolerance threshold.'

I'm always trying to bring the conversation around to rugby.

JP goes, 'Dude, you've got to get yourself a pair of hiking boots.'

And Fionn's there, 'Maybe he can steal them from a sleeping woman when we get to Puente la Reina.'

He's still holding on to a lot of hurt.

'Which reminds me,' I go, putting my plastic bag on the table, 'does anyone fancy a bit of lunch?'

JP's like, 'Ross, I am not touching that food.'

And Oisinn goes, 'Me neither. It was a shitty thing to do on that girl.'

I'm there, 'All the more for me,' as I stort emptying the contents of the bag onto the table.

'What the fock is that?' Christian suddenly goes.

I'm there, 'I think she said it was, like, duck *liver* pâté?'

'Not that,' he goes. 'I'm talking about that shit there – in the Ziploc bag.'

I suddenly notice the bag that he's talking about. I pick it up. It's, like, stuffed to bursting point with what looks very much to me like –

'Jesus Christ,' Fionn goes. 'Are those . . . ashes?'

I'm there, 'They, em, certainly *look* like ashes?' as I suddenly experience this horrible, sinking feeling in my stomach.

'Shit the focking bed,' Oisinn goes. 'Ross, that's Vivica's focking sister.'

'You know what you have to do,' Fionn goes.

This is after we've had a night to sleep slash drink on it.

He's like, 'Seriously, if there's any humanity in you at all.'

In fairness to Fionn, he always knows the difference between right and wrong.

I'm like, 'Fock that, I'm not going back.'

He goes, 'You don't have to *go* back. She's walking the same route as us. She's going to be somewhere here in Puente la Reina. Just go and look for her and tell her you made a mistake.'

'What, I was stealing food from her bag and I accidentally stole her dead sister?'

'Yes, because that's what happened.'

'I'm not doing that. No focking way. Don't worry, I have a plan.'

'What's this plan?' Oisinn goes.

I'm there, 'Well, she mentioned that she was doing the Camino as, like, a promise to her sister, right? So she was obviously planning to sprinkle her ashes somewhere when she got to the end.'

Christian's like, 'Yeah? And?'

'Well,' I go, 'I'll sprinkle her ashes for her.'

JP's there, 'Sprinkle them where?'

I'm like, 'I don't know – isn't there some, like, big church that I heard one of you mention?'

Fionn goes, 'Are you talking about the Santiago de Compostela Cathedral?' which is, like, classic Fionn.

I'm there, 'Yeah, no, quite possibly – so I was thinking I could just, like, tip her out there.'

'Tip her out there?' Fionn goes, clearly horrified by this idea.

'What if that *wasn't* the promise she made to her sister?' JP goes. 'What if she's planning to keep on walking all the way to Finisterre – to sprinkle the ashes in the Atlantic? It's, like, an extra few days of walking.'

I'm like, 'Okay, I'm definitely not doing that. Maybe I'll bring her home and tip her into Bulloch Horbour. I mean, it's all the same sea, isn't it? I'm presuming it all links up?'

Fionn's there, 'Do you not see that this is exactly what happened between us?'

'In terms of?'

'You doing something shitty and then trying to weasel your way out of it.'

'I don't see how they're similar at all.'

'You have the opportunity to do the right thing here and once again you're choosing the easy way out because you don't want to face the music.'

'Okay, that's a serious stretch to say the two things are similar.'

'Can we at least take her off the table?' Christian goes.

Yeah, no, we're sitting in the Casa Mortija and the sight of the ashes is definitely putting me off my potato omelette.

I'm there, 'Can I put her in *your* rucksack?'

Christian's like, 'No, you focking can't.'

I look at the others and they're all just, like, shaking their heads.

'Fine,' I go, 'I'll carry her myself. I'll finish the food and I'll throw her back in the plastic bag.'

JP's phone storts vibrating on the table then. We can all see that it's, like, Delma trying to FaceTime him – except he makes no move to answer it?

I'm there, 'Dude, are you not going to get that?'

He's like, 'No . . . I can't . . . face her?'

'Is it because you did the dirt on her?'

He goes quiet for about thirty seconds, during which time we're all just staring at the phone as it – yeah, no – rings out.

I'm like, 'Dude, I'm not going to tell her that you rode that Dutch bird – and I don't think any of these goys will either.'

'JP,' Fionn goes, 'that Bible verse had nothing to do with you. It's just a coincidence that it happened to be about, well –'

'Adultery,' Christian goes, looking like he's about to vom.

'You don't understand,' JP goes. 'I can't face her because . . . Jesus Christ, I can't bear to look at her any more.'

Like I said, she's some focking sight with the big banjoed mouth on her.

He goes, 'I don't think I'll ever be able to . . . make love to her again.'

On the upside, with those lips, I'd say she's got a sucking action like a focking airplane toilet. But I don't say that to him. He's not in the mood to hear about silver linings.

Instead, I go, 'Just close your eyes and think about, I don't know, Zendaya or Kelly Piquet.'

He roars at me then. He's like, 'I don't want to think about Zendaya or Kelly Piquet! When I have sex with my wife, I want to think about my wife!'

That causes more than a few punters to look at us over the tops of their café con leches and their whatever elses.

I'm there, 'Dude, you can't keep blaming me for what happened.'

He goes quiet again.

Then he's like, 'I don't blame you for what happened. I blame . . . me.'

I'm there, 'In terms of?'

'Delma had been talking about having work done for weeks before you ever said it to her about her mouth.'

'I just happened to mention that you'd a thing about mickey lips.'

'I knew she was massively insecure about the age difference. She was talking about having work done. And I didn't exactly talk her out of it. As a matter of fact –'

'What?'

'I used her laptop one day to look up images of Lindsey Wixson – then I deliberately left the page open for her to find it.'

I'm there, 'And you let me think it was *my* fault?' and I make an actual lunge for him across the table.

Oisinn grabs a hold of me, pinning my orms.

I'm like, 'You focker! You focking, focking focker!' which – again – draws a lot of eyes on us. It's not what you'd call pilgrim language.

JP's there, 'Ross, wait – there's something else that I have to get off my chest.'

I'm like, 'What, there's more?' and bear in mind that Oisinn is still holding me *back* at this stage?

JP's there, 'When Father Fehily was talking about adultery –'

'He wasn't talking about adultery,' Fionn goes. 'It was just a random quote from the Bible. How could he have known that you were going to sleep with that Dutch girl?'

JP goes, 'I wasn't thinking about the Dutch girl . . . Ross, I slept with Sorcha.'

I'm like, 'What? When?' because I'm literally stunned.

'It was years ago,' he goes. 'You two were on a break at the time.'

I'm there, 'That's not an excuse.'

Which is horseshit, of course – it's always worked for me.

He goes, 'She'd just found out you were riding a woman in Cabinteely. In Highland Grove.'

I'm there, 'It was Prospect Lawn. Wait a minute, that was just before our fifth wedding anniversary.'

He looks away. He knows what's coming next.

I'm there, 'It was you! *You* were the one who gave my wife gonorrhoea!'

There are literally gasps in the café. Which is understandable. Fionn tries to point out that there are priests and nuns present. But I make another lunge for JP and this time even Oisinn – one of the best front-rows to ever play the game at Irish schools level, bear in mind – can't hold me back.

I put my two hands around his throat and I stort trying to literally throttle the focker. He manages to push me off him and I go flying backwards onto my orse, sending tables and chairs spilling every-where. I jump up and go at him again, throwing punches at him – missing with most of them – while calling him every this, that and the other under the sun, while he uses his orms to cover up.

Then Oisinn, Fionn and Christian manage to pin my orms to my sides and pull me away from him.

'You gave my wife gonorrhoea!' I go. 'You gave my wife gonorrhoea!'

The manager dude tips over to us and says something to us in Spanish, which presumably means he wants us to leave.

'Oh, fock,' Oisinn goes. 'Oh, fock! Oh, fock! Oh, fock!' and I notice that he's looking down at our feet, where the Ziploc bag con-taining Vivica's sister's ashes has spilled all over the floor.

7.

Quantum of Taurus

No one has spoken a word in the two hours since we set off for Estella, which is apparently our next stop. Yeah, no, I'm walking at the very back of the group – my blisters are in absolute agony – while JP is walking at the very front, and the others are all spread out on the road between us, acting almost like a *buffer*? And, like I said, no one is saying shit. Day five on the road and we're already completely and utterly sick of the sight of each other.

What the fock was Father Fehily thinking?

I've got my phone out and I'm scrolling through Ronan's – yeah, no – Instagram account, looking at photos of him and Avery and Rihanna-Brogan in Disneyland Paris. There's, like, a picture of them eating toffee apples while wearing Mickey and Minnie Mouse ears and one of them sitting in this, like, giant teacup. There's a picture of them standing in front of Sleeping Beauty's castle and there's one of them screaming as they come flying down Splash Mountain. I'm suddenly grinning like an idiot and I don't know if it's just seeing Ronan and his new girlfriend and his daughter having so much fun together or if it's the sight of Rihanna-Brogan with her orm around Donald Duck's waist and a plaster on her face from where she had her borstal mork lasered off.

I look up and I notice that the goys have all stopped walking and are standing in a little, I suppose, scrum just ahead of me on the road.

I catch up with them and I'm like, 'What the fock is going on?'

JP's there, 'Your *girlfriend* is walking just ahead of us,' and I really don't like the way he says the word girlfriend because nothing happened between us, because she was horrendous.

I'm there, 'I presume you're talking about Vivica?'

And he's like, 'Yes, I'm talking about Vivica,' and he has some focking nerve using that tone with me. 'You're welcome, by the way.'

I'm there, 'What do you mean?'

'Well, I could have said nothing and let us catch up with her,' he tries to go. 'Or even called her back. And then you'd have had to explain what you're doing with her sister.'

Yeah, no, we managed to pretty much scrape most of the ashes up off the floor and put them back into the bag, although unfortunately there's little bits of omelette and flaky pastry in there now too.

I'm like, 'What, you want me to be grateful to you now, do you?'

I swear to God, he goes, 'Well, yes, I focking do.'

Fionn's there, 'Okay, this has gone far enough. Ross, we're going to catch up with her and we're going to give her back her sister's ashes.'

I'm like, 'We can't – look at the focking state of them.'

Yeah, no, I can see a contact lens in the bag as well and – Jesus Christ – possibly even a cigarette butt.

Fionn goes, 'Ross, do you have any idea what that poor girl is going through? She made a promise to her sister –'

I'm there, 'And I'm keeping that promise. Dude, it's not like I've tipped her down the sink or something. I'm going to bring her to Santa-wherever-we're-going and I'm going to give her a proper focking send-off – we're talking prayers, we're talking hymns –'

'Is that a cigarette butt in the bag?' JP goes.

I'm like, 'Hey, you were the one who knocked over the table and spilled it everywhere.'

He goes, 'That's because you attacked me.'

'That's because you gave my wife gonorrhoea. And there I was feeling bad because Delma's ended up with a mouth like a . . . I don't even want to *say* what?'

'You didn't feel bad. You didn't feel bad at all.'

'Okay, I'm *going* to say it. A sex doll. She has a mouth like a sex doll. And it wasn't my fault at all. But you having sex with my wife, on the other hand –'

'You were on a break. You rode a woman in Cabinteely.'

'I rode women everywhere! Everywhere!'

'Well, she was upset. She came to me.'

'Oh, yeah, and you were only too happy to console her – and your mickey riddled with focking knob-rot.'

'This is going to achieve nothing.'

'Who gave it to you?'

'Why is that important?'

'Hey, I'm the one asking the questions here. Who gave it to you?'

'Vicky Wiley.'

'Vicky Wiley? I don't even know who that is – *or* what school she went to.'

'She worked in the cor pork of the Ilac Centre. I think she might be from The Naul.'

'I don't give a fock where she's from. I'm more interested in where she's been. So she gave it to you and you gave it to Sorcha – and Sorcha gave it to me?'

'Ross, the story that Sorcha told you has fock-all to do with me. You should talk to *her* about it.'

'Oh, I will – trust me.'

Fock, my blisters are absolutely killing me now. I hobble over to the side of the road and I sit down on a wall.

A group of walkers – pilgrims, whatever – walk past us and they go, '*Buen Camino!*' and I'm like, 'Yeah, whatever,' because that shit is *already* storting to get old?

I take off my right Dube and I can't believe what I'm seeing. There's, like, a humungous hole in the sole of it – as in, it's worn right through. I whip off the other one and – yeah, no – it's, like, the same story.

Oisinn goes, 'Dude, you're not going to be able to walk any further in those.'

Fionn's there, 'He's right. We've got three weeks of walking ahead of us.'

I'm like, 'Well, they're the only shoes I happen to have. So what am I supposed to do?'

'You could abandon,' Fionn goes, 'and go home. Lot of people do. There's no shame in it.'

I'm like, 'Yeah, no, you'd love that, wouldn't you? You didn't even want me here in the first place.'

Christian reaches into his rucksack and pulls out a naggin of vodka.

I'm like, 'Dude, you'd want to lay off that, seriously.'

He unscrews the top and takes a long swig. We all look at each other, thinking the same thing – what can we do here?

JP goes, 'Christian, is this how you want to go back to Lychee?'

He's just like, 'Focking . . . Lychee,' like he's – I don't know – *sick* of her or something?

I'm there, 'Whoa, what's wrong? Things not so great in Influencer Paradise, huh?'

He doesn't say shit.

'Because to look at the two of you on Instagram,' I go, 'you'd swear you were Prince Harry and Meghan focking Morkle in the first throes of it.'

'Ross –' Oisinn goes, trying to get me to shut up so that Christian can talk.

He goes, 'It's the whole, you know, sex thing.'

I actually laugh. I'm there, 'Don't tell me that she's one of these focking celibates that I heard about on the radio. Because if you're not getting any, with the amount of shit she gives you –'

JP's like, 'Fock's sake, Ross. Let him talk.'

Christian takes another mouthful of voddy. He goes, 'If there's one thing I've learned from Lychee –'

Aport from how to take a decent focking photo, I think – but I don't say it.

'– it's that, when it comes to sex,' he goes, 'we are basically repressed.'

Oisinn's like, 'Who's repressed?' because *he* has sex with men, bear in mind – well, *a* man – and there's nothing wrong with that.

'Our generation,' Christian goes. 'We might as well be our parents.'

I'm there, 'So, like, what sort of shit is Lychee into – as in, what sort of things does she do to you?'

'She likes extreme sex,' he goes. 'I'm talking about, like, *weird* stuff?'

I'm there, 'Okay, just to get the ball rolling, I was with a nurse from Bellewstown who asked me to lie underneath a glass coffee table while she took a shit on it. It was a nice table as well. I think it might have been from Habitat.'

'Well, Lychee likes choking me,' he goes. 'And she likes *being* choked. To the point of, like, blacking out. She wants to hurt me and she wants me to hurt her.'

'But if you're not comfortable doing those things,' Fionn goes, 'why don't you just tell her that?'

He's there, 'Because I'm afraid of –'

'Losing her?' Oisinn goes.

She'd be no loss – trust me. She's gorgeous to look at but she's got nothing but focking dust motes between her ears and that's saying something coming from me.

Christian goes, 'Sex with Lauren was, you know, pretty ordinary – and predictable.'

I'm thinking, No focking surprises there.

'She liked me to go on top,' he goes. 'And she didn't like me talking during it because she said it disturbed her concentration. She let me go down on her once when we were both drunk in Westport and she tapped out after, like, twenty seconds.'

'And you're saying it's totally the opposite with Lychee?' Oisinn goes.

'Every time we do it, it's like I'm in a focking porn movie and she's directing it.'

Fionn goes, 'I was actually reading a very interesting orticle in the *New Yorker* about how online porn has changed young people's expectations of sex,' trying to make it all about him as usual. 'I'm talking about males *and* females.'

I'm there, 'Christian, tell us more about the shit she makes you do. You said it was like being in a porn movie.'

'Like I said,' he goes, 'she's big into pain – feeling it and dishing it out. And when we're, you know, doing it, she keeps telling me about different friends of hers who she's fantasizing about at that exact moment.'

I'm like, 'Fock.'

He takes another swig of the voddy, finishing the bottle in, like, three mouthfuls.

'But then, like Fionn said,' he goes, 'I'm wondering is that just the new normal? As in, is that what sex is like for people in their twenties?'

I'm there, 'Give us some more examples of the things she makes you do – the weirder, the better.'

'The worst thing she makes me do,' he goes, 'is feel like she really, really hates me. I mean, the things that come out of her mouth during sex, you wouldn't believe. But then, the next day, if I accidentally misgender somebody on the TV, or if I use a word that the woke crowd have decided is no longer acceptable, she turns into this pious, sanctimonious, almost nun-like figure, talking about the offence that I've caused and how she's been triggered.'

Oisinn shakes his head. He goes, 'I don't know what to tell you, Dude.'

I'm there, 'I do. Drop her like a lap dancer with a dry cough.'

'Ross –' Oisinn goes.

'I'm serious. She's too young for you to be sexually compatible, Dude. End of conversation.'

Fionn goes, 'Will we walk?'

And I'm like, 'Yeah,' because Vivica will be halfway to – and bear in mind that geography was never my strongest subject – but *Romania* by now?

And the most incredible thing happens then. I notice that JP has taken off his hiking boots and he's, like, removing the insoles from them.

'Here,' he goes, suddenly handing them to me, and I don't know what to say, so I'm just like, 'Thanks.'

I slide them into my Dubes, then I put them on, getting down on one knee to tighten the laces. And, as I'm standing up, I notice that JP is offering me his hand.

'Bygones?' he goes.

And, of course, I can't leave him hanging. It's the bro code. So I shake his hand and I'm like, 'Bygones.'

Sorcha answers on the sixth ring and she sounds definitely *not* a happy bunny? As a matter of fact, I'm wondering did JP text her to tell her that I'd probably be ringing.

She goes, 'Ross, I have a very busy afternoon ahead of me,' on the major defensive, 'so you'd better have a good reason for ringing – like an accident or something.'

I'm thinking, That's focking lovely, isn't it?

I'm like, 'Too busy to talk to your husband of, I don't know, however many years it was – minus the five you chopped off when you told the press that we were leading separate lives?'

She goes, 'You always led a separate life,' and I'm thinking, The absolute focking hypocrisy of it.

I'm there, 'So – yeah, no – what has you so supposably busy?' trying to come up with a way of bringing up the subject of her adultery.

She goes, 'If you must know, I have a meeting with the Taoiseach over my proposal to limit the number of miles that Irish citizens are permitted to fly and drive each year. He wants to introduce exemptions for certain people – his friends essentially – and I've decided that I'm going to make a stand.'

I'm like, 'I'm sure you'll get a big *clap* for that.'

She's there, 'What's that supposed to mean?' because she seems genuinely confused by it.

I'm there, 'I'm just saying, if you get the clap, then it will have been fully, fully deserved.'

She goes, 'Are you drinking?'

The answer is yes because I'm sitting outside a little trattoria in a village called Los Arcos with a pint of the local piss in front of me and the sun beating down on my head.

I'm there, 'No, I'm not drinking at all. Are you not going to give me a *clap* for that?'

I'm thinking, Why isn't she taking the focking bait here?

She goes, 'Well, you're obviously having an *amazing* time on the

Camino if the only thing you can think to do at three o'clock on a Wednesday afternoon is ring your ex-wife and act like a weirdo.'

I'm like, 'I *know*, Sorcha.'

'Know what?' she tries to go. 'What are you talking about?'

I'm there, 'I know that you rode JP – and that's how you ended up with gonorrhoea on our fifth wedding anniversary.'

Oh, it's a real conversation stopper – especially given that she had me on speaker phone.

She goes, 'For fock's sake, Ross,' suddenly scrambling for the phone. 'I'm in the cor with my dad.'

I'm there, 'Hey, if you're too important to pick up the phone to me, that's your problem.'

'I can't believe we're having this conversation.'

'Well, believe it. JP spilled his guts out to me. He thought Father Fehily was talking to him from beyond the grave, telling him to own it, so he did.'

In the background, I can hear her old man going, 'Hang up on him! He's not a port of your life any more, Dorling.'

I'm like, 'So – you and JP, huh?'

She goes, 'You and I were on a break at the time. You had sex with a woman in Highland Grove.'

I'm there, 'I had sex with a woman in Prospect Lawn. Why does everyone keep saying Highland Grove?'

I can hear her old man going, 'He's nothing but a deceitful ignoramus – like father, like son, I'm sorely tempted to add.'

I'm there, '*He* still buys your act, of course, doesn't he? Thinks the sun shines out of your orse and you've never put a foot wrong in your entire life. Of course, we all know that's horseshit now.'

'What does it matter any more, Ross?'

'It matters because – as usual – you tried to take the moral high ground. You had sex with my friend. He gave you gonorrhoea – and you gave it to me.'

'Well, what does it say about our marriage that I automatically assumed that I got it from you?'

'It says that you're an absolute hypocrite who pretends to be whiter than white.'

'How do you even know that I gave it to you and not the other way around?'

'Because JP told me he got it from Vicky Wiley.'

'Who's Vicky Wiley?'

'Why does that even matter? She worked in the cor pork of the Ilac Centre. The point is that she gave him the clap. He gave you the clap. And you – even though butter wouldn't melt in your pretty much mouth – gave *me* the clap?'

'I'm about to hang up. I'm sick of this conversation.'

'But it suited you – because of my rep – to pretend it was the other way around. So *I* was the one who ended up having to listen to the big lecture from Doctor focking – what was her name?'

'Doctor Gopalakrishnapp.'

'Yeah, no, her. I had to listen to her giving out shit to me for not wrapping my wobbler. I wouldn't mind, I actually *wore* a johnny that night in Prospect Lawn. Here, I'm just remembering, I also paid for the antibiotics – yours *and* mine.'

'Well, I'll Revolut you the money as soon as I hang up on you.'

I'm there, 'I can't believe I had to come all the way to Spain to find this out – that you slept with one of my friends.'

She goes, 'Ross, you slept with all of my friends. And, by the way, while I have you on the phone, my sister has been saying some – oh my God – *very* random things over the past few days. As in, like, dropping some very dork *hints* about stuff?'

Oh, shit.

I'm there, 'Er – in terms of, like, what?'

'She sent me a photograph of her scan,' she goes, 'and a message saying, oh my God, doesn't my baby look like Ross?'

'And, em, does it – in your view?'

'It's a three-month-old foetus, Ross. How the hell do I know if it looks like you? I'm more interested in why she's saying it?'

'Yeah, no, it's a mystery to me too.'

'For once in your life, give me an honest answer to a question, Ross. Is there a chance that my sister's baby is yours?'

Imagine her old man listening to this conversation. He's got some serious questions to ask himself as a father.

I'm there, 'Of course there isn't. The fock do you take me for?'

She goes, 'Right, I don't think either of us would object to my saying that this conversation is over.'

And then she just, like, hangs up on me.

We're all in, like, cracking form this morning – *and* in fine voice, even if I say so myself. We're giving it:

> *If I had the wings of a sparrow,*
> *If I had the orse of a crow,*
> *I'd fly over Clongowes Wood College,*
> *And shit on the bastards below!*
> *Shit on, shit on, shit on the bastards below-below!*
> *Shit on, shit on, shit on the bastards below!*

If you close your eyes, it could be 1999 again, and I mean that in an obviously *good* way? I've made my peace with JP and the rest of the goys are sort of, like, talking to me again, even if they haven't totally forgiven me yet.

> *If I had the wings of a sparrow,*
> *If I had the orse of a crow,*
> *I'd fly over Belvedere College . . .*

It's, like, day eight of the walk and we're heading for a place called something-something – oh, yeah, no, it's called Navarrete and the reason I remember is because I once provided, let's just say, stud services for a girl from Navan who chewed Nicorette.

She studied Ag Science in UCD.

I look over my shoulder and I notice that Fionn has fallen a good – I want to say – *fifty* metres behind the rest of us on the road. I decide to hang back for him – or stall the ball, as my eldest son would say, although he'd say, 'Stoddle the boddle.'

Fionn looks wrecked and we've only been walking for, like, an hour and a bit.

I'm there. 'I'm surprised at *you*. You're usually the one haring ahead, telling the rest of us that we have to be in the next town by midday if we want a bed.'

He goes, 'I'm just feeling a bit heavy-legged today.'

I'm tempted to ask him if he's getting his period.

I'm there, 'But you trained for this, didn't you? I saw you myself. On Ballinclea Road. You're obviously not as fit as you thought.'

'I'm sure I'll be fine again tomorrow,' he goes. 'Like I said, my legs feel a bit heavy and I'm feeling a bit of strain in the small of my back.'

I'm like, 'Maybe you're getting your period.'

I just think, Fock it – I might as well say it.

I'm there, 'My feet are still in flitters, by the way.'

He goes, 'I didn't ask.'

'Well, just in case you were wondering. I might hang back and walk with you, if that's okay?'

'Hey, it's a free country – at least it has been since Franco died.'

I think that's supposed to be some kind of joke, but it blows like tumbleweed across the road in front of us.

Ahead in the distance, we can still hear the faint sound of the goys singing:

> If I had the wings of a sparrow,
> If I had the orse of a crow,
> I'd fly over Gonzaga College . . .

I'm there, 'Gonzaga, pack of focking pricks. Hey, it's just like 1999 all over again, isn't it?'

He goes, 'You say that like it's a good thing.'

'Of course it's a good thing. Dude, those were the best years of our lives.'

'Were they, though?'

'You're just saying that now because you're on the blob.'

'I'm serious, Ross, what was it all about – all that school rivalry bullshit? I mean, Castlerock College versus Clongowes Wood – it was hordly a battle of civilizations, was it?'

'We focking hated those goys.'

'No, we didn't – we were just told to hate them.'

'Dude, even today, if I'm introduced to some randomer I've never met before and I ask the obvious question, "What school did you go to?" if the answer is Clongowes Wood, I walk away. I don't even say another word. I turn my back on them and I walk away.'

'Does that not say more about you?'

'Meaning?'

'Ross, there are, like, four teachers working in Castlerock College now who all went to Clongowes.'

'Well, they shouldn't be there. The fockers should have been weeded out at the interview stage.'

'And they're all brilliant teachers and perfectly nice people.'

'I think the sun is storting to get to you. You'd want to throw a hat on or something.'

'Ross, I'm serious. What Father Fehily did to us – it scorred us for life.'

'He didn't do anything to us – except turn us into a group of incredible, incredible rugby players who would have died for each other on and off the field.'

'He pitted us against other schools.'

'Wanker schools.'

'He taught us that we were some kind of master race.'

'There wasn't a team in the country who could touch us.'

'He taught us to look down on women, the socially deprived, people who came from the so-called wrong postcode.'

'He was preparing us for life.'

'Well, I'm just saying that's not the kind of principal I'm going to be.'

'Then I think it's fair to say that Castlerock College's Leinster Schools Senior Cup drought is going to continue for another decade.'

'So what, though?'

'So what? This isn't even you talking. It's that girlfriend of yours. The famous Ciara Casaubon.'

'It has nothing to do with Ciara.'

'Horseshit.'

'Yes, she happens to agree with me that we need to end this obsession we have in Ireland with defining people by what school they went to.'

'Of course she does – she went to King's Hos.'

He stops walking. Not because I've said something that's out of order. She definitely went there – she might have even been in the same year as Leo Varadkar. Yeah, no, it's just because the dude is totally out of breath. He takes off his rucksack and leans it against a wall.

I'm there, 'Dude, if you all of a sudden *hate* Father Fehily –'

He goes, 'I don't hate him.'

'Well, if you suddenly disagree with everything he stood for, then why are you here?'

'I don't know. I genuinely do not know.'

The goys are way, way, way out in front now. In fact, their singing is suddenly like a whisper:

> *If I had the wings of a sparrow,*
> *If I had the orse of a crow,*
> *I'd fly over St Mary's College . . .*

Suddenly, out of nowhere, I hear myself go, 'Dude, you've got to forgive me – for what I did.'

He's there, 'I can't.'

'I've paid my price.'

'You paid no price.'

'I lost my wife. I lost my home. I lost my job. Dude, I led the Ireland women's team four fifths of the way to a Grand Slam – who knows what my next gig would have been. I'm guessing that Leo Cullen was only days away from making the call. And now that's all gone. I mean, who the fock would employ me now?'

He stares at me for a good, like, twenty seconds and for a moment I think he's actually weakening. But then he doesn't say shit. He picks up his rucksack and swings it onto his shoulder. I watch him wince. His lower back is obviously in a bad, bad way. I remember he hurt it against Gerard's, of all schools, back in the day – some focking inbreeder from out that way stuck his knee into it about five seconds *after* Fionn scored a try and he's had trouble with it on and off ever since.

God, I focking hate Gerard's and everyone who ever went to it.

I'm there, 'Dude, do you want me to carry your rucksack for you?'

Straight away, he's like, 'No, I don't.'

'Dude, even for the rest of the day? Look, I'll throw it up on my back here – and you can carry Vivica's sister.'

Yeah, no, I've still got the Ziploc bag with the ashes in it.

He's like, 'It's fine,' then he pulls the strap around his other shoulder, again wincing with the pain, then off we go again in the direction of, I don't know, Navan, Nicorette, Navarrete.

'Are you absolutely certain this is the place?' JP goes.

Fionn's there, 'Saint Francis Borgia,' staring at the map that Father Fehily gave him. 'That's what it says here.'

JP goes, 'But there's supposed to be, like, a *convent* here?'

Fionn's like, 'Yes, I know that, JP.'

Oisinn's there, 'So where is it?'

Fionn ends up totally losing it with them then. He goes, 'I don't focking know. I'm following the map like the rest of you. Actually, do you know what? You look after the map,' and he practically throws it at JP.

Christian – hungover to fock – goes, 'What's wrong with you? Have you got your period?'

I'm there, 'No, his back is in flitters.'

Fionn's like, 'It has nothing to do with my back. I just think this stupid treasure hunt that he's sent us on is a waste of time.'

Christian goes, 'Well, why did you come?'

And Fionn's there, 'I don't focking know.'

'I don't think it's a waste of time,' JP goes, looking down at the map, then looking around him, like he's expecting a humungous convent building to appear out of suddenly nowhere.

We're somewhere on the road between Azofra and Grañón and we're surrounded by just, like, vineyords?

'Wine, wine everywhere,' as I said when we stopped about an hour ago, 'and not a drop to drink,' except no one laughed.

Fionn, Oisinn and Christian are still sore with me for one reason or another.

'There's a house,' JP goes, squinting his eyes into the far distance. 'Come on, let's go and knock on the door.'

So we end up walking up this long, I don't know, asphalt road that seems to go on forever. I turn around to Fionn and I go, 'I'm going to track down the Gerard's prick who did that to your back and I'm going to deck him. That's a promise. I'll find out where he's working now. It could be in HR. It could be in IT. I'll walk into wherever it is he works and I will deck him. And he won't even know why he's *been* decked. He'll be lying on the ground, looking up at me, going, "Why me? Why have I been singled out for a deck-ing?" and I'll be like, "If you don't know now, then you never will."'

Fionn doesn't say thanks. He doesn't say shit. I can see from his face that he's still really struggling with his rucksack.

Finally, we reach the gaff and it looks like the house from quite literally *Father Ted*. We all just look at each other, then JP shrugs, walks up to the door and rings the bell.

No one answers. But then this woman in her maybe sixties walks around the side of the house, clutching a handful of what look very much to me like spring onions. She ends up getting a fright when she sees us there.

She's like, '*Oh Dios mío!*' which I know, from listening to Sorcha back in her Spanish debating days, is *their* equivalent of like, 'Oh! My God!'

'*Lo siento!*' Fionn goes. '*No queríamos asustarte.*'

The woman's like, 'What do you want?'

She obviously has a few words of English – thanks be to fock.

JP's there, 'We're looking for a convent. It's on this map we have – even though the map *is* pretty old.'

'The convent is gone,' the woman goes, stating the obvious. 'It was knocked down perhaps twenty years.'

'There's probably no point in asking you about – well, we were looking for a Sister Casilda?'

'Casilda is dead for seven years. Of bad cancer. My name is Arantxa. I am her niece.'

We're all like, 'Oh, er, bummer – but nice to meet you anyway, Arantxa.'

She goes, 'There is something *I* can help?' and I love the way she speaks English. Like one of the many cleaners my old dear has sacked over the years.

JP goes, 'We're, em, walking the Camino. We're sort of, like, following in the footsteps of our old rugby coach and he told us that he left a letter with Sister Casilda to give to us.'

'What is the name of the man?'

I'm there, 'Er, Denis? As in, like, Denis Fehily?'

'Denise!' she goes. 'Father Denise!'

I actually laugh out loud. I called Denis Hickie 'Denise' one night – I was absolutely shit-faced and I kept challenging him to a race down South William Street – and one of his mates ended up grabbing me in a headlock.

Arantxa's there, 'Always, Casilda talks about Denise. They are –' and then she makes, like, a *writing* motion?

'Pen pals,' Fionn goes.

She's like, 'Yes! This!'

JP's there, 'This letter that he supposedly left for us, is there any chance that it still exists?'

'When she dies,' Arantxa goes, 'Casilda has not a lot. Come here,' and she leads us around the side of the house to this, like, pretty much Shomera, or whatever the Spanish equivalent might be. We follow her inside, even though there's not a massive amount of room in it. It's absolutely roasting in there and it smells, I want to say, *musty*?

She points out two boxes and goes, 'That is all of Casilda's things.'

I'm there, 'What, that's, like, everything she had in the world?'

Christian's like, 'She was a nun, Ross. What were you expecting her to have – a Nespresso and a NutriBullet?'

I just give him a filthy and go, 'Again, I think you need to lay off the booze – it's turned you mean, Dude.'

'You can look,' Arantxa goes, waving her orm at the boxes, then she goes back to – *not* a euphemism – but tending her onions.

JP opens one box and Oisinn opens the other. They both stort pulling stuff out – the kind of things you'd sort of, like, *expect* a nun to own? We're taking Rosary beads. We're talking holy water bottles. We're talking pictures of, like, Jesus and Mary and that whole crew.

Oisinn goes, 'Look,' and he's suddenly holding up a stack of letters, which are tied together with, like, a red ribbon.

I'm there, 'Are they from, like, Father Fehily?' and he flicks through them like he's, I don't know, fanning himself in the heat.

He goes, 'It's definitely his handwriting.'

We all look at each other. I know we're all thinking the exact same thing. Will we read them?

'Have you lost your focking minds?' JP goes. 'They're someone else's private letters. Anyway, I think I've found what we're looking for.'

He's holding up – yeah, no – an envelope, which is the same size as the last one and on the front of it is written 'Castlerock College, Camino Walk, 2019'.

I'm like, 'Okay, we've got what we came for – let's get the fock out of here.'

We wave at Arantxa, who just waves back at us. She seems to have zero interest in whether we found what we were looking for, but then JP waves the envelope at her and she just goes, 'Good! Adios!'

We find our way back to the main road again and I'm there, 'So when are we going to read this one?'

But no sooner have I said it than I hear the sound of paper tearing and I notice that JP suddenly has the envelope open.

Again, it's a single sheet of paper. And, again, it's another quote from the famous Bible. JP gives it the old left-to-right.

'It's from John 15,' he goes – like this should automatically mean something to the rest of us.

Fionn's there, 'Go on, let's hear it. Let's hear what else Father Fehily has to say to us – from beyond the grave.'

So JP ends up just reading it.

He's like, '*As the Father hath loved me, so I have loved you: continue ye in my love.*'

I'm there, 'Well, I think that's a good message for all of us. Especially those of you who are still being a dick to me.'

'*If ye keep my commandments,*' JP goes, '*ye shall abide in my love; even as I have kept my Father's commandments, and abide in his love.*'

I'm like, 'Yeah, no, he's lost me now.'

'*These things have I spoken unto you, that my joy might remain in you, and that your joy might be full. This is my commandment, That ye love one another, as I have loved you. Greater love hath no man than this, that a man lay down his life for his friends.*'

We all just look at each other, shaking our heads, with our bottom lips sticking out, not a clue what it's supposed to mean and how it even applies to us.

Fionn goes, 'Are we going to walk? Or are we going to just stand around here wasting more time?'

So – yeah, no – we're sitting outside this little bor in a town that's literally called Villafranca Montes de Oca, where the only beer they sell – believe it or not – is San Miguel.

I tell the lounge girl, 'Yeah, no, pint of the local piss, then – whatever. I suppose that's the whole *point* of travelling, isn't it? As in, like, experiencing new things? Focking San Miguel, though. Actually, I'll take a jug of it.'

Fionn, Oisinn, JP and Christian decide to stick to the red wine.

Out of nowhere, Fionn suddenly goes, 'So just to let you all know, I'm thinking of abandoning – the walk, I mean.'

We're all like, 'What? You can't do that! What the fock?'

'The last few days,' he goes, 'I've been finding it a bit tough-going. It turns out I'm not as fit as I thought I was.'

JP's there, 'That's because you spent the first week and a bit treating it like a race. Up out of bed and on the road by six in the morning –'

'You have to get to the next village as quickly as possible,' Fionn goes. 'Otherwise, you won't get a bed.'

My jug of San Miguel arrives – thank fock – and I pour myself a glass from it.

Oisinn's there, 'Dude, you can't give up now – not after you've come this far.'

Fionn's like, 'Look, my hip is sore. My back is sore. And I'm storting to feel it in my knee – both knees, in fact. I rang Ciara just now and she said, you know, if I wasn't enjoying it, what was the point of even doing it?'

Ciara. I might have focking known. Yeah, no, Fionn will have told her that me and him have been having the deep meaningful chats on the walk and that I'm slowly worming my way back in there. I honestly feel like he's only a day or two away from telling me that he actually forgives me for what I did and obviously *she* does *not* want that.

I'm there, 'I'll tell you what the *point* is, Fionn. It was Father Fehily's final wish – *that's* the point.'

JP's like, 'Ross is right. He's sent us on this – I'm going to say – *quest* for a reason.'

'Quest?' Fionn goes, at the same time laughing. 'Yeah, thanks for that, Frodo Baggins.'

He's a little bit jorred. He'll be lucky if JP doesn't break his glasses here.

'I'm just making the point,' JP goes, 'that there's a reason we're all here together right now,' and he takes out the piece of paper that Father Fehily left with Sister Casilda, opens it up and smooths it out on the table.

Christian's like, 'Have you figured out what it means yet?'

Fionn just laughs and JP gives him serious, serious daggers.

Fionn's there, 'Look, I'm sorry, I just don't buy the idea that Father Fehily is up there in the clouds – *with* God – directing us on our way, while sending us messages that are supposed to somehow, I don't know, improve us as people.'

'Why do you have to sneer at other people's beliefs?' JP goes. 'Just because you're not spiritual yourself.'

Fionn's there, 'Spiritual?' and – I swear to fock – he actually *laughs*?

JP goes, 'What's so funny about being spiritual, Fionn?'

Fionn's there, 'It's just funny hearing *you* use the word, that's all.'

JP's like, 'In terms of?' and you wouldn't blame him either.

Fionn goes, 'Well, you *say* you're spiritual –'

JP's there, 'I am spiritual.'

'– and yet you invent this bed,' Fionn goes.

JP's like, 'What does the Vampire Bed have to do with my belief in God?'

Fionn's there, 'There's a housing crisis going on in Ireland at the moment and you're exploiting it for your own financial gain,' and then he looks at Christian. 'The two of you.'

I'm like, 'I think what Fionn is trying to say, in a roundabout way, is that we're proud of what you've achieved –'

'No,' Fionn goes, throwing my attempt to make peace between them back in my face, 'I'm saying exactly the opposite of that. We have a situation in Ireland where a whole generation of young people will never, ever own their own homes. And now, thanks to your *wonderful* innovation, they won't be able to lie down at night either.'

JP's there, 'At least we're actually doing something to solve the housing crisis.'

'Yeah,' Fionn goes, 'by stuffing people into wardrobes at night. It's a wonder you haven't been nominated for a Nobel Prize.'

Christian's there, 'Fionn, you're out of order – and we're talking *bang* out of order?'

But it turns out he's only warming up.

He goes, 'Seriously, JP, do you really think you're going to Heaven when you die? And when you get there, do you think God is going to say, "Hey, JP, you're very welcome. Well done, by the way, on the whole people-sleeping-standing-up thing. You remember Denis Fehily, don't you? The so-called man of God who pumped you and your friends full of drugs and turned you into a pack of hateful misogynists just to win a rugby competition?"'

JP stands up and goes, 'I'm out of here – before I deck you.'

But Fionn stands up then and goes, 'I'm going back to the hostel. There's an airport in Burgos. We'll be passing through there tomorrow. I can get a flight from there to Bilbao and then home.'

Off he focks then, limping across the square and back to the place where we're staying, leaving JP literally *shaking* with anger?

I'm there, 'Dude, don't listen to him. He's pissed off because he doesn't have it in his legs any more.'

JP's like, 'Just because he took a vow of poverty by deciding to become a teacher, he thinks that makes him better than the *rest of us?*'

'He was out of order,' Christian goes. 'Again, I'm going to say *bang.*'

It's at that exact moment that a bunch of girls arrive in the bor – we're talking four in total, two of them lookers and two of them not great. I'm guessing they're in, like, their early *thirties*?

'*Buen Camino!*' I go, because I'm really storting to get *in* on it?

They all smile. They're like, '*Buen Camino!*' showing me four sets of Yasmine Bleeth.

There's something about me that women just love.

They look a bit, I don't know, foreign to me, so I try to make myself understood by talking to them the same way I used to talk to my old dear's cleaners.

I'm like, 'Where h'are h'you h'ladies from?'

'Scoatland,' one of the lookers goes – I think she's a ringer for Tracy Spiridakos. 'Just ootsade of Fife.'

I'm there, 'I have h'never been but eet sounds like h'a beautiful place to h'live.'

Oisinn goes, 'They're from focking Scotland, Ross. You can drop the Manuel from *Fawlty Towers* impersonation,' which is uncalled for, I think.

One of the not-exactly-ugly ones – she doesn't look like anyone famous – goes, 'Ah love your t-shirt!'

She's talking to me. I'm glad I washed the thing last night.

I'm there, 'Yeah, no, thanks.'

'So is thus, like, yeer stag paerty?' the other looker goes – think Elizabeth Debicki and you're in the right neighbourhood. She's obviously copped the writing on the back of my t-shirt.

I'm like, 'Yeah, no, this is just a t-shirt I picked up along the way because my own clothes got focked in a bin. Do you want to join us, by the way?'

'Aye,' they go, all looking at each other, 'that'd be nace.'

They tell us their names – the lookers are Anna Hughes and Skye Morton and the ones who aren't great are Maisie Something and Fenella Something Else. We tell them our names as well, then we get chatting about how we've found the walk so far and why we're, like, doing it in the first place.

Skye – the one who looks like Elizabeth Debicki – goes, 'Ah splut up with ma husband sux months ago – bastard was sleeping with ma suster.'

I shake my head and go, 'Why do some men have to do that? They give the rest of us a bad name.'

I'm good. I don't think anyone's denying that.

She's like, 'Well, ma suster wasnae exactly innocent either. Anywee, Ah had a wee breekdoon. I wouldnae have made ut throo if it wasnae for these girdles. Likesay, ma three best friends in the wurdled.'

I smile. She says wurdled the same way as Ronan.

'Ah've always wanted tae dae ut,' she goes. 'Likesay, the Camino. And the girdles said, "See when yee're better, Hon? We'll dae ut thegether."'

'Fair focks,' I go. 'And how are you all mates?'

'We went tae school thegether,' Maisie goes.

I'm like, 'That's the exact same as us!'

We end up having an unbelievable night with them. And they can really put the San Miguel away. We end up genuinely struggling to keep up with them. Like I said, they're a little bit younger than us.

It turns out that Maisie and Skye are both nurses and they have an unbelievable number of stories about people showing up in A&E with things stuck in orifices and the excuses they make, my favourite of which is, 'I was eating chips in the nude, having just had a bath, and I forgot that the ketchup bottle was on the coffee table when I sat down.'

Then Fenella – who, it turns out, is an air-hostess – goes, 'Dae any of yee know any gid dranking games?'

I'm like, 'If it's drinking games you want, you've come to the right man.'

Christian goes, 'Not Fuzzy Duck again,' because the poor focker can barely say his own name at this stage.

I'm like, 'No, not Fuzzy Duck. Does anyone remember playing Body to Body in Ayia Napa back in the day?'

Yeah, no, we all went to Ayia Napa on holidays one year.

Oisinn remembers it. He explains the rules to the girls. He's like, 'Okay, you get a load of pieces of paper and you write the names of, like, body ports on them. We're talking elbow. We're talking knee. We're talking ankle. We're talking wrist. We're talking ear. You fold them up and you throw them into, like, a beer glass. Then everyone is divided into, like, teams of two and each team takes a turn in drawing two pieces of paper from the glass.'

JP goes, 'You could get, say, ear and elbow. So you'd have to attach your ear to your teammate's elbow, using – I don't know – string or something like that.'

'And what happens then?' it's Maisie who goes.

I'm there, 'That's when it gets really exciting. You set up, like, a load of jugs of beer somewhere. I'm going to suggest that little bor on the opposite side of the square. So then, while attached to your teammate – elbow to ear, ear to ankle, whatever – you have to make your way across the square, pour yourselves a pint each, send it, then make your way back.'

'While someone times you!' Christian goes.

I'm like, 'That's right – and whoever has the quickest time after three rounds is the winner.'

The girls are all like, 'Let's dae ut!'

So we *dae* dae ut. I pop across the square to the other bor – it's called La Parada – and I order, like, eight jugs of San Miguel and two pints glasses. I set them up on a table outside while Oisinn and JP write out the names of body ports on bits of paper and stick them into a pint glass.

We choose boy-girl teams. I end up with, unfortunately, Fenella. She's totally sound, but she has a face like me tasting anchovies for the first time. Christian – lucky focker – ends up with Anna. Oisinn ends up with Skye. And JP ends up with Maisie. I try to persuade Oisinn to swap with me, given that he's gay and it shouldn't matter to him whether his teammate is a looker or not. But he refuses.

Anyway, it ends up being our turn first – as in, like, me and

Fenella. I draw ear and – I swear to fock – *she* ends up drawing *ankle*? It's, like, *the* worst draw of all. It's the Body to Body equivalent of Saracens away. So I end up having to get down on my knee, then Oisinn uses Anna's hair bobbin to attach Fenella's ankle to my ear.

She goes, 'Hoo are we supposed tae cross the square like this?'

I'm there, 'I have to crawl and you have to hop on one leg.'

Christian gets the stopwatch on his phone ready.

He goes, 'Three, two, one . . . GO!'

So – yeah, no – we cross the square exactly the way I described it, with me down on all fours and Fenella hopping along next to me with her ankle fixed to my ear. And it ends up being very hord on my knees because I'm wearing, like, shorts and the square is cobbed.

The goys stort cheering us on. Suddenly, there's, like, Rock chants going and men just bleeding red and black, left, right and centre.

We reach the bor on the other side of the square and we each pour ourselves a pint of San Miguel, send it, then we cross the square the exact same way.

Of course, everyone in the entire square is, like, suddenly glued to the spectacle and now they're, like, cheering us on, even though they probably don't even know the object of the whole exercise.

We get back to the bor we were in and – I swear to fock – my knees are actually *bleeding*?

I'm like, 'Time?'

And Christian goes, 'One minute, fifty-eight seconds!'

It's a shit time and the fearsome competitor in me knows it. All I can do is hope for a better draw in the next two rounds.

It's, like, Oisinn and Skye's turn next. Oisinn draws knee and Skye draws – would you focking believe it? – knee as well. The easiest draw you could possibly ask for. Focking Scorlets at home.

Christian goes, 'Three, two, one . . . GO!'

It ends up being an un-focking-believable night. Huge. Some of the greatest horseplay of all time.

I'm there, 'You heard I won, did you?'

Fionn's like, 'Won? Won what?'

Yeah, no, we're walking through this, like, forest on the way to our next stop, which is, like, Cordeñuela Riopico. It's, like, a four and a half hour walk and me and Fionn are once again at the back of the field, the two us in absolute ribbons. My blisters are focking killing me and I think I'm very nearly at the stage where I'm going to have to take a pin to them. Although I think it's also fair to say that we're all feeling a bit on the delicate side after the shenanigans of the night before.

I'm like, 'The inaugural San Miguel Cup.'

This obviously means fock-all to him and of course there's no reason why it *should*? Yeah, no, it was a definite you-had-to-be-there moment.

I'm like, 'We played Body to Body with this gang of, like, *Scottish* girls? Check out my knees.'

Yeah, no, they're still bleeding.

I'm there, 'You remember we played it in Ayia Napa? Anyway, me and this girl called Fenella – not great, before you ask – got ankle and ear in the first round and we were bottom of the leaderboard, but we turned it around and ended up beating Christian and Anna – an absolute focking lasher, by the way – by literally two seconds after three rounds.'

He doesn't seem remotely excited by any of this talk. Again, it's obviously because he missed out on the craic.

I'm there, 'Anyway, I was thinking of telling the Past Pupils Union about it and making it into, like, an annual competition for anyone doing the Camino thing. I was thinking of even getting a tattoo saying "San Miguel Cup Champion 2019", but then I remembered what I said to Garret – as in the husband of Claire from Bray of all places – about people who go away on holidays and get tattoos. Pricks and wankers were my exact words.'

I notice that he's, like, wincing again.

I'm like, 'Are you okay, Dude?'

'My back's getting worse,' he goes. 'And my hip.'

He stops – there in the middle of the forest.

I'm there, 'Dude, give me your rucksack. I'm not taking no for an answer. Let me carry it for you – at least for one day.'

This time, he lets me take it from him and – yeah, no – I swing it onto my back.

'So,' he goes, 'I probably owe JP an apology – for some of the things I said last night?'

I'm there, 'Yeah, no, you were a focking dick to him alright.'

'I know it's not an excuse, but I'm just tired. And sore. And I'm missing Hillary.'

'Are you serious about abandoning when we get to –'

'Burgos. Yeah, I've had enough. I'm missing Ciara as well.'

It really is true that there's someone for everyone. I wouldn't touch the girl with a twelve-foot canoeing paddle and I'm sure there are a lot of girls who would feel the same way about Fionn. The vast majority of them, as proven by his track record.

I'm there, 'So – yeah, no – it's obviously serious between you two?'

He nods. He's like, 'Yes, it's serious.'

I resist the temptation to tell him that I think he could do better. He couldn't. He knows it and I know it.

I'm there, 'Are you thinking in terms of, like, marriage and shit?'

He goes, 'I don't know. I mean, I'd love that – but, just between ourselves, it's kind of complicated.'

It's great that he's suddenly, like, confiding in me again.

I'm there, 'Does it have anything to do with what I said about her snowballing Gussie Grennan in Hollywood Nights? Because I remembered it wasn't actually her.'

He's like, 'No, Ross, it has nothing to do with that. If you must know, she's still struggling to get her head around the whole me-already-having-a-kid thing.'

I'm like, 'Hey, you had that kid with my literally wife. If I can get my head around it, then so can she.'

And he smiles at me – for possibly the first time since the whole me-getting-him-put-on-the-sexual-offenders'-register thing came out – and he goes, 'I suppose you have a point.'

He goes quiet for a bit, then he goes, 'I want you to know that I do appreciate it, Ross.'

I'm like, 'What?'

'How, well, cool you were with the whole thing. I mean, like you said, another man fathered a baby with your wife. And not only did

273

you forgive us both, you allowed me to move into your home so that I could be in Hillary's life.'

'I don't know what I was thinking. I must have been focking mad.'

'Don't minimize it, Ross. I want you to know that, whatever about all this other stuff between us, I still appreciate that.'

'Yeah, no, don't mention it.'

'And I haven't forgotten that it was you, more than anyone else, who was there for me when I had my cancer.'

'Dude, that's what people who played rugby together do for each other.'

'Yes, but they also give each other's names and addresses to the police when they're arrested for indecent exposure.'

'It's swings and roundabouts, Fionn.'

He stops walking, takes a deep breath, then goes, 'Ross, I've decided to forgive you.'

I'm like, 'Seriously?' absolutely focking delighted.

He sticks out his hand for me to shake it. But I don't. Well, I *sort* of do? I grab his hand and I pull him into, like, a proper focking bear hug, there in the middle of this – like I said – forest.

Up ahead on the path, I notice that the rest of the goys have all stopped for a drink of water and a rest. They look back at me and Fionn, two men just hugging it out, and they're obviously thinking, *that* is why rugby is the greatest sport in the world.

It turns out that Fionn isn't done yet. Next, he walks up to JP and he goes, 'I said some things last night –'

JP's like, 'Dude, it's forgotten. We were all shit-faced.'

'I said some things that I wish I didn't say and drink is no excuse. It was very wrong of me to say what I did and I'm very sorry. Can you forgive me?'

JP's like, 'On one condition.'

'What's that?'

'That you keep on walking. That you don't abandon.'

Fionn smiles. Yeah, no, he's obviously happier now that he's found some mug to carry his rucksack. He goes, 'I'm not going home,' and then he sticks out his hand. JP accepts it, then *that* ends up turning into a bear hug as well.

Christian smiles and slaps the two of them on the back, although Oisinn, I notice, is just like standing there, staring into the, I don't know, trees, not paying us any attention.

I just happen to go, 'What happened to *you* last night?'

He looks at me with a big paranoid head on him – obviously has a dose of the fear.

He goes, 'What's that supposed to mean?'

I'm there, 'Well, I noticed this morning that you weren't in your bed and also that the thing hadn't been slept in. Unless you got up earlier and made it. Which I seriously doubt.'

I'm only ripping the pistachio out of him, but he ends up instantly losing it with me.

He goes, 'What focking business is it of yours, Ross?' and he pretty much *roars* the words at me? 'The man who got my entire house cleaned out and then focking lied about it.'

'The fock is wrong with you?' I go.

Oisinn goes, 'I slept with one of the Scottish girls last night.'

I'm there, 'What?' instantly jealous. 'Which one?'

'Is that actually relevant?' he goes.

I'm there, 'I'd just love to know – as a matter of interest. Was it Skye?'

'Yes,' he goes, 'it was Skye.'

'I thought so. She was sitting on your knee when I staggered out of the pub at whatever time it was. Sorry, so what's the big deal here?'

They all just stare at me in – whatever the actual word is – *misbelief* or *disbelief*?

'He's upset,' JP goes, 'because he cheated on Magnus.'

I'm there, 'It's not *really* cheating, though, is it? He's, like, gay. It'd be cheating if he rode a dude. That's how I'd be squaring that one with my conscience. If I had a conscience. Am I right, Ois?'

But Oisinn says fock-all back to me. He just storts walking again – at a fair old clip – in the direction of Cordeñuela Riopico.

Christian – I swear to fock – goes, 'Handled with your trademork sensitivity, Ross.'

Then I look at Fionn – again, the focking nerve of him – because he goes, 'Ross, that was a very ignorant thing to say.'

I take his rucksack off my back and I just drop it on his pretty much toes.

'Here,' I go, 'you can carry your own shit. It's digging into my shoulders.'

Fock it.

I actually say it out loud while suddenly stopping dead in my tracks.

I go, 'Fock it!'

The goys are like, 'What?'

I'm there, 'Fock it! Fock it! Fock it! Fock it! Fock it! Fock it! Fock it!'

'What happened?' Fionn goes.

And I'm there, 'I left Vivica's sister's ashes in that coffee shop where we had breakfast this morning.'

They're all just standing there looking at me with their mouths wide open in shock. It's like the time I broke into the staffroom in Terenure College and took a shit in the kettle.

'Well, we can't go back,' Christian goes.

But Fionn's there, 'We *have* to go back.'

Christian's like, 'Back to Tardajos? You must be focking joking. We've been walking for, like, two hours.'

Fionn goes, 'It's someone's ashes.'

Oisinn's there, 'I thought you didn't believe in God.'

'I don't,' Fionn goes.

Oisinn's like, 'Well, then, they're just ashes, right? Like ashes from a fire grate? They don't *mean* shit.'

I'm there, 'I think Oisinn maybe has a point. The dude in the coffee shop has probably already focked them in the bin. And I presume the rubbish eventually gets dumped into the sea.'

'We have to go back for the ashes,' JP goes. 'It's the right thing to do.'

Christian's like, 'How far is it to Castrojeriz?'

Fionn goes, 'It's about another three hours – maybe three and a half?'

Christian's there, 'We've already been walking for two hours. So now we're going to walk two hours back to Tarjados, then two hours back to where we are now, then three and a half hours to Castrojeriz?'

I'm like, 'How many hours is that – in total, like?'

'Nine and a half hours,' Oisinn goes. 'We'll be focked. And we won't get a bed in Tarjados either.'

I'm there, 'Plus, I'm wearing Dubes, bear in mind. My feet are already in focking flitters.'

JP loses his shit with me then. He goes, 'Ross, you stole the ashes. You said you'd take responsibility for them, remember?'

Christian's there, 'That's a good point. Why do we all have to go back? Why can't Ross go back on his own?'

This dude used to be my best friend, bear in mind.

I'm like, 'All I did was try to help your son, who was being sextorted – and you need to get over that fact.'

He whips out his hipflask and takes a mouthful from it.

'Let's put it to a vote,' Fionn goes. 'I say we go back. Christian?'

Christian's there, 'I say we keep walking.'

'Oisinn?'

'Keep walking.'

'JP?'

'Go back.'

'Ross?'

I don't say shit. Because – according to my maths – it's all down to me.

JP goes, 'Ross, we went to Paris – all of us – to sprinkle Father Fehily's ashes in the city he loved more than any other city in the world. What would he say if he knew you were going to let someone else's ashes be thrown into the trash?'

I take a deep sigh.

'Fock's sake,' I go. 'Fine, we'll go back.'

So – yeah, no – we turn around and we retrace our steps through the countryside and back to Tarjados.

Oisinn is in an absolute fouler today anyway. His conscience is still eating away at him, and I think he's also genuinely confused about why he did what he did. We've been walking for about an hour when he suddenly goes, 'I'm wondering now am I bi –'

'As in, like, bisexual?' I go.

He's like, 'Yes, Ross, bisexual.'

I'm there, 'Look, I'm kind of scared of saying anything for fear of putting my foot in it again, but did you enjoy it – as in, having sex with Skye?'

'Yes,' he goes, 'I enjoyed it.'

I'm there, 'Then it sounds very much to me like you're into both – as in, like, men *and* women?'

He just shakes his head – like the whole thing is somehow *my* fault.

'Shit!' JP goes, suddenly stopping. 'Is that Vivica?'

I end up nearly soiling myself.

I'm like, 'Where?'

He's there, 'Up ahead – walking towards us. Do you see her?'

Even from, like, a hundred yords away, I can see that it's her.

Fionn goes, 'Why don't we just explain the whole situation to her?'

I'm like, 'What, I accidentally took her dead sister's ashes while I was stealing food from her rucksack and I left them on the chair in a coffee shop called Cucaracha's?'

Fionn's there, 'Ross, we're about to bump into her – what other choice do we have?'

I'm like, 'We'll take a short cut through this field,' and before any-one can raise an objection I'm suddenly climbing over this, like, five-bor wooden gate.

Of course, they don't want to have to explain what happened to her sister's ashes any more than I do, so they all throw their ruck-sacks over the gate and follow me into this field of just, like, grass.

Fionn is looking at his phone, going, 'Okay, if we walk through this field and then one, two, three, four, five more fields, we can shave about twenty minutes off the walk back.'

I'm there, 'See? It's all good.'

But it's not long before Oisinn storts pissing and whingeing again.

He's like, 'I have to tell Magnus.'

I'm there, 'What, that you're bi –'

'No,' he goes, 'that I had sex with someone else,' and he suddenly whips out his phone.

I'm like, 'Dude, don't do it.'

He goes, 'I'm doing it,' calling up the number.

I'm there, 'Dude, can I just remind you that you two are about to possibly bring a baby into this world? Don't throw it all away over one stupid mistake.'

He's suddenly holding the phone to his ear, going, 'Magnus?'

I launch myself at him. I was one of the best tackling backs in the history of Irish schools rugby, and that was according to Tony Ward. I hit him in the midriff, instantly winding him and knocking him to the ground. His phone flies out of his hand and I grab it and kill the call.

He climbs to his feet – still struggling for breath – and goes, 'It's *your* focking fault anyway,' which sort of, like, takes me by surprise.

I'm like, '*My* fault? The fock are you talking about?'

'This was supposed to be a pilgrimage,' he goes. 'You've turned it into, like, a Leaving Cert holiday.'

I'm there, 'Oh, so it's *my* fault we met those Scottish birds? We had a cracking night with them.'

'It wasn't *supposed* to be *craic*,' Christian then pipes up. 'It was *supposed* to be a journey.'

I'm there, 'What, and I'm responsible for you being back on the drink as well, am I?'

I put Oisinn's phone into my pocket and I turn to walk away.

Oisinn goes, 'What did you mean when you said me and Magnus were *possibly* going to have a baby?'

All of a sudden, I hear Fionn go, 'Oisinn! Do not! Make! Any! Sudden! Movements!'

I'm thinking, What the fock is he on about?

When I turn around, I discover the answer very focking quickly. Oisinn is standing on his own, a little bit away from the rest of us. And about twenty metres behind him is the biggest bull I've seen in my life. And he doesn't look happy. When have you ever seen one that did? But this dude looks especially pissed that he's got five randomers traipsing through his field.

Fionn goes, 'Oisinn! Don't panic! But there is a bull! Standing! Right behind you!'

Oisinn spins around in fright and lets out a sort of, like, girlie scream. The bull sort of, like, snorts at him in reply and the whole time he's also giving him the big-time evil eye. Oisinn storts to back away from him, holding his two hands up in surrender.

He's going, 'Nice bull!' talking to him like he's a dog. 'Take it easy!'

The bull puts his head down and storts sniffing the ground. I don't know why but I know he's getting ready to chorge. He storts, like, *pawing* the ground then with one of his, like, front *hooves*?

'Oh, fock!' Oisinn goes. 'Goys, he's going to focking gore me!'

That's when I suddenly act. Without even thinking, I shout, 'Hey, bull – over here, orsehole!' and I whip off my famous tuxedo t-shirt, holding it out in front of me like a matador's cape.

Now, the bull is suddenly looking *my* way?

I'm like, 'Oisinn, run! Same as the rest of you! Go, go, go!'

They don't need to be told a second time. They absolutely peg it towards the gate.

I stort walking in a circle around the bull, showing him my t-shirt. And, even though it's not red, he seems pretty focked off all the same.

I'm there, 'You want some? You want some of this – you ugly focking animal!' all these lines coming back to me from the time I played front-row for Seapoint against Bruff. 'I'm not scared of you, you scaldy-faced, Limerick fock!'

He chorges at me then, covering the ground between us far quicker than I expected. He goes to jab his two horns into me. Instinctively – if that's a word? – I literally grab the bull by the horns and at the same time I jump, allowing myself to be flipped up into the air.

I land on my back with a hell of a thump. And by the time I climb to my feet again, the bull is standing about ten metres in front of me and getting ready to chorge at me for the second time.

The goys are shouting, 'Run, Ross! Run!' from the safety of the road. Unfortunately, I don't have that option because he's standing between me and the gate.

'You think you're hord?' I go. 'You're going to be playing your rugby in Division 2C of the AIL next season, you focking inbred, culchie gimp.'

Again, I wave the t-shirt in front of him, Matador-style. Again, he chorges at me. This time, I'm ready for him. Just as he reaches me,

I jump to the right, pull the t-shirt away and punch him hord on the bridge of the nose.

I don't know whether it's, like, shock or the power of the punch, but, as he passes me, his two front knees buckle and I take that as my opportunity to run.

I run faster than I've ever run before. And I can tell from the, I don't know, desperation in the voices of the goys that the bull is back on his feet and coming after me.

They're going, 'Run, Ross! Don't look back! Run! Run! Run!'

I put my two hands on the top bor of this, like, iron gate and I leapfrog over it and land on the road, a split-second before the bull smashes into it with his head.

'You can't scrummage for shit, you cabbage-eating ape!' I shout, still high on the adrenalin of it all. 'And your old pair are brother and sister!'

Oisinn ends up being right. By the time we reach Castrojeriz, there's not a bed to be found. The main hostel – or *municipal albergue*, as Fionn insists on calling it – is full by the time we arrive there at, like, seven o'clock that night. But Oisinn's not complaining. I saved the dude's life.

He goes, 'You literally did, Ross. I mean, that thing would have gored me to death if it wasn't for your quick thinking.'

I'm like, 'Yeah, no, thanks,' loving being the hero of the hour, but at the same time playing it *cool*?

'Magnus would be a widower,' he goes, 'bringing up our baby all on his own.'

I'm there, 'Hmmm,' as I examine the Ziploc bag containing Vivica's sister's ashes. Yeah, no, the dude in Cucaracha's guessed what they were and kept them safe underneath the counter.

That was some day.

With nowhere to stay, we've decided to sleep rough – in other words, on the actual street. Yeah, no, it's a beautiful, warm evening and the goys all have sleeping bags, although Oisinn is determined to give me *his*?

He's going, 'Dude, take it – please.'

281

I'm there, 'Where will you sleep?'

He's like, 'I don't give a fock. I'm only alive right now because of you.'

I go, 'Yeah, no, it's definitely one way of looking at it.'

JP unzips his sleeping bag and goes, 'Well, at least we know what Father Fehily's last message meant now.'

I'm like, 'What are you talking about?'

He's there, 'Are you shitting me? *Greater love hath no man than this, that a man lay down his life for his friends.*'

Fock. I hadn't actually thought about it. None of us had.

'It's just a coincidence,' Fionn goes – because he has to steal the limelight from me. 'By the way, you might like to know, we've been walking for, like, two weeks today. So you could say we're halfway through our pilgrimage.'

No one says shit. It's a real tumbleweed moment.

I'm there, 'It was some focking size of a bull, wasn't it?' trying to bring the conversation back to me. 'Did you see me actually deck him with a punch? That'll be some story to tell back in The Bridge, won't it? Can you imagine Heaslip hearing that?'

All of a sudden, Oisinn storts – yeah, no – sobbing.

He's like, 'There I was giving you a hord time about getting all of our shit stolen. But that's just, like, stuff. It doesn't mean anything – not compared to my life. I mean, I literally could have been killed,' even though I'm the only one who was in any *real* danger?

'I'll tell you what,' I go, 'I will take your sleeping bag – if the offer still stands.'

I just think, fock it, I deserve it.

I'm there, 'It's a pity none of you thought to take a picture of the incident. Because the Kearneys will refuse to believe point-blank that it even happened.'

I throw Oisinn's sleeping bag down on the street and I climb into it.

JP laughs. He's like, 'This reminds me of that Christmas when we spent the night sleeping out on College Green to raise money for the homeless.'

'That was another one of Father Fehily's ideas,' Christian goes.

I'm like, 'Yeah, no, it was a great thing to do,' even though I remember me, Christian and Oisinn abandoning after an hour to head for Iskander's and then Brogan's.

In fairness, it was focking freezing.

I'm there, 'How many tonnes are we saying that bull weighed? Two? Three? Actually, what even *is* a tonne?'

Fionn again has to bring the conversation back to him, though.

He's like, 'Oisinn, I've got a ground sheet in the bottom of my rucksack that I can give you to sleep on,' and he storts pulling shit out of the thing.

He's trying to be the hero of the hour. Too late, of course. I'm thinking, Where were you when I was – as the Bible said – laying down my life for my friend?

'What the fock?' Fionn suddenly goes. 'What the –'

Christian's like, 'What's wrong?'

And Fionn's there, 'What the fock is this at the bottom of my rucksack?'

He reaches into and he pulls out – hilariously – three humungous rocks.

He's like, 'Who put rocks in my focking rucksack,' and then – this will tell you what he's focking like – he automatically turns his head and stares at me.

He goes, 'It was you, wasn't it?'

I'm there, 'You couldn't just let me have my moment, could you? You couldn't let me be the man of the hour.'

He's suddenly lost for words. All he can say is like, 'Why? Why would you do something like that?'

I'm there, 'So me and you could talk. My feet were focked from walking in those shoes. And you were walking miles ahead. I thought if I could just slow you down, then we might be able to have a chat and fix shit.'

'But you watched me walking in absolute agony,' he goes, playing the sympathy cord. 'I told you that my back was killing me. And my hip was sore. And my knees were sore.'

In fairness to the rest of the goys, they do seem pretty shocked by this.

I'm there, 'Well, the good news is that there's fock-all wrong with you. It was just the rocks that were slowing you down.'

This comes as no consolation to him. I don't know why I thought it would.

He goes, 'You're completely focking amoral, aren't you?'

I've no idea what that even is, so the joke is on him.

I'm there, 'Hey, we sorted shit out, didn't we?'

He just shakes his head. He's like, 'I can't believe I actually forgave you.'

I'm there, 'Compared to other shit I've done on you, this is small beer. You could do with getting a sense of perspective, like Oisinn there has got.'

He's there, 'You use people. You manipulate them,' and then he looks around at the rest of them, all snuggled into their sleeping bags. 'Are you goys not going to say anything?'

Oisinn goes, 'Fionn, he saved my life today.'

And I'm there, 'The rough with the smooth, Dude. The rough with the smooth.'

8.

The Man with the Olden Nun

As I possibly mentioned earlier, I have a very, very high tolerance threshold for, like, *pain*? You're talking about a man, remember, who sustained a famous labral tear against Terenure College, causing my hip to pop out of its socket. Yeah, no, I shoved it back in again, after three mouthfuls of brandy from Father Fehily's hipflask – even though I was only in, like, First Year at the time – then I carried on playing for another twenty minutes, scoring a pushover try, before passing out from the pain, just seconds after successfully converting the thing. Even as I was being stretchered from the pitch, I still had enough strength in me to sing, 'You're Gick – and you know you are! You're Gick – and you know you are!' although I *am* allowing for the fact that I may well have been pissed.

But it has to be said that even the pain I felt that day – in a match that is still remembered to this day as the Templeogue Road Massacre – pales when compared to the agony that I'm in right now.

We're sitting outside a little wine bor in a village called Frómista and that's when I decide to inspect the damage. I slip off my right Dube, tear off my sock and put my foot up on my left knee to check out the sole.

'Jesus Christ!' Oisinn goes when he sees it. He throws his hand over his mouth. He looks like he's about to vom – and he won the Iron Stomach contest three years running when we were in UCD. He ends up having to close his eyes and turn away. 'Focking hell!'

I check it out. Yeah, no, there's a blister on it that's the size of the mouth of a pint glass and it's full of something that I presume to be pus. It seems to be moving of its own accord, throbbing up and down like my old dear's Adam's apple.

Fionn – like the others – can't bring himself to even *look* at it? He goes, 'Are you not in pain?'

And I'm there, 'Hey, since when has the prospect of pain ever stopped the Rossmeister General in his tracks? I stood in front of a rampaging bull, can I just remind you?'

Jesus, it's focking sore, though. I take off the other Dube and sock and my left foot – if you can believe it – looks even worse. Like the right, it's definitely infected and I can nearly hear the germs humming away beneath the hord surface of the blister.

I'm there, 'There's only one thing for it.'

Christian – of all people – goes, 'You're going to have to abandon,' and he's shit-faced, of course.

I'm like, 'I'm not abandoning.'

He goes, 'There's no way you're going to make it to the end.'

And I'm there, 'Yeah, now you sound like the Order of Malta ambulanceman who tried to persuade me to come off against Terenure College back in the day and ended up getting very nearly decked by me.'

Fionn – wouldn't you know it – goes, 'Ross, we've still got two weeks of walking ahead of us. There's no way you can do it with your feet in that state.'

I'm like, 'Yeah, you'd love me to quit, wouldn't you? You *and* Christian. Just because I've managed to worm my way back in with JP and Oisinn and you're terrified that I'll worm my way back in with you.'

JP goes, 'Ross, your feet look very, very infected. You could end up getting septicaemia.'

I'm there, 'That's why I'm going to burst these blisters.'

They all just wince – like me when I see a woman in a tux.

I'm like, 'Man up, will you? Oisinn, I watched you eat a bowl of Whiskas smothered in toothpaste, followed by six Weetabix soaked in ketchup.'

He goes, 'I know,' still refusing to look at my feet, 'but even so.'

I'm there, 'Okay, I'm going to need something shorp,' and I make a grab for Fionn's – yeah, no – pilgrim stick, which has a pointed end on it.

Fionn tries to grab it off me, but I'm stronger than him, even with two bad feet.

He goes, 'Ross, do *not* use my stick to burst those blisters. I'm serious.'

I'm like, 'Whatever, Dude. JP, I'm going to need something stronger than whatever piss this is we're drinking.'

Yeah, no, we're drinking red wine.

I'm there, 'Get me a lorge brandy, will you? Matter of fact, get me a focking bottle.'

Fionn goes, 'Ross, I'm sure if you held off for a few minutes, I could find you a pin. It would probably be a lot less sore going in and at least it would be sterile.'

JP arrives out with a bottle of Hennessy – my old man's favourite. I take it from him and I knock back four mouthfuls, coughing after each one. I put my right foot on my left knee again, then I take Fionn's – again, hilarious – pilgrim stick and I point the end at the blister.

I count myself down, we're talking three, two, one, but for some reason I can't *do* it? Yeah, no, my nerve for some reason *fails* me?

I'm there, 'Okay, someone else is going to have to do it.'

Fionn goes, 'Ross, I'm serious, it would be a lot easier and a lot safer if you used a pin.'

But I'm not listening to him.

I'm there, 'Oisinn, will you do it?'

He just shakes his head – not a focking chance.

I'm like, 'Mr so-called Iron Stomach 1999 to 2001? I saw you eat pubic hair on a cream cracker. We all turned out to support you.'

He's there, 'I still can't do it.'

But I'm like, 'Dude, I saved your focking life,' and that gets him, of course. 'You owe me.'

His expression changes from one of disgust to one of – I want to say – *resignation*? I hand him the stick and I take one more slug from the brandy bottle. He holds the thing like a spear, with the business end about six inches away from my blister.

I'm there, 'Now, don't hold back, Dude. Make sure you – AAARRRGGGHHH!!!!'

Yeah, no, I don't get a chance to finish my instructions before he jabs the point of the stick into the blister and – I shit you not – the thing bursts like a focking water balloon, showering Oisinn's face in yellow-green pus.

I'm still going, 'AAARRRGGGHHH!!!'

'Jesus Christ,' he goes, wiping his mouth with his free hand. 'Jesus focking Christ.'

I recover from the initial pain and realize that my foot feels less sore – there's definitely less pressure coming from inside.

Oisinn goes, 'I think I swallowed some,' helping himself to a mouthful of brandy to take away the taste.

I'm there, 'Okay, stop being a focking wuss, will you?'

But then the whiff hits us. It's focking vile. And definitely the worst thing I've ever smelled since the time I put a dead rat under the spare wheel of Fionn's Hyundai Ioniq – just because.

'I think I'm going to be sick,' JP goes.

Christian ends up *being* sick. He turns away from the table and spews all over the ground, pebble-dashing the rucksack of a German woman trying to enjoy a quiet glass of Rioja at the next table. She gets up and moves, looking at us like we're scumbags, which to an outsider we probably *are*?

I'm there, 'Okay, now the next one,' and I put my left foot up on my right knee.

This time, Oisinn stands to the side of me to make sure he escapes the splashback. He stands there with the stick poised and his eyes closed.

I'm like, 'Dude, you're going to end up disembowelling me! Open your focking– AAARRGGGHHH!!!'

Before I'm ready, he's jabbed me with the thing and the second blister has burst open like the world's shittest piñata.

I'm like, 'AAARRRGGGHHH!!!'

This time, it's Fionn who ends up getting discharge in his face. A disgusting yellow globule of it flies ten feet across the table and splatters his glasses like something you'd see on – and Christian's eldest would be a better judge of this – but *gay porn*?

He takes his glasses off, going, 'For fock's sake!'

290

I'm like, 'Fock, that was sore!'

But, again, the pain storts to – I don't know – subside once the swelling goes down. I go to put my socks back on.

JP's like, 'Ross, you have to sterilize your feet.'

I'm there, 'What?'

He goes, 'They're going to become infected again.'

He reaches into his rucksack and he whips out a t-shirt. He grabs the bottle and he soaks it in brandy – I'm like, 'Jesus Christ, go easy – there's sober people in Africa!' – then he hands the thing to Oisinn.

Did I mention that the smell was horrendous? Quite a few of our fellow pilgrims have focked off, leaving their drinks unfinished, without so much as a *'Buen Camino!'*

Yeah, no, Oisinn gets down on his knees and presses the alcohol-soaked t-shirt to the sole of my right foot, then my left. As he does so, he storts – I'm not making this up – *crying?*

I'm like, 'Dude, what the fock? I watched you eat peas and Mormite on a pancake.'

He goes, 'You saved my life,' and as he says it, he takes my socks and he pulls them onto my feet.

I'm there, 'Er, I know I did,' and I'm looking at the rest of the goys as if to say, what the fock?

He goes, *'Greater love hath no man than this,'* and he's literally blubbing now, *'that a man lay down his life for his friends.'*

I'm there, 'Oisinn, it's cool. I'm just going to say the word rugby and we'll leave it at that.'

He sits down again. I pick up my shoes and I look down at them. There's, like, enormous holes in the soles of both. The insoles that JP gave me have worn through. I grab two beer mats from the table and I stuff one into each. Then I put them on again.

JP goes, 'Ross, you should ask in the hostel if they have any hiking boots lying around. Sometimes people leave them behind if they abandon.'

I'm like, 'No, I storted the walk in Dubes and I'm going to finish it in Dubes.'

Oisinn goes, 'I wasn't prepared to do the same for you, Dude.'

He looks at me, tears still streaming down his face.

I'm like, 'What are you shitting on about?'

He goes, 'There was one night – I don't know if you remember – on Nassau Street, when you got jumped by those skangers.'

I'm there, 'You don't know if I remember? Dude, I had the words Nike Air Max tattooed backwards on my forehead for about a focking year afterwards.'

He goes, 'The thing is, Ross, I blame myself for what happened to you that night.'

I'm there, 'Dude, you weren't even there. You were still in Renords, getting off with Nuala Carey off the weather.'

'I wasn't.'

'What?'

'I left Renords just after you, Ross. I was running after you – see did you want to share a taxi home. And I watched you get . . . jumped.'

I'm literally stunned.

'So you *were* there?'

'I was hiding in the doorway of, I'm pretty sure, Kilkenny Design.'

Now I'm literally fuming.

I'm there, 'You watched me take a hiding – and you did nothing?'

He goes, 'There were too many of them.'

I'm like, 'There were four of them. The focking size of you, Oisinn. The two of us could have possibly taken them.'

He goes, 'I know. I've carried that guilt around with me for nearly twenty years.'

I'm there, 'I stood in front of a focking bull for you!' jabbing my finger in his general postcode. 'I stood in front of a focking bull!'

I would get up and deck the dude if it wasn't for the fact that I'm too focking pissed to trust my legs.

What the focking fock?

Yeah, no, I wake up with *the* most unbelievably itchy legs. The backs of them feel like they're on actual fire. I stort scratching, tearing my skin with my nails, but it doesn't do any good. Then suddenly it's the backs of my orms that are itchy, then my actual back.

Like I said, I'm like, 'What the focking fock?'

I hop out of the bed.

JP's already awake and he's like, 'What's the story, Dude?'

I'm there, 'I'm focking itchy all over. It's like I've been, I don't know, bitten by something.'

'Bed bugs,' Fionn goes, putting on his glasses. 'Oh focking hell!'

He's seen my back, as well as the backs of my orms and legs.

I'm like, 'What?'

He goes, 'Ross, you need to see it for yourself.'

So – yeah, no – I head for the jacks. There's some randomer in there ahead of me, washing his jocks in the sink.

I'm there, 'Get the fock out.'

He's like, 'I *beg* your pardon?' because I'm pretty sure he's German.

'I said get the fock out,' I go, then I grab his jocks out of the sink and fock them out the door.

He tells me I'm an orsehole, which I can live with, then off he focks. I stand with my back to the mirror and check out my reflection over my shoulder.

Oh, focking, focking fock.

My back, my orms and my legs are covered in clusters of sores, which are, like, an angry shade of red. I go at them again with my fingernails, giving them a serious going-over, but it doesn't bring me any relief.

I go back out to the goys and I'm like, 'I've been bitten to fock.'

Fionn's there, 'I told you. It's bed bugs.'

'Did any of you get bitten?'

'No, because we brought sleeping bags with us.'

'So you *knew* – about the bed bugs?'

Jesus Christ, I didn't even know they were real – I thought they were a makey-uppy thing, as in, 'Night, night, sleep tight,' and blah, blah, blah.

He goes, 'Do you have any idea how many people might have slept on that mattress before you?'

I don't even want to think about it.

He's there, 'Of course, I could have given you my ground sheet to sleep on – if you hadn't put rocks in my rucksack.'

I stort clawing at the backs of my orms. Jesus Christ, it's agony.

I'm there, 'Has anyone got any Sudocrem?'

But, of course, only women carry that shit around with them.

I look at Fionn. I'm there, 'Have *you* got any Sudocrem?'

He's like, 'No, I don't.'

I'm there, 'Fine – fock you all, then,' and I grab my tuxedo t-shirt off the radiator and I pull it on me. It's still damp from me washing it just before I went to bed and it feels cool against my back.

Oisinn walks in then. I hadn't even noticed that he wasn't here. He holds up a plastic bag and goes, 'I got sandwiches – for our breakfast.'

I'm there, 'Is there a *chicken* one in there?' putting the emphasis on the word chicken.

'No, it's *jamón y queso* or tuna, I'm afraid.'

'You should definitely have *chicken*, Oisinn.'

'There's no chicken, Ross. I told you, it's ham and –'

'I'm saying *you're* the chicken, Oisinn – *you're* a focking chicken. Are you not picking up on that?'

He goes, 'Jesus,' at the same time pulling a face, 'what happened to your orms?'

JP's like, 'He got bitten by bed bugs.'

'Fock,' he goes – in fairness to him, 'does anyone have any Sudocrem?'

I'm there, 'Can we just get on the road already?'

Yeah, no, according to Fionn, today is a three-and-a-half-hour walk to a place called – hilariously – Carrión de los Condes, although we've to make a stop along the way to collect another one of Father Fehily's letters.

'It's going to involve a slight detour at Población de Campos,' Fionn goes, pushing his glasses up on his nose. 'Although I'm wondering should we –'

Oisinn's like, 'What?'

'– well, *bother*?' Fionn goes.

JP's there, 'Why *wouldn't* we bother? If Father Fehily went to the trouble of leaving messages for us –'

Fionn goes, 'Look, maybe it's because I'm not a believer. I don't *have* what you'd call a spiritual side. But I really think you're reading too much into these so-called messages.'

JP's like, 'How do you explain it, then? That first one – about adultery. That was aimed at me.'

Fionn goes, 'How did Father Fehily know you slept with Sorcha?'

Oisinn's there, 'And the one about laying down your life for your friends – that spoke directly to me, Fionn.'

I go, 'Bock, bock, bock, bock – bwaaahhhkkk!!!' making a sound like a chicken.

Fionn's there, 'It's like picking shapes out of cloud formations – you're seeing what you want to see.'

JP's there, 'Well, I vote that we carry on collecting the messages.'

Fionn's like, 'Fine,' and we walk on in silence, eating our sandwiches, while I stop every few seconds to claw at my orms and legs and back.

We walk for, like, an hour, maybe two, then we come to a fork in the road and Fionn tells us that the gaff we're looking for involves a forty-minute detour, which is fine by me. We walk along the banks of a river until we eventually come to what looks like a model village, as in, it's full of small cottages and it's a bit – I want to say – *picturesque?*

As we're walking up the main drag, we hear the sound of bells.

Fionn goes, 'Well,' looking up from Father Fehily's instructions, 'we're not going to need directions anyway.'

We follow the sound of the bells to a small church at the far end of the village. I'm still scratching myself, by the way. The more I think about it, the more my skin feels like it's crawling with bugs.

We make our way to the church, which it turns out is called the Church of Saint Genova. We walk in. The place is empty. There's the usual churchy smells of candles and wet coats.

JP goes, 'The steeple is on that side – which means the bell-ringer must be –' and he pushes open a door. 'There.'

Yeah, no, he's right. There's a dude with a round, smiley face, jet-black hair and humungous eyebrows to match and he's pulling on a giant rope. He doesn't say shit to us, just smiles at us and carries on ringing the bell for a good, I don't know, sixty seconds, nearly blowing out our eardrums in the process.

He finally finishes and lets go of the rope, although the bells continue to hum for a good, like, minute after he's stopped ringing them.

'*Buenos días!*' the dude tries to go – your guess is as good as mine.

Fionn goes, 'Er, Periko Uralde?'

The dude's eyes go wide. He's like, 'No, no, no! English?'

'Er, Irish,' JP goes.

The dude's there, 'No, I speak English?'

'It'd definitely help,' I go.

He's like, 'Okay, Periko is my – how you say? – *late* father.'

I'm there, 'You're doing very well.'

'I like to practise my English,' he goes. 'Periko – my father – was the bell-ringer here for fifty years. Now, I am the bell-ringer. My name is Ricardo.'

JP goes, 'It's nice to meet you, Ricardo. We were sent by Father Fehily, who was our former headmaster and rugby –'

'Ah, Denis!' he goes. 'How is Denis? He is very old, I am expecting.'

I'm like, 'He's, em, very dead,' which doesn't come out as funny as I *thought* it would?

'Of course, of course,' he goes, 'he was my father's age. They walk the Camino together. They were good, good friends.'

JP goes, 'He, em, said he left something here for us – a letter?'

'The letter!' the dude goes – suddenly excited. 'You are the boys! He says you must get this letter! The last words my father speaks to me is, "Look after the letter from Denis! One day, someone will come for!" and then he dies! Come, come, come, come, come,' and he sort of, like, beckons us to follow him, which we do – out of the church and across the road to this, like, tiny bungalow, where he seems to live on his Tobler.

He invites us into the gaff, then into a tiny kitchen. He tells us to sit down at a sort of, like, rustic table, puts a glass in front of each of us, then puts a jug of lemonade – 'Made in the home!' he goes – in front of us, before he disappears into the next room to find the letter.

I'm sitting there, knocking back the lemonade and scratching the backs of my orms.

'You're only going to make it worse,' Fionn goes.

I'm there, 'Says the man who had a ground sheet but let me sleep in a dirty bed.'

A second or two later, Ricardo arrives back, holding the letter. He hands it to JP, who tears it open like it's focking Oscars night. He pulls out the piece of paper inside and – again – gives it the old left-to-right.

'Well?' it's Oisinn who goes. 'Is it another quote from the Bible?'

JP nods.

He's like, 'It's from the Book of Genesis. It's the story of God telling Abraham to sacrifice his son, Isaac.'

I'm there, 'Random.'

Christian goes, 'What does it, I don't know, mean?'

JP hasn't a Scooby-Doo – like the rest of us.

All of a sudden, I notice that Ricardo is watching me claw at my orms. He looks a bit – I'm going to be honest here – *fearful*?

He goes, 'What is?' and he points with a sort of, like, limp finger.

I'm there, 'Don't sweat it, Dude, it's just a few – yeah, no – bites.'

He goes, 'I cannot have fleas here.'

I'm like, 'Er, they're not fleas, Dude. They're bed bugs. Totally different thing. I presume. Although until a few hours ago, I didn't know they even existed.'

'You must go,' Ricardo goes – suddenly looking at me like I'm unclean. 'You must take your fleas outside.'

Jesus Christ, he's obviously some kind of germ freak. We all stand up from the table.

'Well,' Oisinn goes, 'it was a pleasure to meet you, Ricordo,' but the dude doesn't shake his hand and refuses to take his eyes off me until I'm outside the gaff.

'You must understand,' he goes, 'not to be rude, but fleas I do not like.'

I'm there, 'I don't have focking fleas.'

JP follows the rest of us outside, reading from the Bible passage. He's like, *'God said to Abraham, "Take your son, your only son, who you love – Isaac – and go to the region of Moriah. Sacrifice him there as a burnt offering on a mountain I will show you."'*

I turn around to Ricordo and I go, 'You wouldn't have any Sudocrem, would you?' but he's already closed the door in our faces.

Without wanting to sound like Fionn – blogging his way around the internet cafés of South America while normal people his age were out chasing their hole – the walk from Carrión de los Condes to Terradillos de los Templarios ends up being – yeah, no – pretty alright.

We're walking along a road with, like, yellow fields of wheat on either side of us and a dork blue sky overhead.

Oisinn goes, 'Looks like it might rain.'

I'm like, 'Yeah, thanks for the weather update, Oisinn. I forgot you once got off with Nuala Carey. Oh, wait a minute, you didn't! You just pretended you did so that –'

My phone rings before I get a chance to finish the gag. I check the screen. It ends up being Roz, so I answer it, giving her a big, friendly, 'Hey, babes, what's the story?'

She goes, 'Hi, how are you?'

'Yeah, no, all is good – *ins an* 'hood.'

'Don't call me babes, by the way. I'm not one of your Mount Anville girls.'

'Fair enough.'

'How's the walk going?'

'Yeah, no, it's fine. The scenery is, em, nice.'

'Nice? Wow, Ross!'

'I'm just saying – if that's your kind of thing, then, yeah, it's nice.'

'And what about the goys? How are things there?'

'Oh,' I go, at the top of my voice, just so they all hear me, 'we're getting along like a house on fire.'

She's there, 'That's good.'

'Yeah, no, you wouldn't believe the things that have come out of some of their mouths while we've been walking.'

I suddenly stop to rub my back off a telegraph pole.

Roz goes, 'Are you okay there, Ross?'

I'm there, 'Yeah, no, I'm just scratching here. I got bitten by bed bugs, by the way.'

'Oh my God!'

'*Exactly* that! Although I'm not surprised – some of the shitholes we've slept in along the way.'

'Did the others get bitten?'

I'm like, 'No, they all have sleeping bags,' and then I raise my voice so that JP *especially* can hear me? 'Speaking of itches, though, JP slept with Sorcha and gave her an STD.'

There's, like, silence on the other end of the phone.

I'm there, 'Like I said, you wouldn't believe the shit that's come out so far on this trip. And Oisinn – who was busting my balls about getting all of his shit stolen – had a confession of his own. He was hiding in the doorway of Kilkenny Design when I got the shit kicked out of me by some random skobies back in the day. Claimed originally that he was busy getting off with Nuala Carey off the weather, but that was horseshit.'

Again, she doesn't say anything – probably in shock, like me.

I'm there, 'Anyway,' because I don't want the conversation to be all about me, 'how are you? Do you miss me?'

She's like, 'Of course I do.'

I'm there, 'Yeah, no, I miss you too,' although I make sure to keep my voice low, so the goys don't hear me. 'How's, em, Sincerity? Is she still seeing that Jonah dude?'

'Yeah, they're still seeing each other. She's very upset, though.'

'Oh, yeah?'

'She and Honor had a huge fight. Honor told her she wanted all of her clothes and make-up back.'

I'm thinking, Fair focks, Honor. Fair focking focks.

I'm there, 'That's, em, terrible.'

'She said that Sincerity was a total nobody when she met her,' she goes, 'and that she rescued her from Dorksville.'

'Sounds like she, em, really opened up on her – we're talking both barrels.'

'She sent her a text saying, Let's see how much Jonah likes you when you're back in your plain Jane, dorky clothes.'

'And does he? Still like her, I mean?'

'I presume so – well, she hasn't dropped the clothes and the make-up back yet.'

'So the jury is still out, seems to be what you're saying.'

All of a sudden, out of literally nowhere, the heavens open, and we find ourselves walking, out in the open, in *the* heaviest downpour I have literally ever seen. We're getting absolutely lashed on.

I'm like, 'Roz, I have to go, okay?'

The goys are already running. I hear JP go, 'There's a born over there! Let's see can we shelter in it!'

So – yeah, no – that's what we end up *doing*? I end up getting there first. That's what an unbelievable competitor I am, that even with my feet still in ribbons and my back and legs covered in bites, I'm still quicker than any of them off a standing stort.

We're all soaked to the skin by the time we reach the shelter of the born. I end up having to whip off my tuxedo t-shirt to wring the water out of it. And that's when I notice that we're, like, not alone in the born.

There's, like, five older dudes in there, sitting on what look – to this South Dublin man's eyes – to be bales of hay.

They're like, '*Comment ça va?*'

They're obviously Spanish.

I give them a wave, meaning hello.

Fionn – who speaks several languages fluently – storts spraffing away to them in words they understand. They seem to be sound, insofar as I'm any kind of judge. They're around our age and from the smell I can't help but notice that they're smoking – and this brings me right back to my unsupervised access days with Ronan as a child – but *hash*?

'*Voulez vous?*' one of them goes, offering me a blast of his, I suppose, *joint*? And even though I always said no whenever Ronan tried to get me to smoke the shit – he was only eight and I was trying to set a good example – I end up thinking, Fock it, Ross, you're on your holliers.

So I take it from him and I take what Ronan used to call a blast from the thing. It's strong shit as well and I feel instantly light-headed.

Fionn does some more of his foreign talking with them and it turns out they weren't speaking Spanish at all, but French, a language I supposably learned in school.

I'm there, 'So why do you *speak* French if you're *from* Spain?'

Fionn goes, 'They're not from Spain, Ross – they're speaking French because they're from France,' but I have to admit that I'm struggling to keep up and it's possibly the hash.

Fionn makes the introductions. He's like, *'Je m'appelle, Fionn. Il s'appelle Oisinn. Il s'appelle Christian. Il s'appelle JP. Et il s'appelle Ross.'*

The goys are called Dominique, Marius, Didier and Philippe and it turns out – unbelievable – that *they* played rugby together as *well*? From the time they were, like, thirteen. You could almost say they're France's equivalent of *us*?

Fionn goes, 'Didier is asking us why we decided to walk the Camino together.'

I'm there, 'I'll answer this one, Fionn,' and bear in mind we've all got a joint between our fingers at this stage. 'We have coach. His name is Father Fehily. He is dead. Sad time. He leave us money in will. He say when we are forty, we should walk Camino together.'

'Ross,' JP goes, 'they're focking French, not Native Americans,' which everyone seems to find hilarious – although maybe, again, it's just the hash.

'Et vous?' Fionn goes. *'Pourqoui est vous marcher le Camino?'*

It's, like, Dominique who answers. I have literally no idea what he says in reply, but I notice that he places his hand on his hort and he storts speaking in an, I don't know, *sad* tone?

I take another puff on my, I suppose, hash cigarette. Jesus, Ronan wasn't wrong about this stuff being tremendous.

'Dominique has a brain tumour,' Fionn goes – typical him, suddenly bringing the mood down. 'He says it's inoperable. He has – at most – twelve months to live.'

'Non, non, non!' Dominique goes, because he must cop our

reaction. *'Je ne suis pas miserable! Comprendez-vous?'* and then he says some other shit.

Fionn's there, 'He says he's not unhappy. He says this is port of his bucket list – to spend a precious month in the company of his three best friends in the world, three men who soldiered alongside him on the rugby field, three men for whom . . . he would lay down his life.'

While he's saying all of this, I'm just staring at Oisinn, who's sitting on a – again – bale of hay a few feet away from me, with a joint burning between his fingers and a big, dumb look on his face.

I stand up and I walk over to him.

He's like, 'Dude, if you're going to deck me, please just get it over with. Deck away. I deserve it.'

But I don't deck him. Instead, I throw my orms around him and I pull him close to me. And – again – it might well be the drugs talking, but I end up going, 'I focking love you, Dude.'

And although his face is buried in my chest, over the sound of the rain drumming on the roof of the born, I hear him go, 'I love you, Dude.'

Oh, rugby. I've said it before and I'll go on saying it. Oh, rugby, rugby, rugby.

'So, like, who was this Abraham dude?' I go. 'It's not Abraham Lincoln, is it? I don't know why I've got that name in my head.'

Fionn just rolls his eyes. Like he said, he doesn't believe in the whole God thing – thinks it's a waste of time. But I'm prepared to keep an open mind on the subject.

He's like, 'No, it's not Abraham Lincoln,' acting the real dick.

We're sitting on the wall of a bridge over a small stream, an hour outside of somewhere-or-other – Mansilla de la Mulas, according to Fionn, who's in chorge of the map.

'He was a prophet,' JP goes. 'Some people believe that it was to Abraham that God revealed that the Jews were the chosen people.'

Fionn's there, 'Yes, *some* people believe.'

I'm like, 'So what happened? Did you say that God told him to top his own son?'

JP looks down at the piece of paper in his hands and storts reading it. He's like, 'When they reached the place God told him about, Abraham built an altar there and arranged the wood on it. He bound his son, Isaac, and laid him on the altar, on top of the wood. Then he reached out his hand and took the knife to slay his son.'

I'm there, 'Seriously? What the fock?'

'But the angel of the Lord called out to him from Heaven: "Abraham! Abraham!" "Here I am," he replied. "Do not lay a hand on the boy," the angel said. "Do not do anything to him. Now I know that you fear God because you have not withheld from me your son, your only son."'

I'm like, 'Bit of a dick move by God, wasn't it?'

'He was testing Abraham's faith,' JP goes.

Fionn's like, 'Yeah, there's no historical evidence that Abraham ever existed. The world of Genesis is about as real as Tír na nÓg.'

I actually thought Tír na nÓg was real. I don't say anything, for fear of looking stupid, although I make a quiet vow to myself to Google it when we get to the next hostel.

Oisinn goes, 'So who do we think this one is aimed at?' handing me his Bobble to drink from.

Fionn's like, 'It's not *aimed* at any of us. But any one of us is capable of reading whatever we want into it.'

JP reads it again – except this time to himself. He goes, 'Now I know that you fear God because you have not withheld from me your son, your only son.'

'Fock!' Oisinn suddenly goes.

I'm like, 'What?'

He's there, 'Look who's coming!' and I look up the road to be greeted by a sight that almost stops my focking hort.

It's Vivica.

'Fock's sake,' I go. 'I thought we lost her a week ago. Why won't she just fock off?'

The ashes, by the way, are stashed in Oisinn's bag. I got sick of carrying them and I guilted him into taking them for me. He still owes me, in fairness.

I'm like, 'What are we going to do?'

Christian's there, 'You mean, what are *you* going to do, Ross?' and this from my supposably best mate in the world.

Oisinn goes, 'Ross, you better make yourself scarce – and quick.'

There isn't time to make a run for it. She's, like, fifty feet away and – yeah, no – she'll see me. So instead I decide to hide under the bridge. I throw my two legs over the wall and drop down into the stream, landing with a splash and a . . .

'FOCK!'

I end up landing on a rock and I manage to turn my ankle and fall backwards into the water.

I'm like, 'FOOO –' but then I put my hand over my mouth to stifle my cries, lying on my back on the bed of the stream, with the water washing over me, because I can suddenly hear Vivica's voice, just overhead.

She's going, 'So where is he?'

They're all like, 'Who?' in fairness to them.

I manage to get to my feet and I hop a few paces so that I'm under the bridge and out of sight. I can still hear her voice. She sounds mad.

She's there, 'That asshole friend of yours. Neville Archeson . . . ston – if that even *is* his name.'

I'm thinking, How the fock did I come up with that in the heat of the moment? That's some very impressive thinking on my feet.

She goes, 'Which I seriously doubt, by the way, because I looked him up on Facebook, Twitter, LinkedIn.'

Oisinn's there, 'Yeah, no, Neville doesn't *do* the whole social media thing?' and he's being a real bro to me, in fairness to him. 'He doesn't believe in it.'

'So where is he?' she goes. 'Fucking asshole.'

JP's there, 'Oh, he's, em, gone back to Ireland.'

'Ireland?' she goes – she sounds angry enough to kill. 'Why?'

Christian's there, 'He found the going too tough,' which is a real dig at me. 'So he quit. He's a quitter.'

It takes every bit of self-control I have to stop myself from shouting, '*I'm* a quitter? When Leinster were sixteen points down to Northampton at half-time in the 2011 Heineken Cup final, who wanted to leave and go to the focking pub? And who said no, because he fully believed that Leinster were capable of turning it around in the second half?'

I hear Vivica go, 'He stole something from me.'

Oisinn's like, '*Stole* something? What was it?'

'My sister's ashes,' she goes.

JP's there, 'Her ashes? Why would he steal your sister's ashes? Think about what you're saying.'

'I don't know,' she goes. 'All I know is that we were all together in the hostel that night, then you guys left the next morning and someone had taken food from my bag, along with my sister's ashes.'

Oisinn goes, 'That doesn't sound like Ross – I mean Neville. He's been my friend since we were, like, twelve – and he would never do something as shitty as that. Never.'

It's a lovely thing for me to hear, even though it's obviously bollocks. I notice that Fionn and Christian are staying silent on the question – two focking dicks.

She goes, 'So if Neville didn't steal them, then who did?'

JP's there, 'Could have been anyone. Maybe someone else in the hostel took it, thinking it was food.'

She goes, 'You fucking tell Neville that I want my sister's ashes back,' and she storts – oh, shit the bed – crying her eyes out. 'Can you get that message to him – please?'

There's, like, thirty seconds of silence then. I'm standing there up to my mid-shin in water, my ankle absolutely throbbing.

Then I hear Oisinn go, 'You can come out now, Neville! She's gone!'

Ronan and Avery have taken Rihanna-Brogan to Venice. Yeah, no, I'm looking through his Instagram account and there's a photograph of the three of them in – I'm pretty sure it's called – a *gondola*?

I show it to Oisinn. I'm like, 'That's Ronan and his girlfriend – we're talking Avery.'

'I didn't know she was black,' he goes, taking the phone from me.

I'm there, 'Er, African-American is what you're *supposed* to say?'

'No, you can say black,' JP goes. 'It's perfectly acceptable.'

I'm thinking, Who even knows any more?

Oisinn's like, 'Oh my God, they're so in love.'

I'm there, 'Yeah, no, I think she's a ringer for Gugu Mbatha-Raw – if that's not racist.'

'Look at this one of them at the Colosseum,' Oisinn goes. 'The way they're looking at each other.'

Fionn goes, 'When is he storting in Horvard?' because he always finds a way to bring the conversation around to education.

I'm there, 'September. The two of them. They're just doing a tour of Europe before they stort. Avery's always wanted to see it. It's, like, whatever you're into.'

Oisinn hands me back my phone and asks me how my ankle's holding up. Yeah, no, I really thought I could hopefully walk the soreness off but, if anything, it's made it worse and now I'm sitting outside a little restaurant in León with the thing propped up on a stool and I'm holding ice cubes against it to try to bring down the swelling.

'You can't walk on that ankle for ten more days,' Fionn goes. 'You're going to have to go home.'

I'm like, 'Dude, I get it. You don't want me here. But I'm not abandoning.'

He goes, 'You can always come back another time to finish it. A lot of people do the Camino over the course of two or three years.'

I'm there, 'JP, give me a blast of that, will you?'

Yeah, no, the French dudes we met in the hay born gave us a humungous lump of hash and, while I would normally be very much *anti* working-class drugs, it's definitely helping with the pain. JP hands me the cigarette. I take two long drags off it – and before I know it, I'm grinning like an idiot.

Ronan really was right about this shit.

'I'm going to finish it with Lychee,' Christian – out of literally nowhere – goes. He looks gee-eyed and miserable.

Fionn's there, 'Christian, you really should lay off the drink,' because he's throwing it down his Ant and Dec like there's no tomorrow.

'She's a focker,' he goes. 'She's a focking . . . *focker*.'

I go to hand him the – again, so random – *joint*, but he refuses it.

JP's like, 'The girl is twenty-whatever, Christian. It's a generational thing.'

'And you and Delma isn't?' Christian goes.

JP's there, 'It's easier to be with a much older woman than a much younger woman.'

'Why?'

'I think we can understand people of Delma's age because we all have parents. But Lychee's generation – let's be honest, they're a focking mystery to us.'

I'm there, 'Tell us a bit more about the sex thing, Christian,' because he's highly unlikely to remember this conversation tomorrow. 'Tell us about some of the other shit she makes you do.'

'She's a focker, Ross,' he goes, his eyes spinning like pinwheels. 'She's a focking . . . *focker*.'

I'm there, 'Has she ever pissed on your face?'

'Hello there!' I hear a voice suddenly go.

I look up and – yeah, no – there's a woman standing there. She's in her maybe early thirties with short, dork hair, deep, brown eyes and a big, gummy smile.

She sort of, like, sniffs the air, then goes, 'Is that what I think?' and she has an accent that sounds quite possibly German.

I'm like, 'Errr –,' because we have no idea who she even *is*?

She goes, 'If it is what I think, I would very much like some.'

Like I said, she's an absolute cracker, so I go, 'Yeah, no, fair enough,' and I hand her the joint. She closes her eyes and storts – holy fock – sucking on the thing like a Louth man siphoning diesel from an engine.

'Oh, is so good,' she eventually goes, handing it back to me. 'At home, I smoke all the time. But for almost three weeks now, nothing.'

I'm there, 'So where's home?' because I'm nothing if not a great conversationalist.

She goes, 'Denmark,' and I just nod, wondering is it a real country or one she's just made up on the spot.

Fionn's there, 'Yes, Ross, it's a real country,' trying to make me look like a fool.

I'm like, 'I know it's a real country. I've heard of it, okay? So what's your name?'

She places her hand on her, I don't know, breastbone and she goes, 'I am Stine. And my friends –' and she looks over her shoulder at two birds in shorts with rucksacks, who are watching us from the other side of the road. 'Janni! Maja!'

The two birds cross over the road. One of them is blonde, about six feet tall and looks like a model, while the other one is shorter with big glasses and – I'm not even sure if I *have* to say this? – not great in terms of looks.

I'm there, 'So which one is Janni and which one is Maja?' ever the people-person.

It turns out that Janni is the model and Maja is the lagoon donkey.

'Sit down,' I go, 'join us,' which they're only too happy to do.

Maja, I notice, takes the empty seat next to Fionn. She obviously knows her level.

'I very much like your t-shirt,' Stine goes, taking the joint from me again. She blows smoke from her mouth and smiles at me in a definitely *flirty* way? 'So, you are getting married?'

I'm like, 'No, yeah, this is just something I picked up in a hostel we stayed in,' and I stand up and show her the back. 'I don't even know who Desmond is.'

She seems quite shocked by this.

I'm there, 'The walk was kind of a last-minute thing for me. I arrived with literally nothing.'

She smiles. I'm picking up on the fact that she's into me.

She goes, 'You are a true pilgrim,' and then she turns to the others. 'A true pilgrim travels with no possessions and lives off the charity of others.'

'Well, he's certainly been doing that,' Fionn goes.

No one laughs – talk about a tumbleweed moment.

Stine finishes the joint and stubs it out in the ashtray. She goes, 'You have more?' because she's a focking fiend for the stuff.

Oisinn takes out the massive lump that the French dudes gave us. He's like, 'Plenty more,' and Stine's face lights up. I'm storting to think she might have a problem.

'You are a true pilgrim,' she again goes as she rolls another joint. I watch her run her tongue along the length of the cigarette paper and I'd be lying if I said there wasn't some port of me that wishes that paper was my nipple.

'So, what university do you lecture in?' Fionn goes.

Him and the bomb-sniffer are getting on like a something, something, something.

Yeah, no, I can always tell when Fionn is into a girl because his cheeks go all red and he storts cleaning his glasses with the corner of his shirt. That's usually my cue to move in there and clean his plate for him. But he's welcome to this girl. I'd love to see him do the dirt on the famous Ciara Casaubon.

'I have to say,' he goes, 'Kierkegaard has always been one of my go-to philosophers.'

'Uh-oh!' Janni suddenly goes. 'Maja, here is your brother!'

I look around and there's a dude walking towards us who looks weirdly familiar. He storts saying something to the girls in – I don't know – I want to say *Denmorkish*?

'In English, please,' Stine goes. 'These are our new friends. This is Ross, Oisinn, Christian, JP and Fionn,' which is a serious feat of memory given the way she's smoking that shit. 'Boys, this is Maja's brother, Rasmus.'

I catch him just glowering at me and I laugh because I suddenly recognize him. He's the dude who was washing his jockeys in the sink the other day when I focked them out into the hallway.

I'm like, 'What's the *craic*, Dude?'

He doesn't answer – although he looks like he wants to kill me.

He goes, 'So now you are doing drugs, yes?'

Maja's like, 'Oh, please, Rasmus, you are not at work now.'

Stine's there, 'Rasmus is a motorcycle cop.'

Which the dude obviously takes exception to, because he goes, 'I am a police officer.'

'Traffic police,' Stine goes.

The dude responds like he's having his manhood questioned.

'It is my job to uphold the law,' he goes. 'All laws.'

Stine's like, 'Not in this country.'

I'm picking up on the fact that he's into Stine in a major way.

He's there, 'We go to bed. It is a long walk to Villar de Mazarife.'

Stine goes, 'Then you go to bed, Rasmus. Sweet dreams.'

The dude gives me a serious filthy, then he points at me and goes, 'You are asshole!'

He turns on his heel and focks off.

Stine goes, 'I am so sorry. I went out with Rasmus for one year and he cannot accept that it is finished.'

I'm there, 'Yeah, no, he's possibly also pissed off because I focked him out of the bathroom the other day when he was washing his boxers.'

Janni laughs. She goes, 'This was you? For two days, it is all he talks about as we walk! This man with fleas who bursts into the toilet while he is washing his clothes.'

I'm there, 'Er, these *aren't* flea bites, by the way? They're bed bugs, in case you're wondering. And they're not even itchy any more.'

'Let's get some wine here,' Janni goes, then she goes inside to order a bottle.

Stine smiles at me.

'You are very handsome,' she goes.

I'm like, 'Do you think so?' pretending that the thought has never occurred to me in, like, nearly forty years of existence on this planet we call Earth. 'I've never heard that before.'

She laughs. 'Okay,' she goes, 'this I find very difficult to believe!'

We end up sitting there, shooting the shit for, like, two or three hours before she propositions me – direct and to-the-point.

'So, are you married?' she goes.

I'm like, '*Was* married. We've been separated for a few months – or a few years, according to the story she put out.'

She's there, 'And do you have someone new?'

This is it, I think. The first proper test of my loyalty to Roz, not counting the bird I brought back to Oisinn and Magnus's gaff.

'Yeah, no,' I hear myself go, 'I have, like, em, a *girlfriend*, I suppose.'

She puts her hand on my knee. She's like, 'You do not sound so sure, Ross.'

I think about it for a good, like, ten seconds, then I go, 'No, I'm sure, Stine. I'm one hundred per cent sure.'

She smiles at me – no hord feelings – and goes, 'Pity – another life perhaps.'

I look at Fionn and I notice that him and Maja are sort of, like, holding hands under the table – as in their fingers are, like, intertwined.

'You know,' I hear Maja say quietly, 'the theory of the nexus between thesis, antithesis and synthesis is often wrongly ascribed to Hegel, when it was in fact the idea of Johann Gottlieb Fichte.'

And, as she's saying it, I can't help but notice that Fionn has a massive focking tentpole in his khakis.

So it's, like, the following morning and we're having breakfast in a little café – we're talking me, we're talking JP, we're talking Oisinn and we're talking Christian.

Fionn ends up being a no-show. Yeah, no, he didn't come back to the hostel last night either.

JP goes, 'He must have ended up with that Maja.'

I'm there, 'He needed his hole. I can't wait to tell the famous Ciara.'

Oisinn goes, 'Ross!'

I'm like, 'I'm not going to tell Ciara.'

I am going to tell Ciara, but I'll make it look like a slip of the tongue.

JP goes, 'It's, em, very out of character for Fionn, isn't it? I've never known him to be a cheater.'

Oisinn's there, 'Goys, I think he's going through something. Has anyone noticed he's been very touchy – especially since we collected that last letter from Father Fehily?'

I'm like, 'Let's just hope that whatever that bird does to him improves his mood.'

I knock back a mouthful of coffee.

'And what about you?' JP goes.

I'm like, 'In terms of?'

'Er, turning down Stine?' he goes. 'I mean, she was gorgeous, Ross.'

'Yeah, no, I noticed.'

'And you said no to her. I wouldn't have believed it if I hadn't seen it with my own eyes.'

I'm like, 'I'm in a relationship, goys,' and I notice that both JP and Oisinn look away. I didn't mean to make them feel bad. 'I did have a wank thinking about Stine – when we got back to the hostel.'

'Yeah,' Christian goes, 'we heard.'

'I don't think *that* counts as cheating. Here, I'll give you a good laugh, though – when I finished off, I used Fionn's t-shirt to mop the knuckle children off my stomach.'

JP goes, 'Which t-shirt?'

I'm like, 'Yeah, no, the purple one with the shell symbol on the front. It was drying on the radiator.'

'That's *my* focking t-shirt!'

'Well, *I* didn't know.'

'For fock's sake, Ross.'

You'd swear it was the first time I ever used an item of his clothing to clean up after myself. I feel like nearly telling him to grow up.

I'm like, 'I'll wash it for you when we get to, I don't know, wherever.'

'Villar de Mazarife,' Christian goes.

'Exactly – although I suppose we can't get on the road until Fionn finally shows his face. She must be doing all sorts to him. By the way, I could have totally got in there if I'd wanted – ruined his focking chances. But I didn't. Because I'm a mate. And because she was a bit of a focking gorgon.'

JP goes, 'I can't believe you focking jizzed on my t-shirt.'

I'm like, 'Yeah, grow up, JP. How much of my jizz have you seen over the years? Jesus Christ, we played rugby together.'

He ends up just shaking his head – like I'm an *animal* or something? He pushes his Spanish omelette away. In fairness to him, it'd be hord to stomach anything with eggs in it after what he's just heard.

I grab his plate and I horse into whatever's left.

Oisinn turns around to JP and goes, 'So have you decided what you're going to do?'

JP's like, 'Do?'

'Yeah, no,' Oisinn goes, 'are you going to tell Delma about doing the dirt on her?'

That knocks him down a rung or two – Mr High and focking Mighty.

'Maybe,' he goes. 'I mean, I don't *want* to tell her. And not because I'm scared to tell her. I just think it'll be very hord for her to hear, especially after –'

After he dropped a load of hints to her to get her face done and she's ended up looking like the kind of woman you inflate with a foot pump.

He goes, 'What about you? Are you going to tell Magnus?'

Oisinn – believe it or not – nods. He's like, 'I nearly told him on the phone two nights ago, but I decided I should wait until I go home.'

I'm there, 'You're focking mad. Oisinn, you and Magnus have got a quite possibly baby on the way.'

'It's not a quite possibly baby,' Oisinn goes. 'You've seen the scan, Ross.'

I'm there, 'Exactly. So, what, one or other of you is going to bring up this child alone just because you had a drunken fumble – quite possibly for old time's sake – with a girl? You're a focking idiot – and you are as well, JP.'

'Why?'

'Because we're in focking Spain. There's no chance of Magnus or Delma finding out about what happened. And you're going to risk everything you have at home – for what exactly?'

'Well, I happen to think that honesty is important in a relation-ship,' JP goes.

I'm there, 'If you thought honesty was important in a relationship, you wouldn't have done the dirt in the first place. You just need to become better at managing your guilt, Dude.'

JP suddenly stands up. He goes, 'Okay, I can't think about any-thing else except that jizz-covered t-shirt stuffed into my bag. I have to go and get rid of it.'

315

Yeah, no, this is one of those cafés that make you leave your ruck-sack outside.

I'm there, 'I said I'd wash it. I honestly think you're making a bigger deal of this than it *needs* to be?'

That's when Fionn decides to finally show his face.

I'm there, 'So did you ride her?'

But he avoids the question. He goes, 'What's wrong with JP?' because one was walking in as the other one was walking out.

Christian goes, 'Ross wanked on his t-shirt.'

I'm there, 'I didn't wank on his t-shirt. That makes it sound sexual. I had – yes – a wank and I used his t-shirt to clean myself up afterwards. I actually thought it was yours, Fionn.'

The dude is in foul form – another one who could do with getting control over his conscience.

He goes, 'Let's just get on the road, can we?'

Suddenly, JP walks back into the café with a worried look on his face. He goes, 'It's gone, goys – someone's stolen my focking rucksack.'

For the first two hours of the day, we walk in mostly silence. My ankle is in a serious jocker, so I'm limping along. Once or twice, I try to strike up a chorus of . . .

> If I had the wings of a sparrow,
> If I had the orse of a crow,
> I'd fly over St Michael's College –

. . . except no one is in the mood.

JP's like, 'I can't believe it. I've lost everything.'

Oisinn goes, 'Shit, was your passport in the bag?'

'No,' he goes, 'I keep that in my pocket. Fock's sake, though. Who would want to rob my clothes?'

Fionn's there, 'There's a lot of poverty in this region.'

I'm like, 'I'd love to see their faces when they pull out your t-shirt with my yoghurt all over it.'

No one laughs.

'So are you going to tell Ciara?' I go.

Yeah, no, I'm talking to Fionn now.

He's there, 'Tell her what?'

I'm like, 'Er, tell her that you rode someone else last night? I'm *presuming* that you rode her. Unless you spent the whole night talking about, I don't know, Keerstersturd.'

'It was Kierkegaard.'

'Boring the focking ears off each other. You really met your match there, didn't you? Must have been like riding the female you.'

'I've already *told* Ciara.'

'What?'

'I rang her this morning. Before I came to find you.'

That's Fionn all over. He always, always, *always* does the right thing – the focking mug.

'That's very disappointing,' I go. 'I was looking forward to having that over you and now you've taken that pleasure away from me.'

'How did she take it?' Oisinn goes – he's clearly still toying with the idea of telling Magnus about his own bit of extra-curricular.

Fionn's like, 'Not well. She hung up and that was that.'

I'm there, 'She was bet-down, by the way – as in, the one you rode? A focking hippofrogamus.'

It's absolutely roasting today – possibly the hottest day of the walk so *far*? – and my famous tuxedo t-shirt is soaked through with sweat. Suddenly, up ahead on the road, I notice a police cor pulled over. As we approach, two dudes – yeah, no, *policemen*? – get out and put their hats on.

JP goes, 'It's the Feds. I can tell them about my shit being stolen!' and up to them he casually saunters.

He goes, '*Hablas inglés?*' and the two dudes just shake their heads.

Fionn storts banging on to them in Spanish, telling them about the stolen rucksack and the two dudes nod slowly, pretending to actually *give* a fock? Then *they* stort asking questions, not about the bag, but about *us*?

Fionn goes, '*Irlanda*,' and then he's there, '*Por el Camino*,' and then he's like, '*Tres semanas*,' and then he goes, '*Drogas?*'

I notice him biting his lip – he looks suddenly worried about something.

I'm there, 'Dude, what's the Johnny Magory here?'

Fionn goes, 'He's telling us to place our hands on the side of the police car.'

'Er, *why?*'

'He said they have reason to believe that we're carrying drugs.'

Suddenly, I feel a shove in my back and one of the dudes storts shouting at me in – again – Spanish. I place my two hands on the cor and he storts patting me down. He hears the rattle of plastic in my pocket. He slips his hand inside and he whips out – yeah, no – a banana burka, still in its wrapper.

I give him a wink and go, 'Case I get lucky,' and I can tell that he's not a fan. He shoves me away, then he grabs JP and he storts frisking *him?*

Out of the corner of his mouth, Oisinn goes, 'We're focked.'

I'm like, 'What are you talking about?'

He's there, 'I've got that humungous lump of hash in my rucksack.'

And that's when the truth suddenly hits me – hits us *all?*

I'm there, 'Focking Rasmus – he tipped off the Feds.'

Next, the dude gives Christian the same treatment, shaking him down, while the other dude gets on the radio and says some shit in Spanish.

'He's calling for another cor,' Fionn goes. 'They're obviously going to take us to the station.'

Oisinn's like, 'The shit is in the very bottom of my bag. Will I see can I get it out and fock it away?'

'It's too risky,' I go. 'This dude on the radio isn't taking his eyes off us.'

Oisinn turns to Fionn. He's like, 'What's the worst they can do to us – we're not talking about jail time, are we?'

Fionn's there, 'I've no idea. I think the drug laws are very strict over here.'

Oisinn's there, 'Fock!'

The second cor arrives. Two birds get out – very disappointing, if you're wondering – and they throw the three rucksacks into the boot. They order me and Oisinn into the back of their cor, while Fionn, JP and Christian get into the back of the other one.

We're driven for, like, fifteen minutes to this small town. Oisinn storts shitting his pants. He's going, 'I can't go to jail. I'm about to be a father,' and for a split-second I consider telling him that, er, he's possibly *not*?

But I don't. Instead, I go, 'We could tell them that it belongs to Fionn.'

He's like, 'What? Why?'

'We could say he needs it for, like, medicinal reasons. Sorcha's granny had a friend who smoked it for glaucoma. They'll believe that of Fionn. Blind focker.'

We pull up outside a one-storey, flat-roofed building with a sign outside saying 'Policía'.

I'm there, 'This must be the cop shop.'

Oisinn – in a sorcastic voice – goes, 'Do you reckon?'

And I'm like, 'Hey, I'm not the one in possession, Dude. *You* are?' and that softens his cough.

We're ordered out of the cor and we're escorted inside, along with the others. There's lots of people in there, all banging on in the local lingo.

I turn to Fionn. Without moving my lips, I go, 'Pretend to have glaucoma.'

He's like, 'What?'

'Yeah, no,' I go, 'sort of, like, pat the air in front of you as you're walking – like you can't see. We're going to say you smoke it for medicinal reasons.'

He's like, 'Don't be ridiculous.'

So I'm there, 'Christian, pretend to be blind, will you?'

We're brought into an interview room by the four cops who brought us in – the two dudes and the two fugly manstrosities. Christian – in fairness to him – bumps into a desk and then a water cooler, knocking it over and spilling water everywhere.

There's a long, boardroom table in the room. The three ruck-sacks are placed on it by the same dude who patted us down and I notice that he's now wearing rubber gloves.

He searches Fionn's rucksack first. He reaches in and storts pull-ing items out of it. His glasses case. A book – wouldn't you focking know it? – called *Don Quixote*. Then a tub of –

'Focking Sudocrem!' I shout, turning to Fionn. 'You focking *had* Sudocrem!'

The cop doing the search shouts something at me in Spanish, presumably telling me to shut the fock up. But I've lost it.

I'm there, 'I was focking killed with the itch. For three days and nights, you watched me tearing at my skin to try to get some relief. And all the time, you had focking Sudocrem in your focking –'

I grab him by the front of his shirt and I'm about to deck him with a punch, except the three other Feds in the room jump on me and stort trying to pull me away from him.

I'm there, 'Just let me get one dig in – break his focking glasses.'

Oisinn goes, 'You can't hit him, Ross – he's blind, remember?'

And Christian's like, 'Er, I thought *I* was the blind one?'

When order is eventually restored, the dude finishes searching Fionn's rucksack. There's fock-all of interest in it. The same with Christian's. The last one he opens is Oisinn's. As he undoes the zip, we're all kacking it to one degree or another. I notice that Oisinn's hand is shaking and even my own hort is pounding like Wade Dooley has just come home to catch me wanking into his home aquarium.

Again, the cop dude storts taking all of his things out piece by piece and placing them on the table. His water bottle. His sleeping bag. His Swiss ormy knife. And then . . .

Nothing. The bag is empty. The dude turns it over and shakes it and nothing falls out.

'Oh my God,' JP suddenly whispers, 'I've just remembered – the stuff was in *my* rucksack.'

I laugh. I'm like, 'What?'

He goes, 'Oisinn, you left it on the table of the restaurant last night. I picked it up and threw it into my bag.'

Which was then stolen.

There's, like, a furious discussion then between the four Feds – again, in the local language – at the end of which, one of the women is like, 'You are free to go.'

I'm there, 'What, just like that? After what you just put us through? Five innocent men! You haven't heard the focking last of this! Do you know who my old man is? He's, like, the leader of Ireland!'

'Ross,' Fionn goes, 'enough with the Gerry Conlon act. Let's take the win and get out of here.'

We leave the interview room. As we're walking through reception, another police dude walks in. There's, like, a kid with him, who's a bit rough-looking – reminds me a bit of Ronan at eight, right down to the tight jeans and the Christmas jumper in the middle of the focking summer. The cop is holding him by the ear. And in the other hand, I notice, is JP's rucksack.

He's like, 'Hey, that's my –'

But Oisinn shoves him in the back and goes, 'No, it focking isn't – remember?'

JP is in absolutely no doubt in terms of what happened.

'It was Father Fehily,' he goes. 'It was divine intervention.'

Fionn's there, 'What, he *made* that child steal your rucksack, knowing that we were going to be stopped by the police?'

I'm like, 'How else would you explain it?'

'That's easy,' he goes with a shrug. 'It was coincidence.'

We've stopped on the road because I'm putting new beer mats into my shoes.

Oisinn's like, 'There *are* no coincidences.'

JP's there, 'Father Fehily wants us to make it all the way to Santiago de Compostela.'

But Fionn goes, 'So you believe that dead people are controlling events on Earth from some spirit world, but you don't believe in coincidences?'

I'm there, 'I don't know about coincidences, but I've always felt that Father Fehily was watching over me.'

'Really?' Fionn goes – and I watch his face turn suddenly puce. 'Do you want me to tell you a secret about Father Fehily? Do you want to know the truth about this so-called man of God?'

Me and the goys are all looking at each other – yeah, no, something has clearly rattled the dude.

JP's like, 'What are you talking about?'

'He was having an affair,' Fionn goes. 'With Sister Casilda. For forty years.'

I'm there, 'How could he have been having an affair? Er, he was a *priest* – and she was a *nun*, remember?'

'Because he was a focking hypocrite,' Fionn goes. 'That's how.'

I'm like, 'Whoa, be careful, Dude. He was a huge mentor to me in terms of my rugby.'

JP goes, 'You stole his letters from Casilda's niece?'

Fionn's there, 'Yes, I stole them. And I read them.'

JP goes, 'Show them to me.'

Fionn's like, 'I don't have them any more. I burned them – two nights ago.'

JP's there, 'What, so we're supposed to just believe –'

'He poured out his feelings for her,' Fionn goes. 'Page after page. What he was a going to do to her the next time he saw her.'

I'm like, 'What, dirty stuff?'

'Yes, Ross,' he goes, 'dirty stuff.'

I'm there, 'How dirty are we talking?'

He's like, 'Filthy, Ross.'

Oisinn goes, 'Fionn, you had no right to read those letters.'

But Fionn's there, 'But I did anyway – so here we are.'

I'm like, 'Can I just interject here and say the word rugby?'

Fionn laughs – but not in a good way.

He shakes his head and goes, 'Rugby is not a justification for everything, Ross.'

I'm there, 'You're angry. You don't know what you're saying.'

He goes, 'What good did it do any of us? All that turning us against kids from other schools – just for his own amusement.'

I'm like, 'Dude, you're talking like Castlerock v Terenure, Blackrock v Michael's, Mary's v Belvedere, don't matter.'

He goes, 'They *don't* matter!' and that's when he suddenly loses his shit in a major way. He takes his pilgrim stick and he storts smashing it off the wall on which I'm sitting.

He's going, 'You focking hypocrite! You focking –!'

SMACK!

'– focking –!'

SMACK!

'– *focking* –!'

SMACK!

'– hypocrite!'

The stick snaps in two. He turns around to me then, tears off his glasses and goes, 'Ross, punch me in the face.'

I actually laugh.

I'm there, 'Dude, I'm not punching you in the face.'

He's like, 'Come on, Ross. Like you said, I watched you scratching yourself for three days and nights and I had Sudocrem in my bag all the time. Punch me in the face.'

I'm there, 'Dude, I'm not punching you in the face. Anyway, if I was going to do it, I'd want to do it while you were *wearing* your glasses.'

I have an irrational hatred for his glasses. He puts them back on him and goes, 'There! Go on, hit me now! I deserve it!'

I can feel my right hand forming a fist. I really do hate his glasses – what *is* that?

Christian goes, 'Fionn, what the fock is going on with you?'

And that's when the tears come. He's suddenly, like, bawling his eyes out. Again, we're looking at each other and it's, like, what the fock? Fionn is usually a rock of sense. Three weeks on the road, living out of a rucksack, have obviously sent him doo-focking-lally.

JP puts his orm around him. He's like, 'Is it because you did the dirt on Ciara?'

But he doesn't answer. He keeps crying and crying, then under his breath, he goes, 'It's about me.'

Oisinn's like, 'What's about you? The fock are you talking about?'

'Abraham sacrificing Isaac,' he goes. 'It's about me.'

I'm looking at the others and I'm like, 'I thought you said the Bible was horseshit?'

'So who did *you* sacrifice?' JP goes.

Fionn looks me in the eye. I'm actually putting my shoes back on.

He goes, 'Ross, when we were in First Year in school, you were accused of cheating in a Biology exam.'

I'm like, 'Yeah, no, the prick Lambkin found cog notes on the floor and he claimed they were mine.'

'They weren't yours,' he goes.

I'm there, 'I know they weren't mine. The joke was that I couldn't read or write at the time, but I couldn't say it, because I didn't want anyone to know.'

He goes, 'They were my cog notes, Ross.'

I'm like, 'What?'

He goes, 'They were *my* cog notes.'

I can't believe what I'm actually hearing.

I'm like, 'Dude, you watched me do a month's detention –'

He's there, 'You didn't do a month's detention. Hennessy saw to that.'

'But you never said anything. You let me be labelled a cheat.'

'I knew that I had a very good chance of winning the Young Scientist of the Year competition. I was worried that Lambkin would stop me from representing the school. I just figured that, well, you weren't exactly academic –'

I'm so angry that I'm actually *shaking*?

I'm there, 'I can't believe you made me feel bad about getting you put on the sex offenders' register. This is worse.'

He goes, 'Well, I don't think it's worse, Ross.'

I'm there, 'I was just a kid,' and I'm screaming at him now, 'accused in the wrong. And you stood by and watched me take the rap for your shit.'

He goes, 'Ross, please, just punch me in the face.'

And I just think, Yeah, no, why not?

9.

Camino Royale

Fionn looks miserable. He's got the beginnings of two black eyes from where I decked him and a piece of – yeah, no – gaffer tape wrapped around the nose of his glasses, holding the two sides together. I can never seem to break the glass like they do in the cortoons. I'm wondering is there, like, a special *technique* involved?

'You maybe shouldn't have hit him,' Oisinn goes.

I'm there, 'He begged me to hit him.'

'Only because he thought it would make him feel better.'

'Hey, it's not my fault that it didn't work. I'll give it another go if he wants.'

I've got blisters again. Same spot – as in, like, right on the balls of my feet, but also one on each of my big toes and I'm walking on my pretty much heels to save them from touching the ground. Today is, like, one of the longest walking days so far – we're talking six hours supposably, to a town called Astorga. The scenery is fine – again, if that's what revs your engine. It's, like, very green, full of hills and all the rest of it. It's warm this morning, but it's, like, drizzling rain, which is nice and cooling.

I look over my shoulder at Fionn. Loud enough for him to hear, I go, 'The focker deserved it anyway.'

He doesn't let himself get drawn in – says fock-all.

I'm there, 'Did you catch that, Fionn? Or can you not hear with your glasses in bits?'

He goes, 'Yes, I heard what you said, Ross.'

He suddenly stops for a rest – so the rest of us do too.

I'm there, 'I mean, the more I think about it, the focking balls on you, Fionn. Trying to make me feel bad for what I did and you've been holding on to that secret for all these years.'

JP goes, 'Ross, there is no moral equivalence between what you did and what Fionn did.'

I'm there, 'Now say that in English.'

'You got him labelled as a sex offender,' JP goes, 'and very nearly cost him his job.'

Fionn's there, 'Ross is right. What I did was every bit as bad.'

I'm like, 'Thank you, Fionn. Every teacher in that school – not just Lambkin – had it in for me from that day onwards.'

'They had it in for you,' Christian goes, 'because Hennessy went to the Supreme Court to have the school's disciplinary procedures declared unconstitutional.'

JP's there, 'And because you never went to classes. You were always outside practising your kicking. And because Fehily protected you – I mean, how many teachers did he sack for bringing up your non-attendance?'

I'm like, 'But *why* was I outside practising my kicking? Because from the moment I was accused of cheating in that exam, I was labelled – yes, *labelled*, JP – as a bad egg and a thicko. When I look back on it now, that was my – in fairness to me – *Sliding Doors* moment?'

'How?' Oisinn goes.

I'm there, 'I'm just saying that if Fionn had stuck his hand up, as I was being frogmorched out of the exam hall, and said that they were *his* cog notes, my life might have turned out differently. It might have been *me* winning the Young Scientist of the Year competition.'

No one says anything.

I'm there, 'It might have been *me* getting maximum points in the Leaving Cert.'

They're letting a hell of a lot go here.

I'm like, 'It might have been *me* getting degrees. And Master's – Masterses – and Ph focking D's.'

'Ross is right,' Fionn goes.

'About the Young Scientist of the Year competition?' Oisinn goes.

He'll be next in line for a decking if he's not careful.

Fionn's there, 'What I mean is that I gave Ross his bad name. And, once he had that, his life was lorgely determined.'

'That's right,' I go. 'I was seen as a loser who was only good for one thing – and that was my ability to kick a rugby ball between the posts from literally any angle or distance.'

I'm trying to stay angry here but I'm getting goosebomps saying it.

Fionn – out of nowhere – goes, 'I'm going home.'

I'm like, 'What?'

'I'm going back to Ireland,' he goes.

Oisinn's like, 'When?'

He's there, 'Now.'

That's when I realize that we're standing next to a bus stop.

He goes, 'There's a bus that goes from here to León. I can catch a flight there to Madrid and a connection to Dublin.'

JP's there, 'Fionn, you can't quit now. We've come this far.'

Oisinn and Christian are saying pretty much the same thing.

They're like, 'Dude, we're going to be in Santiago de Compostela in just over a week.'

He goes, 'I've got to get back home. School is starting again soon.'

All of a sudden, I hear the approaching rumble of a bus.

Fionn's there, 'This is me,' and he sticks out his hand like a man who's been using public transport all his life.

The bus pulls up and the driver gets out. Fionn hands him his rucksack and the dude throws it into the belly of the bus.

'Well,' Fionn goes, 'this is goodbye.'

He offers Oisinn his hand, but Oisinn grabs him in a bear hug. He's like, 'I'm going to miss you, Dude.'

It's a bit OTT, if you ask me.

JP gives him a hug as well and goes, 'God speed, Fionn.'

He's like, 'Thanks, JP.'

Then it's Christian's turn. Again, it's a hug and the dude is like, 'I wish you didn't have to go.'

Fionn's there, 'Thanks, Christian.'

'We've still got one more letter to collect,' Christian goes.

Fionn's there, 'No offence to any of you, but I wish I'd never come. Good luck with the rest of the walk.'

Fionn looks at me then – it's a sort of, like, fleeting *glance*?

I'm there, 'Don't even think about it, Dude. Get on your bus and fock off back to Ireland.'

He just nods. He knows I'm talking sense. He climbs the steps with a sad look on his face.

JP goes, 'Ross, say something!'

I'm there, 'What is there to say?'

'Ask him not to go,' Christian goes.

I'm there, 'I actually *want* him to go?' except as I watch him make his way down the bus, I suddenly realize that I *don't*?

Maybe it's just that I want to make him feel bad for longer. Or maybe it's just that I'm going to – I don't know – *miss* him?

The door closes. The driver pulls out onto the road and off he goes. Suddenly I find myself haring after the bus in my focked Dubes, my feet hurting like a focking motherfocker.

I'm slapping the side of the thing and I'm roaring, 'Stop the bus! Stop the bus!' at the top of my voice.

The driver obviously doesn't hear me because he puts his foot down on the accelerator and he's suddenly disappearing into the distance. I'm, like, waving my orms like a drowning man trying to attract the attention of a passing ship and I'm shouting, 'Come back! Come back!'

And that's when the most unbelievable thing happens. The driver must see me waving at him in his rear-view because the bus all of a sudden *stops*?

JP's like, 'Go and get him, Ross!'

I don't need to be told twice. I cover the ground like Tadhg Furlong attacking the opposition twenty-two.

When I reach the bus, the driver opens the door. I walk up the steps.

'H'wait!' I go – again, like I'm talking to one of my old dear's domestics. 'Hw'one meennet.'

Fionn is sitting halfway down the aisle, already deep in conversation with – wouldn't you know it? – the ugliest woman on the bus. He's surprised to see me coming, although shocked is possibly *more* the word?

I'm like, 'Hey.'

He's there, 'Hey.'

'Answer me this,' I go. 'Why does the glass in those things never break?'

He sort of, like, smiles to himself. He goes, 'Because it's not really glass. It's fifty per cent glass and fifty per cent plastic.'

I'm there, 'That's good for me to know.'

He goes, 'Ross, what do you want?'

I'm there, 'I want you to not go home. I want you to stay with us and finish the walk.'

He's like, 'Ross, it was a bad idea from the stort.'

I'm there, 'Dude, I still think JP's right. I think Father Fehily is directing this whole thing.'

'If he is,' he goes, 'he's got a sick sense of humour.'

I'm like, 'Fionn, don't go – please!'

Some American dude, who's pissed off that we're stopped, goes, 'Hey, what kind of romantic comedy bullshit *is* this?'

The woman sitting beside Fionn goes, 'Shut your mouth! Can you not see he is talking to his lover?'

I'm there, 'We're not lovers. Get that out of your heads now.'

'Ross,' Fionn goes, 'I thought I'd feel better if I told you the truth about what I did. But I don't.'

I'm like, 'Dude, I forgive you.'

He goes, 'Why, though?'

And I'm there, 'Because . . . rugby.'

The American dude is right – utter dick that he is. This *is* like the final scene of a romcom – something with Ryan Reynolds and Rachel McAdams in it.

Fionn goes, 'Rugby isn't the answer to everything, Ross.'

I'm like, 'That's where we differ.'

Fionn looks away. He's still determined to go home.

I'm like, 'Rug-by! Rug-by! Rug-by!' and I'm clapping my two hands together and looking around me, trying to get everyone onboard to join in the chant.

Soon, pretty much everyone on the bus is going, 'Rug-by! Rug-by! Rug-by!' even though they've no idea why. They just get caught up in the moment.

Fionn storts laughing – can't help himself – and shaking his head.

I stick out my hand. I'm there, 'Dude, let's put it behind us. All of it.'

He shakes my hand – I shout at the driver, 'This man is going to need his rucksack!' – and I pull Fionn to his feet to loud cheers from pretty much everyone onboard.

As we're getting off the bus, I hear Fionn's mate go, 'So, so romantic. Now, they will go home and make beautiful love!'

I stop, turn around to her and I go, 'It's a rugby thing. And it's very far from gay – trust me.'

JP goes, 'This is the place,' meaning the place where we're supposed to collect Father Fehily's fourth and final, I'm presuming, *Bible* quote?

The place ends up being a – believe it or not – chicken form on the road to Ponferrada.

We're, like, literally walking through a yord filled with chickens to reach the front door, which happens to be open.

'*Hola?*' Fionn goes, shouting into the house, which focking stinks, by the way. There's, like, chickens in the hall. They seem to have the run of the gaff. '*Hola?*'

All of a sudden, a woman appears in the hallway, wearing – I shit you not – wellies and a house coat. She lets out a loud screech and chases the chickens out of the gaff, waving her orms madly in the air. We have to jump to one side as they come flapping past us, quite literally shitting themselves as they do.

It's only then that the woman cops us standing there. She's what I would have called, in less politically correct times, an absolute focking boot. She glowers at me. She's, like, seventy or eighty years old and she has – I'm not making this up – one big eye and one small eye. She says something to me in Spanish that sounds *definitely* threatening? When I don't respond, she says something else in Spanish and then disappears inside the house.

I turn to Fionn and I'm there, 'What's the deal?'

Fionn goes, 'I'm going to be honest, I'm having a little bit of trouble with her dialect, but she was going back into the house to get either her *escuela* –'

330

'Which means what?'

'It means primary school.'

'Or.'

'Or her *escopeta*, which now that I say it seems more probable.'

I'm there, 'So what's an *esco*, I don't know, whatever-the-fock?'

Suddenly, I don't need the translation, because I'm staring down the barrel of what I straight away recognize – being the father of a son who pestered me to buy him one every Christmas and birthday – as a shotgun, although the one Ronan wanted was of the sawn-off variety.

I'm like, 'What the fock? What the actual fock?' because – like I said – she's pointing it at *me* and she's, like, roaring at me.

Christian and Oisinn are like, 'Holy focking shit!'

And I'm there, 'Fionn, talk to her – please!'

Fionn says something to her in a calm voice and she says something back to him in an angry voice and then – oh, focking fock – she cocks the thing, we're talking *chuck-chuck*, which is never a sound you want to hear.

I'm like, 'Fionn! Jesus Christ, keep talking to her, will you?'

Fionn says some more Spanish words to her and she says some shit back in a thankfully calmer voice.

Fionn goes, 'It's okay, goys. She thought we were the bailiffs and we'd come to throw her out.'

She lowers the shotgun and I'm thinking, Who knows what would have happened here if I hadn't persuaded Fionn to get off that bus?

All of a sudden, some dude comes out and snatches the shotgun out of the woman's hands. He says something to her in Spanish and I'm like, 'Dude, what the fock is this crazy old bint doing with a gun?'

He goes, 'Inglesa?'

JP's like, 'Yeah, no, Irish, but we *speak* English?'

The dude goes, 'Not worrying. Is not loaded,' but then he cocks the thing and he's like, 'Oh, *is* loaded, yes. I am sorry. Is for chickens.'

JP goes, 'Dude, we're looking for a man named Abel Aduriz.'

He's there, 'You are looking for him? What is your business with Abel Aduriz?'

I'm in favour of turning around and getting the fock out of there right now.

JP's like, 'Er, we're walking the Camino –'

'Fucking tourists,' he goes, with genuine contempt, and then, 'Sorry – forgive, forgive. Father Abel is my great-uncle. He is dead-ing.'

Fionn's there, 'Oh, we're very sorry.'

He goes, 'No, no, not correct – he is *dying*. You want to see?'

I'm there, 'Do you know what? We might pass on that offer and get back on the road – what do you think, goys?'

JP's like, 'Our old school principal –'

'And rugby coach,' I make sure to go.

JP's there, 'He left an envelope with, er, Father Abel that he was to give to us when we walked the Camino.'

'You come,' the dude goes. 'All of you come.'

He opens the door wide and we all step into the house, which smells of piss and mushrooms. He leads us into a dork bedroom at the end of a hallway, where five or six people – including two priests – are sitting around the bedside of this dude, who looks like he's about a hundred and ten years old. There's, like, candles burning everywhere.

Fionn goes, 'Jesus, when he said he was dying, I didn't think he meant . . . *literally* dying?'

JP's like, 'Goys, I think we've basically crashed his *deathbed* scene?'

The dude who let us in says something to the old dude in Spanish. I know little or nothing about foreign languages, but I recognize one or two words, mainly 'Irlanda' and 'rugby'.

And the dude in the bed – who looks *already* dead to me? – suddenly comes to life. Yeah, no, he opens his eyes and I watch him lift his hand, slowly and shakily, and he says something in a whisper.

'The drawer,' Fionn goes. 'He's pointing at the chest of drawers over there.'

The dude who let us in tips over to the – like he said – chest of drawers. He storts pulling the drawers open, storting with the top one.

The dude in the bed whispers something.

Fionn goes, 'He's saying it's in the bottom drawer, tucked inside his Bible.'

The dude who let us in opens the bottom drawer, finds the Bible and whips the envelope from out of the back of it. He hands it to JP.

JP goes, 'We're really sorry to have crashed in on you like this.'

And that's when one of the two priests at the dude's bedside goes, '*Está muerto*,' and, for the second time this afternoon, I don't *need* a translation?

JP goes, 'We'll, em, leave you to it. Sorry for your loss,' and we all sort of, like, moonwalk our way out of the room.

Once we're outside, we're all like, 'Fock! Focking fock!' because it was one of *the* most intense experiences we've ever shared together not on the rugby field.

Oisinn goes, 'I can't believe that the final words he spoke were to say where he hid Father Fehily's letter. I mean, it's almost as if he was waiting for us to come before he died.'

JP's there, 'So, Fionn, do you still doubt that Father Fehily is somehow guiding us?'

He doesn't answer.

I'm like, 'Dude, all *I* know is that if I hadn't dragged Fionn off that bus, I would have been a dead man back there.'

JP tears open the envelope, whips out the piece of paper inside, opens it out and gives it the old left-to-right.

'It's John 8:32,' he goes.

I'm there, 'Which one is that again?'

'*And you will know the truth*,' JP goes, '*and the truth will set you free.*'

I'm like, 'What, that's it?'

'Yeah,' JP goes, 'just one line.'

Christian's like, 'I don't think I'll ever get the smell of that house out of my nostrils.'

And I'm there, 'Yeah, no, about that – just to let you know, goys, when that crazy old lady was pointing that shotgun at me, there's a very definite chance that I may have – totally understandable in the circumstances and I hope it will never be mentioned again – pissed my shorts.'

JP just blurts it out – and it comes right out of left field.

He's like, 'I'm giving up the business.'

We're all there, 'What?'

Yeah, no, we're sitting on two pork benches in the main square in Villafranca de Bierzo, well into the last week of our walk, passing a bottle of – random, I know – *Pernod* between us?

He's there, 'I'm giving up the vertical bed business.'

I'm like, 'No way.'

This is clearly news to Christian, his supposed business portner, because he looks at him – shit-faced again, by the way – and goes, 'The fog are you talking about?'

JP's there, 'I'm sorry, Christian – I've decided that I'm out.'

Oisinn goes, 'What do you mean by out, JP?'

He's like, 'I'm resigning as the Joint Managing Director of the company and I'm selling my shareholding in the business. Who has the bottle?'

I'm like, 'I do,' and I hand it to him.

I sniff the air. I can smell piss. I should have possibly washed these shorts this morning but I thought they'd keep for another day.

Christian's there, 'Without even consulting me?'

Oisinn goes, 'Dude, you came up with a revolutionary idea that could potentially solve not only Ireland's accommodation crisis but the world's refugee crisis – get people to sleep . . . standing up.'

I'm like, 'It's genius.'

JP's there, 'It's immoral.'

Nobody says shit. They're obviously thinking what I'm thinking – as in, what the fock is wrong with that?

Although Oisinn goes, 'Can anyone else smell piss?'

I'm there, 'No, definitely not.'

JP's like, 'I came up with the idea of treating human beings as units – that's what I actually called them – to be stacked like plates in a dishwasher. And I made tens of millions of euros off the back of other people's misfortune.'

I'm there, 'Dude, you're saying that like it's a *bad* thing?'

But Fionn ends up letting me down in a major way. He goes, 'I, for one, support you, JP. As you know, I always had misgivings about treating homelessness as a space issue rather than a failure of social policy.'

Fock him for making *me* look bad.

Christian goes, 'So, what, you're out – and that's it? Give me that fogging bottle.'

I'm there, 'Christian, I think you've had enough.'

He goes, 'I want more than enough!' and he roars it, then snatches the bottle out of JP's hands. 'Give me that fogging thing.'

JP's like, 'Christian, I hoped you'd understand –'

But Christian goes, 'What the fog am I supposed to do – huh?'

JP's there, 'You're still joint Managing Director. You still have equity in the business.'

Christian goes, 'I can't run a fogging business!' and then he takes a long slug from the bottle like he's trying to quench a day's thirst with the stuff.

I'm like, 'You definitely can't run a business if you carry on drinking like you've been drinking since we got here. What's wrong with you, Dude?'

He ignores this and instead continues to focus his anger on JP.

He's there, 'So what are you going to do with all your fogging ill-gotten gains then? Are you going to give it to fogging charity?'

JP goes, 'I might. I was thinking of setting up a foundation –'

'Fogging Bill Gates,' Christian goes. 'Fogging . . . prick.'

Oisinn's there, 'I think what Christian is trying to say, in a round-about way, is that maybe you've come to this decision – you know – too *hastily*? You're obviously on some kind of spiritual journey at the moment. You might change your mind in the cold reality of returning home.'

'To your fugging ugly wife,' Christian goes. 'Face like the inside of a baboon's orse.'

I'm like, 'Christian, you're bang out of order – and I *mean* bang?'

'How much?' Christian storts shouting. 'How *much*?'

JP's there, 'It's probably a few hundred million. I might set up a fund to help children from working-class backgrounds to go to Blackrock College and Mount Anville.'

I'm like, 'Oh, that'd really piss them off. That'd be money well spent. I'd nearly Revolut you money now.'

Christian goes, 'I wasn't fugging talking to you?' and that's when I realize that when he was asking, 'How much?' he was talking to two women in their – definitely – early fifties, who may or may not be hookers. They're standing on the other side of the square, talking to each other out of the side of their mouths. They're both wearing white shoes with black tights, a dead giveaway the world over.

I'm there, 'Christian, what about your supposed girlfriend?'

He goes, 'Fog her – stupid fogging –' and he hands Oisinn the bottle. 'Fionn, what's *how much?* in Spanish?'

Fionn's there, 'Christian, you're very drunk. Why don't you –'

Christian's like, 'What the fog is it?'

Fionn goes, 'It's *cuánto cuesta?*'

'Cunta –'

'Cuánto . . . cuesta. But I really don't think you should –'

'Cuánto cuesta. And what's sex?'

I'm like, 'Dude, I'm not sure you're going to need that. They don't look like they're selling ice cream.'

'Fionn,' he goes, 'what's sex?'

Fionn's there, '*Relaciónes sexuales.*'

Then off Christian focks, muttering under his breath, '*Cunto cuesta . . . relaciónes sexuales?*'

I shout after him. I'm like, 'What about Lychee?' but he just blanks me.

'I wonder who it is?' JP goes.

Oisinn's like, 'What do you mean?'

JP's there, 'Father Fehily's latest Bible version. Who is it aimed at?'

Oisinn's like, 'It's got to be either Ross or Christian, right?'

I'm there, 'What did it say again?'

'*And you will know the truth,*' JP goes, '*and the truth will set you free.*'

We all sit there and watch Christian, across the square, disappear down a laneway, hand in hand with one of the two hookers.

I'm there, 'I never thought I'd hear myself say this, but we've come away on holidays – and I'm the only one of us who hasn't done the dirt.'

'The Miracle of Santiago de Compostela!' Oisinn goes, lifting the Pernod bottle as a kind of toast.

And – yeah, no – we all crack our holes laughing.

I'm there, 'I'm the only one out of the five of us who hasn't done the dirt yet.'

Roz doesn't seem as pumped to hear this news as I *thought* she'd be?

She goes, 'What do you mean by yet?'

I'm there, 'Sorry, I mean to say at all. That's not to say I haven't had opportunities. One or two absolute crackers put it on a plate for me. I had literally no interest. The rest of them have all been with other people. Oisinn rode a woman and Christian rode a prostitute.'

'For fock's sake!' Oisinn goes.

Yeah, no, he and the rest of the goys are earwigging my conversation while I'm washing my piss-stained shorts – finally getting around to it – in the sink.

'What happened to what goes on tour stays on tour?'

I'm there, 'She's hordly going to tell your significant others.'

Roz goes, 'I actually bumped into Delma this morning in the Butler's Pantry in Blackrock.'

I'm like, 'Jesus! Is she still shocking-looking? No offence, JP.'

JP looks around – not a clue. He's like, 'What?'

'Her face just looks so, I don't know, ortificial,' Roz goes.

I'm there, 'I don't know why she couldn't have just left herself alone. JP, by the way, was the one who encouraged her to get work done – not me. The sexist bastard.'

She's like, 'Oh, he must feel awful.'

I'm there, 'Hey, all I care about is that I'm off the hook.'

She goes, 'When are you home?'

I'm there, 'Yeah, no, Sunday.'

She's like, 'Anyway, look, I don't want to bother you with this while you're away –'

I'm there, 'Er, yeah, no, it's fine – continue.'

She goes, 'Sincerity broke it off with Jonah.'

I'm like, 'Oh, right,' and at the same time I silently punch the air and mouth the word, 'Yes!'

She goes, 'Yeah, she misses Honor's friendship. And she realizes she jeopardized that by being with Jonah, even though she knew that Honor really liked him.'

What a focking mug, I think.

I'm there, 'That's, em, very good of her.'

'Anyway, I miss you,' she goes.

And I'm like, 'I miss you too.'

That ends up setting the goys off in a major way. They're like, 'Whoooaaahhh!!!' because they've never witnessed this – I'm going to say – *romantic* side to me before?

Jesus Christ, I'm going to ride her like Tiger Roll, though.

She's like, 'I better let you go. Good luck today.'

And I'm there, 'Yeah, no, see you on Sunday, Roz.'

I hang up while the goys make kissy sounds, then I wring the water out of my shorts and throw them on me.

Oisinn goes, 'You can't wear them wet, Ross.'

I'm like, 'Why not? They'll dry out in an hour or two. Has anyone tried waking Christian yet?'

Oisinn's there, 'I'll go,' and – yeah, no – off he heads.

I catch Fionn smiling at me. I'm like, 'What?'

He goes, 'You really like her, don't you?'

I'm there, 'Yeah, no, I'm on the record as saying that she's a ringer for Allison Williams except with a smaller –'

He's like, 'I'm happy for you, Ross.'

I'm there, 'Oh, em, thanks.'

There ends up being an awkward silence then, so I go, 'It'll happen for you, Dude.'

It won't. He'll die alone.

I'm there, 'I'm sorry it didn't work out with you and Ciara – even though I think you can do better.'

He can't. She was exactly his level.

I'm like, 'At least you've still got little Hillary.'

He nods. He's there, 'Yeah, I've really missed him. I just want to concentrate now on being the best father and best school principal that I can be.'

What a focking recipe for misery, I think.

I'm there, 'Fair focks, Dude. Fair focking focks.'

Oisinn steps into the room then with Christian following behind him, looking a bit sheepish and – yeah, no – *limping*?

I'm like, 'Did you catch something – off one of those hookers?'

'No, I think I've aggravated the facet joint injury I picked up against Newbridge College back in the day.'

I'm like, 'Focking Newbridge. Fock those inbred, diesel-supping, porsnip-eating alpaca jockeys – fock every one of them.'

He limps over to JP and goes, 'Dude, I just wanted to say sorry.'

JP's there, 'It's not necessary.'

Christian goes, 'It is necessary. I was out of order.'

I'm there, 'Why don't I just say rugby and we'll leave it at that?'

But Christian *doesn't* leave it at that? He goes, 'You've made me a very rich man. I'll never have to worry about things like paying a mortgage and putting my kids through third-level education.'

'That's music to *my* ears,' I go. 'I spent your eldest's college fund paying off those blackmailers – the little focking perv.'

JP's there, 'Dude, you invested in my idea when no one else believed in it. I just don't want any port of it any more. This pilgrimage has persuaded me that there's a new and quite possibly spiritual path opening up for me.'

Christian sticks out his hand. He's like, 'No hord feelings.'

They shake it out, then Fionn goes, 'Come on, let's get on the road. It's a four-and-a-half-hour walk to Triacastela. We'll get breakfast somewhere along the way.'

I'm like, 'Yeah, no, I'm cool with that.'

He goes, 'Triacastela means three castles. It used to be the site of three castles, although none of them remains today.'

The five of us step outside to see the most incredible sunrise any of us has ever seen. The sky is, like, red and orange and purple and yellow. It's so random.

I say it as well. I'm there, 'That sky is, like, so random,' and everyone agrees.

We stort walking into the morning ahead.

We've only been on the road for, like, twenty minutes when Christian all of a sudden stops, his face twisted in agony.

He goes, 'Aaarrrggghhh!!!' and – yeah, no – he's clearly in a lot of pain.

I'm there, 'Dude, are you okay?'

He just shakes his head. He's like, 'I can't.'

I'm there, 'Can't what?'

'Goys, you're going to have to go on without me.'

'Dude, it's just three more days. Fionn, show him the map.'

He stops and he holds onto a wall made up of just, like, rocks laid on top of each other. Yeah, no, he's in a serious jocker.

He goes, 'Ross, I don't think I can walk another ten steps.'

I'm there, 'You're not giving up – not this close to the end.'

'I have no choice.'

'You always have a choice. What did Father Fehily used to tell us? Pain is temporary. Quitting is permanent.'

'Physically, I can't do it. Jesus, the pain.'

'Does anyone have any painkillers?'

'I've got some Solpadeine,' Oisinn goys.

I'm there, 'Give him two Solpadeine.'

Christian goes, 'Solpadine won't help me walk –'

I'm like, 'You're not going to walk.'

'What do you mean?'

'We're going to carry you.'

Oisinn's like, 'Carry him?'

'Yeah, no,' I go, 'on our backs. We'll take it in turns to give him a piggy-back. I'll do fifteen minutes, then you, then JP, then Fionn – if he's capable.'

Christian's there, 'I can't let you do that.'

But I'm like, 'Dude, we are Castlerock! We leave no man behind!'

Christian is not as light as he was back in his days as – I'm going to say it – quite possibly the best centre in schools rugby in the mid to late 1990s. Yeah, no, he's been no stranger to the China Sichuan in

Sandyford since he storted coining it in and after two days of helping to carry him I'm really storting to feel it in my thighs.

I'm like, 'Oisinn, how long have I had him on my back now?'

'Five minutes,' he goes.

I'm there, 'So, em, how long until it's your turn?'

He's like, 'Ten minutes.'

Christian goes, 'Ross, you don't have to carry me,' focking guilt-tripping me. 'I'll go home.'

I'm there, 'Hopefully, a day or two of rest from walking will do the trick in terms of your back.'

'*And you will know the truth,*' JP goes, '*and the truth will set you free.*'

I'm there, 'Have we figured it out yet?'

He's like, 'Well, it's aimed at either you or Christian.'

All of a sudden, Christian storts singing and I can't resist joining in:

If I had the wings of a swallow,
If I had the orse of a crow,
I'd fly over CBC Monkstown –

'Fock!' I go. 'Who's got the ashes?'

Oisinn's like, 'I've got them here, Dude,' and he shows me the Ziploc baggie.

I'm there, 'Thank fock. Thought I'd lost them.'

'I have to say,' Fionn goes, 'I'm quite impressed that you've brought them this far.'

I'm there, 'What, you thought I'd have flushed them down the toilet or something?'

I would have totally flushed them down the toilet except I'd never hear the end of it.

I'm like, 'If I commit to doing something, I do it. How many minutes now, Oisinn?'

He's there, 'Six.'

'*And you will know the truth,*' JP goes, '*and the truth will set you free.*'

Christian's like:

If I had the wings of a swallow,
If I had the orse of a crow,
I'd fly over Cistercian College –

I'm like, 'Goys, let me hear those voices!'

Shit on, shit on, shit on the bastards below-below.
Shit on, shit on, shit on the bastards below.

'Speaking of rugby,' I go, 'I was doing some of my famous deep thinking last night.'

JP's like, 'No wonder you're tired today.'

I'm there, 'You're focking hilarious. Yeah, no, I was thinking about my – again – *Sliding Doors* moment, when Fionn there blamed me for cheating in that exam.'

'I didn't blame you for cheating,' he tries to go. 'I cheated and I let you take the blame for it – which, now that I say it, is pretty much the same thing.'

I'm there, 'You don't have to keep apologizing. No, I was thinking that if I'd gone on to win the Young Scientist of the Year competition –'

'You were never going to win the Young Scientist of the Year competition,' Oisinn goes.

I'm there, 'Okay, if I'd just gone on to be a focking nerd like Fionn there – no offence, Dude – reading books, morning, noon and night, I might not have been the rugby player that I was. So, in a way, I should be thanking you.'

He's like, 'Right.'

'I mean, not literally,' I go. 'I'm not thanking you. But I should be. Does that make sense?'

Fionn's there, 'Who knows?'

Oisinn goes, 'So what's everyone most looking forward to when they get home? Fionn, you first.'

'Seeing Hillary,' he goes. 'I knew I was going to miss him, but I had no idea how much. I was talking to Eleanor –'

His sister Eleanor, who I've ridden twice.

342

Fionn turns around and gives me a filthy. He's like, 'Why is that relevant?'

I'm there, 'Sorry, I didn't mean to say it out loud.'

He doesn't like being reminded.

He goes, 'I've asked her to bring him to the airport. I've butterflies in my stomach when I think about it.'

'I'm looking forward to seeing the boys,' Christian goes, 'but I'm also looking forward to having a Chinese. Crispy salt and chilli squid, pan-fried chicken dumplings, pepper-flavour rib-eye beef –'

I'm like, 'How long is it now, Oisinn?'

He goes, 'Two more minutes.'

JP's there, 'I'm looking forward to seeing Isa obviously. And, well, Delma. But the thing I'm looking forward to most is putting my money to use helping people.'

I'm like, 'You're a focking mug.'

'What are you talking about?'

'You should spend it on yourself. Do the shit that you've always wanted to do.'

'I want to help people.'

'That's why you're a focking mug.'

He goes, 'What about you, Oisinn?'

He's like, 'Well, I'm looking forward to seeing Magnus obviously. But the thing I'm most excited about is, well, the baby.'

Oh, shit.

'I'm so excited for you,' JP goes. 'Fatherhood is the best thing I've ever experienced.'

I'm there, 'Obviously you mean non-rugby-related?'

'No,' he goes, 'it's way better than anything I ever experienced on the pitch.'

I'm like, 'Steady on, Dude.'

'I agree,' Fionn goes. 'Being a parent is the greatest responsibility but also the greatest privilege that any of us will ever know.'

Christian's like, 'Hear, hear.'

I'm there, 'I'd still make a case for rugby.'

Oisinn whips out his phone and goes, 'Hey, did I show you the picture that Magnus sent me last night?'

I'm there, 'There's no need, Dude. I find other people's pictures boring.'

But he holds the thing in front of my face and it's a – yeah, no – picture of Sorcha's sister with her hand on her bump. I'm thinking, Oh, fock.

He goes, 'That's our little son or daughter in there! In all truth, I've never felt anything like it before.'

Oh, focking, focking fock. I'm going to tell him. I have to tell him.

'*And you will know the truth,*' JP goes, '*and the truth will set you free.*'

I'm like, 'Oisinn, I have something to –'

But Christian ends up beating me to the punch. He's like, 'It's about me.'

I'm there, 'What?' and I suddenly stop walking.

He goes, 'Ross, put me down,' so I do.

Oisinn's like, 'What do you mean it's about you?'

The dude takes a deep breath.

'Ross,' he goes, 'I have something to tell you.'

I have a feeling I'm not going to like it.

I'm there, 'Go on.'

He looks away. He's like, 'Ross Junior wasn't looking at gay porn. It was . . . me.'

I'm there, '*Excuse* me?'

He goes, 'Lychee wanted us to have a threesome.'

I'm there, 'I presume we're talking about a devil's threesome?'

One with two horns.

'Yes,' he goes, 'a devil's threesome. With her friend Darius.'

I'm there, 'What, the YouTuber who went down the bannisters on a skateboard?'

He's like, 'He's more of a TikToker than a YouTuber. Anyway, I've never, you know, done anything like that. And she told me I should maybe watch some videos –'

I'm there, 'So it was *you* who was getting sextorted?'

He's like, 'Yes, but I didn't know that until you brought it up at the borbecue.'

I'm there, 'But why didn't you say something?'

He goes, 'I don't know. I was embarrassed. I didn't want Lauren and her family and friends to know that I was watching gay porn. No offence, Oisinn.'

The dude's like, 'Er, none taken.'

Fionn goes, 'So you let people think it was your teenage son?'

He stares at his feet, with his head down.

Fionn's there, 'Well, no wonder you're drinking like you are.'

Christian goes, 'I can't live with the guilt.'

I'm there, 'Hang on, you focked me out of the house that day.'

He's like, 'I know.'

I'm there, 'You said you never wanted to talk to me again.'

'I'm sorry,' he tries to go.

I'm like, 'You were my best friend in the world. And you took your friendship away. And all the time, you and focking Lychee knew the truth.'

He goes, 'She didn't want me having anything to do with you anyway – over the whole indecent exposure thing.'

I'm there, 'It was a focking mooner!'

'Even so,' he goes, 'she thought me being friends with you could hurt my brand identity.'

Oisinn's like, 'Your what?'

Christian goes, 'My brand –. Doesn't matter.'

I'm there, 'Okay, I'm going to deck you now, Christian.'

JP goes, 'You're not going to deck him, Ross.'

'The funny thing is,' I go, 'I *am*?' and I throw a punch at him.

Christian steps to the side to evade it – fock-all wrong with his back – and I end up punching Oisinn, who drops the Ziploc bag, which then bursts open, spilling Vivica's sister's ashes all over the road again.

'I rang Lauren,' Christian goes, 'and I told her everything.'

I'm there, 'And did she apologize – to me, I mean?'

'Er –'

'In other words, no.'

This is us sitting outside a bor in a town called – apparently – Arzúa. It's our last night before we arrive in Santiago de Compostela tomorrow.

He goes, 'Look, you did give her a very inappropriate birthday present. I mean, anal focking beads, Ross.'

I'm there, 'Which weren't even mine to give.'

'There were children present. Then you told her in front of a room full of people that her son was watching gay porn.'

'That's because I didn't know it was you. And you could have said something but didn't.'

'I know. Look, Lauren isn't sorry – but *I* am?'

JP goes, 'Dude, tell him you forgive him. Be the bigger man.'

Christian's like, 'Come on, Ross. I told Lauren the truth. I finished it with Lychee. I picked up all the ashes – well, most of them.'

Poor Vivica's sister. Yeah, no, she's there in the middle of the table – the bits of her we could save, along with quite a few pebbles and dirt from the road.

He goes, 'So am I forgiven?'

I'm like, 'Yeah, no, whatever. I'm sorry about you and Lychee. Even though she was an idiot. And a bitch.'

'She was too young for me. I don't know what I was thinking.'

I'm there, 'I never thought I'd hear myself say this, but looks aren't everything. Actually, now that I hear myself say it, it's horseshit.'

I offer him my hand.

I'm there, 'Put it behind us?'

And he's like, 'That'd be great – thanks, Ross.'

I'm there, 'Drink?'

He goes, 'No, I'm going to, em, stick with water from now on.'

'I wasn't offering. I was asking you to get me one. Matter of fact, get another bottle of red, will you?'

Into the bor he goes.

JP's there, 'Go easy on him, Ross.'

I'm like, 'I won't go easy on him. I'm telling you, there's been quite a few – I want to say – *relevations* on this trip, hasn't there?

Between you having sex with my wife and Fionn getting me blamed for cheating in an exam and Oisinn letting me get the shit kicked out of me outside Renords, and now Christian. And just to think, a month ago none of you was even talking to me. It's almost like Father Fehily sent us on this pilgrimage to show you what a bunch of focking hypocrites you are.'

JP's there, 'Is that it? Is that why Father Fehily sent us here?'

'I told you,' Fionn goes, 'you can read into those Bible verses whatever you want to read.'

All of a sudden, my phone rings. I check the screen and it's, like, Honor?

I answer by going, 'Hey, Honor, how the hell *are* you?'

She's like, 'Oh my God! Sincerity and Jonah are, like, *finished*?'

I'm there, 'No focking way?' cracking on that I don't know shit.

She goes, 'Apparently, she finished it with him because she, like, values my *friendship* too much?'

I'm like, 'That's a nice thing to hear, isn't it? Are you going to give her a call?'

'Er, *no*?' she goes. 'She can fock *right* off, the back-stabbing bitch.'

I'm there, 'Er, okay.'

She goes, 'Jonah is – oh my God – *devastated*? He just texted me!'

I'm like, 'Hey, it sounds like it might be good news for you.'

She's there, 'Oh my God, I'm going to be *such* a good friend to him! Do you know why? Because the High School Rathgor Fifth Year Formal is coming up and I know for a fact that he was going to invite Sincerity.'

I go, 'So you're hoping to, what, pick up her sloppy seconds?'

She's like, 'Focking right I am.'

I'm there, 'But, like, he doesn't fancy you, Honor – as in, you two are just friends, right?'

She's like, 'So? Friendship can actually turn into something stronger, Dad.'

She's talking out of her orse, of course. I should maybe tell her, except I don't have the hort.

'Anyway,' she goes, 'I have to go. We're, like, talking to each other on WhatsApp here. I am being *such* a shoulder for him,' and then she hangs up on me.

Christian arrives out with a bottle of wine. He puts it in the middle of the table.

Fionn's there, 'How's your back?'

Christian goes, 'Yeah, no, it's not too bad now. I think it was just a tweak.'

'Do you think you'll be alright to walk tomorrow?'

'If I have to walk to Santiago di Compostela on my hands and knees, I will.'

I'm there, 'That's good – because you're not getting a piggy-back off me.'

Oisinn goes, 'So what was everyone's favourite moment of the trip?'

'For me,' JP goes, 'it has to be Ross getting flipped by the bull.'

I'm there, 'Staring down a bull, you mean. The rest of you pissed your pants.'

Oisinn goes, 'My favourite is Ross actually pissing his pants when that old biddy pointed the shotgun at him!'

I'm like, 'Oh, it's not me saving your life, is it?'

'Smoking hash with the Danish girls,' Fionn goes. 'I enjoyed that.'

I'm there, 'What about you riding one of them? The only ugly one of the three? Was that not a highlight? Or *did* you ride her?'

He doesn't say shit. He's very discreet. Which can be very focking annoying.

'For me,' Christian goes, 'nothing can beat the thrill of getting out of that police station without being chorged.'

I'm there, 'Not even having sex with a hooker?' which is childish of me, I know – but then I just think, Fock it. Might as well say whatever's in my head. 'Did you mention that to Lychee, by the way?'

JP picks up the bottle and pours us each a glass of wine.

Fionn goes, 'I'm glad you persuaded me to stay, Ross. I'm glad I didn't go home.'

Christian's there, 'I'm glad I didn't too.'

JP holds up his glass of wine and goes, 'Well, goys, it's been an absolute pleasure walking with you. I think it's fair to say that we're all a lot wiser after what we've been through these past four weeks. And even if – as Fionn says – those Bible verses were vague enough to be read any way we wanted, I think Father Fehily's plan was just to bring us all closer together. And in that, I think it's fair to say that he succeeded.'

I nod.

'To Father Fehily,' Oisinn goes, lifting his drink in a toast.

I notice that Fionn doesn't touch his glass.

Oisinn's there, 'A hypocrite maybe, Fionn. But a human being. And the best damned human being that any of us will ever have the privilege to know.'

Fionn nods and picks up his glass.

'To Father Fehily,' Oisinn goes, 'with thanks.'

I'm there, 'I couldn't have said it better myself. Except I probably would have mentioned rugby.'

We're, like, an hour outside Santiago de Compostela when it finally happens. The sole of my right Dube works itself loose and suddenly it's flapping open and closed like a fish's mouth. Oisinn gives me an elastic band and I snap it onto the thing.

I'm there, 'Won't be too much longer now, goys,' and I am literally talking to my shoes.

Yeah, no, it could be sun-stroke. It's unbelievably hot this morning.

Fionn offers me his Bubble and I knock back a mouthful of water. Oisinn asks how everyone else is doing.

Christian says his back is storting to hurt again but he's determined to push through the pain barrier. JP says his feet feel like blocks of wood. Fionn says he feels like he could sleep for three days solid. As for Oisinn, the dude looks like he's lost about two stone since we storted this walk and his skin is all soft and saggy like a tortoise's neck.

He goes, 'What about you, Ross?'

I'm there, 'Yeah, no, the ankle is throbbing a bit, but, as Father Fehily used to say, there are two types of pain – one that hurts you and one that teaches you. Actually, has anyone got any more Solpadeine?'

Oisinn gives me his last two.

Fionn's like, 'Have a look at this, everyone,' so – yeah, no – we all stop and check out this, like, satellite map on Fionn's phone. 'That's how far we've walked.'

There's, like, a red line on it showing our route.

I'm there, 'Is that Spain?'

He goes, 'Yes, Ross, that's Spain.'

'I'll take your word for it.'

'What do you mean, you'll take my word for it?'

'I just expected it to be more –'

'More what?'

'I don't know. It just doesn't *look* like Spain to me?'

'What did you expect Spain to look like? A pair of castanets?'

He's pushing his focking luck.

I'm like, 'No, not a pair of castanets – just not like that.'

'Well, that's Spain,' he goes.

I'm there, 'Agree to differ.'

'No, we won't agree to differ. It's not a subjective question, Ross. *That* is Spain.'

'Whatever, Dude.'

I think the tiredness is getting to us all. We're all sick of the sight and the smell and the sound of each other. We're all sick of the sight and the smell and the sound of ourselves. We walk on in silence.

'Okay, everyone,' JP suddenly goes, 'what's everyone looking forward to eating when we get home? I'm talking about your fantasy first meal when you arrive home tonight.'

'Delma does a beautiful roast,' JP goes. 'Eye of beef, potatoes roasted in duck fat, Yorkshire puddings –'

Fionn's like, 'It'd be the Old Spot in Sandymount for me. The roast chicken. And all my family are there with me. And obviously Hillary.'

Oisinn's there, 'Magnus always wakes me on Sunday morning with smashed avocado on sourdough toast.'

'You'll be lucky,' Fionn goes. 'I read the *Irish Times* online this morning and apparently there isn't an avocado in the country. It's because of Irexit. We've your old man to thank for that, Ross.'

I laugh along. Seriously, though, he's going to get his glasses broken again if he's not careful.

Christian goes, 'For me – believe it or not – it'd be McDonald's with Ross Junior and Oliver. Eating whatever we want from the menu, then telling them to pretend to their mother that we had a proper meal, because she'd go focking apeshit.'

We all laugh. Lauren really is the worst.

I realize something then. We're supposedly talking about food but we're really talking about the people we've missed. I know that's deep but it's just how my mind sometimes works.

'For me,' I go, 'it'd be my old dear's cooking,' and there's, like, a wobble in my voice when I say it. The others definitely hear it as well.

Christian puts his orm around my shoulder and goes, 'It's alright, Ross.'

I'm there, 'I focking love her food. Even though I'd never tell her. In case she got a big head. I usually say it's focking revolting –'

He goes, 'I'm sure she knows you don't mean that.'

'– but then I always clear my plate and I ask her if there's any more.'

'There you are, then – see?'

'And she always smiles like she knows I love it but I'm incapable – or uncapable – of giving her a compliment.'

'How is she?'

'She's not good, Dude.'

He nods. He's there, 'I've seen her on the balcony – videos of her.'

'She's turned herself into a laughing stock,' I go. 'But the old man is happy to pretend it's not happening.'

'Why don't you do something about it?'

'In terms of?'

'Well, if your old man isn't going to stop it, then maybe *you* should – as her son.'

I know that what he's talking is sense.

Onwards we go. The sun is beating down on our heads. JP storts talking about his foundation. He says he's been jotting down ideas into his iPhone. He says that a country as small and as prosperous as Ireland shouldn't have a homelessness problem and that he's come up with a number of initiatives to solve it that don't involve people sleeping standing up.

'Providing homes for everyone,' he goes, 'should be the base camp of our ambition as a caring society.'

I think it's him who needs the intervention.

Oisinn puts his hand on my back. He's there, 'You okay?'

I'm like, 'Yeah, no, thanks, Dude. It's just weird watching her, I don't know, slowly disappear from the world.'

'I can't imagine.'

'Oh, well.'

'So you and Roz Carew, huh?'

'Yeah, no, it's all good.'

'It's weird to think of you being with someone other than Sorcha.'

'Dude, you've seen me with hundreds of girls other than Sorcha. It's being with girls other than Sorcha that broke up our marriage.'

'You know what I mean. I'm talking about permanently. It was always Ross and Sorcha. It's going to take some getting used to. How are the kids dealing with it?'

'Yeah, no, weirdly well. Honor's obviously taken *my* side? I *was* worried about Brian, Johnny and Leo, but it kills me to say that their behaviour has improved like you wouldn't believe since Sorcha's old pair storted looking after them. Two focking dicks.'

'I ran into them one day in Dundrum and – no offence, Ross – but I couldn't believe they were the same kids who were –'

'Banned from Tayto Pork? Focked out of the Disney Store on Grafton Street? The subject of a Joe Duffy phone-in show about antisocial behaviour amongst children?'

'Well, yeah, now that you say it.'

'Dude, I'm storting to wonder if it was possibly my fault.'

'Ross, you have no questions to ask yourself as a father.'

'I don't know about that. Were they acting out because I didn't give them the stable home that every child needs?'

'Dude,' he goes, 'if I turn out to be even half the father that you've been to your children, I'll be a very happy man.'

And that's when I decide that it's time to tell him the truth.

I'm like, 'Dude – about Sorcha's sister's baby. Look, I know you're going to laugh at this –'

He won't laugh at this.

I'm there, 'There's an outside possibility –'

'WHOOOAAA!!!' a voice behind me suddenly goes.

It's, like, JP.

Then Christian and Fionn say the same thing.

They're like, 'WHOOOAAA!!!' and they're looking into the mid-distance with, like, humungous smiles on their faces.

I follow their line of vision. And there, towering over the skyline, shimmering like gold in the midday sun, are the twin spires of Santiago de Compostela Cathedral.

I suddenly burst into tears. I've no idea why. But I'm suddenly bawling like a child. I turn around to the goys to apologize only to discover that they're crying too.

We step into the cathedral and it's – no other word for it – *humungous*?

I try to remember how to make the sign of the cross. I'm like, 'Hooker, full-back, blindside flanker, openside flanker.'

JP sort of, like, chuckles to himself. He goes, 'That's exactly the way I remember it.'

The pews are, like, packed with pilgrims, who've walked the same walk as us and who smell just as bad. But there's, like, a lightness about everyone, as if a weight has been lifted.

It feels, I don't know, *spiritual*?

People are kneeling down in the pews, praying out loud in all sorts of different languages. There's a smell of – I think it's the word – *incest*?

Yeah, no, there's this massive incest-burner – it's, like, three times the size of the Ken Cup – and it's swinging back and forth on a heavy chain and making the whole place smell – again – incesty.

'Anyone interested in saying a prayer?' JP goes.

I'm there, 'Yeah, no, whatever,' and even Fionn – the least religious of us all – just nods his head and we all follow JP into a pew near the front.

JP gets down on his knees. He knows all the steps – studied to be a priest at one point, bear in mind – and we just copy him.

I'm there, 'Are we saying our own prayers in our heads or are we going to –'

And that's when JP goes, 'Father Fehily, if you can hear us, which I know you can, we just wanted to say a big, big thank-you for sending us on this pilgrimage. Thank you for the Bible verses. I don't know how you chose them but they were perfect, and they spoke to each one of us individually.'

Out of the corner of my mouth, I go, 'Dude, tell him that I didn't get one.'

JP's there, 'What?'

'As in, there were only, like, *four* envelopes? Ask him does he have a message for me.'

JP goes, 'Ross was wondering if you had a message for him?'

A few seconds pass.

I'm there, 'Well?'

He goes, 'Well what?'

I'm like, 'What did he say?'

Oisinn goes, 'It's not a focking séance, Ross. He can't hear him.'

I'm there, 'Well, just tell him that if he has anything to say to me, then I'd love to hear from him.'

JP goes, 'Father Fehily, thank you for taking us on this journey,' and then he launches into – fock's sake – a decade of the Rosary.

We all close our eyes for it. I'm not going to lie – at one point, I actually nod off. It's been a long few weeks.

'Okay, let's go,' Oisinn goes. 'Ross, wake up.'

I open my eyes very suddenly and I find myself staring at the back-rest of the seat in front of me. Various people have, like, corved words into the wood. But I'm staring at one word – and it gives me literally chills.

I'm there, 'Rugby.'

Christian goes, 'Ross, wake up,' because I have been known to say the word in my sleep.

I'm like, 'I am awake. Goys, look.'

Christian's there, 'What are we looking at?'

'Look what someone has written,' I go, 'in the wood there. I asked Father Fehily to send me a message – and there it is! Rugby.'

Fionn leans closer to it, then he goes, 'It says Ruby.'

I'm there, 'He obviously spelt it wrong – maybe as a joke. Yeah, no, because he knows how thick I am and I couldn't write my own name at fourteen.'

'Or,' Fionn goes, 'maybe someone named Ruby walked the Camino and wanted to commemorate the achievement by corving their name into the wood.'

I'm there, 'You choose to interpret it however you want, Dude. I know what I believe. That's my message. Rugby. He knows it's exactly what I'd want to hear.'

JP stands up then. He goes, 'We'd better go and collect our certificates and then think about heading for the airport.'

So – yeah, no – we *all* stand up then.

I'm still a bit freaked by the whole rugby/ruby thing. I'm thinking, If Father Fehily was alive and I'd called on him to act as a character witness for me in my court case, I like to think that's exactly what he would have told the judge.

He'd have just gone, 'Rugby.'

My hort is literally pounding at this thought.

We step out into the aisle and I'm there, 'I've just got one thing left to do. Here, hold this, will you?' and I hand Oisinn the famous bag of ashes.

I walk up the aisle towards the – I suppose – *altar*? I lean on the gord rail and I take off my Dubes – first the right, then the left. And I leave them there, on the steps leading to the altar.

'Oh, Lord,' I go, 'please accept these sacred shoes, which have carried me to this holy place, as a sacrifice to you.'

As I'm walking away, some random priest dude storts shouting at me in, I'm guessing, the local lingo.

Fionn goes, 'Ross, he's telling you that you can't leave your shoes there.'

And I'm there, 'Can't I, Fionn? *Can't* I?'

Oisinn hands me back the bag of ashes. We step outside and we queue up – me in just my socks – for our certificates to say that we completed the famous Camino.

JP goes, 'In the cathedral, while we were praying, I really felt Father Fehily's presence. I felt like he was there with us.'

Christian goes, 'I felt it too.'

I'm there, 'Er, *rugby*? Could he have *made* it any more obvious?'

'Maybe if he'd put in the letter G,' Fionn goes – a focking last-word freak. 'If he'd actually *written* rugby, in other words, instead of Ruby.'

I'm handed my certificate. Oisinn points out that it's the first certificate I've ever got, having failed to get my Junior and Leaving. I laugh along, pretending to find it as hilarious as the others.

If he takes his shoes off then falls asleep on the flight home, he'll find out what focking funny is.

'I suppose we'd better stort making our way to the airport,' Fionn goes.

I'm there, 'Hang on, I've to get rid of these first,' meaning the ashes.

Christian's like, 'What are you going to do with them?'

I'm there, 'I was going to just tip them out here.'

'You can't do that,' Fionn goes.

I'm like, 'Dude, a promise is a promise.'

'What he means,' Oisinn goes, 'is that you can't just turn the bag upside-down in the middle of the square.'

I'm there, 'Dude, that's exactly what I *am* going to do?' and I unzip the bag and turn it upside-down.

What I haven't factored into this decision is that there's a bit of a *breeze* blowing across the square. The ashes get caught on the wind and all of a sudden I hear the sound of coughing and spluttering behind me. I also hear one or two voices go, 'What the fock?'

I turn around and there's a group of, like, Americans staring at me with angry faces and – yeah, no – I can't help but notice that they're covered in ashes.

They're literally spitting them out and I'm storting to pick up on the vibe that we should maybe get the fock out of here now when all of a sudden I recognize one of the group.

Oh, shitting focking shit-fock – it's Vivica.

She's got ashes all over her mouth and in her hair and I'm like, 'Okay, goys, will we see can we grab an Uber?'

But deep down I know that there's no escaping this scene. She sees the empty Ziploc bag in my hand and she goes, 'You focking asshole!'

I'm there, 'Can I just remind you that this is supposably a place of worship?'

She's like, 'Those were my sister's ashes!'

The Americans all gasp. They're easily shocked. These are the people who voted for Donald Trump, bear in mind.

I'm like, 'It's what she would have wanted.'

'How dare you?' Vivica goes. 'You don't know what my sister wanted.'

An elderly dude behind her, who's obviously swallowed some, is leaning over with his hands on his thighs and he's literally vomiting her sister's ashes onto the ground. I'm thinking, You're not focking helping here, mate.

I'm there, 'I just presumed she wanted you to tip them out here.'

Jesus Christ, I can see bits of ash in her mouth and on her focking eyelashes.

'Tip them out here?' she goes. 'She wanted me to bring them home to her.'

I'm like, 'Bring them home to her? Is that not her?' and I wipe a few flecks of ash off her chin.

'No, they were volcanic ashes that I collected in Santorini,' she goes. 'My sister is a geophysicist.'

I'm there, 'You said your sister was dead.'

She goes, 'I have five sisters.'

I suddenly feel like the world's biggest mug. I'm there, 'I can't

focking believe I lugged those focking things from one side of Spain to the other.'

And that's when I hear sniggers from Oisinn, JP, Christian and – yeah, no – even Fionn.

I'm there, 'What, you all knew?'

Oisinn's there, 'Vivica told us the story the night we met her.'

'And you didn't think to tell me?'

'Where would the fun be in that?'

Vivica goes, 'You're a fucking asshole, Neville Archeson . . . ston!' and slaps me hord – very hord – across the face.

Which makes the goys laugh even horder.

Oisinn goes, 'Sorry about that, Neville!'

I am one hundred per cent definitely shitting in his shoes on the flight home.

10.

The Goy Who Loved Me

Honor tells me that I look like shit. Which I know is her way of telling me that she missed me.

I'm like, 'Thanks, Honor.'

'No,' she goes, 'you genuinely, *genuinely* look like shit? And – oh my God – you focking stink.'

I'm there, 'Well, I've been on the road for a month, Honor. I'm looking forward to a shower, a hot meal and a warm bed.'

I glance at Helen when I mention the hot meal. It's an unconscious thing, except she doesn't take the hint.

She goes, 'Where are your shoes, Ross?'

I'm there, 'Yeah, no, I left them on the altar in Santiago de Compostela Cathedral.'

She's like, 'Why?' and I'm thinking, All these focking questions when she could be doing me steak and chips – either one of them.

I'm there, 'I don't *know* why I did it. It felt like the right thing to do at the time and I just went with it.'

'So you came home from Spain,' she goes, 'in your socks?'

I'm there, 'I didn't walk, Helen. We got a taxi to the airport. I was planning to buy a pair of shoes in the airport but then we had to run to catch our flight. I'll tell you what I'd do serious damage to right now – a plate of steak and chips. Or even a full Irish.'

Again, neither of them seems to hear me.

Honor goes, 'Oh my God, I got my dress today!'

I'm like, 'What dress?'

'Er, my dress for the High School Rathgor Fifth Year *Formal*? Do you want to see it?'

'Maybe I should eat something first. It's looking like Deliveroo at this stage, isn't it?'

She focks off upstairs to throw on the dress.

Helen's there, 'She's very young, isn't she? To be going to a Fifth Year Formal, I mean.'

I'm like, 'I wouldn't sweat it, Helen. The dude who's bringing her has zero interest in her. He's already friend-zoned her and she just can't take the hint.'

She's not the only one around here, I think.

Erika arrives home then. I was about to ask where she was when she suddenly walks into the kitchen, looking all lovely, like she's hurting nobody.

I'm there, 'Erika, looking well!' and – yeah, no – it possibly comes off as a bit sleazy.

She goes, 'Oh, you're home. What the fock are you wearing?'

'It's a tuxedo t-shirt. Yeah, no, someone left it behind in one of the fleapit hostels we stayed in. Long story. Any chance of a hug?'

'No,' she goes, 'you stink.'

I'm there, 'I was just telling Helen that the three things I'm most looking forward to are a shower, a good night's sleep and then, somewhere in between, a hot meal.'

She goes, 'Forget it, Ross.'

'Excuse me?'

'I'm not focking cooking for you.'

Helen goes, 'Is that what you were hinting at, Ross?'

I'm there, 'I genuinely wasn't hinting, Helen. Yeah, no, I'll fix myself something,' and I tip over to the fridge.

I reef open the door and I end up getting a bit of a shock. The shelves, which are usually – I don't know – *laden* with stuff, are suddenly empty.

I'm like, 'Er, what day do you do the big shop again, Helen?'

She goes, 'I did it today.'

I'm there, 'So, like, where is everything?'

'The supermorket shelves are empty,' she goes.

Erika's like, 'This is what your father has done to the country.'

I'm there, 'He's your father as well.'

'You can't get camembert,' Helen goes. 'Or figs. Or Porma ham.

Or grapes. Or avocados. Or olive oil. Or grapes. Or mozzarella. Or red wine vinegar.'

Erika goes, 'The shops say they're running out of coffee. Coffee, Ross!'

I'm there, 'Fock!' and I slam the fridge door closed. 'So it looks like it's going to be Deliveroo, then.'

Erika goes, 'You won't get anything at this stage. It's nearly midnight.'

I'm like, 'Fock's sake. Where are you coming from, by the way? Hot date, was it? Who's the lucky man? I hate him already!'

Jesus Christ, I'm wondering do I maybe need counselling.

She goes, 'I went to Roundstone to see Sea-mon.'

I'm like, 'So how is she?'

'Paranoid,' she goes. 'She's still convinced that they're going to kill her and make it look like an accident. I mean, she practically wrapped herself around me when I was trying to leave.'

'Jesus, I would have paid good money to see that.'

'See what?'

'Her wrapped around –. Sorry, forget I said anything.'

Luckily, my *phone* all of a sudden rings? I check the screen and – yeah, no – it's Sorcha.

I'm there, 'Look who it is,' showing it to Erika. 'She probably just wants to say welcome home and blah, blah, blah.'

So I answer it.

I'm there, 'Hey, Sorcha – the wanderer returns, huh?'

The first words out of her mouth are, 'What the fock, Ross?'

I'm there, 'Er, I'm not a hundred per cent sure what this *about*, Sorcha?'

Oh, shit, I think. Does she know about her sister?

She goes, 'I can't believe I have to find out about it on Instagram!'

I'm there, 'Is this something to do with your sister, Sorcha? Because if it is, bear in mind, she's always been full of sh–'

'I'm talking about Honor, Ross. She posted pictures on Instagram of her shopping for a dress – for some boy's Fifth Year Formal?'

'Yeah, no, she's going with a dude named Jonah. High School Rathgor before you ask.'

'She's fourteen years old, Ross.'

'I know how old she is, Sorcha.'

I didn't know how old she was – good information to have, though.

She goes, 'She's just storted her Junior Cert year. She is *not* going to a Fifth Year Formal.'

I'm there, 'Nothing is going to happen, Sorcha. I was just saying to Helen, this dude is way out of her league. They're just mates.'

'Oh, I'm overreacting – am I, Ross? Just because I don't want our teenage daughter being made pregnant by some rugby focking jock?'

'Rugby jock? Will you listen to yourself? He's High School Rathgor, Sorcha – they haven't won a Leinster Schools Senior Cup since 1973.'

'She's still a child, Ross.'

'He's only, like, a year or two older than her. And like I said, he wouldn't touch her with a ten-foot borge –'

All of a sudden, the kitchen door swings open and Honor walks in, wearing her dress.

She's like, 'Well? What do you think?'

'Oh my God!' Erika goes.

Helen says it as well. She's like, 'Oh my God!'

Sorcha's still on the line, by the way. I have her in my ear going, 'What's happening, Ross? Why is Erika saying, "Oh my God"?'

I'm there, 'Sorcha, I have to go.'

She's like, 'Don't you hang up on me! Don't you focking hang up on me!'

I hang up on her and I just stare at my daughter standing there in her – yeah, no – ballgown. And suddenly it's my turn to say it.

I'm like, 'Oh my God!'

Honor's there, 'How do I look?'

And I go, 'Like a movie stor, Honor. Like an actual movie stor.'

'So did you miss me?' Roz goes.

The answer should be obvious. I've got a horn on me like a roll of wallpaper.

I'm there, 'Big time. And I didn't *do* the dirt in the end. The only one out of all of us.'

She's like, 'So you said.'

'Which is huge for me, Roz. I'm giving myself massive pats on the back here.'

We stort kissing again. We're standing in her kitchen in Goatstown, by the way. She has her back against the two-door, American-style refrigerator and I'm squeezing her wabs through the cashmere of her sweater like I'm testing mangoes for firmness.

'Oh God!' she goes – absolutely loving it. 'That feels so good! That feels *so, so* good!'

I'm there, 'So did *you* miss *me*?'

'Oh my God, so much,' she goes. 'Like you wouldn't believe. Like you wouldn't actually –'

Then her lips are on mine again. Her mouth tastes of cool mint dental floss and elderflower gin.

'I was thinking, we might have normal sex now,' I go, seriously worried about disappointing her, 'then do the whole tantric thing the *next* time we see each other?'

She's like, 'No, let's eat first.'

I'm there, 'Eat?'

'Yes,' she goes, 'I'm going to do you griddled peaches with prosciutto and Roquefort.'

I'm thinking, Don't bother – seriously, don't bother.

'Although I've had to swap out the Roquefort for Cashel Blue,' she goes, pulling the griddle pan out of the drawer.

I'm there, 'Yeah, no, because of the whole Irexit thing.'

'And it's going to be bacon instead of prosciutto. And pears instead of peaches.'

'Still sounds great.'

She pours oil into the pan and tilts the thing at different angles to spread it around. Then she chops the pears and throws them into it.

I'm there, 'So how are things with you?' sitting down on a high stool with a length of Wavin pipe in my chinos. 'What have you been up to?'

She goes, 'Not a lot. Raymond was here yesterday.'

I'm there, 'Was he indeed?' trying not to sound jealous.

'Yeah, he offered to help me paint the bedroom. I think it helped take his mind off things. They're saying his mother only has days left.'

'That's, em, a bummer.'

She opens the fridge – like Helen's, it's pretty much *empty*? She holds up a lettuce.

'It's going to have to be plain old butterhead instead of rocket,' she goes. 'Is that okay?'

I'm there, 'Yeah, no, it's all good.'

She chops up the lettuce, then she sort of, like, crumbles up the blue cheese. There's something on her mind. I can tell.

'So, em, can I talk to you about something?' she goes.

I'm like, 'Uh-oh, this sounds serious.'

'It's not *that* serious.'

'Go on – let me be the judge of that.'

'Sincerity saw on Instagram that Honor bought a dress.'

'Yeah.'

'She said that Jonah is taking her to the Fifth Year Formal.'

'Yeah, no, just as mates.'

'Sincerity is very upset.'

'Er, *she* finished with *him*, Roz?'

'That's because she was trying to save her friendship with Honor. But Honor's still not talking to her – and now she's ended up going to the Fifth Year Formal instead of her.'

'She let herself be played, Roz. She's going to need to toughen up if she's going to make it in the big, bad world.'

She puts the salad in front of me. I've zero interest in it.

'She was up all night, crying her eyes out,' Roz goes.

I'm there, 'Sounds like she has it bad for him,' and I pick up my fork.

'She keeps listening to all *their* songs,' she goes. 'Reading back over his WhatsApp messages.'

'We've all done it.'

'I said to her why don't you text him and tell him you made a mistake and you want him back?'

'And what did she say?'

'She doesn't want to upset Honor – especially with school starting again tomorrow.'

She looks up from her plate.

She goes, 'It's disgusting, isn't it?'

I'm there, 'I'm not really hungry.'

For food anyway.

She's like, 'No, it's disgusting. It doesn't work without peaches and rocket. And balsamic vinegar, of course – another thing you can't get for love nor money.'

I don't know if it's the mention of love but we're suddenly giving each other the eye across the table. She smiles at me and goes, 'Let's take this somewhere more comfortable, will we?'

I'm there, 'I wouldn't say no.'

I follow her up the stairs, my eyes fixed on her gorgeous orse, which suddenly reminds me of the Mastercord symbol – two perfect circles – in her black, Lululemon yoga pants.

We lie down on the bed and there's more kissing. She stares really intensely into my eyes. I stort unbuttoning the fly of my chinos.

'No, wait,' she goes. 'Let's take our time, remember?'

I'm like, 'Er, okay.'

She's there, 'Breathe.'

I *am* breathing, though.

I stort going at her gongas again, first over the bra, then under it, until her nipples are so hord you could hang a brace of pheasant off them, ready for plucking.

She's kissing my mouth, my neck, my face, while pulling the plonker off me, and several times I'm convinced I'm about to cream my boxers. But at the very last second, she stops and whispers in my ear that she's been dreaming about this for weeks.

'Me too,' I go – another subtle reminder that I didn't do the dirt on her. 'I'm actually gagging for it.'

We've been doing the whole foreplay thing for a good, like, half an

367

hour, when Roz all of a sudden stops bringing the little man's wind up, removes my hand from under her sweater and rolls onto her back.

I'm there, 'What's the Jack?'

She goes, 'I'm just not feeling it tonight.'

I'm like, 'Feeling it? You seem pretty turned on to me. Jesus, you could hang a brace of pheasant off your –'

'What I mean is, I just can't *get* there – to the mental plane where I need to be to properly enjoy it.'

I'm there, 'What did you think of my suggestion earlier that we have just regular sex first – just to clear the pipes out, if that's not too disgusting a phrase? Then we can go back to the tantric thing at a future date?'

'No,' she goes, 'I'm sorry. I'm too distracted.'

I'm like, 'Distracted? Distracted by –'

The penny drops. She's talking about Sincerity.

She goes, 'I've never seen her so upset.'

I'm there, 'Come on, Roz, everyone gets their hort broken at some stage. It's port and porcel. Do you want me to put my hand back up your top?'

She's like, 'Ross, she really, really likes this boy. I actually think she's in love.'

I realize what's going on here. Roz is playing me just like my daughter played hers.

'I'll tell you what,' I go, 'why don't I have a word with Honor?'

And she's like, 'Thanks, Ross. That would be a huge weight off my mind.'

So – yeah, no – it's, like, a Wednesday afternoon and I've collected Honor and the boys from school. Today is one of my famous un-supervised access days and I've taken them up Killiney Hill for a walk, even though Honor says she finds walking – oh my God – so focking boring.

So we're sitting on the grass in front of the Witch's Hat. Honor has her nose stuck in her phone, while Brian, Johnny and Leo are climbing the concrete blocks to the top of the pyramid and shouting, 'I'm the king of the castle!'

I'm there, 'So how was your first day back at school?'

Honor goes, 'Oh my God, *everyone* in Mount Anville is talking about how Honor O'Carroll-Kelly has been invited to an actual Fifth Year Formal! It's never happened to anyone in Third Year before!'

I'm like, 'That's, em, great for you. And how's Sincerity taking the whole thing?'

'Who *gives* a fock?'

'Yeah, no, good point. Very good point, in fact.'

'She's a focking sappy bitch. I only let her hang out with me because I wanted things to work out between you and Roz – and that's only to piss off my so-called mother.'

She goes back to her phone again.

I'm there, 'But you're only going to this Formal as Jonah's mate, right?'

'That's what he thinks,' she goes. 'But wait until he sees me in my dress.'

'It's a nice dress. I'll admit it.'

'I'm going to make him totally want me.'

'Right.'

'What? What do you mean by that?'

'I don't know if I'm all that comfortable with the age difference.'

'I'm fourteen and he's sixteen.'

'Yeah, no, that's a massive gap.'

'It's a good job that I don't give two *focks* what you think?'

'Okay, look, cords on the table, Roz was saying that Sincerity is still majorly keen on him.'

'Then why did she finish with him?'

'Because she thought it'd help repair her friendship with you.'

'That was her mistake, then – the back-stabbing bitch.'

I'm there, 'It's just that she likes him, Honor, and *he* likes *her* –'

'Oh my God!' she goes. 'Oh! My literally! God!'

I'm like, 'What?'

She's there, 'Roz has cut you off, hasn't she?'

I'm like, 'Don't be ridiculous. That's crazy talk.'

'Yes, she has,' she goes. 'She's refusing to have sex with you until you persuade me to let her sappy bitch of a daughter have Jonah back.'

I'm there, 'Honor, I'm not sure I'm one hundred per cent comfortable talking to you about this subject.'

She's like, 'I'm right, aren't I?'

And what can I say except, 'Yes, you're right.'

'Oh my God,' she goes, 'I actually really admire Roz for that. She's obviously a woman who's used to getting what she wants.'

I'm there, 'So what do you say?'

But she's like, 'I say tough shit. I'm going to the Formal with Jonah and I'm going to make him fall in love with me.'

There's an angry mob outside the gates of the Áras. We're talking, like, three or four hundred of them and there's a line of Gordaí – all linking orms – stopping them from climbing the fence.

They're shouting, 'Stop Irexit!' and 'CO'CK out! CO'CK out! CO'CK out!'

They're holding, like, banners and placords saying shit like, 'Liar!' and 'Give Us Our Stor Back!' and 'We love EU!'

I drive up to the gate. The Gorda dude in the box recognizes me and opens the gate for me while his colleagues hold the crowd back.

'The fock is all this about?' I go.

He's like, 'It's democracy in action, I suppose.'

I'm there, 'Is there nothing you can do to stop it?'

He goes, 'I think your father already has that in hand, don't you?'

Someone in the crowd obviously recognizes me because I hear a dude shout, 'Look, it's the focking idiot son – the one who took his penis out in a focking pub!'

I'm about to shout that it was actually my orse when something suddenly hits the front passenger window. Fock, it's an egg. It's followed by another one, which hits the windscreen, then another, which explodes off the bonnet.

'You better get out of here,' the Gorda dude goes. 'I don't think you're too popular with them.'

I'm there, 'They're clearly not a rugby crowd.'

'Privileged prick!' another voice goes as yet another egg cracks off the rear windscreen.

I put my foot down, then drive through the gates and up to the gaff. I throw the cor in front of the house and in I go.

It's actually my old dear I've come to see, except there's no sign of her. I check the nursery, but Astrid says she hasn't seen her this morning. I check her bedroom with my hand over my eyes so as not to accidentally see her in a state of undress – I'm obviously scorred from my childhood – but she's not in her bed and she's not in the drawing room either.

I tip into the kitchen, where Bruno, the French chef that she poached from l'Gueuleton, is preparing the lunch.

I'm like, 'Dude, have you seen the old dear?'

He goes, *'Non!* And I am surprised because this morning she does not ring to ask for this!'

He holds up one of my old dear's signature pomegranate bellinis in a pint glass – and that's when I stort to get *really* worried?

I'm like, 'Dude, no one has seen her.'

He just, like, shrugs – the way French people sometimes do.

It's only then that I decide to go looking for the old man. Up the stairs I go. Just as I reach the landing, my phone rings. It's, like, Sorcha.

She goes, 'Ross, I meant what I said. Honor is *not* going to that boy's Formal.'

I'm like, 'Sorcha, I don't have time for this.'

I hang up and I make my way to the old man's office. It's, like, *his* voice I hear first – big foghorn of a thing, so loud it nearly loosens my focking molars.

He's going, 'What in the name of God do these bastards want?'

I stand outside the door and – again – have a sneaky listen.

'A People's Vote,' Hennessy goes.

The old man's like, 'A People's Vote? The people already voted! They voted to leave!'

'Well, now they want a Second Referendum.'

'A Second Referendum, ladies and gentlemen! A Second Referendum – quote-unquote!'

'They're saying they were lied to.'

'Of course they were lied to! If people are going to go around believing all the nonsense that spews from the mouths of politicians during the course of an election campaign, well, maybe they don't deserve the vote!'

'The shortage of imported food items, especially French and Dutch cheeses, as well Spanish and Italian cured meats, has radical-ized a rump of Remainers. But it's the disappearance of avocados that has pushed a lot of people over the edge.'

'Good Lord! But *we're* okay for those things, are we, Old Scout?'

'Yes, Taoiseach, we have our own private importation channel.'

'You're sending the Government jet, aren't you?'

'Yes – although I think it would be prudent not to mention this to the Minister for Climate Action.'

'Oh, God, yes! Lambay Rules, as they say at sea! Can't we shoot these people, Hennessy – with rubber bullets or something?'

'If you're asking me for a legal opinion, then, yes, we can and it can be arranged. But from a political standpoint –'

'Not a good idea?'

'It might inflame the situation. Like I said to you, the people are very angry.'

'What, because they can't get avocados? No one in Ireland had bloody well heard of them until twenty years ago!'

'If you don't mind my saying, Taoiseach, there have been more – shall we say – teething problems with Irexit than we might have anticipated.'

'Such as?'

'Reneging on our sovereign debt means that no one in the inter-national markets will lend us any money.'

'Can't we just get more from our friends in Russia?'

'We've asked. So far, nothing.'

'But we gave them our oil and our gas! We gave them thousands of acres of trees! We're allowing them to build a bloody well city in Donegal!'

'They've asked us to be patient. But, well, the Exchequer is running out of money and other countries no longer trust us enough to trade with us.'

'Good Lord!'

'The empty supermarket shelves – like I said, they're making people nervous and Amnesty International has expressed *grave* concern that the Dáil hasn't sat in seven months.'

'It's not our fault that someone decided to burn the building down! Speaking of which –'

'What?'

'The girl is due to stand trial soon! We have no idea what she's going to say on the stand! But one thing's for sure – it's not going to be good for us!'

'Don't worry about it.'

'I'm *very* worried about it!'

'It's all in hand.'

'Well, whatever it is you're planning, make sure to keep me out of the loop! I think if my cross-examination in front of the Mahon Tribunal proved anything, it's that the less I know, the more plausible my denials will sound!'

'In the meantime, you might need to make some concessions, Taoiseach – just to quell the public anger.'

'What kind of concessions, old bean?'

'Some of our *green* initiatives might have to go.'

'The Minister won't be happy.'

'These things were only meant as a diversion anyway.'

'She doesn't know that, though.'

I suddenly stick my head around the door.

I'm there, 'Sounds like *someone* is having a shit day? I'm focking delighted for you both.'

The two of them pretty much levitate with the fright.

Hennessy goes, 'How long have you been standing there?'

And I'm like, 'Don't worry. Most of it went over my head as per usual. You've got an even bigger problem, though. The old dear is missing.'

The old man goes, 'Missing?'

I'm there, 'She's not in the nursery. She's not her in bedroom. She's not in the drawing room.'

'Did you speak to Bruno?' the old man goes.

I'm like, 'Yes – and she didn't drink her breakfast.'

Now, like me, the old man is suddenly concerned. He stands up from his desk. He's like, 'Where the hell could she be?'

And that's when his *phone* all of a sudden rings.

He answers. He's like, 'Yes? Ah, Security! Hello, Security! She's where? Good Lord! No, leave this to me! Thank you!'

The old man puts the phone down.

He's like, 'It seems she's down at the front gate – talking to the protesters!'

'*Talking* to them?' Hennessy goes.

The old man's there, '*Addressing* them!'

Hennessy's like, 'Oh, Jesus!'

They rush out of the office and down the stairs, with me following closely behind. Out of the house and down the gorden we run towards the fence. I can see the old dear standing there in just her dressing gown and slippers and she's shouting at the protesters through the railings.

She's going, 'Why can't you just eat things you *can* buy in the supermorket – like turnips and cabbages?'

A man on the other side of the railings with a big angry head on him goes, 'She's like the Irish Marie Antoinette – let them eat turnips? I wouldn't say you're eating turnips in there, are you?'

'We don't need to eat turnips,' she goes. 'My husband sends the Government jet to France, Spain and Italy to get all the food and wine we need. There are no food shortages here.'

The old man goes, 'That's enough, Dorling! Don't say another word!'

The dude with the angry head goes, 'Ah, look who it is! The man who promised us a bright new future if we voted to leave the EU! And his son who waves his wanger around in public at the drop of a hat!'

The old man puts his orm around the old dear and goes, 'Let's go back to the house, Dorling, and put you back in bed.'

She's there, 'I was *in* bed – it was their shouting that disturbed me.'

'Is it true?' this random woman – not great – in a bubble jacket shouts through the railings. 'Are you sending the Government jet all over Europe to make sure you don't suffer like the rest of us?'

The old dear goes, 'Yes – and because the plane flies under the flag of a sovereign state, we don't even have to pay customs chorges.'

This news is too much for the woman in the bubble jacket. I watch her pull an egg from her pocket and shape up to throw it at the old dear. In that moment, without a thought for my own safety, I jump in front of her and I end up taking the egg full on the face.

It's followed, very quickly, by a second egg, then a third, then a fourth, then a fifth, until I'm being absolutely pelted with the things from all directions.

It's only then that the police decide to weigh into the crowd with their batons. As they're cracking heads beyond the railings, the old man helps me up off the ground.

He's like, 'An act of pure heroism – eh, Hennessy?'

Hennessy says fock-all.

We walk back to the gaff. The old dear is muttering under her breath now. She's going, 'Why can't they eat potatoes and turnips? It's what peasants have eaten for hundreds of years. What makes them so special?'

I'm like, 'Dude, she needs to be in somewhere.'

The old man's there, 'Don't be ridiculous, Ross. Rest is all she needs. And, like you said, she could do with getting a bit of break-fast inside her.'

But then Hennessy, at the top of his voice, goes, 'Taoiseach!' and the old man turns around, like he recognizes that tone, like he knows that his best mate isn't focking around. 'For once in his life, your idiot son is right. It's time.'

'Oh my God,' Honor goes, 'you're, like, all over social media!'

I'm there, 'Am I?' pretending that I don't know.

Yeah, no, Roz rang me last night to tell me how my heroics had gone down on Twitter and Instagram. I think she's falling a little bit in love with me.

Honor's like, 'Everyone is sharing the video of you jumping in front of Fionnuala to stop her getting egged.'

I'm there, 'You don't have time to think in a moment like that. You just act.'

'Some of the comments!' Honor goes, scrolling through them on her phone.

I'm there, 'Okay, give me some of the highlights.'

'This girl is like, *What a way to come back from being cancelled! A month ago, he was a convicted pervert –*'

I'm there, 'Pervert is a bit strong.'

Jesus, Roz never mentioned that one.

Honor goes, 'Then she says, *Now I can't help but think he's kind of hot.*'

I'm there, 'I'll try not to get a swelled head.'

She goes, 'Oh my God, this person says, *I know what you mean. When he was in court for flashing, I actually wanted to punch him in the face – but now I kind of fancy him, even if it's in a dumbass rugby-jock kind of way.*'

I'm like, 'What's her name?'

She goes, '*His* name. It's a boy.'

I'm there, 'Okay, move on. Not that there's anything wrong with that. Anyway, look, I wanted to talk to you about –'

She's like, 'Dad, I'm *going* to the focking Formal, okay?'

'Not about that,' I go. 'It's about, well, your grandmother.'

'She wasn't hurt, was she?'

'No, she wasn't hurt, Honor. But she's going to have to go in somewhere.'

'What do you mean by *in* somewhere?'

'Into, like, a nursing home.'

'Why?'

'Because she's losing her mind, Honor.'

Honor looks sad. She absolutely adores the woman. But, at the same time, she nods – it's almost as if she *knew* this day was coming?

She goes, 'I love the way she's a bitch to people – especially her cleaners and waiters in restaurants.'

I'm there, 'You'll still be able to visit her, Honor. It's just that she needs round-the-clock care.'

'What's going to happen to the children?'

'I suppose Astrid will go on looking after them. I don't know is the honest answer.'

All of a sudden, there's a ring on the doorbell.

Honor's like, 'I'm not answering it.'

I'm there, 'Leave it – Helen will get it.'

I'm right. Twenty seconds later, I hear Helen open the front door, then the hallway is suddenly filled with voices.

It's like, 'Ah, how's she cutten, Heden? You're looken weddle, so you are!'

Honor jumps up off the sofa. She's like, 'Oh my God, it's Ronan!' and she practically *runs* from the room?

I follow her out.

She's hugging him and she's going, 'Oh my God! Oh my God! Oh my God!'

He's laughing. He's there, 'Howiya, Hodor? Did you miss me?'

'Oh my God!' she goes. '*So*, so much!'

Yeah, no, Rihanna-Brogan and Avery are *also* standing there?

I'm there, 'Avery, how the hell are you? How was the trip?'

She gives me a hug and goes, 'Awe-some!'

She's *so* American.

Then I give Rihanna-Brogan and Ronan a hug as well.

I'm like, 'Why didn't you tell us you were home?'

'We waddanted to suproyse yous,' Rihanna-Brogan goes. 'Daddy, cad I gib Hodor and Ross their pressedents?'

Ronan's there, 'She's arthur buying yous sometin in Paddis – you're godda lub it!'

Rihanna-Brogan reaches into her – wouldn't you focking know it? – *holdall* and pulls out two berets.

'Oh! My God!' Honor goes, putting hers on her. 'I love it! Dad, put your beret on!'

So – yeah, no – I do. Rihanna-Brogan takes a photograph of us in our matching berets, looking like two knobs.

'Come down to the kitchen,' Helen goes. 'Will you have something to drink?'

Avery's there, 'Do you have, like, matcha tea?'

Matcha focking tea. Like I said – typical American.

Helen goes, 'We may have something like that,' and we all head down to the kitchen, me and Honor still wearing our berets.

'Hee-or, Rosser,' Ronan goes, 'how was the walk?'

I'm there, 'Yeah, no, all good.'

'Yous all fidished it, did yous?'

'We did.'

'Some stordies, I'd say – wha?'

'Yeah, no, quite a few. But what goes on tour –'

'Stays on tooer.'

'Christian was with a hooker. That's all I'm saying. And Oisinn, who's supposedly gay, was with a woman.'

There's, like, silence in the kitchen in response to that.

I'm there, 'The other two did the dirt as well. I was the only one who didn't – although that information doesn't leave this kitchen.'

Helen is rooting through the press. She goes, 'We have *mint* tea, Avery, if that's any good?'

And Avery's like, 'That would be so nice – thank you.'

Honor's like, 'Ronan, I'm going to the High School Rathgor Fifth Year Formal next week?'

He's there, 'Shurden, I know – I geb the pitcher of your thress a Like on Instagraddam.'

She goes, 'I'm the first, like, Junior Cert student in the history of Mount Anville to ever be invited to a Fifth Year Formal.'

Ronan's like, 'Is she not a bit young to be going to didder dad-dences, Rosser?'

I'm there, 'Ro, you of all people should know that I have absolutely no control over what my kids do.'

Everyone laughs. I'm not even joking.

'So how was Europe?' Honor goes. 'I want to know everything. What did you see?'

Ronan's there, 'We saw Paddis. We saw Rowum. We saw Athiddens.'

Avery's like, 'We saw Berlin. We saw Prague. We saw Budapest.'

'Disneyladdend Paddis,' Rihanna-Brogan goes. 'The Eifuddle Tower. The Codosseum.'

I'm there, 'Sounds like you really enjoyed yourselves.'

I notice Ronan and Avery looking at each other across the free-standing island, absolutely lost in each other's eyes – just so obviously in love.

And Avery goes, 'I had the time of my life.'

I can't believe what Jamie Heaslip is telling me.

He's like, 'We've none, Rosser. We've no Heineken.'

I can see my reflection in the mirror behind the bor. It's like he's just told me that he's agreed to become the forwards coach at Munster.

I'm there, 'Dude, what are you saying? Do you need to change a barrel or something?'

'No,' he goes, 'I'm saying we can't get it. It's because of Irexit.'

Seriously – my face. I look like I'm having a stroke. I *could* be having a stroke.

I'm like, 'Dude, you're not making any sense.'

'They've closed the brewery in Cork,' he goes. 'And we can't get it from Amsterdam because of the whole EU thing. Do you want a Hanijan?'

I'm there, 'Do I want a what?'

He's like, 'A Hanijan. It's Chinese.'

He points to one of the pumps. I shit you not, there's a logo on it that *looks* like the Heineken logo, except it says – Jesus focking Christ – Hanijan.

I'm there, 'No, I do not want a focking Hanijan. Come on, goys, let's hit the Horse Show House,' because it's supposed to be Christian's birthday. 'Madigan Square Gorden, here we come.'

'They've only got Hanijan as well,' Jamie goes – and it's a hord thing to hear from one of your all-time heroes. 'Same with Crowes and everywhere else. You won't get Heineken anywhere in this country.'

JP goes, '*I'll* try the Hanijan,' letting me down in a big-time way.

Then Oisinn and Fionn say they'll try the Hanijan as well. Jamie looks at me then, eyebrows raised.

I'm there, 'I'd sooner die of thirst. I'll just have nothing.'

Oisinn goes, 'So how has everyone been?' and I think he's asking Christian specifically.

Christian's like, 'I'm good. I've reset the clock. My name is Christian Forde. I'm an alcoholic and I've been sober for twelve days.'

I'm there, 'Well, I'm going to be joining you, Dude, if the nearest thing to Heineken is focking Hanijan.'

'It's actually quite nice,' Fionn goes, looking at me over the top of his pint, while the others nod their approval.

JP's like, 'I can't actually tell the difference.'

I'm there, 'Well, I'll never know because I'd sooner drink my own urine. So what's the story, Christian. Have you seen the famous Lychee?'

He's like, 'Yeah, no, just to tell her that I wanted the house back.'

Yeah, no, he bought a gaff in Harold's Cross for her and her influencer mates to use as – and this is an actual *thing*? – a collab house, where they basically sit around all day, dreaming up shit, which they call 'content', to post on Instagram and TikTok.

Oisinn's there, 'How did she react?'

Christian goes, 'About as well as you'd expect. She called me a focking dream-stealer and said I was a sad, pathetic, old man who was just trying to stop her from living her best life.'

I'm there, 'That's exactly what Honor said to me when I refused to let her get botox for her thirteenth birthday.'

'Then Lychee posted a video on TikTok,' he goes, 'saying all the same stuff about me, but this time in tears.'

JP's like, 'You're better off out of it, Dude.'

I'm there, 'Where's, em, Delma, by the way?'

He's like, 'She's in Roly's. She's having dinner with Belle and Bingley.'

'I'll never *not* find those names funny,' I go. 'I'm just warning you.'

He's there, 'She's going to pop in afterwards.'

I'm like, 'What's the story with her face? Have you gotten used to it?'

He's there, 'Yeah, I'm actually storting to like it.'

'I suppose it's a bit like when you get a bang on your cor,' I go. 'You kind of get used to the damage – to the point where you actually stop *noticing* it?'

Oisinn's there, 'I think what Ross is trying to say is that it's what's on the inside that really matters.'

I look away without saying shit. Oisinn has always been a better liar than me.

I raise a pint of imaginary Heineken and I go, 'Here's to us, goys. It was great walking with you.'

They all return the toast.

JP's like, 'Amen to that!'

Christian's there, 'We're definitely a lot closer now because of it.'

'Which was Father Fehily's plan,' JP goes, 'whether you believe the clues were real or not.'

Even Fionn ends up having to agree.

I'm there, 'Oisinn, is Magnus coming in?'

He goes, 'Yeah, no, he's just porking the cor. He's with Sorcha's sister.'

I have another crack at it.

I'm there, 'Which sister?'

And he's like, 'Er, how many sisters does she have, Ross?'

I'm like, 'Fair enough. Good point.'

'They were in town all day shopping for baby clothes.'

Baby clothes. I fall suddenly silent.

JP's there, 'Did you tell him about –'

He means doing the dirt.

Oisinn's like, 'I did. He just laughed.'

We're all there, 'What?'

'Seriously,' Oisinn goes. 'I might as well have told him I had sex with a Mitsubishi Lancer.'

'What,' Christian goes, 'because it was a woman and not a man, he didn't consider it cheating?'

Oisinn laughs. He's there, 'I know, right?'

I'm like, 'He's a keeper, dude.'

He'd focking want to be. They're married.

Christian goes, 'Fionn, how's school?'

No one cares, but you have to ask – even though I feel like nearly decking Christian for killing the buzz.

Fionn's there, 'Yeah, very good. We've got nearly eight hundred students this year. And we're making plans for going co-ed next year.'

I'm like, 'That's still happening, is it? There's going to be, like, girls in Castlerock?'

'Yes,' he goes, 'it's still happening. Although there's a huge amount of work to do between now and then.'

All of a sudden, Magnus and Sorcha's sister arrive. It's, like, hellos all round, then Magnus asks Jamie Heaslip for a pint of Carlsberg.

'No Carlsberg,' Jamie goes. 'Do you want a Hanijan?'

I'm there, 'I wouldn't focking bother, Magnus.'

Oisinn's like, 'It's actually really good.'

'Yesh,' Magnus goes, 'I'll try one of thoshe,' making *me* look focking petty.

I'm there, 'Seriously, I'd rather die of –'

And I suddenly stop because Sorcha's sister has her hand on my orse and she's squeezing my left butt cheek like it's a focking stress ball.

'So how did you get on?' Oisinn goes.

Magnus is like, 'We shpent – oh my God – sho much money. We bought a lot of clothesh.'

JP's there, 'All neutral colours, I presume?'

'No,' Sorcha's sister goes, 'because I am absolutely convinced that it's going to be a boy.'

Oisinn's like, 'Really?'

'Honestly,' she goes, 'I just know! Also, he's going to be a rugby player. He's going to be a –' and then she's like, 'Ross, what position did *you* play again?'

I swear to fock, I can feel my face turn red. It's actually burning.

'Er, out-half – number ten,' I go, somehow managing to get the words out. 'But I was equally capable of doing a job in the centre or at full-back and running the game from there.'

My hort is pounding like you wouldn't believe. It's a massive relief when Roz suddenly arrives, with her ex, Raymond, and his current wife, Grainne, in tow.

Roz walks over to us and kisses me. She's still not putting out, by the way – still claims that she can't 'get there' while her daughter is so upset – but I'm pretending that it doesn't bother me.

Raymond gives me a handshake and a hug and introduces me to Grainne, who works for the Maple Group in Fiduciary Services and looks like an older version of Olivia Deeble, except she's from originally Lusk.

I'm there, 'Yeah, no, it's great to meet you.'

Raymond's like, 'What are you drinking, Ross?' because he's actually one of the soundest dudes you could ever meet.

I'm there, 'I'm not drinking, Dude. They've no Heineken.'

He's like, 'No Heineken?'

Oisinn goes, 'We're all drinking Hanijan. There's very little difference.'

'I'll take a Hanijan,' Raymond tells Jamie Heaslip, then Roz and Grainne both say they'll have a Hanijan as well and I'm left to feel like a spare prick.

'So,' Raymond goes, 'I believe Sincerity and Honor had a bit of a falling-out.'

I'm like, 'Yeah, no, over a boy,' and I smile at Roz.

She looks incredible tonight.

'Unlikely to be the last broken heart, unfortunately,' Raymond goes – like I said, he's cool. 'That's teenage girls for you.'

We all end up breaking into little huddles then. I end up standing there – sober, by the way – shooting the shit with Raymond, Grainne and JP, who's telling us about selling his stake in the Vampire Bed business and using the money to do good works. Grainne thinks this is such a – not a word – but *selfless* thing to do.

I ask Raymond how his old dear is doing because I'm nothing if not a conversationalist.

He's like, 'She's in palliative care – so it's any day now.'

I'm there, 'Yeah, no, I'm going through something similar with my own old dear at the moment.'

'I read about the egg-throwing incident,' he goes. 'I don't care how you feel about Ireland leaving the EU – to attack a defenceless, old woman like that.'

I'm there, 'She's, em, going into, like, a home this weekend.'

Raymond's like, 'That must be very hord for you.'

I'm there, 'Yeah, no – thanks, Dude.'

'Oh my God,' Grainne suddenly goes, slapping her hand over her mouth. 'Look at that poor woman's face.'

I don't even need to look to know that it's Delma she's talking about. I look at JP.

It's, like, *awk*-ward!

She's got the famous Belle and Bingley with her. She walks over to JP and kisses him with her focked mouth, which is when Grainne realizes that she's put her foot in it in a major, major way.

I decide that's a good moment to go for a slash. I've got about a metre of piss in the hose and I head for the jacks, giving Roz a big wink and a smile as I pass.

She gives me a big Allison-Williams-but-not-as-annoying smile.

Ten seconds later, I'm standing at the old urination station, draining the sleepy weasel, as they say, when all of a sudden Raymond walks in and joins me at the trough. He whips his out as well – it'd be weird if he didn't – and he storts having a slash beside me.

'You make her very happy,' he goes – this is, like, mid-stream? 'I'm talking about Roz.'

I'm there, 'Er, yeah, no, thanks,' because it's weird listening to each other's toilet noises.

He goes, 'She's dated other goys, but I've honestly never seen her like this before. I mean, she's giddy these days.'

I'm there, 'Yeah, no, I'd love to think I've played even a small port in that,' like I'm being interviewed by focking Gerry Thornley or something. 'And let's just hope it, er, continues into the future.'

He goes, 'I'd say the sex is great, is it?'

I'm like, 'Er . . .'

He's there, 'You don't have to answer that. I miss the sex. She's an absolutely tigress between the sheets.'

I shake the last drop out of the little lad, then button my fly and make my way over to the sink to check out my hair in the mirror. Five seconds later, he joins me. He switches on the hot tap and washes his hands. I decide that I probably should do the same.

He's there, 'I'm only pretending to be happy for you, of course.'

I'm like, 'Excuse me?'

'The nice goy thing,' he goes, 'it's just an act. You see, the truth is that I don't want to see her with someone else, especially not someone who makes her happy. So I'm putting you on notice, Ross, that I am going to do everything in my power to break you two up.'

'Have you taken a lover?' the old dear goes.

She's talking to – believe it or not – Honor.

I'm there, 'No, she hasn't taken a lover. She's fourteen years old. She's telling you that she's going to a Fifth Year Formal.'

The old man's like, 'Do you mind my asking –'

'High School Rathgor,' I go. 'And they're only mates. He's got, like, zero interest in her.'

Honor's like, 'For now.'

This is us in the back of the old man's *limo*, by the way? Kennet is driving and we're bringing the old dear to what we're all calling her new home in Powerscourt.

'Take my advice, Honor,' the woman goes, 'take plenty of lovers.'

Seriously, she sounds like something from a Jane Austen movie.

Honor's there, 'I will, Fionnuala.'

I'm like, 'If you do, I don't want to focking hear about it.'

The old dear goes, 'Where are we, Chorles?' because – yeah, no – I don't think she has a clue what's actually *happening* here?

The old man's there, 'We're in Wicklow, Dorling!'

'Wicklow,' the old dear goes – like she's trying to place it. 'Wicklow. Wicklow. Wicklow.'

I suddenly get this, like, flashback to when I was – I don't know – maybe ten years old and we sent my dog, Doyler, to Wicklow to this, like, formyord where there were loads of other dogs for him to hang *out* with? This for some reason reminds me of that.

I'm there, 'I was just thinking about Doyler – do you remember the little Jack Russell that I had when I was a kid?'

'Oh,' the old dear goes, 'the one I ran over in the cor?'

I'm there, 'Excuse me?'

The old man's like, 'Don't listen to her, Ross. She forgets.'

'He chewed the leg of my ormoire,' she goes.

I'm there, 'You told me he went to a form.'

Honor's like, 'Oh my God!' at the same time laughing. 'Oh! *My* God?'

The old dear goes, 'Oh, that was just a story that your father told you to stop you from crying. I threw him in the rubbish.'

Suddenly, Honor stops laughing and there's, like, a deathly silence in the cor, until I go, 'Congratulations on destroying the country, by the way,' and I'm obviously talking to my old man. 'Er, Hanijan?'

'Hanijan?' the old man goes. 'What on earth are you talking about, Ross?'

I'm there, 'It's rip-off Heineken. It comes from focking China. It's the only beer you can buy since you dragged us out of the EU.'

He's like, 'Nobody said that Irexit wouldn't be without its challenges, Kicker!'

Over his shoulder, Kennet goes, 'We're neerdy theyor, T . . . T . . . T . . . T . . . T . . . T . . . Teashocked. The entradence is c . . . c . . . c . . . c . . . cubben up on the left.'

He swings the wheel and we turn into the grounds of this, like, stately home. We drive up this, like, long gravel driveway. The grounds are – yeah, no – spectacular.

The old dear is looking around her like me at the Assets Model Agency Christmas porty 2005.

She goes, 'It's beautiful! Look at these trees, Chorles! Who lives here?'

I'm looking at the old man, thinking, Have you even told her yet?

'Chorles,' she goes, 'whom are we visiting?'

He's there, 'All will be revealed, Fionnuala!'

We pull up outside. Kennet jumps out, runs around the cor and opens the door for the old man and the old dear.

He's like, 'Th . . . Th . . . Th . . . Th . . . Theer you are now, Fidooda!'

The old dear gets out and goes, 'Oh! Is this Jackie Lavin's house?'

I turn to the old man and I'm like, 'Are you focking serious? Are you saying she doesn't even know what's happening here today?'

He goes, 'Ross, please don't make this any more difficult than it needs to be!' and I notice that the dude has got, like, tears in his eyes.

I could count on the fingers of one hand the number of times I've seen my old man cry. The day that Declan Kidney's Ireland won the Grand Slam. The day that Seán FitzPatrick was declared bankrupt. The day that women were allowed to become members of Portmornock Golf Club.

He wipes his tears away with the palm of his hand, then he gets out of the cor. Honor gets out too, then I get out.

A woman steps out of the front door. She goes, 'You're very welcome!' with her head cocked to one side. 'You must be Fionnuala!'

The old dear's like, 'You must be new. Could I have a lorge Gin Sling sent to my room, please? Jackie keeps a bottle of Tanqueray just for me.'

The woman smiles at her in, like, a *patronizing* way? Then she leads her and the old man inside. Kennet takes the old dear's matching Louis Vuitton luggage set out of the boot and carries it into the place. I walk up to the door with Honor walking a step or two behind me. I turn around to her. I can see she's upset.

I'm there, 'Are you okay?'

She just nods. Her bottom lip is sticking out.

I'm there, 'It's for the best, Honor. She needs, like, round-the-clock care.'

She nods again.

I'm there, 'We can visit. All the time. You and me, Honor.'

We walk in. The old dear's expression has changed. Now she looks, I don't know, worried. There's, like, old dudes moving around on walking frames and old dears going around in wheelchairs.

She's like, 'Who are all these people, Chorles? Is Bill having one of his frightful Murder Mystery nights?'

The old man goes, 'Fionnuala, this is where you live now, Dorling!'

She's like, 'Where I live? What are you talking about, Chorles? And where the hell is my Gin Sling?'

'Fionnuala,' the old man goes, 'you haven't been yourself lately! You've been forgetting things! You've been getting muddled! And it was felt, by one and all – including the famous Hennessy – that what you needed was twenty-four-hour care, the kind that can only be provided by full-time professionals who are trained in the field!'

Her mouth falls open. It's finally dawned on her what's happening.

She's there, 'Chorles, I don't like it here – please, take me home!'

Suddenly, I can feel tears pouring from my own eyes.

'Fionnuala,' the woman in chorge goes, 'come on, I'll show you to your room.'

The old dear's like, 'Chorles?' in this, like, pleading voice. 'Chorles, I want to go home!'

He's like, 'You *can't* go home, Fionnuala! This *is* your home now!'

She goes, 'Well, can it be *your* home too?'

He's there, 'I can't stay here, Fionnuala! I have a country to run!'

She's like, 'What country?' and she has literally no idea.

Honor turns on her heel and runs out of the place, sobbing her hort out.

'Chorles,' the old dear goes, sounding seriously distressed now, 'you can't leave me here!'

He doesn't something un-focking-forgivable then. He just goes, 'I'm sorry,' then turns and runs out of the place.

She looks at me then – with her little girl lost face.

'Ross,' she goes, 'please take me home. I want to go back to my beautiful, beautiful babies.'

I throw my orms around her and we stand there for a good, like, sixty seconds, the two of us just sobbing our horts out.

I'm there, 'I'll come and see you – all the time,' and then *I* turn to go?

She shouts after me, 'Tell Honor to have lots of affairs, Ross. Lots and lots of affairs.'

And over my shoulder, I shout, 'Yeah, no, I will.'

I go outside. Honor is sitting in the back of the cor, with her hands over her eyes, crying her hort out. The old man is leaning against the cor, sucking on a Cohiba the size of an airport security wand, tears all over his face.

I end up totally losing it with him.

I'm there, 'That's how you say goodbye to her?'

He goes, 'It's like Irexit, Ross – it's painful in the short term but necessary nonetheless!'

I'm like, 'How the fock can you compare the two things? And what about the kids?'

He's there, 'I expect we'll hire more nannies.'

He knows what I mean, though.

I'm like, 'You brought six children into this world –'

'Yes, we did,' he goes. 'Out of love. And no one could have envisaged this would happen.'

I'm there, 'I focking envisaged it! I said it! She was nearly seventy and already losing her morbles.'

'Ross,' he goes, 'it's been an emotional day! I think it's time to go!'

I get into the back of the cor and I put my orm around Honor and tell her that everything's going to be okay. I notice Kennet looking over his shoulder at me with a literally *smirk* on his face?

I'm there, 'What are you so happy about – you focking stuttering fock?'

And he's like, 'J . . . J . . . J . . . Joost gorra birra good news, Rosser. N . . . N . . . N . . . Nuttin to b . . . b . . . b . . . b . . . botter yisser head about.'

Poor Jonah. He's sitting on the edge of Helen's sofa, absolutely crapping himself. I asked him if he wants a beer and he says no thanks, he doesn't drink, which comes as a massive relief to me because (a) he's only sixteen years old and (b) I'm down to my last six sticks of Heineken.

'Is, em, Honor nearly ready?' the dude goes, tugging at the neck of his dress shirt.

Erika's there, 'You know what girls are like, Jonah. It takes as long as it takes.'

There's suddenly a ring on the doorbell. Erika goes outside to answer it, leaving me on my own with the dude. It's a bit awkward.

I'm there, 'So let's get this straight – you don't actually fancy Honor, do you?'

I'm just trying to get it from him on the record before he sees her in that dress.

He goes, 'Er, well, we're just, like – you know – *friends*?' obviously not wanting to insult me.

I'm there, 'And that's great. All I'm saying is that you can see a girl in a dress and be absolutely blown away by her in the moment. But the moment doesn't last. The next day, she's back in her Juicy Couture tracksuit pants – no make-up – and you're thinking, What the fock have you done to the girl I was with last night? Do you know what I'm saying?'

He's like, 'Er, not really, no.'

Out in the hallway, I can hear Sorcha going, 'Where is he? Where is this boy?' and five seconds later she bursts into the living room.

Jonah stands up and goes, 'Hello, Minister,' and – I swear to fock – he sort of, like, bows his *head* to her? 'I have to say, I'm a huge, huge fan. You're the main reason I want to study Renewable Energy and Environmental Finance when I leave school.'

He didn't mention that he was a fan of mine, can I just say?

Sorcha goes, 'Oh, how lovely,' immediately smitten by him.

She's very easily taken in. She married me, bear in mind.

He's there, 'You've done more for the future of the planet than any politician alive.'

She's like, 'Well, thank you.'

The dude could ask for Honor's hand in marriage right now and she'd go, 'Fire away!'

I notice Sorcha and Erika exchanging sly looks at each other. It's majorly awkward. They used to be best mates.

Sorcha goes, 'How have you been, Erika?'

Erika's like, 'Fine. You?'

All of a sudden, I hear Honor coming down the stairs.

I'm there, 'Are you ready? Jonah's been sitting here for the last twenty minutes.'

She shouts, 'Just wait a minute, will you?' and I hear her open the front door. Then I hear voices in the hallway.

I'm there, 'What the fock is going on?'

Ten seconds later, the living-room door opens and in walks Honor – still in her Juicy tracksuit bottoms.

I'm there, 'Honor, I'm supposed to be dropping you and Jonah to the school. Are you getting ready?'

'No,' she goes, 'because he's not going with me.'

All of a sudden, she opens the door wider and in walks Sincerity, followed by Roz.

Jonah's like, 'Sincerity!'

And Sincerity goes, 'Jonah? I didn't know you were –'

Honor's there, 'Jonah, I know you don't like me in, like, *that* way? I'm cool with that. And I know you two are absolutely mad about each other and I'm cool with that too. So that's the reason I rang your mom, Sincerity, and asked her to bring you here. Because *you're* going to the Fifth Year Formal with Jonah.'

Sincerity is, like, bowled over by this. She's there, 'I can't go. I don't have a dress.'

Honor's like, 'You're going to wear *my* dress. Come on, I'll do your make-up as well. And don't tell anyone I did this. I want people to still think I'm a bitch.'

Erika goes, 'I'll give you a hand,' because she clearly doesn't like being around Sorcha.

So that leaves Jonah in the living room with me, Sorcha and Roz. It's, like, majorly awks standing there with my still technically wife and the woman who I'm hopefully back riding.

Sorcha goes, 'How are you, Roz? Are you still doing yoga three mornings a week?'

And Roz is like, 'I'm fine – and yes, although it's actually *four?*'

Sorcha's phone all of a sudden rings. She's there, 'Sorry, I have to take this.'

She answers. She's like, 'Good evening, Taoiseach,' then she listens for about thirty seconds and goes, 'What do you mean, I have to pull back on my legislative agenda?'

Roz mouths the words to me, 'Can I have a word?' and she sort of, like, flicks her head in the direction of the door.

I'm there, 'Yeah, no, cool,' and I follow her out into the hall, then outside to the front gorden.

She goes, 'I just needed to see you on your own.'

I'm there, 'Er, riiigghht,' because she seems to have something on her mind.

'I was talking to Raymond,' she goes.

I'm like, 'And?'

'He really likes you, you know?'

'Does he now?'

'It means so much to me that you two got along so well in The Bridge that night.'

'Did you bring me outside to tell me that?'

'No, I brought you outside to tell you –'

That it's over. That's what I'm expecting.

'That I love you,' she goes. 'I've been putting off saying it for a while, but I was standing in the living room there looking at you and I was thinking if I don't tell him now, I'm going to burst!'

I laugh. I'm there, 'I love you too, Roz.'

She smiles at me. I move in for the kiss. We're going at it for, like, twenty or thirty seconds when I suddenly hear a voice, 'Moy Jaysus, will you leeb it out, Rosser – wha?'

I burst out laughing and I open my eyes. He's standing at the front gate with a – yeah, no – *rose* in his hand?

I'm there, 'Roz, this is my son.'

She turns around and smiles at him as he walks up the pathway to the house.

'The famous Ronan,' she goes.

He's there, 'Ine arthur hearden a lorra bout you,' and he kisses her on both cheeks.

I'm like, 'He hasn't, Roz. I've told him very little. I swear.'

He's there, 'I came to see Hodor in her thress. Brought her a rowuz.'

I'm like, 'Honor's not going. Sincerity's going instead.'

'Oh,' Ronan goes, looking confused.

Roz is like, 'I'll just go and check how they're getting on. Lovely to meet you, Ronan,' and she heads back into the gaff.

I'm there, 'How the hell are you?'

He goes, 'Ine game-ball, Rosser.'

I'm like, 'Avery not with you?'

392

He's there, 'She's arthur going back – to Amedica.'

I'm like, 'Oh – when are you going back?'

And that's when he says it.

He goes, 'Ine not going back, Rosser.'

I'm like, 'What do you mean? What about Horvord?'

He's there, 'Ine not going to Heervard. Ine mooben back hee-or.'

I'm like, 'What the fock are you talking about?'

'The thrip that we took arowunt Eurdope,' he goes, 'that was joost me and Avoddy saying goodbye.'

I'm there, 'Goodbye?' and that's when the penny suddenly drops.

Jesus Christ, no wonder Kennet couldn't wipe the focking smile off his face.

I'm there, 'You did a deal – with Hennessy.'

He goes, 'I'd no utter choice, Rosser.'

I'm there, 'He got at the judge. That's why the dude let me off.'

It had fock-all to do with rugby.

He goes, 'You couldn't have dudden toyum, Rosser. I could see it in you. You wouldn't have lasted pissing toyum in jayult.'

I suddenly let a scream out of me, loud enough for the whole of Ailesbury Road to hear.

I'm like, 'Nooo!'

I'm like, 'FOCKING NOOOOOOOOO!!!!!!!!'

Epilogue

I don't know what the fock I'm doing here. But I'm here anyway. Even though *she's* not?

Yeah, no, it's, like, three days later and I'm back in the Áras. I barely even remember the drive here. It's like the cor was on automatic pilot or some shit.

The nursery is empty – as in, there's no sign of my brother and sisters, we're talking Hugo, we're talking Cassiopeia, we're talking Diana, we're talking Mellicent, we're talking Louisa May, we're talking Emily. There's no sign of Astrid either – or, well, of *her*.

So – again – why the fock did I come here this morning? I could see the old dear if I wanted. All I'd have to do is drive down to Wicklow. But then I've no idea whether she'll be having one of her good days or one of her, well, *other* days. So maybe *that's* why I'm here – because I prefer to remember her the way she used to be?

I can actually smell her, if that's not too weird a thing to say about your own mother. There's, like, a cloud of *Soleil Neige* by Tom Ford and Gunpowder Gin hanging over the room. I make my way over to the ormchair where she spent so many mornings and afternoons, watching those six babies that she helped bring into the world, sometimes thinking about the miracle of life, sometimes wondering, 'Who the fock owns those kids?'

I touch the orm of the thing, where her hands used to rest, then I sit down in it.

On a little table next to it, there's a cocktail list. I read down through all the drinks. Rum Cobbler. Planter's Punch. Gin Ricky. Vodka Stinger. Whiskey Swizzle. And I get an instant flashback to my childhood. *My little borman*, as she used to call me. I could mix every single one of these drinks right now without even having to check the ingredients.

Outside the window, I can hear squeals of excitement. I stand up and I make my way over to it and look out. Down below, I can see the children toddling around the lawn, with Astrid and presumably two new nannies running around after them. I smile to myself.

Beyond the fence, I notice, the crowd of protestors is getting lorger and angrier. They're chanting, 'People's Vote! People's Vote! People's Vote!'

That's when I all of a sudden smell cigor smoke. I turn around and there, standing in the doorway, is Hennessy Coghlan-O'Hara.

I end up losing it with him there on the spot.

I'm like, 'You focker! You focked up my son's future!'

But he goes, 'You focked up your son's future.'

I'm there, 'He was going to Horvard! Focking Horvard! And now he's home, working for you!'

He's like, 'Hey, it was his decision. And he did it for you. He did it because you told him you couldn't face going to jail, you little pussy.'

I go, 'I'll get you back, Dude. Godfather or not, I will have my focking revenge.'

He laughs, then his expression turns suddenly serious.

He's there, 'Don't threaten me, you little turd. We are in bed with some very, very dangerous people. You have no idea what we're fucking capable of.'

He turns and walks away.

I suddenly realize there *is* no reason to be here. I head outside and back to the cor and I point it in the direction of Ailesbury Road.

A dude on the radio says that the Government is planning to pull back on many of the promises it made as port of its Green agenda in the wake of the last General Election. He says that plans to place a cap on the number of air and road miles that Irish people are permitted to travel each year have been scrapped and that the Government is also considering lifting its ban on cow- and sheep-breeding.

I'd say Sorcha is having an absolute shit-fit about that. Still, she's learning a very valuable lesson – don't trust my old man.

I'm actually, like, *chuckling* to myself?

And that's when the dude on the radio says that Gordaí are investigating the circumstances surrounding a single-cor collision in Roundstone, County Galway, in which a woman in her early thirties has died.

Acknowledgements

Huge thanks to my good friends Alan Kelly and Martin Doran, two true pioneers, who walked the Camino so that I might know The Way. Thanks to my editor, Rachel Pierce, and my agent, Faith O'Grady. Thanks to Alan Clarke for your extraordinary artwork. Thanks to all the team at Sandycove, especially Michael McLoughlin, Patricia Deevy, Cliona Lewis, Brian Walker, Carrie Anderson and Aimée Johnston. Five real-life people made cameo appearances in this book. I want to say an enormous thank-you to the real Bryan Hickson, Anna Hughes, Deco Gahan, Hugo Mangan and Jane Murphy for your incredibly generous support for some causes that are very dear to my heart. Thanks to Bryan Hickson and Anna Hughes (as well as Neil Hughes) for your generosity towards GOAL Global, Deco Gahan for you contribution to Suicide or Survive, Hugo Mangan for your support of the Irish Youth Foundation and Fighting Words, and Jane Murphy for your kindness towards LauraLynn, Ireland's Children's Hospice.

Lastly, thanks to my family and, most of all, my wonderful wife, Mary McCarthy.